"I might

The subtly accented baritone, as deep and sensual as the purr of a tiger, vibrated along Tessa's nerves.

The man standing behind her was strikingly tall with dark hair and the coldest slate-colored eyes she'd ever seen. His chiseled features—a square jaw, straight nose and high Slavic cheekbones—were too strong to be called handsome, but his very presence exuded power and masculinity.

He was a stranger—surely she'd remember if she'd ever met such a man. But something about him seemed familiar.

Tessa found her voice. "I beg your pardon," she said. "Did you just offer to help me?"

"I couldn't help overhearing," he said. "I'll be taking off for Anchorage in a few minutes. There's plenty of room in the plane. You're welcome to come along."

There had to be a catch. She would never get into a car with a strange man. Would getting into a plane, especially with her precious babies, be any different?

"My plane's a private craft." He spoke as if sensing her hesitation. "But I happen to be a co-owner of this charter company. They can vouch for me." He spoke like a man accustomed to getting his own way.

How could she refuse, when this might be her only chance to get to Anchorage with the twins?

"Yes," Tessa said, taking the plunge. "I'd be happy to accept your very kind offer."

* * *

Stranded with the Boss
is part of the No.1 bestselling series from Mills & Boon®
Desire™—Billionaires and Babies: Powerful men…
wrapped around their babies' little fingers.

STRANDED WITH THE BOSS

BY
ELIZABETH LANE

Published in Great Britain 2015
by Mills & Boon, an imprint of Harlequin (UK) Limited,
Eton House, 18-24 Paradise Road, Richmond, Surrey, TW9 1SR

© 2015 Elizabeth Lane

ISBN: 978-0-263-25281-1

51-1015

Harlequin (UK) Limited's policy is to use papers that are natural, renewable and recyclable products and made from wood grown in sustainable forests. The logging and manufacturing processes conform to the legal environmental regulations of the country of origin.

Printed and bound in Spain
by CPI, Barcelona

Elizabeth Lane has lived and traveled in many parts of the world, including Europe, Latin America and the Far East, but her heart remains in the American West, where she was born and raised. Her idea of heaven is hiking a mountain trail on a clear autumn day. She also enjoys music, animals and dancing. You can learn more about Elizabeth by visiting her website at www.elizabethlaneauthor.com.

One

"**A**re you telling me that lawsuit's still going to trial?" Dragan Markovic glowered from behind his massive desk. "We've offered the blasted woman everything short of the moon. Why won't she settle?"

The young lawyer, part of the Trans Pacific corporate team, was visibly nervous. He fiddled with his pen. A bead of sweat gleamed on his forehead. "According to her attorney, it's not just about money. Miss Randall wants the public to know how unfairly she was treated. She's determined to make sure no female employee is ever again fired because of pregnancy."

Dragan's scowl darkened. "She wasn't fired because she was pregnant. I was given to understand that Miss Randall was fired because she couldn't perform her job."

"That's what we'll be telling the judge. Her work involved trips to the Far East. The pregnancy was too high-risk for that kind of travel."

"So why wasn't she given a desk job for the duration?"

The lawyer flinched. "That's what her lawyer is going to argue. The firing was her supervisor's call. It seems there was some friction between them."

With a muttered curse Dragan rose from his massive leather chair and turned to gaze out the floor-to-ceiling window. His top-floor, corner office gave him a sweeping view of the Seattle waterfront, lined by acres of warehouses, piers and gigantic cranes. Two huge container ships, with the Trans Pacific logo on their bows, were moored along the company dock waiting to be loaded with cargo. Beyond them, the gray waters of Puget Sound lay shrouded in September fog.

Dammit, he had a company to run. He didn't have time to deal with Miss Tessa Randall—a woman he'd never met, nor cared to—and the lawsuit that threatened to smear Trans Pacific's reputation in the media. Why couldn't she just take the money, sign the nondisclosure agreement and go away?

"As I remember hearing, she gave birth to twins," he said.

"That's right. Identical twin girls. Sixteen months ago." The lawyer wiped his glasses and replaced them. "They were born seven weeks early. By then her insurance had been terminated. The medical expenses—"

"We've offered to cover those," Dragan snapped.

"I know. But her lawyer's talking about demanding punitive damages, claiming the stress of losing her job caused Miss Randall to go into premature labor a month later."

"Can they prove that?"

"They'll no doubt try. This could get nasty—and expensive." The lawyer shuffled his papers. "If I could offer a suggestion, Mr. Markovic?"

"Go ahead."

"I know you don't like getting involved in these matters. But if you could meet with Miss Randall face-to-face, maybe even offer her an apology on behalf of the company, she might be willing to—"

"That's out of the question." Dragan swung back to face him. "I don't have time and I don't owe the woman a personal apology. When's the court date?"

"A week from today. Since Miss Randall worked out of our Alaska office, the civil trial's being held in Anchorage. There's still time for you to—"

"I said no. Just handle it. That's what you and your associates are paid for. If you can't do your jobs…" Dragan let the implied threat hang on the air. "That will be all for now."

"Yes, Mr. Markovic. We'll do our best." Clutching his paperwork, the lawyer actually backed out of the office.

As the door clicked shut, Dragan turned toward the window again. Muttering a few choice curses in his native Croatian, he gazed into the gathering fog. For two cents he'd fire the whole hot-shot legal team and hire one seasoned attorney who knew how to work the system. As it was…

The melancholy wail of a foghorn echoed through the glass. Reminding himself that he was wasting time, Dragan returned to his desk, switched on his computer and brought up Tessa Randall's archived personnel file. He hadn't bothered to read it earlier. But now that his legal team seemed to be stalled, maybe it was time he took a look.

Her photo showed a tousled redhead, surprisingly pretty, with challenging hazel eyes. Even on paper, the woman looked damn sexy.

Her marital status was listed as single, with no indication of a marriage or divorce in her six years with the company. Since she'd become pregnant, there had to be a story behind that—a story that wasn't mentioned in her file. What the file did contain was a stack of sterling performance reviews. Not only did Miss Randall speak fluent Japanese, but she was highly valued as a contract negotiator. With so much Trans Pacific cargo—chiefly lumber, steel, and other building supplies—going to Japan, she wouldn't have been an easy employee to replace.

Intrigued, Dragan read the rest of the file. There were no details about her dismissal, only the date. That was a puzzle. Could part of the record have been deleted?

The last entry showed a current address in Bellingham, Washington, a college town across the Sound from Seattle. Wherever she was living now, she'd have to show up in Anchorage for the trial. The question was did he care enough to clear his calendar to be there, too?

Dragan closed the file and switched off the computer. He'd hoped his legal team could handle what he'd once viewed as a simple settlement issue. But he could feel himself being sucked into the drama. Facing Miss Tessa Randall, in or out of court, might be the only way to strengthen his case and prevent damage to Trans Pacific's reputation. But before it could happen he needed a plan—and a way to find the missing pieces of her story. If he discovered that she'd been wronged he would do the decent thing, but only on his own terms. Whatever happened, nobody was going to blacken his company's name.

Nobody.

Bellingham, Washington
Six days later

This couldn't be happening.

Tessa fumbled in her purse for a bottle of ibuprofen,

wrenched off the lid and glanced around the bustling air-charter terminal for a drinking fountain. Seeing none, she gulped two tablets dry, gagging slightly as they went down.

Weeks ago she'd booked a single seat on the Alaska Airlines flight to Anchorage. Her parents had agreed to watch the twins for a few days while she attended the hearing for her lawsuit. Then her mother had tripped and broken her foot. To make matters worse, Tessa's lawyer, Helen Carmichael, had warned her that if they went for punitive damages, the proceedings could drag on for weeks. Left with no choice except to take her toddler twins with her to Anchorage, Tessa had called the airline and tried to reserve three adjoining seats. There were no additional seats available.

Helen, a silver-haired marvel of efficiency, had booked a charter flight for Tessa and the twins and arranged for housing and a daytime nanny in Anchorage. Problem solved. Or so Tessa had thought—until now.

Fighting tears of frustration, she strode down the corridor toward the waiting area, where her friend Penny, who'd driven her to the airport, was keeping an eye on the twins.

Strapped into their side-by-side stroller, Maddie and Missy were getting plenty of attention from passers-by. Dressed in identical pink coveralls, with their blue eyes and flame-colored curls, they were truly adorable. But when they were tired they could be cranky little hellions.

They were tired now.

At the sight of their mother they started to cry, bucking against the safety harnesses that kept them in the stroller. The closer Tessa came, the louder they screamed. Their little arms reached out toward her, Missy begging to be picked up and cuddled, Maddie just wanting to get loose and run.

Tessa's headache was getting worse and the ibuprofen wasn't working fast enough.

"What's wrong?" Penny, a perky blonde with a husband and three school-age children, gave her a concerned look.

Tessa shook her head. "You're not going to believe this. My flight's been canceled. Some kind of trouble with the plane."

"Well, if it's their plane at fault, don't they have to get you another flight?"

"So far all the people behind the counter have done is shrug and roll their eyes. I'm going back in there again and pitch a fit until I get some results. It may take a little time. I just wanted to give you a heads-up."

"Don't worry about me. I've got all the time you need." Penny glanced at the two fussing babies. "Maybe if we wait, the little munchkins will wear themselves out and go to sleep."

"I put some snacks and juice in the diaper bag," Tessa said. "That might help settle them down. Sorry about this, Penny. I know you've got other things to do."

"Don't worry about it. And don't come back here until you've got another flight."

The twins screamed louder as Tessa walked back down the corridor. Their cries tore at her heart but turning around to look at them would only make things worse. What a mess. Maybe she should've settled for the generous amount the Trans Pacific lawyers had offered her. But as Helen, a fiery advocate for women's rights, had reminded her, there was more at stake here than money. Her lawsuit would make an example of Trans Pacific and set a precedent for future cases.

Squaring her shoulders and setting her jaw, she marched up to the check-in counter for Northwest Charter Air, where she'd left her luggage. "This is an outrage," she said.

"I have a ticket and a reservation. I'm not moving from this spot until you find me another flight to Anchorage."

The middle-aged woman behind the counter shook her head. "I'm sorry. We're booked solid. There's no other plane avail—"

"I might be able to help you." The subtly accented baritone, as deep and sensual as the purr of a tiger, vibrated along Tessa's nerves, as if someone had brushed a velvet-clad fingertip down her cheek. She turned with a startled gasp.

The man standing behind her was strikingly tall with dark hair and the coldest slate-colored eyes she'd ever seen. His chiseled features—a square jaw, straight nose and high Slavic cheekbones—were too strong to be called handsome, but his very presence exuded power and masculinity. He was simply dressed in jeans, a muted plaid wool shirt and lambskin jacket, but the watch on his wrist was a high-end steel Rolex, sleek and expensive.

With his flinty eyes and Eastern European accent, he could have played the sexy villain in a Hollywood spy movie.

He was a stranger—surely she'd remember if she'd ever met such a man. But something about him seemed familiar. Was he an actor? Maybe a newscaster she'd seen on TV? He hadn't introduced himself. Had he assumed she'd know who he was?

Tessa found her voice. "I beg your pardon," she said. "Did you just offer to help me?"

"I couldn't help overhearing," he said. "I'll be taking off for Anchorage in a few minutes. There's plenty of room in the plane. You're welcome to come along—at no charge, of course."

"You're sure?" Tessa wavered on the edge of uncertainty. The man's offer had come as an amazing stroke of luck. But there had to be a catch. She would never get into a car with a strange man. Would getting into a plane, especially with her precious babies, be any different?

"My plane's outside." He spoke as if sensing her hesitation. "It's a private craft. But I happen to be a co-owner of this charter company. If you're worried about your safety, Miss Burris, here, can vouch for me, can't you, Marlene?" He glanced at the woman behind the counter.

"Oh, yes," she simpered. "Absolutely, sir."

"So make up your mind, miss. We need to leave before the fog comes in." He spoke like a man accustomed to getting his own way.

How could she refuse, when this might be her only chance to get to Anchorage with the twins? "Yes," Tessa said, taking the plunge. "I'd be happy to accept your very kind offer."

"Fine." He glanced down at her stacked luggage, which held more clothes, snacks and diapers for the twins than things for herself. "Are these your bags? I'll have them put aboard."

"Yes, thanks. But right now I need to get something. I'll only be a couple of minutes."

Tessa raced down the hall toward the waiting room. She should probably have told her rescuer about the twins. But now that she'd agreed to go, she didn't want to take a chance on his changing his mind. He'd said there was plenty of room. And even in a small plane, the flight from Bellingham to Anchorage couldn't take more than a few hours. How big an imposition could two little children be?

Such a riveting man. Why did that chiseled Slavic face seem so familiar? Where had she seen it before? In a magazine? Maybe on TV? If she didn't remember his name soon she would have to swallow her embarrassment and ask him.

* * *

Dragan watched her hurry away, admiring how her tan slacks clung to her shapely little rump. Too bad the pending lawsuit made bedding her a bad idea. She was definitely his type—petite, curvy and spirited. He imagined she could be a little wildcat between the sheets. Maybe after the trial, if things worked out to everyone's satisfaction…

He shook his head, amused by the predictable wanderings of his mind. He was a shamelessly physical animal who enjoyed pretty women. As long as a lady didn't expect anything beyond a few dinners and nighttime romps, then maybe a diamond bracelet as a parting gift, that was enough for him. Emotions and other such complications were a waste of time and energy.

As for love, if there even was such a thing, it had no place in his world. Now that his uncle—who'd brought him to America after Sarajevo and raised him as a son—had passed away, he had no one left who was truly close to him. No family, no personal attachments of any kind. Dragan was comfortable with that. It made everything simpler, leaving him free to concentrate on the shipping business he'd inherited and forged into an ocean-spanning empire.

His new private plane sat fueled and waiting on the tarmac. Dragan gave orders for a worker to put Miss Randall's luggage—one large suitcase and two smaller ones—in the cargo bay behind the seats. He could tell from the way the man lifted them that they were heavy. The lady must've brought enough clothes, shoes and makeup for a long stay in Anchorage. He could only hope she wouldn't need them—that they'd be able to come to a quick, amicable agreement.

Turning toward the window, Dragan surveyed the thirty-six-foot craft from its single turbo propeller and fifty-two-foot overhead wing to its gleaming tail. The

Swiss-built Pilatus P-6, known as the Porter, was engineered for short-distance takeoffs and landings, making it ideal for Alaska. This one was just out of the shop, where it had been custom fitted with floats above the wheels and heavy-duty tires for landing on rough ground. With these additions, the plane could take him almost anywhere he wished. Dragan looked forward to trying out his new toy, especially with a sexy redheaded passenger aboard.

But this wasn't a pleasure trip, he reminded himself. If he couldn't charm Miss Tessa Randall into a fair settlement of her lawsuit, they'd be facing each other in court.

If it came to that, the gloves would be off. His lawyers would use every dirty trick in the book to discredit her. And her attorney, Helen Carmichael, whose reputation as a feminist ball-buster was widely known, would do her damnedest to portray Trans Pacific as a company that exploited women and cast them aside in their time of need. No matter the outcome, a court battle was bound to be ugly—unless the delicious Miss Randall agreed to settle.

Had she recognized the stranger who'd offered her a flight? Since she'd showed no sign of it, Dragan could only conclude that she hadn't realized who he was. That in itself wasn't surprising. Trans Pacific was a huge company. As its CEO he tended to work behind the scenes, dealing only with upper-level supervisors. He couldn't say for sure if he'd even visited the Anchorage offices in the years she worked there.

She was bound to learn the truth about his identity eventually. But it might be wise to keep it from her until they were in the air. Otherwise, all this trouble—tracking her plans and then showing up here in time to cancel her charter and offer his services—could be for nothing.

He glanced at his watch. Miss Randall had been gone several minutes. She was probably just in the ladies' room, but he needed her to hurry. The fog was rolling in across the Sound. For safety's sake, he needed to take off and get above it before the airport became blanketed in a cloud of gray-white mist.

He was about to go looking for her when he heard the ring of her low-heeled pumps on the tiled floor. Relieved, he turned toward the sound—and stopped cold, as if he'd run into a concrete wall.

Dragan had always prided himself on being able to handle any situation. But, heaven help him, he wasn't prepared to handle this.

Tessa Randall was pushing a baby stroller—one of those ungainly contraptions with two seats side by side. Strapped into those seats, their cornflower eyes taking his measure as if sizing up their next victim, were two toddler-size girls with hair as red as their mother's.

Two

Tessa caught the displeasure—and the surprising flicker of panic—in the stranger's glacial eyes. Most people dissolved into smiles and silly talk at the sight of her adorable twins. But this man was staring at them as if she'd just wheeled in a pair of ticking bombs.

He cleared his throat in the silence. "Well, this is unexpected," he said.

Tessa lifted her chin to meet his gaze. "It's not like I can just leave them behind. And you did tell me you had plenty of room."

He exhaled a long breath as if mentally counting to ten. "So I did. Your bags are already on the plane. But I don't know if that big stroller will fit. And you can't hold your babies on the flight or let them run loose. They'll need to be strapped into the rear seats. Can you manage that?"

"No problem. Their stroller seats double as car seats. They can be lifted free and buckled into place. With the seats gone, the stroller folds flat."

"I see." He glanced at the twins.

Maddie was struggling to wiggle out of her harness but Missy returned his gaze, looking up at him with a smile that would melt a heart of ice.

This stranger's heart, however, must've been carved from solid granite. "We're wasting time," he growled, turning away. "Weather's moving in. Let's get going."

He held the door while Tessa pushed the stroller outside to the nearby plane. The sleek silver-white craft, with its long, tapered nose, looked new and expensive. During her six years of work in Anchorage, she'd seen plenty of bush planes—mostly Beavers, Otters, Cessnas and Pipers—but never one quite like this, with a custom undercarriage that featured both floats and wheels.

He opened the passenger door. "Unfasten the stroller seats. Then climb in. I'll pass them up to you."

He was clearly accustomed to taking charge. Tessa saw no reason to argue with him when his suggestion made sense. And, anyway, she was still relieved he hadn't kicked up more of a fuss about allowing the twins on his plane. She released the levers that fastened the seats to the strollers then stepped onto the float to boost herself into the cockpit.

"Careful." He reached out a hand to steady her, his fingers strong and cool. Tessa clasped them for balance as she swung upward, feeling the electric contact between them. By the time he let go, her pulse was fluttering. Between her pregnancy and caring for the twins, she'd almost forgotten what a man's touch felt like.

Had the compelling stranger been thinking of seduction when he'd offered her a lift? If so, she could thank her twins for dousing that idea. She wasn't looking for a hot one-night stand. If and when she let a man back into her life, it would be someone kind and responsible, someone who wanted to make a life-long commitment and who'd be a good father to her little girls.

Inside, the plane smelled like a new car. The seats were butter-soft beige leather, the wood-grained instrument panel a polished array of dials and gauges. Whoever her rescuer was, he wasn't poor.

Looking down from the doorway, she waited as he lifted Maddie in her car seat and carried her toward the plane. The twins were old enough to recognize a strange situation and react. Maddie broke into an ear-splitting howl. Her sister followed suit.

"Good God! Here, take her!" He thrust the screaming baby upward into Tessa's outstretched hands. Setting the car seat safely down, she turned to take a frantic Missy from the man's arms. The pained look on his lordly face left no need for words.

Tessa busied herself with buckling the twins securely into the two rear seats of the plane. They were still howling, their little cherub faces splotched with tear stains. Tessa wiped their runny noses, kissed them and murmured a few vain words of comfort. When she looked out the open door, the plane's owner was wrestling with the stroller frame. Scowling, he glared up at her. "How the devil do you fold this thing?" he demanded.

"There's a release button on the handle. Try pushing it," Tessa said.

He tried again and managed to make it work. After stowing the stroller and closing the door, he walked around to the other side and took his place in the pilot's seat.

"You're flying the plane?" she asked, surprised.

He glanced back at her, one dark eyebrow quirked upward. "Do you have a problem with that?"

Tessa shook her head.

"Then sit down and buckle up." He indicated the seat next to him. "We're about to take off."

Willing herself to ignore the twins' cries, Tessa slid into the front passenger seat and clicked the belt buckle.

In profile, her pilot looked even more familiar than before. Who was he? This was getting ridiculous. Once they were in the air she would have to ask him.

"Here." He handed her a set of headphones with an attached mike. "Put these on. They'll cut down on the engine noise and let us talk without having to shout."

Tessa took the headphones. Before slipping them on, she glanced back at her daughters. They were still crying but she could tell they were winding down. They'd been awake long enough to be exhausted. With luck they'd soon fall asleep.

Her mysterious pilot had put on his own headphones. He checked the gauges and then switched on the power. The propeller spun to life with a roar of smooth-running power. Tessa glanced back at the twins. They were wide-eyed but didn't seem upset by the noise. Maybe it was like riding in a car, which usually tended to settle them down.

Humming like a high-end European sports car, the plane taxied past the hangars and out onto the runway. Tessa's pulse skittered. She held her breath as he opened the throttle and pulled back on the wheel. The sleek craft rocketed down the runway, left the ground and soared into the air.

As it climbed, wind battering the fuselage, doubts assailed her mind. What if she'd made a foolish mistake, trusting her life and the lives of her precious children to this arrogant stranger? What if he meant them harm, or lacked the competence to get them safely to Anchorage? She should have held out for a charter flight. Surely they would have been able to find something to accommodate her if she'd given them enough time.

As the plane leveled off from its steep climb, she began to breathe again. The man at the controls appeared to be a skilled pilot. His hands moved with a sureness born of experience. His expression radiated calm confidence. She still wasn't certain he was safe, but at least he was competent.

As if sensing her gaze, he glanced toward her. In that brief instant something about the light on his face and the set of his mouth struck her like a thunderbolt.

She knew who he was.

Until today she'd never met him face-to-face. But she'd seen his photo on company bulletins when she'd worked for Trans Pacific. He was the CEO, secretly referred to as "The Dragon" in part because of his name but mostly because of his management style.

He was Dragan Markovic, the man whose company she was suing.

Dragan leveled off at ten thousand feet and eased the Porter to a cruising speed of one hundred and thirty-two miles an hour. If the weather held, they should make it to Anchorage before dark. The time included a stop in Ketchikan for refueling and maybe a quick snack, eaten on the run.

He'd been flying since his late teens and was no stranger to handling small planes. In the past couple of summers he'd flown big-money clients to the company-owned lodge on a hidden inlet northeast of Petersburg for salmon fishing. But this was his first long-distance flight in the new Porter. So far, so good. At least as far as the plane was concerned.

He glanced to the right, where his pretty, redheaded passenger sat in grim silence, hands clasped in her lap.

Was she nervous about the flight or was something else bothering her?

Dragan had hoped to draw her into a conversation. But the lady wasn't making things easy. "Are you all right?" he asked, speaking into the mike. "Not getting airsick, are you?"

"I'm fine." He could hear the tension in her breathing. "But I can't help wondering what you have in mind for us, Mr. Markovic."

So she had figured it out—and she wasn't happy.

Dragan weighed the wisdom of speaking in his own defense then rejected the idea. He'd learn more if he let her take the lead.

"Why didn't you tell me who you were?" she demanded.

He stalled for time, checking the instrument panel. "If you'd known, would you have come with me?"

"Certainly not. I'm not even supposed to be talking to you. My lawyer would have a fit if she knew about this." Turning in her seat, she glanced back at the twins.

"Knowing your lawyer's reputation, I can imagine that. How are your babies doing?"

"Fine. They're fast asleep." She settled back into the seat. "Would you have invited me along if you'd known I came with so much baggage?"

She was sharper than he'd expected. Dragan managed an edgy laugh. "I plead the Fifth."

"I saw the look on your face when I showed up with my twins," she said. "You don't like children much, do you?"

Dragan blocked the images that sprang up in his memory—sharp-boned faces, haunted eyes—images he'd spent the past twenty years trying to forget. "No comment," he said.

"Then what do you have to say about tricking me onto your plane?" Her tongue gave a disapproving click. "You said you own the charter company…did you have something to do with my flight being canceled?"

There was no good way for him to answer, so he stayed silent.

Her voice was even frostier when she spoke again.

"Kidnapping's a federal offense, Mr. Markovic, especially now that you've crossed the U.S. border. That's Canada down below us."

"I didn't kidnap you. I offered you a lift to Anchorage. You accepted, and that's exactly where we're headed. We'll be landing before nightfall. Call me Dragan, by the way."

She was silent, her rose-petal lips pressed together in a thin line. Dragan could sense the tension building in her, the outrage, the fury. When the explosion came he was braced for it, but her words still stung.

"Of all the arrogant, low-down, presumptuous, high-handed tricks—" The words ended in a sputter. She stared down at her clenched hands. "How could you do this with a clear conscience? How could you just manipulate me into coming with you?"

"The question you should be asking isn't how. It's why."

"All right. Why?" She gazed straight ahead into the skyscape of drifting clouds. "Suppose you tell me."

Dragan made a show of checking the altimeter while he thought out his answer. "There are two sides to every story," he said. "Before we face off in front of a judge, I wanted to hear yours."

"You could have just offered to take me out to dinner." Her voice was flat, stubborn.

"Would you have accepted? You said you weren't supposed to talk to me—a restriction that I find absolutely absurd. How are we supposed to settle matters if I can't even find out what's truly bothering you until it's all dragged out in court? As it is, you have a captive audience here.

You can say anything you like—swear at me, call me every vile name in the book if you want."

"Don't tempt me. I don't work for you anymore."

"That's a shame, considering your great performance reviews. Somebody must've thought you were doing an excellent job."

"You read my file?"

"Of course I did."

"Then you know that before I was fired for supposedly not being able to handle the work attached to my position, I applied for a desk job in the Seattle office. It would've been a step down, but with the babies coming, I couldn't travel and I wanted to be closer to my parents in Bellingham. I filled out the papers but I didn't even get an interview. The next thing I knew I'd been fired."

"Actually, I didn't know that. None of that was in your file." Dragan remembered noticing what had appeared to be missing information.

"That doesn't surprise me," she said. "Maybe you should pay more attention to what's going on in your company, Mr. Markovic. It's not just about the bottom line. It's about the people."

Her words burned like the jab of a hot poker. Stunned for an instant, he recovered his voice. "It's Dragan. And I hope you're prepared to explain what you just said."

She shrugged. "You'll hear it all tomorrow—in court."

Dragan held his tongue, hoping she'd say more. But she'd lapsed into stubborn silence. The lady was tougher than he'd expected—and smart. Too smart to discuss the case with a man she saw as the enemy. He had to give her points for that.

Not that he was about to give up. Whatever it took, he was going to crack Tessa Randall's protective shell and discover the real story behind her lawsuit.

But wanting to settle the lawsuit wasn't all that was mo-
tivating him. Tessa had gotten to him in a way few women
did. He wouldn't be satisfied until he knew what made the
sexy redhead tick.

Tessa gazed downward through the cockpit's wrap-
around window. She'd taken a fair number of flights between Seattle and Anchorage, but always by commercial
jet and usually with her nose in her laptop. Only now, at
a slower speed and much lower altitude, did she realize
what heart-stopping views she'd missed.

Glacier-carved peaks, dotted with jewel-like hanging
lakes, rose out of pine-carpeted slopes. On the right, the
ocean stretched to the horizon. The coast between was a
maze of wooded islands and sun-sparkled inlets. "Magnificent," Tessa murmured, forgetting she was wearing a mike.

"Isn't it?" Dragan's deep, gravelly voice came through
the headphones, startling her. "Amazing what nature can
do, given a few million years."

"Seeing country like this makes me want to forget all
the ugliness and pettiness in the world." Tessa forced a
chuckle. "Of course, that's not possible these days, is it?"

He banked the plane to give her a dizzying view of a
waterfall. The wing tilted then leveled again. "How did
you come to speak Japanese?" he asked.

It seemed a safe enough question for her to answer. "I
was an air force brat. Our family was stationed in Japan for
a few years. We had Japanese babysitters and watched Japanese TV. Later on I went part-time to a Japanese school."

"We?"

"My big brother and I. He's married now, works for a
bank in London. My dad and mother live in Bellingham."
Tessa knew he was trying to draw her out, probably hoping
she'd slip and give him some detail he could use against

her. She would have to weigh everything she told him. But talking about her family seemed a harmless enough way to pass the time.

"I take it your parents are enjoying their granddaughters," he said.

"Oh, yes. My mother was going to watch the twins while I went to Anchorage, but she broke her foot. Now that the girls can walk, it takes a lot of chasing to keep up with them." She glanced back over the seat to make sure her daughters were still sleeping.

"What are their names?"

"Madelyn and Melissa, but we call them Maddie and Missy." Tessa loved talking about her twins. She was so proud of them.

"They look exactly alike to me. How the devil do you tell them apart?"

"It's easy. Missy has a little mole on her ear. But even without that, once you get to know them, you can tell by their personalities. Missy's the snuggly one. Maddie's the little explorer. Turn your back and she's gone. Now that they know their own names, it's even easier to tell which one is which."

He paused a moment, as if weighing the next question. "Would it be too personal if I asked about their father?"

Yes, Tessa wanted to say. But if she gave a dismissive answer, he might imagine that the full story was something he could use against her, like a married lover or a pick-up in a bar. The truth would serve her best.

"He was my fiancé, a journalist. We'd planned to get married when he came back from his assignment in the Middle East." Tessa swallowed the lump that rose in her throat. Even after two years it hurt to talk about Kevin. "He was killed in Yemen, in a car bombing. At the time it happened, I didn't even know I was pregnant."

"I'm sorry."

"After he died, I didn't want to go on. But my babies pulled me through. They gave me something to live for."

"You've been through a rough time."

"Rough in more ways than you can imagine. That's the reason I'm suing your company."

Her words silenced Dragan like the click of a closing door. For now, it was time to back off. She'd be more likely to open up about her side of the lawsuit if he kept things friendly and didn't push her.

He'd already learned a few things about Tessa Randall. She struck him as an honest woman, interested in more than just grabbing easy money. But what part did her pretty face and seductive figure play in his assessment? Was he thinking like a CEO, protecting his company's reputation, or did he just want to lure the lady into his bed?

Clouds were moving in along the coastline, but the sky ahead looked clear. Like any competent pilot, Dragan had checked the weather forecast before taking off. There was a storm brewing out in the Pacific, but it shouldn't make landfall before tomorrow morning. He had an ample window of time for the flight to Anchorage; and the Porter was performing beautifully, its engine purring like a contented cat.

There was no way to explain the premonition that ran along his spine like the stroke of an icy fingertip; the sense that something dire was about to happen. It was a feeling Dragan recognized from his boyhood years in Sarajevo when shells and mortars would rain out of the sky to explode in hellish bursts of flame. Back then, that danger sense had kept him alive. But why should he feel it now? Everything was fine.

By the time they sighted Ketchikan the twins were

awake and fussing. The floats skimmed the water as Dragan landed the plane and taxied to the fuel dock by the small airport. Across the harbor, the town lay along the narrow edge of pine-forested mountains. Autumn was already setting in. The cruise ships were gone, the dockside souvenir shops closed. Fishing boats plied the waters for the last of the seasonal catch.

While Tessa changed her little girls and fed them snacks from her bag, Dragan ordered the tank filled and walked uphill to the terminal to pay for the fuel. At the snack bar he picked up a couple of sandwiches and some bottled water. On his return, he found Tessa sitting in the cockpit, her babies once more buckled into their safety seats.

"Hungry?" He held up the wrapped sandwiches. "Chicken or ham and cheese. Your choice."

"Either one, thanks. But first I could use a restroom. And I need to dump these somewhere." She held up a plastic bag sagging with the damp weight of what smelled suspiciously like dirty diapers. "Could you keep an eye on my girls for a few minutes? I'll be right back."

Without waiting for an answer she opened the passenger-side door, climbed down to the float and stepped onto the dock. Dragan watched as she tossed the bagged disposable diapers into a trash can and strode up the long ramp to the terminal, her purse slung over her shoulder.

As he wolfed down the ham sandwich, Dragan watched her, admiring the confidence in her long, easy strides. She was a strong woman. She would have to be, to survive what she'd been through. And she was intelligent. He liked smart women—the bland, clingy ones were no challenge. The thought of getting Tessa Randall into bed and driving her wild with pleasure was enough to stoke a simmering blaze in his loins. But it was time for a dash of cold water. He couldn't let his attraction to her distract him from why they were there. Tessa and her lawyer were out to drag the name of his company through the mud. He'd be a fool to let himself forget that.

A cooing sound from the rear caught his attention. He turned in his seat to see Tessa's twins gazing up at him. A nap and a meal had transformed the pair from little screaming monsters to cherubs from a Renaissance painting, with Titian curls and sky-blue eyes.

Dragan tended to avoid children. Their innocence tore at his heart, stirring shadowed memories, sights and sounds he wanted only to forget. He'd vowed never to have children of his own. There was too much suffering in the world, too much danger.

He scowled over the seat at the little girls. The twin on the right smiled and giggled. The one on the left scowled back at him. Tessa had told him they had different personalities. He could see that already.

"So what are you two thinking?" His voice startled the smiling twin. Her blue eyes grew even bigger. Her sister's suspicious frown didn't change. "If you could talk, what would you say to me?"

"Da." The smiling twin—by now he'd guessed she was Missy—began to jabber, making little nonsense sounds that were her version of conversation. When she turned her head, Dragan could see the tiny mole on her earlobe. He'd guessed right.

"So how about you, Maddie?" He addressed her sister. "What do you think of all this?"

"Phhht!" The flawless raspberry was punctuated by an impressive spit bubble.

Dragan couldn't hold back a chuckle. At last, a female who spoke her mind!

"I see you're getting acquainted." Tessa climbed back into the plane and closed the door.

"You're right, they do have different personalities."

"See, I told you. Maddie's quiet and restless like her father. I guess Missy is more like me."

"Snuggly—that was how you described her. Are you snuggly, too?" It would be fun finding out, he thought.

"No comment." She fastened her seat belt and slipped on her headset, as if to shut him out. "Let's get going."

Dragan taxied away from the dock and swung the nose into the rising wind. The plane skimmed across the water and roared skyward. The air was getting rougher now, turbulence buffeting the wing and the fuselage. It was nothing that couldn't be handled, but he'd be relieved when they touched down in Anchorage.

Yet he knew that the time was limited for him to learn all he wanted to know about Miss Tessa Randall. So far he wasn't making much progress.

She'd finished her sandwich and sat silent as the plane rose above the turbulence and leveled off in calmer air. Was she nervous about the flight or had he crossed the line when he'd asked if she was snuggly? Maybe she'd had a talk with herself in the terminal and concluded that she was being too friendly with a man who was planning to rip her apart in court.

The only sound from the twins was Missy's contented babbling. The twins, thank heaven, seemed to like the drone of the engine and the motion of the plane. He could only hope the tranquility would last.

They'd passed over the old Norwegian fishing village of Petersburg and were headed in the general direction of Sitka when Dragan happened to glance at the fuel gauge.

His heart dropped.

The indicator was almost on empty.

Three

Dragan stared at the fuel gauge in disbelief. He'd watched the attendant fill the tank in Ketchikan. Given the distance they'd flown, it should be at least three-quarters full. But he had to trust what the indicator told him. The tank was almost empty.

The plane had to be leaking fuel. Nothing else made sense. Maybe the fuel line had broken or become disconnected, or some unseen object had punctured the tank. The problem might be as simple as the fuel cap coming loose. Whatever it was, he had to get the plane down before the fuel ran out and the engine quit.

Willing himself to keep calm, he glanced at Tessa. She was looking out the window and hadn't noticed the falling gauge. Good. The last thing he wanted was to have her panic. He would try to keep her unaware until he had a plan.

The country below was a vast jigsaw puzzle of islands, inlets and fjords. Landing on water shouldn't be a problem. But if he came down in the wilderness, he'd be marooned with a woman, two babies and no supplies. The plane had a radio, but with a storm coming in, any rescue might be days away. He needed to get his vulnerable passengers somewhere safe.

Clouds were rolling in ahead of the storm, already obscuring his view. He had to make a decision fast.

Petersburg was too far behind, Sitka too far ahead. But the company lodge where he flew wealthy clients might be within reach. He checked the plane's GPS. The lodge was just thirty miles to the northeast. It was their best chance, maybe their only chance.

Banking the plane, he veered sharply to the right. The sudden move caught Tessa's attention. "What's happening?" she demanded. "Why are you turning us around?"

Dragan willed himself to speak calmly. "We're losing fuel—almost out. We need to set down while we can."

"Down there?" She stared out the window at the wild mosaic of forest and water.

"Not if I can help it. The company has a fishing lodge a few miles from here. If we can make it that far, we'll have a safe place to stay until help comes."

For a long moment she was still. Suddenly she turned on him, her hand gripping his sleeve.

"I don't believe you! This is just a trick to keep me away from the trial! Get back on course *now* or so help me, I'll have you arrested for kidnapping!"

"Look at that gauge, Tessa," he snapped. "This is no trick. This is real. Now let go of me and pray that we can make the lodge before I have to land this plane!"

Releasing her grip, Tessa stared at the fuel gauge. The needle was hovering just above the empty line. If this was a trick, it was a convincing one.

The plane had descended into clouds and rough air. A howling wind rattled the fuselage. The craft bucked and lurched, fighting its way downward. The twins began to cry. Tessa yanked frantically at her seat belt, hands fumbling with the buckle.

"What the hell are you doing?" Dragan's voice thundered.

"My babies—"

"They'll be safest right where they are. So will you. Now stay put!"

Tessa braced against the jarring turbulence, eyes scanning the cloud-blurred landscape for some sign of shelter. She could see nothing below but water and trees, with a few open patches of what she guessed to be bog. A flock of white gulls swooped past the plane, just missing the windshield.

Dragan's hands were steady on the controls. Only a muscle, twitching along his jaw, betrayed his unease. With the clouds moving in, it was getting harder to see the ground. He had to be depending as much on the GPS as on his vision. His grim expression told her he had yet to find what he was looking for. Knowing he needed all of his concentration for the task, she kept herself as silent and still as possible so she wouldn't distract him.

Even with the headset on, Tessa could hear her twins crying above the drone of the plane. It was all she could do to keep from ripping off her seat belt and rushing back to clutch them in her arms. But Dragan was right. They were safest as they were, and so was she.

"There it is. Two o'clock." Dragan's voice, crackling through the headset, startled her. Through the trees in the direction he'd indicated, she glimpsed something flat and brown at the foot of an inlet. Then it was gone, hidden by the clouds. "Hang on," he said. "We're going in."

He'd spoken none too soon. As the plane banked right and angled into its final descent, the engine sputtered and stopped.

The sudden stillness was terrifying. Tessa forgot to breathe. Could they make it as far as the inlet or would they fall short and crash into the trees? What would happen to her babies?

Time seemed to stop as the plane glided down through clouds and battering wind. The floats raked the treetops. There was a split second of air before the plane skimmed the water and came to rest like a settling bird, twenty yards from the beach.

Rain spattered the windshield. Beyond the waterline, Tessa could make out thick pines half screening a substantial log building. Wherever they were, at least they'd have shelter.

Dragan switched off the engine and lifted away his headphones. His breath whooshed out in a powerful exhalation. "You can see to your babies now," he said. "Try to keep them quiet while I radio for help."

The twins were wailing at the top of their lungs. Tessa flung off her belt and scrambled back to the rear seat. At the sight of their mother, their cries diminished to whimpers. Unbuckling their harnesses, she lifted them onto her lap and hugged them fiercely close. Holding them this way had been easy when they were tiny. Now that they were active toddlers it was different. Missy flung her little arms around Tessa's neck, hanging on as if she never wanted to let go. Maddie was already struggling to get down and explore the plane.

Love burned through Tessa like the stab of a hot blade. Her little girls were her whole life. What would she have done if they'd come to harm?

From the cockpit she could hear Dragan on the radio,

shouting through the static at somebody on the other end. The relief that had swept through her when the plane landed was congealing into cold rage. Dragan's skill as a pilot may have just saved their lives. But it was his reckless, high-handed behavior that had created the danger in the first place. The crash landing could have killed them all—including her precious babies.

If he hadn't shanghaied her onto his flight by interfering with her plane, she'd be well on her way to Anchorage now, looking forward to a good meal and a comfortable night's rest before the trial. Instead, *almost as if he'd planned it*, she and her twins would be stuck with this domineering alpha male in the middle of nowhere, maybe for days, until help arrived.

So help her, when she got back to civilization, Dragan Markovic would pay for this. He thought he'd had trouble before the flight, but she was just getting started. She would show him what *real* trouble was.

Meanwhile, she and her little ones would be dependent on him for their survival. The only sensible course of action would be to rein in her anger and cooperate. But it wasn't going to be easy—when she could barely look at him without wanting to slap his arrogant face.

The radio reception had faded into static. Frustrated, Dragan switched it off. With luck it was just the weather interfering with the signal. He would try again later. For now he could only hope that somebody on the other end had heard his shouted transmission, giving their location and their need for help. Cell phones, he already knew, were useless here.

At least the twins had stopped howling. He leaned around the pilot's seat to see Tessa cradling them in her arms, looking as fiercely protective as a tigress. "Is everything all right back there?" he asked.

"So far." Her cheerful reply sounded forced. "How did you fare with the radio?"

"The reception was bad, but I think I managed to send our position before it cut out. If we're lucky we could be seeing a rescue plane in the next few hours. But don't count on it. There's a big storm moving in. We could be here until it blows over."

She pressed her lips together, as if biting back a caustic reply. If she was furious, he couldn't blame her. His actions had likely caused her to miss the trial opening and put all their lives in danger. At least she was making an effort to be civil.

"Another question," she said. "How are we supposed to get from here to solid ground? Will we have to swim?"

"Tomorrow morning when the tide's out we could walk. But don't worry, there's a faster way."

Moving past her into the rear of the plane, he found and opened the yellow valise that held the plane's emergency raft. Raising the cargo door and dropping the sea anchor, he gripped the tether line and tossed the raft down to the water. With a loud hiss it self-inflated, rocking on the slight swell next to the plane's float. A chilly wind rippled the water.

"Ladies first," he said. "Take the minimum you'll need for now. I'll get the heavy things later."

Slinging her purse and the pink-quilted diaper bag over her shoulder, Tessa rose with the babies and stumbled her way to the cargo bay. "Hang on to the girls," she said. "Once I'm in the raft, you can pass them down to me."

Dragan hesitated. He hadn't held a baby since he was a boy in Sarajevo. But this was no time for memories, especially those he wanted to forget. He reached toward her, hoping he could manage two squirming toddlers long enough to get them safely into the raft with their mother.

"Here." Tessa stepped close to him, her arms loaded with wiggly little redheads. "Take them and hold on tight. They won't bite you, but they might try to get loose. Whatever happens, you can't let them fall."

Dragan caught the flash of worry in her deep hazel eyes. She was trusting her precious children to his inexperienced hands. She had every reason to be nervous.

One baby would have been easy enough to hand off. Two babies were a different matter. Dragan worked an arm around Missy, trying to ignore the intimate contact as the back of his hand slid over Tessa's warm breast. Missy wailed and seized her mother's neck in a frantic clasp, refusing to let go.

Giving up for the moment, he tried Maddie. She went to him readily, but as he lifted her against his chest, the stink that rose to his nostrils was unmistakable. "Good Lord," he muttered. "This one needs changing."

"She's a baby. Deal with it." Tessa looked frayed. "Give her back. I've got a better idea. You're taller than I am. You climb into the raft and I'll pass the girls down to you, one at a time."

"Good idea." Dragan wondered why he hadn't thought of it himself. Handing the reeking Maddie back to her mother, he took the purse and diaper bag, looped the handles over his shoulder and climbed down onto the float. The raft was a step below, secured to the plane by the tether.

From the door he could see Tessa buckling Missy into her safety seat. She managed to do it while balancing Maddie between her arm and her hip, a remarkable feat. Dropping the bags into the raft he kept his weight on the float and held up his arms for Maddie.

The transfer was going to be tricky. The raft wasn't made for standing, and he couldn't risk putting Maddie down there by herself. He would need to take both twins, sit on the float with them and shift from there into the raft.

Maddie came to him without a fuss. Bracing his senses against her rank aroma, he circled her with his left arm. By the time he had a firm grip on her Tessa had unbuckled Missy and was ready to hand her down. Dragan could see the worry in her eyes as she passed him her whimpering child. She was trusting him only because she had no other choice.

Tessa watched, holding her breath as Dragan, with one twin under each arm, managed to maneuver from the float to the raft without a spill. Now she stood alone in the plane, looking down at them from the cargo door. Clouds were drifting across the inlet, graying the afternoon sunlight. The wind was getting stronger and colder.

Dragan placed the babies next to him and covered them with his leather jacket. When Maddie tried to crawl away he pulled her back and held her by her pink coverall straps. "Give me your shoes, Tessa," he said. "You'll have better footing without them."

She stepped out of her low-heeled tan pumps and tossed them one at a time. He caught them with his free hand. "We'll need the tether undone," he said. "Untie it and bring it with you. I'll come back and close the door later."

The stout nylon rope was looped around a grip handle next to the cargo door. Tessa untied it and, with the end in her hand, climbed gingerly onto the float. By now the raft was rolling on the wind-whipped water. The next step wasn't going to be easy.

"Give me your hand," Dragan said, leaning toward her. She'd put one foot onto the inflated side of the raft and was just reaching for him when a harsh gust blasted across the inlet. The plane rocked. The float pitched upward, lifting away from the raft. Caught between, Tess lost her footing and tumbled into the water.

It was cold. Deathly cold. Tessa was a fair swimmer, but in the few seconds before she broke the surface and caught Dragan's outstretched hand she was chilled to the bone. Her teeth chattered as he pulled her into the raft.

"Here—" He yanked off his flannel shirt and wrapped it around her shoulders. "Hang on," he muttered. "We've got to get you someplace warm."

The raft kit was equipped with a collapsible paddle. Snapping it together, he pushed hard for the beach.

Tessa huddled with her twins and watched his broad shoulders labor under the gray thermal T-shirt he wore. He was pushing against the wind, making slow but steady progress. Under the woolen shirt, her skin felt clammy. Her fingers and toes were numb. She'd heard enough stories about cold Alaskan waters to know that she could have died of hypothermia in minutes if he hadn't pulled her out. Even on the raft, freed from the water, she wasn't out of danger. Her wet clothes were turning icy in the wind. She was worried about her little girls, too. Dragan's leather jacket was giving them some protection, but they needed to get indoors and get warm.

She could see the lodge through the trees. Even at a distance she could see that it was no paltry wilderness cabin. Solidly built of logs, it was the size of a large one-story home with a tall stone chimney and a covered porch running along the front. The windows had been shuttered for the winter. The door would be securely locked.

Would Dragan have the key? If he'd brought it along that would be a sure sign he'd planned this whole misadventure. If he could keep her away from Anchorage, her testimony at the trial—perhaps the trial itself—would have to be delayed. Worse yet, the trial could go ahead without her, and without her testimony to give weight to her claims, she'd lose her case.

But that wouldn't be the end, she vowed. If this little escapade cost her a victory in court, she would do everything in her power to make Dragan pay for it.

A narrow floating dock led from the sloping beach into the water. By the time Tessa had found her shoes and put them on, the raft had bumped against the side. The dock was an easy step above the raft. After climbing up, Dragan secured the tether to a capstan and reached down for the twins.

Wrapping the squirming Maddie in the leather jacket, she passed her up to his waiting arms. Missy came next. This time she went to him willingly. Tessa followed, her purse and diaper bag slung over her shoulder.

"Can you make it to the lodge all right?" he asked.

"I'll be fine. Just hang on to the girls and keep them warm." Tessa's feet were too numb to feel the ground beneath her shoes, but she forced herself to put one foot in front of the other.

He walked beside her; the twins snuggled against his chest, still covered by his leather jacket.

"The lodge looks closed up," she said. "Will we have any trouble getting in?"

"Don't worry. I have a key."

Tessa had thought she couldn't get any colder. But a jolt of frigid rage penetrated all the way to her heart. So he *did* have the key. He could have planned this all along, luring her onto the plane and then faking an emergency to strand her and her children in the middle of nowhere.

The front steps of the lodge were carpeted with dead needles from the surrounding lodgepole pines, but the covered porch was swept clean. A raven, scolding from the roofline, flapped into the trees as Dragan handed off Maddie and fished a ring of keys out of his pocket.

The heavy front door was secured with a cast-iron hasp and an industrial-weight padlock. Without a pause, Dragan chose a key from the half dozen on the ring and thrust it into the lock, which parted with a well-lubricated click.

Lifting the lock free of the hasp, Dragan swung the door open and ushered Tessa into a rustic Shangri-La.

The great room encompassed a sitting area in front of a huge stone fireplace, with a dining table and wet bar at the far end. Double swinging doors concealed what she assumed to be the kitchen. A hallway opening off one side led, presumably, to the bedrooms and bathrooms.

The layout of the lodge wasn't surprising. It was the construction of the place that made Tessa catch her breath. Seen in the faint light that fell through the shutter vanes and the open door, massive trees, stripped of their bark, supported the cathedral ceiling of the great room. The chandelier that hung from the center beam was a rustically elegant filigree of twisted wood and glass that had probably cost more than she would earn in a lifetime. The floors were dark wood, the thick sheepskin rugs almost floating on their polished surface. The cream-colored leather divans grouped around the fireplace looked as soft as baby skin. The surface of the coffee table was a slab of black marble. The tall windows, if uncovered, would have offered a view of the inlet through the trees.

The place was spectacular—but one thing it wasn't was warm. Tessa's skin had shrunk to goose bumps beneath her wet clothes. Her teeth were chattering.

"Come on!" Dragan took her arm and led her down a hallway lined with doors. "While you get out of those wet clothes, I'll light the fireplace and turn on the water. The pipes have been drained for the winter, so it'll take a few minutes. You can use the bathroom but you won't be able to flush the toilet until the tank fills. And I'll need to turn on the propane tank to heat the water and run the stove." He paused outside one of the doors. "This room should do you fine. You'll find some thermal underwear and wool socks in the dresser drawer and a warm robe in the closet. Put them on. This is a summer lodge. There's no heat except the fireplace." He opened the door and disappeared back the way they'd come.

The twins were getting heavy in her arms. They'd been unusually subdued since they'd come inside—awed, perhaps, by their strange new surroundings. Tessa carried them into the room and set them on the bed. They'd soon need to be fed and changed, but she'd be useless to care for them if she didn't get out of her wet clothes first.

The queen-size bed was covered with a dark-green, down-filled comforter that matched the window drapes. The twins loved the fluffy softness. Happy to be out of their confining seats, they tumbled, rolled and giggled as Tessa stripped off her wet clothes and hung them over the shower rack in the bathroom. She was soaked to the skin. Even her bra and panties had to come off. In the dresser she found several sets of new thermal underwear, still sealed in plastic bags. Choosing the smallest size, she pulled the shirt over her head and stepped into the drawers. They were too big, and the fly in front told her they were made for a man, but they were soft and warm, and she was in no condition to complain. The waist had a drawstring. She tightened it to fit, rolled up the ankles and opened a packet of thick wool socks.

As she was pulling them on, she heard the gurgle and rush of water in the adjoining bathroom. The taps, she realized, would have been left open when the pipes were drained for the winter. She raced into the opulent marble bathroom to shut them off. At least Dragan had made good on his promise to get the water running right away.

But she'd been a fool to trust his offer to fly her to Anchorage. Blast the man! Once they were safely out of this place, she was going to give him a piece of her mind! The robe in the closet was black cashmere. It glided around her as she slid her arms into the sleeves and tightened the sash. It was too big for her, but so decadently soft that it was a pleasure to wear. She took a moment to roll up the long sleeves, then turned back to check on her twins. Missy was sitting on the bed, watching her with wide blue eyes.

Maddie was nowhere in sight.

Tessa glanced around. There was no cause for panic. She'd closed the door firmly behind her when she'd entered the room. Hadn't she?

She swung toward the door, her heart creeping into her throat. The door stood partway open. Preoccupied with the babies and her wet clothes, she must have failed to close it all the way, leaving just enough edge for Maddie to catch with her tiny fingers. The little scamp was an accomplished Houdini.

Snatching Missy off the bed, Tessa flung the door all the way open and peered up and down the hall. No Maddie. She'd made a clean getaway—into a house filled with unknown dangers.

"Maddie!" Tessa called. "Come back here! Come back right now!"

There was no answer.

Four

After he'd turned on the water, Dragan made a fire in the fireplace, opened the valve on the propane tank behind the lodge and lit the pilot lights on the stove and water heater. That done, he went out to the equipment shed to check the generator. The machine that powered the house had been drained of fuel and covered for the winter. There was no gasoline. Sam, the Tlingit caretaker who'd spent the summer in a cabin on the property, would have taken what was left of it when he'd departed for his island home after the season was over.

Closing the shed door and locking it, Dragan headed back toward the house. He and his reluctant guests would have no electricity for their stay. But at least they'd be warm. There was plenty of firewood and the propane would allow them to take hot baths and heat the emergency supply of canned and freeze-dried food that stocked the pantry shelves.

But what were Tessa's twins going to eat? Dragan mouthed a curse as the question struck him. There was no baby food in the house and no fresh milk. Not only that, the place wasn't equipped for small children. There were no cribs, no playpens, no high chairs, no toys—and certainly no reserve supply of disposable diapers.

This was going to be a nightmare!

He could only hope his radio transmission had gotten through and that a rescue plane would soon come to fly them to Anchorage, or at least to deliver some fuel for the Porter.

Meanwhile, he'd be damned if he was going to play nanny. The twins would be Tessa's problem, not his. Babies stirred emotions he never wanted to feel again. The less he had to do with them, the better.

The light was already fading above the trees. He would need to locate a supply of candles or a lantern. Otherwise they'd soon be stumbling around in the dark. There was a flashlight in the plane, as well as Tessa's suitcases and his own bag. He'd hoped to get everything in the morning, when the tide would be out, and he could check for the cause of the fuel leak. But with the storm coming, he'd be smart to take the raft now to get the luggage and secure the plane as best he could.

Tessa seemed to think he'd planned this misadventure. Nothing could be further from the truth. If he'd known he was going to end up stuck in the middle of nowhere with three troublesome redheads, he wouldn't have come within a mile of her and her two little imps.

On the back porch, he stomped the mud off his shoes before opening the door to the kitchen. He'd seen small bear tracks and fresh scat near the equipment shed; maybe a half-grown cub snooping around. Not much to worry about as long as everything was securely locked and no food was left out. For now, at least, he'd spare Tessa the news of this latest discovery. She was already under enough stress.

He'd moved into the shadowed kitchen and had just turned back to lock the dead bolt when he heard a subtle sound behind him. Startled, he jerked around to see a stubby little figure with a mop of russet curls gazing up at him.

"Phhht!" Maddie had passed judgment on him again.

"What the devil are you doing in here, you little scamp?" Dragan dropped to a crouch beside her. It hadn't occurred to him that the twins could walk. Until now he'd only seen them carried.

"Noz." She reached out and poked his face. He hadn't known they could talk, either. Surprise. But there was nothing surprising about the familiar stink that rose from under her pink coveralls. Miss Maddie had clearly escaped before her mother had had a chance to change her diaper.

Rising, he edged around her and headed toward the dining room. "Come on," he said, beckoning. "Let's go find your mom."

"Phhht!" Ignoring him, Maddie began tugging at the door to the cabinet under the sink—the cabinet that held detergent, bleach, drain cleaner, mouse bait…

Dragan had never been into sports, but he scooped her up like a halfback seizing a fumbled ball, gripping her under one arm as he strode out of the kitchen. Thanks to Maddie and her sister, he would have to childproof the whole damned lodge, starting with that cabinet.

In the entry he ran into Tessa. Dressed in the black cashmere robe, she was holding Missy, eyes darting this way and that with a frantic look. Relief lit her face when she saw that Dragan had her daughter.

"For God's sake, take her!" Dragan muttered. "She smells like a—" He groped for the right word.

"Like a messy baby." Tessa took Maddie with her free arm, arching slightly backward to balance both twins with the aid of her hips. Dragan found the pose strangely sexy, although he couldn't say why. "Thank goodness you found her," she said. "Where was she?"

"In the kitchen, trying to open a cabinet full of toxic cleaners. You can't just let your children run around by themselves here. The place isn't safe for toddlers. It's dangerous."

"You think I'd just turn them loose?" Her hazel eyes flashed. "Keeping an eye on these two is a full-time job. As a mother, I take that job seriously. Maddie's getting out of the bedroom was an accident. It won't happen again."

"Fine." He met her defiance with a scowl. "As long as you're here, what will you do about feeding those two? There should be an emergency stash of cans and freeze-dried meals in the pantry, but there's no baby food."

"They can eat regular food as long as I mash it up. But I'll warn you, they're picky little eaters, *and* they usually make a mess."

"Then I guess that's your problem." He started toward the front door then paused. "I'll be taking the raft back to the plane to get our luggage and close the cargo door. I won't be long."

"Please don't drown." Her words followed him as he headed for the door. Was she joking or was she worried about his safety? He'd bet money she was most concerned about being stranded here if something were to happen to him.

"Drowning's more your specialty." Leaving her with those words, he closed the door and walked out onto the porch. Looking to the west he could see thick, black clouds roiling above the treetops. The front was moving in fast. There was no time to waste. He needed to get the luggage inside and secure the plane. Once the storm struck it would likely be too late.

* * *

Tessa stood a moment, clasping her twins and staring at the closed door. Wind rattled the shutters that covered the front windows. Dragan wouldn't have an easy time out there, paddling the clumsy raft out to the plane, loading the luggage and bringing it back. Worse, it could be dangerous. She remembered the awful sensation of icy water closing over her head, then Dragan's strong hand pulling her up into the raft. If he happened to slip now, he would be alone, with no one to help him. He could freeze or drown.

But worrying about him wouldn't help—especially with two toddlers to care for. Both twins needed changing, and they'd soon be getting hungry. The pink quilted bag held a half-dozen disposable diapers, some wipes, two fresh outfits, two bibs, sippy cups and miniature spoons, and what was left of the snacks she'd brought along—mostly crackers, cereal, cheese sticks and a little juice. Dragan had mentioned canned and freeze-dried food. She could only hope it included something her fussy babies would eat, and that there'd be enough to last until they made it out of here.

She carried the girls back to the bedroom, closed the door—firmly, listening for it to click—and spread a towel on the bed. As a mother, she'd had enough practice changing messy diapers to do it efficiently. Within a few minutes both twins were wiped and changed, the soiled diapers sealed in a plastic bag. She would leave them in their coveralls for now. After supper she could bathe them and put them to bed in the pajamas she'd packed in her luggage— the luggage Dragan was risking his life to bring inside.

Outside, the wind had risen to a howl. Rain—no, it had to be hail—peppered the shuttered windows like buckshot. She pictured Dragan fighting his way through the storm, wind and hail battering his rugged face. How long had he been gone? He'd walked out the door maybe fifteen minutes ago, but it already seemed like hours. She felt guilty at the thought of him out there alone, but there was no way she could have offered to help him. She couldn't leave her babies.

The bedroom was chilly. Scooping up the girls she carried them into the great room. Shadows had deepened inside the lodge. Tessa had tried the light switches earlier and discovered there was no power. But the crackling blaze in the big stone fireplace cast a glow and gave off welcome heat. A metal screen, she noticed, had been placed on the hearth to contain the sparks and keep little explorers away from the flames.

Pulling a blanket off the back of a love seat, she sank into the pillow-soft leather upholstery. With her twins nestled on either side and the blanket tucked around them all, the feeling was almost cozy. But Tessa's worries kept her from relaxing.

Tomorrow morning the trial was scheduled to start in Anchorage. What would happen when she failed to show up? The lawyers for Trans Pacific would be ready to charge ahead, with or without Dragan. But Helen would be frantic, not knowing where her client was. And the judge would be outraged that the plaintiff hadn't cared enough to show up. He—or she—could throw the case out of court, leaving Tessa with damaged pride, no job prospects and a teetering mountain of medical bills.

Maybe she should have called Helen from Ketchikan to let her lawyer know she was with Dragan. Or better yet, maybe she should have ignored Helen's advice and agreed to the settlement. If she lost the case, her only recourse would be to file for bankruptcy—or more likely, file a personal suit against Dragan Markovic. After what he'd done today, she could probably win.

As if the thought could summon him, the front door burst open, letting in a blast of icy wind and hail. Dragan stumbled inside, reeling under his burden of suitcases. Jumping to her feet, Tessa raced to the entry, braced against the door and managed to push it closed behind him.

Dragan released his hold on the luggage. Suitcases clattered to the floor around him. He looked as if he'd barely made it up the dock to the lodge. His hair and eyebrows were frosted with hail, his damp clothes plastered stiff against his body.

"You've got to get warm!" She flung off the roomy cashmere robe, wrapped it around him and pulled him toward a chair next to the fire. "You could've frozen to death out there!"

He shrugged. "Stop fussing. I'll be fine. It needed to be done."

She stepped back as if he'd physically pushed her. "Well, thanks for bringing in the bags, at least. If you'll tell me what to do, I'll start supper while you warm up. You said something about freeze-dried meals. Does the stove work?"

"The stove's ready to go. Emergency food's in the pantry off the kitchen. Nothing fancy. Lots of spaghetti as I remember."

"Wonderful! My girls love spaghetti!" They also loved making a spectacular mess with it. When Tessa fed them in their high chairs, they usually needed a bath when they were finished. Feeding them at the table was going to be a challenge. But she wouldn't bother Dragan with that detail right now.

"I guess there'll be directions on the packages, right?" she asked.

"There should be. What about these two?" He glanced at the twins. They were snuggled on the love seat, both of them looking drowsy.

"I think they're about to nod off," she said. "If you don't mind keeping an eye on them, I'll be just a shout away."

He hesitated then nodded. "Here, take the flashlight. You'll need it to see what you're doing. And you'll want to do something about that cabinet under the sink. Maddie almost had it open."

"I will." She took the flashlight he gave her. "Thanks for reminding me about the cabinet." Tessa hurried through the swinging doors into the kitchen. She was a fair cook, but she'd never prepared freeze-dried food. She could only hope the twins would eat it.

The pantry was well stocked. One shelf held cartons of high-end, freeze-dried food in both family and individual-serving sizes. Another shelf held canned fruit and vegetables along with packaged biscuit and cookie mixes and some basics—salt, sugar, rice, baking soda, powdered milk and cocoa mix. The milk and cocoa would be a godsend if she could get her girls to drink them.

Choosing a family-size carton of spaghetti and meatballs, she focused the flashlight on the directions. They looked simple enough. Just add water and cook. With a little creativity she could put together some tasty meals.

But what was she thinking? She wouldn't be staying long enough to need to make several meals. All she really wanted was to get out of there. With any luck, the storm would be gone tomorrow and the rescue plane Dragan had called for would arrive to take her and her twins away. After that, the only place she wanted to see Dragan Markovic was in a courtroom.

Dragan shrugged out of the black cashmere robe and peeled off the damp thermal shirt he wore underneath. After laying the shirt on the hearth to dry, he slipped the robe back on and tied the sash. The cashmere was soft against his skin and smelled faintly of Tessa—not perfume, but a subtle, womanly aura that he found strangely erotic. He liked the idea that she'd worn it before he put it on. There was something sexy about a woman in a man's robe.

The twins on the love seat remind him of sleepy kittens. Maddie's curly head drooped lower. Her eyes closed. Dragan waited for Missy to do the same, but no, she was watching him, her gaze so pure and innocent that Dragan had to look away.

He was hoping she'd give up on interacting with him and go to sleep like her sister. Instead she scooted to the edge of the cushion, slid her little sneaker-clad feet to the floor and toddled toward him. Dragan felt something shrink inside him. He tried ignoring her, but she came straight to his knees, gazing at him as she reached up with her small, plump arms.

"Da!" she said.

She was making a clear demand to be picked up. "Forget it," Dragan said, scowling down at her. "Can't you see I'm not a baby person?"

"Da?" Her lower lip quivered. Her round blue eyes welled with tears. Heaven help him, she was going to cry. Lord, not that. Anything but that.

He reached down and lifted her onto one knee, holding her as if she were made of glass. Dragan had helped Tessa carry the twins earlier. And he'd carted Maddie away when the little rascal had gone for the kitchen cabinet. Each time he'd managed to think of the girls as pieces of baggage to be lifted and moved. But this was different. Missy was a living, breathing, vulnerable child who'd come to him in complete trust. Her nearness ripped through the wall of his memory like a jagged blade.

Sarajevo. The children.

Pushing against his rigid clasp, Missy wriggled closer.

Her warm baby smell crept through Dragan's senses, stirring the well of pain he'd buried at seventeen, when he'd come to America and immersed himself in a life of plenty. By some miracle he'd survived the brutal four-year siege by Serbian forces under the dictator Milosevic. So many others hadn't—friends, family and so many children, especially small ones like the little girl on his lap.

The only way to move on had been to shut down his emotions and will himself not to care.

"My, don't you all look cozy!" Tessa came in through the swinging kitchen door, arriving just in time to rescue him. "The spaghetti's in the oven. It'll be ready in fifteen minutes. Oh, and I found this lantern in the pantry." She held up a red metal camp lantern with a glass chimney. "There's fuel in it, and plenty of wick, but I couldn't find any matches."

"There's a box on the mantel. Take this young lady, and I'll do the honors." Dragan thrust Missy toward her, trying not to show his relief when Tessa put the lantern down and took her daughter in her arms.

"I can tell Missy likes you," she said. "She's usually a little shy with strangers."

"After today I'm hardly a stranger." Dragan busied himself with the lantern, removing the glass and touching a match to the wick. The flame spread a soft glow, deepening the shadows in the room.

"You seem to have a way with children," Tessa said. "Do you have any of your own?"

"No, and I don't plan to." Dragan avoided her eyes as he replaced the chimney on the lantern and set it on the mantel. "Whatever you think you may have seen, I'm not parent material."

Tessa smiled. She looked surprisingly hot in those oversize gray thermals with the fly in front. The thought that she had nothing on underneath triggered a pleasant zing of arousal, though it was dampened by the sight of the child in her arms. As much as he'd relish using this time to seduce Tessa, he had a feeling their pint-size chaperones would take every opportunity to get in the way.

"You never know," she said. "I didn't consider myself parent material, either, until these two little munchkins came along. Now they're my whole life." Her expression grew sad and a little wistful. "Their father would've adored them."

"I'm sorry."

"So you said." She lowered herself to the love seat. Maddie blinked awake, looking as cross as a little owl. Tessa reached out and gathered her close, embracing both her twins. "I set the table in the kitchen," she said, changing the subject. "I thought the cleanup might be easier in there."

"Fine. This isn't an occasion for formal dining."

She laughed; a golden sound. "Not quite what you're used to at home, I'll bet."

"Hardly." Dragan thought of his silent penthouse on the Seattle skyline, the meals his housekeeper left in the fridge for him to warm up and eat alone at whatever hour he came home. If he invited a woman up, they would have dinner at a restaurant beforehand. Within days both the dinner and the woman would likely be forgotten.

"The spaghetti should be about done," Tessa said, rising with her twins. "I warmed up some canned string beans, too. They're the closest I could come to a salad. Come on in, and I'll dish it up."

Dragan followed her into the kitchen with the lantern, which he set on the counter. Tessa had tied a dishtowel through the handles of the under-sink cabinet, making it impossible for little hands to open. But feeding the twins would be a different challenge. The small utility table had four adult-size chairs. On two of them, Tessa had arranged tall cans to serve as booster seats. It was a clever idea, but from what he'd seen of her wiggly twins he'd already guessed it wasn't going to work. Neither would anything else he could think of. This meal was destined to be a disaster.

"You take care of your girls," he said. "I'll get the food."

Dragan dumped the heated string beans into a bowl and used a towel to lift the hot spaghetti dish out of the oven. When he peeled back the foil covering, the savory smell filled the kitchen. It looked good, too. Amazing what could be done with freeze-dried food these days.

When he turned around he saw that Tessa had put plastic-coated bibs on the girls and was gripping one with either hand to keep them on their makeshift booster seats. Neither of the twins looked happy. Probably wondering why they didn't have high chairs.

Dragan found spoons for the beans and spaghetti and set the dishes on the table. "Careful, it's hot," he said.

"Look, girls, it's spaghetti! Yum!" Tessa said.

"Getti." Missy smiled and pointed.

Maddie pushed one of the cans off her chair. It clattered to the floor and rolled into the corner. "Dow," she said, beginning to climb.

Tessa met Dragan's gaze across the table. She rolled her eyes in a look of hopelessness.

"You know this isn't going to work, don't you?" Dragan said.

She sighed, grabbing Maddie before she could fall to the floor. "I know. But they've got to eat. There's only one way to do this. We'll have to hold them and feed them on our laps."

As the *we* and *our* sunk in, Dragan cringed inside. Tessa could only feed one twin at a time. She was expecting him to feed the other one. Short of pretending to faint, there was no gracious way he could refuse.

"Missy's the easiest," she said. "You can take her. I'll take Maddie."

"I've never done this before."

"No problem. Just watch me and do what I do." She lifted the teetering Maddie off the remaining cans, sat with her and picked up the toddler-size spoon next to her bowl. With her free hand, she scooped a dollop of cut-up spaghetti onto her own plate and spread it out to cool.

"Getti!" Missy was rocking forward on her chair, reaching for the hot dish in the middle of the table. "Getti!"

Dragan caught her around the waist as the cans toppled off the chair. Sitting, he settled her on his lap and followed Tessa's lead, dishing spaghetti onto his plate and spreading it in a thin layer.

"Getti!" Missy's demand rose. She reached for the steaming plate. Dragan grabbed her hand in time to save her from burned fingers.

"Give her a string bean. They're cool enough." Tessa had done the same thing with Maddie, who was holding her bean, eyeing it with suspicion. She took a bite, made a face and threw it on the tiled floor.

Dragan used his fork to spear a string bean for Missy. She took it and stuck one end up her nose.

Watching her sister across the table, Maddie giggled. "Noz!" She reached for the bowl of string beans and managed to grab one. "Noz!" She stuck it up her own nose, both twins shrilling with laughter.

"That's enough." The steel in Tessa's voice silenced both her daughters. "Give me those." She took the string bean out of Maddie's nose and held her hand out for Missy's. "Let's hope the spaghetti's cooled enough to eat."

Following her lead, Dragan used the side of his fork to

mash the noodles and meat into small pieces, then filled the tiny spoon she'd handed him. "Be ready," Tessa cautioned. "They've gotten used to feeding themselves in their high chairs. I don't know how they'll take to being spoon-fed again."

Dragan lifted the spoon toward Missy's mouth. She reached up to grab it. "No," he said, moving the spoon out of reach and shifting his clasp to pin both her arms to her side. He was half-afraid she'd cry, but the next time he maneuvered the spoon toward her she opened her mouth like a baby bird. "That's it," he murmured, spooning in the food. "Good girl."

"See? I told you that you were a natural with children." Tessa beamed at him.

"She's just hungry, that's all." Dragan imagined a wall of ice, holding back his emotions, holding back his memories. He could do this, as long as he didn't allow himself to think or feel. "If I can make it out to the plane tomorrow, I'll get the safety seats. Then you can buckle your girls in to feed them." And he wouldn't be required to do this ever again.

"That's a great idea." She delivered another spoonful to Maddie's mouth. "I'm just hoping we won't need to improvise much longer. How soon do you think the rescue plane will get here?"

"In good weather, a rescue flight from Sitka could be here in an hour. But in a storm like this one it isn't going to happen." Dragan paused to listen to the roar of the wind outside and the hammering of hail and sleet on the roof. This was Alaska, wild and unpredictable. The storm could be gone tomorrow. But he'd known weather like this to drag on for days, even weeks, making it too dangerous for small planes to fly.

There was no telling how long they could be stuck there.

* * *

Head aching, Tessa wiped a spaghetti string off her cheek. Supper had started out well enough, once they'd gotten past the string beans shenanigans. As long as the twins were hungry they'd allowed themselves to be fed. But they were tired and getting crankier by the minute. Things were rapidly going from bad to worse.

Missy worked an arm loose from Dragan's clasp, grabbed a handful of spaghetti and smeared it in her hair. While Tessa's attention was diverted, Maddie one-upped her sister by shoving her plate off the table. It shattered on the tiles, shooting tomato sauce in all directions.

Now it was Missy's turn again. She took advantage of Dragan's shock to lob another handful of spaghetti onto his chin. The noodles hung down like a scraggly, red-stained beard. His stunned look would have made Tessa laugh if she hadn't been so tired.

"Are we done here?" Dragan took a napkin and wiped his face. His voice snapped with impatience.

"We are done." Tessa rose and snatched up her daughters, one under each arm. "Thanks for your help, and for being a good sport."

"You haven't eaten anything," he said.

"I'm too tired to be hungry. Don't worry, I'll clean up this mess after I've bathed these two and put them to bed."

"Fine. Take the lantern with you. I've got the flashlight."

"You'll have to carry the lantern for me—unless you expect me to hang on to it with my teeth."

Without a word he picked up the lantern, held one swinging door open and walked ahead of her through the dining room and down the hall to the bedroom. His manner stated clearly that he considered his work done for the day.

Tessa followed him, keeping a firm clasp on her squirming daughters. She'd hoped he'd at least offer to clean up the kitchen. But she'd probably emerge from putting the twins down to find him relaxing in front of the fire with a drink in his hand and the kitchen still a mess.

Blast the man. Too bad Missy hadn't upended her spaghetti plate right on top of his arrogant head.

Five

Tessa sat on the edge of the tub, running warm bath water for the twins. There was no bubble bath. They'd be unhappy about that—but some things couldn't be helped.

She was exhausted. All she wanted was to get them clean, get them in their pajamas and get them to sleep. Since there were no cribs in the lodge, they'd be spending the night with her in the queen-size bed. That would be her only hope of keeping them under control.

She'd stripped them down for their bath, stuffing their dirty clothes into the plastic laundry bag she'd brought along. Earlier she'd noticed a washer and dryer off the kitchen, but without electricity the appliances were useless. Washing clothes by hand would be a last resort. In the cool, damp air, cotton garments could take days to dry. She could only hope rescue would come before the twins ran out of clean clothes and disposable diapers.

When she turned off the water she could hear the storm

outside, battering the sides and roof of the lodge. If the weather didn't let up, rescue could take days. Meanwhile she and her twins would be held virtually captive here by the most powerful—and maddening—man she'd ever met.

But powerful or not, Dragan Markovic would pay for this scheme. When she and Helen were through with him, he would curse the day he'd set eyes on her.

While she was filling the tub, the two little imps had escaped into the adjoining bedroom. Now, naked and giggling in the dark, they were chasing each other around the bed. At least, this time, she'd made sure the door into the hall was securely closed.

Setting the lantern on a safe counter, she strode into the bedroom and scooped first Missy, then Maddie, into her arms. "Come on, you little monkeys, it's bath time." She carried her laughing, squirming babies back to the bathroom and lowered them into the warm water.

The twins loved their bath. While they squealed and played, Tessa managed to wash them clean and use the baby shampoo she'd brought along. She was about to drain the water and lift them out of the tub when she heard a rap on the bedroom door.

"Come in," she called. "It's all right."

Seconds later Dragan appeared in the doorway to the bathroom, face washed, shirt changed, looking like an ad from *GQ*.

Pink and sweet as rosebuds, the twins gazed up at him from the tub.

He shook his head. "I can't believe these are the same little barbarians who were fighting spaghetti wars in the kitchen."

"A bath can do wonders." Tessa was suddenly conscious of her own damp, stringy hair and spaghetti-spattered men's thermals. She was a mess. But she didn't owe Dragan an apology for the way she looked. This whole wretched situation was his fault.

"Did you want something?" she asked.

"Only to tell you that the rest of the spaghetti's warming in the oven. Once your girls are asleep, come on back and enjoy a peaceful dinner, maybe even with some adult conversation."

She shook her head. "Thanks for the invitation, but by then I'll be too tired to chew, let alone converse."

"You need to eat, Tessa. And I think we both need to talk."

So you can lobby me not to sue you and your company? No thank you, mister.

"We'll see." Tessa reached for a towel and turned away. The next time she glanced back at the door, he'd gone.

By the time she got the twins dry, diapered and zipped into their one-piece pajamas, Tessa was reeling with weariness. She tucked them into the big bed and lay next to them on top of the quilt. She had to stay with them until they fell asleep. But if she got too comfortable, she might fall asleep herself, leaving the mess in the kitchen to be faced tomorrow.

As she eased one arm across her babies, her empty stomach growled. Dragan's invitation came to mind. She really was hungry. But she'd had enough of the man for one day. If she had to face him, she wanted it to be when her mind was sharp and alert.

She drifted on the edge of slumber. By the time she jerked herself awake, the twins were both asleep. Peeling herself away from them, she eased her feet to the floor. Missy and Maddie usually slept as soundly as little hibernating bears. Hopefully, she'd have a chance to clean up the kitchen and unwind a little before going to bed. Even with the bedroom door closed, she'd be able to hear them if they woke up.

Stumbling into the bathroom, she splashed her face and finger-combed her hair. In the glow of the lantern, which she'd left on the shelf, the mirror reflected red-laced eyes and a tired face. From outside she could hear the storm, still rattling the shuttered windows. What time was it? She'd lost track, but the night was pitch-dark. With luck, Dragan had given up on her and gone to bed.

Taking the lantern, she stepped out into the hall and closed the door behind her. The fire in the great room was still crackling, as if someone had recently added a fresh log. Stepping into the open she could see the dining area. From the table at the far end, white tapered candles cast a flickering glow on the walls.

A shadow moved. Dragan rose from the couch in front of the fire. "I'd almost given up on you, Tessa," he said. "Let's have dinner."

Too stunned to protest, she let him put the lantern up, usher her toward the table and seat her in a high-backed leather chair. The table was set with gold-rimmed white china, cloth napkins and crystal goblets. Next to the candles stood a bottle of wine with a French label. Tessa didn't have to read French to surmise that it was expensive.

"You look surprised," he said.

Tessa glanced down at her grubby thermals. "Surprised isn't the word. If I'd known this was going to be formal, I'd have dressed for dinner."

He laughed. "You're fine. I just wanted to show you there's more than one way to eat freeze-dried spaghetti."

Turning away, he strode through the swinging doors into the kitchen. Tessa glimpsed enough of the room beyond to see that he'd cleaned up the mess the twins had made. Score the man a few points for that; but if he was trying to soften her up, it wasn't going to work.

He came back using a towel to carry what was left of the hot spaghetti. He'd transferred it to a blue porcelain dish, with the string beans nested alongside. Sprinkled with grated cheese, it looked and smelled like something from a nice restaurant.

"How did you manage this?"

"Secrets." He gave her a mysterious smile as he opened the wine and filled her glass half-full.

"I shouldn't. Wine always makes me silly."

"Good." He poured a little more before taking his seat at the head of the table, with Tessa on the right-hand corner. "You must be hungry. You've barely eaten all day."

"Eating takes time and at least one free hand. Since my girls came along, I rarely have either."

"They're sixteen months old, right?" He scooped a generous helping onto her plate.

"Yes. They're small for their age because they came seven weeks early. But as you see, that doesn't slow them down." She shouldn't be talking about the premature birth of her twins, Tessa reminded herself. That was part of the basis for her lawsuit. She mustn't risk saying anything that might damage her case.

"This lodge is amazing," she said, changing the subject. "Was it your idea to build it here?"

He took a sip of wine, his silvery eyes reflecting the candlelight like moonstones. "The man who had it built was an Indonesian, a former prince, who wanted a quiet retreat—and, I suspect, a hideout from his enemies. When Alaska turned out to be too cold for him, I offered to take it off his hands. The company uses it to entertain clients who want to get away from it all and try their hand at fishing. The profits from the deals we've made here have long since made up the cost." He glanced at his plate. "Of course, in addition to a full-time summer caretaker, when we have visitors, we fly in a housekeeper, a gourmet chef and a week's supply of fresh food."

"How did you come to know a former Indonesian prince?" Tessa swirled a strand of spaghetti around her fork and lifted it to her mouth.

"As an international shipper, it's my business to know all kinds of people—not all of them saints." He gazed into his wineglass. "When I bought this lodge the walls were covered with the prince's mounted hunting trophies—antelope, lions, tigers, leopards, a rhino, even an elephant. I ordered them all burned, right down to the horn and tusks."

"I think I might like you for that," Tessa said. "But I'm curious about your reason."

"I'm glad you might like me for something." His mouth tightened in a brief, ironic smile. "As for the reason, they were ugly. I couldn't look at those snarling, staring animals without thinking how they'd suffered and died so one pompous little piss-ant could show off his manhood."

He emptied his wineglass, filled it halfway and poured some for Tessa. "Now I have a question for you. How does a woman who's been wrangling two babies all day, a woman who's been drenched in seawater and spattered with spaghetti sauce still manage to look so beautiful?"

Tessa's face flushed hot. She'd almost begun to feel comfortable with the man, but now the truth slammed home. He was out to seduce her. And worse, part of her—the part that had been without male attention for far too long—was almost tempted to let him.

Quivering, she stood. "I should go."

"Why?" He looked as innocent as a schoolboy. "You've hardly eaten a thing."

"You know why! You think you can ply me with wine

and flattery and I'll fall into your arms and cancel my lawsuit. That's not going to happen. I'm here under duress. You kidnapped me and my children. Or have you forgotten that?"

He shook his head, looking pained. "Sit down and eat, Tessa. Your storming off to bed won't do either of us any good. Ask me anything you want about my intentions. I have nothing to hide."

"All right." She sat again, spine rigid. "You can start by telling me why you interfered with my flight in the first place."

"Fine. I'll talk. You eat. That's the deal."

He leaned back in his chair, the candle flames casting his proud Slavic features into stark light and shadow. Dragan Markovic was her enemy. So why did just looking at the man make her pulse race?

Tessa took a nibble of spaghetti and waited for him to speak.

"To start with, you aren't the first employee—or former employee—to sue Trans Pacific," he said. "A big, high-risk company like ours, we've dealt with sexual harassment issues, wrongful termination, injury, even wrongful death. It's not pleasant but it's a reality of the business."

"So if mine's just another lawsuit, why interfere personally? Why not let your lawyers handle it? I know you've got an army of legal experts at your beck and call."

"That was the plan. But when you turned down our offer of a fair settlement, I got curious and wanted to know why. Was it just a question of wanting more money or was something else involved?"

Tessa sipped her wine, stalling for time. The settlement offer honestly *had* been more than fair. It would have paid her medical bills, allowed her to stay home while the twins were young, and provided company stock for their college fund. She'd been on the verge of taking it when Helen had stopped her. "Think about it, dear," she'd said. "To a company like Trans Pacific, this settlement is a pittance. They'll pay you off, then turn around and do the same thing to some other woman. The only way they're going to change is if we can hurt them—not only their pockets but their reputation."

It had occurred to Tessa to question her attorney's motives. Helen had taken her case on spec. A big award for punitive damages would mean more money for Helen and a victory over such a high-profile company would enhance her image as a champion of women's rights.

But wasn't that what she wanted, too? Tessa asked herself. Getting fired had almost ruined her life. If she could keep the same thing from happening to another pregnant woman, didn't she have the responsibility to go ahead?

"I asked you why you didn't take the settlement," Dragan said.

"That wasn't part of our deal. You talk, I eat. And I'm eating."

"All right." He shrugged. "Believe it or not, I'm a decent person. If you were wronged by my company, I want to make it right. But I won't be taken advantage of. If you and your lawyer are just in this to milk the money, my team will fight you down to the last nickel."

"You still haven't told me why you kidnapped me."

He flinched, as if she'd flung something distasteful in his face. "If that's what you want to call it, fine. First off, I wanted to know more about you. Are you honest? Are you reasonable? Do you have a genuine need for the money or are you just greedy?"

"And have you reached any conclusions?"

"Not yet." He put his wineglass down. His eyes narrowed as he studied her. Did he suspect her of hiding a secret or was he just trying to intimidate her?

She lifted her chin, daring herself to meet his gaze with boldness. "You said 'first off.' Does that mean you had another reason?"

A surprising smile tugged at a corner of his mouth. "More like a delusion. I was actually hoping we might find a way to settle this issue without going to trial. But now that I've met you…" He let the words dangle.

"What?" she demanded.

"You're a proud woman, Tessa Randall. Proud and stubborn. And when it comes to protecting those little girls, you're a tigress. In that lovely redheaded mind of yours, striking a bargain with me would be like striking a bargain with the devil. Am I right?"

"No comment." He was reading her almost frighteningly well, but she wasn't about to let him know it.

In the silence that followed, she could hear the wind howling above the chimney. A chilly draft fluttered the candle flames. Tessa shivered.

He stood, his height looming above her. "It's warm next to the fire. If you've finished eating, we could continue this discussion over there."

Wings fluttered below Tessa's rib cage. She hadn't drunk much of the wine but she was already feeling giddy. Alarms were going off in her head. "I should check on the twins," she said, sliding out her chair.

"Go ahead. I'll be here." He picked up the wine bottle and the two goblets and walked toward the circle of warm light that surrounded the fireplace. As she hurried into the hall, she saw him set the wine and the glasses on the coffee table.

The room was dark, but Tessa could make out Maddie and Missy snuggled in the middle of the bed. Out of motherly habit, she rested a hand on their little bodies to feel the rise and fall of their breathing. It would be smart to stay here with them, she thought. Temptation and even regret waited in the cozy warmth by the fire.

But if she tried to go to sleep now, there was no way her wired nerves would let her rest. She needed to finish the conversation with Dragan and let him know where she stood. She would be pleasant and sociable—but no more wine. Holding her own with the CEO of Trans Pacific demanded a clear head.

She was suing this man and she meant to teach him and his company a lesson they'd never forget. She owed it to her daughters and to any woman who might find herself in a similar situation.

With a last look at her twins, Tessa stole out of the bedroom and closed the door behind her. From the great room, the glow of firelight drew her like a moth to a flame.

Moths got their wings burned, she reminded herself. She would be sure not to let that happen.

Dragan had settled himself in a corner of the leather sofa. One hand held a glass of wine. The other hand lay along the sofa back in an unspoken invitation to join him. Even in the plaid shirt and jeans he wore, he reminded Tessa of some ancient Transylvanian prince whose smile might, or might not, reveal gleaming vampire fangs. The aura of danger only added to his magnetic appeal. She was seized by a sudden desire to know more about this intriguing man.

"How are your little ones?" he asked.

"Sleeping, thank heaven. I love them but they wear me out."

"Then sit down. Have some wine."

"No more wine for me, thanks." Tessa seated herself at a cautious distance. "As I told you, wine makes me silly."

"I'd like to see you silly." His grin flashed. No visible fangs. But her wariness remained.

"Too much alcohol also gives me a headache."

"That won't do." He set his glass on the table. "Can I get you some water—or better yet, make you some coffee? The coffee machine needs power, but there's a jar of instant in the pantry."

"I'm fine. I'll take a rain check on the coffee tomorrow morning." Even with the fire, Tessa felt cold. She shivered, her arms hugging her ribs.

"Here." Dragan rose and pulled a gray afghan off the back of a chair. Bending close, he tucked it around her, lingering as she nestled into its creamy softness. "Better?"

"Yes. Thank you." She waited until he'd taken his seat again. "How soon do you think we'll be out of here?"

He exhaled. "That depends on the weather. Bush pilots won't fly in this." He glanced upward, to where the wind was tearing at the roof. "We could see clear skies tomorrow, or the storm could last for days. But there's one thing I'll promise you."

"What's that?"

"First thing tomorrow, rain, snow or shine, I'm going out to the plane and getting those safety seats for your twins. Then you'll be able to strap them in and spoon-feed them."

You not *we,* he'd said. She gave him a frown. "I take it you don't plan to help."

"I've had my first and last experience with trying to get food down a squirming, spaghetti-throwing toddler. They're all yours."

"You don't like children much, do you?"

"It's not that I don't like them." He paused and shook his head. "I'm just not comfortable with them."

"Having children of your own would fix that."

"Fatherhood is not for me." He shook his head. "After what I've seen of this world, I can't imagine anybody brave enough, or foolish enough, to bring children into it."

Tessa gazed at him, struck not so much by what he'd said as by what he'd implied. Had she'd glimpsed a crack in the wall of ice that surrounded this coldly calculating, very private man?

She chose her next words carefully. "What you just told me—I can't say I understand or agree. But I'd like to know more about why you feel that way."

For a long beat of time he was silent. Sleet lashed the roof. A sap knot in the fireplace exploded in a shower of sparks. Dragan shifted on the leather cushions, glancing down at the empty space beside him. "Come," he said. "Come here."

She hesitated then moved next to him. The more she knew about the man, the better her chance of getting the justice she wanted. She waited for him to speak, but he gazed at the fire in silence.

"You said I could ask you anything," she reminded him.

He shifted toward her, resettling himself with a ragged breath. "I said you could ask about my intentions. But I don't talk about the past. Not even when I'm trapped in a storm with a beautiful, curious woman. If you'd seen what I've seen you'd understand how I feel about children."

His fingertips brushed her shoulder then withdrew, leaving a tingle in their wake. Tessa willed herself to ignore the effect his nearness was having on her. Dragan Markovic was a master manipulator. He knew exactly what he was doing.

Under different circumstances she might not have minded playing along. In the past two years she'd almost forgotten how it felt to be touched intimately by a man. Now Dragan's powerful male aura crept around and through her, stirring responses she'd buried and tried to forget. He was all man—the kind of man who'd know how to give a woman exactly what she needed.

But she'd be a fool to fall under his spell, even for a one-night stand. Dragan was as ruthless as his nickname. The Dragon. He would stop at nothing to wear down her defenses.

She groped to fill the tension-charged stillness. "At least let me ask about your accent. Eastern European, maybe? You don't sound American."

"I'm American in every way that counts. I've been a United States citizen since I was twenty-two But I was born and spent my boyhood in Sarajevo." He paused, gazing into the fire, as if he'd been about to say more then changed his mind.

Sarajevo.

In the wake of his silence, Tessa searched her own memory. She'd been a little girl when that name had been on the TV news. She remembered black-and-white images of exploding bombs, ruined buildings and marching soldiers. Years later, in high school history, her teacher had spent one class period explaining how the country once known as Yugoslavia had splintered into warring political and ethnic factions in a terrible conflict that had lasted four years and cost many thousands of lives.

She could dredge up place names like Bosnia Herzegovina, Kosovo and Srebrenica, along with horror-charged terms like ethnic cleansing and genocide. Sarajevo, she recalled, had been at the heart of the tragedy. But she'd never understood the meaning of it all. It had never touched her sheltered life—until now.

The war had taken place just over twenty years ago. Dragan was in his midthirties now—a good ten years her senior. He would have been a teenage boy back then.

The dark energy that radiated from him now fed Tessa's growing certainty. Dragan had been there.

How had he survived? What had he seen? What had he done?

"I remember hearing about Sarajevo, but I was too young to understand," she said. "Perhaps you could help me understand now." *Then, maybe, I might be able to understand you.*

"No." The word was barely whispered, but it was as if a wall had been thrown up between them.

"You said we were going to talk."

"No. No more talking." His hand reached out to brace her chin, forcing her to look directly into his eyes. They blazed like fire under glacial ice. "The pictures I carry in my head, Tessa—if I shared them with you and put them in your innocent mind, you would never forgive me. It would be the cruelest thing I could do."

Six

Even before it happened, Tessa knew Dragan was going to kiss her. She knew his kiss would be as hard and fierce as he was. And she knew she wanted it—with a rush of wild hunger that swept away every warning.

Maybe this was the smart thing to do, she thought as her head began to spin. Maybe this was the way to get what she wanted. But even as he lowered his mouth to hers, she knew better. She wasn't being driven by rational reasons. She needed him, pure and simple. Nothing else made sense.

A groan rumbled in his throat as he claimed her, his lips tasting of wine, his stubbled beard rough against her skin. He took possession of her mouth as if he'd bought and paid for the right—no tenderness, no coaxing, only a raw, driving desire.

Tessa's response blazed like torched gasoline. Heat rocketed through her senses. Her hands tangled his hair as she pulled him closer, drinking in the taste of him and the musky man-smell of his skin. Her mouth melted against his, softening as she opened to the demands of his thrusting tongue.

The last, lingering voice of common sense whispered that Dragan Markovic was a calculating man who knew exactly what he was doing. But Tessa was too far gone to listen. She would worry about that later. Not now.

Her head fell back as his kisses grazed her throat, moving down to the loose neckline of the baggy thermal undershirt.

She had nothing on underneath—something he would already know. His hands slid up her rib cage to her shoulders, working the loose, stretchy garment up over her head and arms. She arched her back as his fingers moved to stroke her breasts. Her nipples shrank to aching nubs, broadcasting the desire that throbbed and quivered in the depths of her body.

Releasing her, he leaned back, reclined against the cushions and took a moment to study her. She sat facing him, naked above the rolled waistband of the oversize thermal drawers, which bunched around her hips.

His mouth twitched in a lazy grin. "You're absolutely shameless, Miss Tessa Randall," he said.

"I know." She bent to kiss him, stretching her body on top of his. His hands invaded the bunched waist of her drawers to cup her buttocks and pull her in against the rock-hard ridge of his erection.

"This is…insane," she murmured as her hips pressed him through his jeans, triggering waves of exquisite sensation. Heaven help her, but he was huge. How would he feel inside her?

He gave her a rough laugh. "It *is* insane, isn't it? But what would this world be without a little insanity?" He kissed her again as his hands peeled the thermals lower on her hips. Her frenzied fingers yanked at his buttons, opening the front of his shirt.

"Hang on." He eased her away and sat up to strip off his shirt and the T-shirt beneath. His body was muscled like an athlete's, lightly tanned, with a dusting of hair across his chest. Only when he stood to undo his belt did she catch sight of the deep white scar along his side—a scar that couldn't be anything but a long-healed wound from a large-caliber bullet.

She knew better than to ask him about it. It was a relic from his past—the past he refused to talk about.

His belt hung loose, his trousers unfastened to the zipper. "Come here and finish the job, Tessa." His voice was a low rasp.

She'd risen and was reaching for him when a wail rose from the dark recesses of the hallway. First one baby voice, then two. Tessa went rigid. She grabbed for the shirt she'd flung on the back of the couch. Her little ones had awakened in the dark, in a strange room, without her. She had to go to them.

Dragan stood silent while she yanked on her shirt. Should she apologize? No, that would be ludicrous. Just go.

"Will you be back?" he asked her.

"I don't know." Tessa spun away, seized the lantern off the dining-room table and rushed into the dark hallway.

She wouldn't be back.

Dragan pulled his thermal T-shirt over his head, slipped into the plaid wool shirt without bothering to button it and fastened his jeans. Sinking back onto the couch he picked up the wineglass and took a slow sip as he fought to calm the excitement and desire still buzzing in his veins.

Tessa Randall was a beautiful woman, sexy, spirited

and passionate. He would have enjoyed every minute of making love to her in front of the crackling fire. But first and foremost, Tessa was a mother. And there was no way he could compete with the distraction of two demanding little redheads.

Now that his head was clearing, Dragan realized that having sex with Tessa might not be the smartest idea. After all, she was already claiming he'd kidnapped her and her daughters. If she could add to that claim the suggestion that he'd seduced her with the intent of tarnishing her case, no judge on earth could look into those big hazel eyes and believe it wasn't true.

Especially since it almost was.

Swearing under his breath, he placed the wineglass on the coffee table and settled back against the cushions. He would give Tessa fifteen minutes before he threw in the towel and went to bed. The wait would be little more than a courtesy. He knew what would happen.

Alone in the bedroom with her twins, Tessa would come to her senses. She would dismiss what she'd almost done as reckless and foolish, maybe blame herself, more likely blame him. If nothing else, motherly guilt over leaving her precious children would cool her passion like an ice-cold shower.

He'd made it a rule not to date women with young children. Now he remembered why.

He reached for the wine then changed his mind about having more. When he drank, it was mostly to unwind, and he was already getting drowsy. The sexual rush that had charged his body when he'd taken Tessa in his arms was ebbing. In its wake, he felt exhaustion in every bone, nerve and muscle.

Drained by the strenuous day, he slumped against the pillows, gazing into the fire. Tessa's womanly scent lingered in his nostrils. Lord, but she'd been beautiful, leaning above him in the firelight, her ripe breasts swelling and falling with every breath. The thought of what he'd be doing to her right now if she'd stayed was enough to drive a man crazy.

But it was best that she'd gone, he told himself. He should never have waylaid her flight, never let her board his plane with two vulnerable children who had to be watched every waking second.

Children stirred memories of Sarajevo—and emotions he never wanted to feel again.

He was drifting into the old dream. A dream of trudging through a dark tunnel, his boy's body weighed down by the man-size pack he carried on his thin shoulders. Every faltering step threatened to pitch him into the trampled mud. But he couldn't stop to rest. Nor could he fuel his meager strength with the black market bread, cheese, oats, lentils and salt pork he carried. The food was for the children. And at thirteen, he already counted as a man.

Others moved with him in the long, dreary line, loaded down with smuggled weapons and supplies to keep the bombarded city alive. Later on, the hand-dug tunnel would have pipes and cables, steel supports and a solid floor with tracks for carts. But now, in the second year of the siege, the tunnel, which ran from beneath a house in Sarajevo, under the nearby airport and into free territory, was little more than a long, dark hole. Too low and narrow for a big man to stand, it was better suited to the smaller soldiers or to half-grown boys like him who were too young for the Bosnian army.

At the tunnel's far end he could see a pinpoint of light— a lantern, hung as a beacon to mark the end of the two-hour trek. This would be his last run of the night. Minutes from now he'd be free to go home, wolf down a bowl of thin gruel and take shelter with his parents, his younger brother and two little sisters in the cellar of their house.

The boom of an exploding Serbian shell—not close but still deafening—echoed down the tunnel. Startled by the sound, he tripped over his own boots and tumbled forward into the mud.

The shock jarred Dragan awake. He jerked bolt-upright, muscles clenched, heart pounding as he forced himself back to full awareness. It was all right, he reminded himself. He was in the lodge, on the couch, staring into the fire, which had burned down to embers.

The tunnel dream hadn't troubled him in years—so many years that Dragan had dared to hope it was gone. But all it had taken to bring it back was Tessa questioning him about his past. That, and maybe being around her twins.

Getting up, he took a moment to clear the dining-room table and stack the dishes in the sink. At least he'd awakened before the worst part of the dream. But now he was more exhausted than ever. Maybe if he went to bed he could sleep through the night without dreading the memory's return. Maybe the weather would be better tomorrow, and he'd be able to get a rescue plane here—or at least get a decent signal on the radio. Meanwhile, what he needed was rest.

He found the flashlight, checked the outside doors and headed down the hall to his bedroom. Passing Tessa's closed door he paused. It wouldn't hurt to look in on her to make sure she and the twins were all right. If she was awake he could let her know he was going to bed in the next room, and she could call him if anything frightened her.

Not that Tessa struck him as a woman who'd be easily frightened. When it came to protecting her children she'd likely face down a grizzly bear.

Half smiling at the thought, he gave a light rap on the door. There was no answer. He waited a few seconds then cracked the door open far enough to look into the room.

Dressed in a soft flannel nightgown, Tessa lay curved like a mother cat around her babies. He focused the flashlight beam on the wall above them to cast a soft light below. All three were fast asleep, their russet curls spilling over the ivory-damask pillowcases. The little ones looked like angels. The sight of them triggered an ache of yearning for something lost that no longer had a name. And Tessa...

His eyes lingered on her face, the parted lips, the dark gold lashes lying soft against her cheeks. She was so delicious in sleep that it was all he could do to keep from scooping her up in his arms and carrying her to his bed. But there was such innocence to her in that moment— such sweetness in the way she cuddled her precious girls.

His three beautiful redheads.

Strange what a long day could do to a man's thoughts.

Easing the door closed, Dragan turned away and moved down the hall to his own room. A good night's rest would clear his head of dreams and fantasies. By morning's grim light he would see Tessa as she was: the woman who was out for all she could get from his company. And he would see her twins as little nuisances who had no place in his solitary life. The sooner he got them out of here, the sooner he could resolve this mess and move on.

After he'd brushed his teeth he stripped down, pulled a pair of thermal bottoms over his legs and slid into bed. The sheets were chilly, but with the down comforter over him he'd soon be warm enough. Overhead, the storm still raged, howling like a banshee around the chimney top, peppering the roof with hail and sleet. Lulled by the sound he lay gazing up into the darkness until he drifted into sleep.

* * *

Tessa opened her eyes. The bedroom was pitch-dark; the twins snuggled peacefully against her side. The light hand she brushed across their warm little bodies reassured her that they were all right. But something had startled her awake. What was it?

She pushed herself up on one elbow, listening. No wind. No storm battering the lodge. Suddenly she realized what had awakened her.

It was the silence.

Was the storm over? Driven by curiosity, she eased away from her twins and reached for the robe she'd tossed over the bedpost. Slipping it on, she opened the door, closed it behind her and tiptoed out into the hall.

The lodge was eerily quiet and so dark she could barely see her way. The door to Dragan's room was ajar. Peering inside, she could just make out his sleeping body, sprawled belly-down under the comforter. One bare foot hung over the edge of the mattress.

Tenderness tugged at her. He slept like a tired young boy. But Dragan Markovic was no boy, she reminded herself. He was a powerful, manipulative man, as heartless as his nickname. His near-seduction earlier had been just one more tool to control her—and he'd nearly succeeded. Thank goodness her crying babies had saved her from a foolish mistake.

Turning away, she walked along the hall and groped her way toward the great room. There was a little more light in here, but the hardwood floor was cold beneath her feet, the fireplace gone dark as a cave. She shivered, knowing that any heat left from the fire would have already been sucked up the chimney through the open damper.

Anxious to see if the weather had cleared, she tried to peer through the front window. But the shutters, locked from the outside, blocked her view. The only way to look at the sky would be to step out onto the covered porch. It was bound to be cold, but she wouldn't plan to stay more than a few seconds.

Moving to the front door she unlocked the dead bolt and opened the door far enough to slip out. The windless air that met her was like walking into a wall of ice. Her bare feet were already going numb.

Pulling the robe tighter around her she walked to the edge of the ice-glazed porch. From where she stood she could see a nearby lodgepole pine, its branches festooned with needle-like icicles. Beyond the tree, thick, white fog blanketed everything. She couldn't see the sky. She couldn't see the water or the plane. She could barely see the ground at the foot of the steps.

From the direction of the inlet, the cry of an owl sent a shiver up Tessa's back. Cold and anxiety raised goose bumps on her skin. What else was out there beyond the porch, unseen and waiting? She'd spent several years working in the Anchorage office, but she was a city girl. Apart from a couple of tourist outings, she'd never ventured into the Alaskan wilderness. Only now, with the mist closing around her like the fingers of an icy hand, did she sense what a dangerous place it could be.

A low-pitched howl quivered through the fog—one, then another and another, coming closer. Panic surged through Tessa's body. Those blood-chilling calls could only mean one thing. Heaven help her, there were *wolves* out here!

She spun toward the door, wanting only to get back inside. Her feet slipped on the icy surface. She caught herself with one hand, bracing against a nasty fall. Fear clutched at her stomach as she stumbled upright. What if she couldn't get back in? She'd be stuck out here barefoot and barely clad, in the killing cold, with a wolf pack on the prowl.

In the deep shadow of the porch, she collided with something big and solid. A strong arm seized her waist.

"What the devil are you doing out here, Tessa?" Dragan's voice growled in her ear.

"Ch-checking the weather." Her knees had gone limp. Her teeth were chattering. "Dragan, I heard wolves! They're coming! We've got to get inside."

As if on cue, another wolf call echoed through the darkness. From a dozen yards off the side of the lodge came the sound of breaking underbrush, moving away as if some large animal was fleeing into the night.

Dragan's arm tightened around her waist. "It's all right," he said. "The wolves are hunting, but they're not after us. They're mostly afraid of people."

"I'm not so sure I believe you."

"We can discuss that once we get you back inside. Come on, you're freezing."

He pulled her into the entryway and locked the door behind them. Only then did he let her go and step away. And only then did she notice the pistol in his free hand. "Is that loaded?" she asked, staring at the weapon.

"Of course it is. You should have told me you were going out. I would've come with you."

"You were asleep."

"You looked?"

"Yes. You were dead to the world."

"As you see, I'm a light sleeper." He'd flung on a plaid, woolen robe to go outside. The front had fallen open, exposing his bare chest. He looked rumpled and annoyed. He also looked meltingly sexy, Tessa realized. Good grief, had her fright triggered a sudden hormone surge?

"You're shivering." He set the pistol on a high shelf

and led her to the couch. "Lord, you could've at least put on some shoes. Your feet must be half-frozen. Sit while I start the fire."

Or had he started a fire already?

He took time to find the afghan and tuck it around her. Even the slight pressure of his hands as he bent close sent warm tingles through her body. Was he aware of the effect he was having on her? How could he not be?

Moving to the fireplace, he stirred the coals with a poker. A few embers still glowed. Laying on a few sticks of sapwood and kindling, he soon had a cheerful blaze crackling on the hearth.

"Now, let's have a look at those feet." He sat on the ottoman in front of her.

"They'll be fine." Tessa tried to wiggle her bare toes. She could barely feel them.

"Up here. Now." He indicated his lap. Tessa raised her feet. He settled them between his knees. "At least I had the good sense to put on some shoes before I went out there."

Tessa glanced down. His high-end sneakers were unlaced and worn without socks, as if he'd shoved his feet into them before rushing outside. He'd actually been worried about her.

"What woke you?" she asked.

"Who knows? The sound of your footsteps…the door… maybe just a feeling." His strong hands began massaging her feet, squeezing and rubbing her toes. "They're like ice," he said. "Have you ever seen frostbitten feet? They're not a pretty sight."

"I take it you have."

"Yes." He fell silent, leaving Tessa to wonder if she'd crossed into the forbidden territory of his past. Her toes began to tingle, then to warm as the circulation returned. A buzz of pleasure stirred in her throat as his thumbs moved to her arches. "Nobody's ever given me a foot rub before," she murmured. "I could let you do this all night."

Her face flushed hot as she realized what she'd just implied.

The flash of a mischievous grin made his thoughts clear. If he was going to be with her all night, the time wouldn't be spent rubbing her feet. "Did I catch you blushing?" he asked.

"Sorry. It's the curse of being a redhead. My face shows everything."

"Whatever it's showing right now, I like it."

"No comment."

They fell silent as his skilled hands massaged the arches of her feet then moved upward to her ankles. Tessa closed her eyes. Her breath deepened as she felt his touch on her legs. The brush of his fingertips sent ripples of heat up into her thighs. She felt the slickness and knew what it meant. By now they were both aware of where this was leading. They'd been interrupted earlier. Now, neither of them would be satisfied until they'd finished what they'd started.

Leaning forward, he freed a hand, cupped the back of her head and kissed her. His tongue parted her lips, thrusting deep in a delicious pantomime of what he wanted to do to her body. The fingers of his other hand moved up her thigh to brush the wetness then paused. "If you want me to stop, Tessa, you'd better tell me now," he rasped in her ear.

She couldn't have spoken if she'd wanted to.

His fingers moved higher, parting the sensitive folds, finding the tender nub at the center. "Oh…" she gasped, coming hard, pushing against his hand, wanting more. "Yes," she pleaded. "Yes, Dragan."

Without a word he scooped her up into his arms and strode down the hall. She thought fleetingly of her twins, but there was no sound behind the closed door of her room.

With luck her little ones would sleep until morning. For now it was her time—to be a woman, to be a lover. Not until this moment had she realized how much she'd needed it.

He lowered her to the soft bed, pausing a moment to drop his pajama bottoms and add protection before he slipped in beside her.

"Only you could look sexy in this nightgown," he teased as he pulled the flannel fabric up over her head.

"Hey, at least it's warm. I can't say the same for your sheets."

"How's this?" He wrapped his arms and legs around her, enfolding her in the warmth and texture and wonderful man-smell of him. She drank him into her senses, loving the feel of his rugged body against her bare skin.

"I said, how's this?" he murmured against her hair.

"Nice." She wiggled her hips against the jut of his erection. "But I know something that would make it even nicer."

"What's that?"

"Guess," she whispered, shifting enough for her hand to reach down and clasp him.

With a raw laugh he shifted between her welcoming legs. She was ready for him, more than ready. As he slid inside her and began to move a climax shook her so hard that she cried out.

He grinned down at her. "Whoa there! What a woman you are. Since you're so rambunctious, what do you say I let you ride this time?"

Without waiting for an answer he rolled over, bringing her on top. His hands reached up to cup her breasts. "Dammit, but you're beautiful," he muttered.

"It's pitch-dark. But at least you can't see my stretch marks."

"That has nothing to do with your kind of beautiful." He pushed upward, moving deeper inside her. "Make love to me, Tessa."

Slowly, dreamily, she began to move. The sensations that poured through her were so exquisite she wanted to weep. As he urged her faster, she ground hard, harder. He gripped her hips, his breath quickening, rasping, ending in a groan as he finished.

Tenderness washed over her. Moving off him, she bent and brushed a kiss on his lips. "Thank you," she whispered.

His only reply was a contented chuckle as he rolled over and fell asleep.

Dragan stirred awake at dawn. He was alone in the bed. He had no memory of Tessa leaving him, but it was no surprise that she'd gone back to her twins. Before anything else, she was a mother.

But she was more than a mother. She was a warm, loving, sensitive woman—different in every way from the glittering, self-absorbed beauties he dated. Making love to her had been as close to real as anything he'd ever experienced. He couldn't wait to do it again…and again, for as long as they were here.

And then what? Sooner or later their rescue would come. They'd be back in Anchorage, facing each in court—enemies possibly made even more bitter by what had passed between them.

But it wasn't the legal issue that troubled him. After last night he'd be willing to give her the moon if she wanted it. No, the problem went far deeper.

Tessa was a wonderful woman, one he wouldn't mind keeping around for a while. But she was a package deal. And the very sight of her two little imps squeezed his emotions like a cold iron vise. Once he might have had the capacity to love a child—or children. But that had been a long time ago. Sarajevo had destroyed that in him—forever.

Seven

The lodge was quiet, the dawn casting slivers of gray light through the cracks in the shutters. Dragan dressed in silence, layering a thick wool sweater over his shirt and finding the hiking boots and heavy socks he kept in the closet. This morning the tide would be out. Unless the storm had done even more damage than he'd feared, he should be able to walk out to the plane, try the radio again, and retrieve the safety seats for the twins. The little scamps might not like being strapped in for meals, but at least their mother would be able to feed them without starting a food fight.

Tessa's door was closed. She'd earned a good night's sleep, he mused with a secret smile. He could only hope her daughters wouldn't wake her too soon.

He took a few minutes to rebuild the fire, light a match and wait for the kindling to catch the flame. Then, pausing at the shelf where he'd put the pistol the night before, he took it down and tucked it into his belt. He'd spent enough time in the Alaskan bush to know that a man couldn't be too careful.

After unlocking the front door, he walked out onto the porch. A solid bank of fog greeted him. He could barely see the thicket of Sitka spruce that grew a stone's throw to the right of the steps. But at least he could see the ground and the trail that led to the dock. As long as he watched his footing he should be all right.

Everything was covered with a glaze of frozen sleet. The strings of moss that hung from the tree limbs had turned to icicles. The willows drooped with the weight. Dragan had seen storms like this before. If the day was sunny, the ice would be melted by noon. But would the sun burn off the heavy fog? That remained to be seen. The only sure thing was that no sane bush pilot would risk flying into this remote spot until the skies cleared.

A dozen yards down the path he found wolf tracks in the layer of frost that covered the icy ground. The resident pack had come close to the lodge last night, but from what he knew of them, they'd be resting in the deep woods today, most likely with full bellies. Wolves could be bloodthirsty, but at least, unlike some humans he'd known, they only killed for food.

As he passed the high-tide line, he could hear the distant lap of water through the fog. His boots crunched half-frozen seaweed as he walked. Veiled by mist, something heavy was splashing at the water's edge—a fishing bear, maybe the young one whose tracks he'd seen behind the lodge. Best to warn it away. He'd hate to have it charge and be forced to shoot it.

As he walked, he began to whistle, tossing a few stones ahead of him. He was rewarded by the sound of hasty splashing, growing fainter as the creature moved away. So far, so good.

The plane loomed out of the fog, so close that Dragan was startled. Trailing the sea anchor, it was sitting off-kilter as if buffeted by last night's wind. Otherwise it looked undamaged.

What had caused the engine to lose fuel? It took Dragan less than a minute to find the cause. The cap on the fuel tank was hanging by its chain. Either it had been put on loose after the refueling in Ketchikan or it hadn't been put on at all. Dragan swore. A brand-new, four-million-dollar airplane, forced down in the bush because of a damned fuel cap! It was pure luck he'd been within range of this lodge. He and his precious passengers could just as easily have crashed or been stranded in the wild with no food and no shelter except the plane.

Climbing up into the cockpit, he tried the radio. It was working, but the reception was only a little better than last night. All he could do was send out another distress signal and hope it was being picked up. He'd filed a flight plan in Bellingham. But this was supposed to be a hush-hush trip. No one from the company was expecting him in Anchorage. As for Tessa, by now her lawyer, Helen Carmichael, would've discovered that she hadn't taken her original flight. But the frantic woman would have no way of knowing what had really happened to her client and the twins. The bottom line—even once they were missed, nobody would have any idea precisely where to look for them.

This entire debacle was his fault. Whatever happened to Tessa and her daughters because of it would be on him.

Dragan found the twins' safety seats, unfastened the straps that held them in place and climbed out of the plane with them. Later, after the sun came up, he would go back to the plane and try the radio again.

He reached the floating dock and struck out on the path that led toward the lodge. The fog was as thick as ever, the cold so bitter that it reminded him of winters in Sarajevo. He remembered walking the shell-ravaged streets at dawn, after a night of running supplies through the tunnel, his eyes and ears alert for the enemy snipers that lurked in abandoned buildings, picking off people in the streets below. Sniper Alleys, they'd called the worst of those streets—and the running, dodging games he'd played as a boy had become a way of keeping alive.

Those years had been a time of hunger and death, a time of unspeakable losses—his friends, his family...

Dragan had tried hard to block the memories. Most of the time, if he kept himself busy, he could manage it. But here, in the cold, with three vulnerable lives depending on him, the images came crowding back.

In the four years of the siege he'd grown from an innocent boy to a young man who'd armored himself against all emotion except anger. To love was to lose. To care was to hurt. And he'd never found a reason to change.

Now, through the swirling mist, he could see the lodge. He quickened his footsteps, moving as fast as he dared over the icy ground, craving the warmth of the fire, the sound of footsteps, the ring of voices. Anything that might help him forget.

He mounted the steps and, shifting the sturdy child seats to one side, opened the door. The fire he'd built was blazing warmth into the room. From the kitchen came the sounds of baby chatter and the aroma of... *Was it pancakes?*

Replacing the gun on the high shelf, he strode through the swinging doors into the kitchen. What he saw chased the darkness from his mind.

Tessa was standing by the stove in a pastel-plaid flannel robe that she must've brought in her suitcase. Her hair was mussed, her pretty face bare of makeup. She looked as fresh and delicious as a bowl of ripe strawberries—and he could have devoured every bite.

She glanced toward him with a smile, the color deepening in her face. Was she thinking about last night? He sure as hell was. In fact he could use a rematch right now. But forget that. Their two little chaperones were front and center, standing on their chairs, stuffing cut-up pieces of syrupy pancake into their mouths.

"Glad you made it back," Tessa said, behaving as if nothing had happened. "I was getting worried about you, especially since we heard wolves in the night."

"I saw a few tracks, but the wolves are long gone. If I'm slow, it was because of the fog and the ice. But I brought back the seats for your daughters." If she wanted to play it cool, that was fine with him—for now.

"Thanks." She ladled three pools of batter onto the hot griddle. "Those seats will be freezing cold. Let's give them time to warm up before we try them with the girls. Want some pancakes?"

"Sure." Dragan stowed the seats in an out-of-the-way corner. "Your girls seem to be enjoying them. And I see you found them some paper plates. Good idea."

"At least they won't break any more dishes. And at least they can eat pancakes by themselves, even if they make a mess." Tessa reached for a spatula. "Sorry there's no butter. But at least there's plenty of maple syrup. And I mixed some powdered milk for the girls. It's in that blue pitcher. Feel free to have some."

Dragan eyed the twins. They had sticky syrup and bits of pancake all over their hands and faces and in their hair. But they were laughing as they stuffed their little mouths and drank from their sippy cups, thoroughly enjoying themselves. He willed away a poignant twinge of memory.

"What do you say I make us both some coffee?" he asked.

"That would be great. There's hot water in the teakettle, but I've been too busy to do anything with it." She glanced down at her bathrobe. "I haven't had time to do anything with *me*, either. When these pancakes are done, maybe you could keep an eye on the girls while I grab a shower."

"No problem," Dragan lied, thinking he'd rather be caged with a couple of wildcats than be left alone in the kitchen with Tessa's innocent little pixies. "What about your coffee? Should I leave it until you get back?"

"Go ahead and make it while I finish your pancakes. I'll take the cup with me. Black is fine." She took a porcelain plate out of the cupboard for him. After flipping the pancakes, she waited for them to brown then turned them onto the plate. By then, Dragan had spooned the instant coffee into a cup and added hot water.

"Here you go." He handed her the cup and took the plate of pancakes.

"Thanks. I won't be long," she said. "Just let the girls feed themselves. If they want more pancakes, there's a little batter left."

Dragan watched her hurry through the swinging doors. Why did he keep letting Tessa drag him into helping with her twins? He'd made it clear that he wanted nothing to do with children. So why did he find himself standing here, watching the little darlings make a sticky disaster of themselves and the kitchen?

"Da?" Missy gazed up at him with heart-melting blue eyes and pointed to his plate of pancakes. Her own paper plate was empty. Did she want more?

"No problem." He forked one of his pancakes onto her plate, cut it into bite-size pieces and soaked them in maple syrup. Missy picked up a piece with her fingers and stuffed it in her mouth, syrup dribbling down her chin onto her bib.

Maddie glowered from her side of the table. One sticky hand reached toward Dragan's plate. Her own plate had plenty of pancake pieces left, but that didn't seem to make any difference.

Dragan shook his head. "That's not the way it works, Maddie. Finish what's on your plate, then you can have more."

"*Phhht*!" Maddie picked up her paper plate with both hands and upended it onto her head. She grinned as the sticky syrup flowed down through her flame-colored curls. Her sister giggled hysterically.

Now what? Dragan could hear the shower running in Tessa's bathroom. This was no time to call for help. His heart sank. He had no choice except to handle the situation himself.

He snatched Maddie up with one arm, hauled her over to the sink and ran the tap until the water felt lukewarm. The sink was equipped with a sprayer. If he could manage to hang on to the squirming, fussing Maddie, he could use it to get her clean.

The syrup had already begun to thicken. Maddie squalled and kicked as he worked the plate off her hair and held the back of her head under the spray. Dammit, he should have just left the cleaning up for Tessa.

It took a couple of minutes to work the stickiness out of Maddie's hair. By then her clothes were wet, too, and she was howling with pint-size rage. Dragan was just reaching for a kitchen towel to dry her when Missy tried to climb off her chair and tumbled head-first onto the floor. Sitting up she began to scream. A purple welt was darkening her forehead.

Dragan swore, fighting the urge to flee out the front

door and leave them for their mother. That would only make the situation worse.

Leaving Maddie with the towel, he gathered the crying Missy into his arms. Close up the bruise didn't look too bad, but they'd have to watch her to make sure she didn't have a concussion. More scared than hurt, he guessed, Missy had begun to sob. Feeling his own pain at a depth he'd long since buried, Dragan cradled her close. "It's all right, Missy," he murmured, rocking her. "I've got you, girl. You'll be fine."

Little by little, Missy's sobs eased. She snuggled against Dragan's sweater, her gooey fingers kneading the yarn. Maddie, too, had stopped crying. When Dragan glanced around, he saw that she was trying to strip off her damp clothes. Her coveralls were down around her ankles and her pink T-shirt was up around her neck.

"Blast it, Maddie—" He eased Missy away from him, meaning to put her down, but she clung to his sweater, refusing to let go. He was trying to balance her with one hand and control Maddie with the other when the doors swung open and Tessa walked into the kitchen. She was still in her robe, a towel wrapping her wet hair.

Her jaw dropped. "I heard crying. What on earth happened in here?"

Dragan told her in as few words as possible. "I don't know how you do it," he said. "You have those little troublemakers twenty-four-seven and manage like a pro. I can't handle them for ten minutes!"

"I'm their mom. I know what to expect." She gathered Missy close and kissed the bump on her forehead. "She'll be fine. She just needs a little sympathy."

Maddie tugged at the sash of Tessa's robe, wanting attention. Tessa bent and put an arm around her. "You, too, sweetie. Here, let me dry you off."

With her free hand, Tessa unwound the towel from her head and blotted the little girl's dripping hair. "That's what you get for fooling around with your food," she said. "Now we'll have to change your clothes again."

"Do they really understand all that?" Dragan asked.

"They understand as much as they need to." Tessa looked up at him. With damp russet curls framing her pert face, the resemblance to her daughters gave him a jolt. "I'm guessing you've had enough babysitting for now," she said. "I'll take the girls with me while I get dressed. Then I'll come back and clean up this mess. Did you get enough to eat?"

"I'll eat later." All Dragan wanted right now was to escape. "Since we're running low on kindling for the fireplace, I think I'll go out back to the woodpile and work up an appetite."

It had been a long time, but Dragan hadn't forgotten how to split logs into firewood. The chips flew as he swung the ax and landed each blow with a solid *whack!* It felt good to burn off his frustration in hard physical work—and he had plenty of frustration to burn.

Here he was, stuck in the middle of nowhere with an airplane out of gas and three redheads who were driving him crazy—only one of them in a good way. He couldn't get through to anyone on the radio and the weather was nothing but a curse. Stranded here, he was missing the trial, as well as any other business crises that might have come up.

But at least he could whack the hell out of these logs.

He'd do well to remember the reason he'd commandeered Tessa's flight in the first place. Whatever had happened between them, her lawsuit wasn't going to go away. She needed, and perhaps deserved, the money involved. The least he could do was try to learn more about the circumstances and her motives. Maybe now that they'd become lovers, she'd be willing to talk.

With the sun up, the cold was losing its edge. Melting ice dripped from the trees. Smells of moss, rotting wood and damp earth rose from the ground. But the fog lingered like a cottony blanket over the land. There'd be no bush planes searching today, at least not around here.

When Dragan had chopped a fair pile of wood, he used the smaller hatchet to split some of the pieces into kindling. The sap-rich knots, which burned extra fast and hot, went into a special pile. Alaska's weather could be violent and unpredictable. Another storm could blow in at any time. They would need plenty of fuel to prepare them for the worst.

He'd just picked up an armful of wood to carry inside when he happened to glance toward the back porch.

A small, forlorn figure sat on the top step, watching him. By now he knew the twins well enough to guess it was Maddie.

He straightened, feeling an unaccustomed twinge in his lower back muscles. "What're you doing out here, you little scamp?" he demanded. "Where's your coat?"

"*Phhht!*" It was Maddie, all right. Dressed in clean, dry coveralls and a long-sleeved shirt, she didn't seem to mind the cold. It was easy enough to guess how she'd escaped. When he'd gone outside to cut wood, he'd left the back door unlocked. Even if Tessa had thought to latch it, she might not have done so, since it would have meant locking him out.

He walked to the foot of the steps, scowling at her. "We need to get you back inside. It's cold out here, and your mother will be worried. Come on, girl, let's go in."

Maddie didn't budge. Did she want him to put the wood

down and carry her? That was something her snuggly sister might have done, but not Maddie.

"Gah!" she demanded, reaching for Dragan's armful of wood.

"Is this what you want?" Dragan chose a stick of kindling, checked it for splinters and held it out. She took it, looked at it a moment, then tottered to her feet and started across the porch toward the back door.

"Well, I'll be," Dragan muttered, opening the door with his free hand. "You just wanted to help me, didn't you? You're quite the girl, Miss Maddie."

She toddled ahead of him into the empty, clean kitchen, clutching the kindling stick as if it were a precious treasure. They found Tessa in the dining room, dressed in jeans and a black turtleneck. She'd moved a chair out and was bending to look under the table. Seeing them, she straightened so fast she nearly bumped her head. "Oh, thank goodness!" she gasped. "I've been looking all over for her."

"She showed up on the back porch," Dragan said. "We'll need to keep that door locked. Otherwise she's bound to wander out again."

Maddie toddled up to her mother. "Gah?" She held out the kindling stick.

Tessa smiled, bending to hug her. "Why, thank you, Maddie, for bringing that inside. Why don't you go show it to Missy? She's over there on the chair."

As Maddie scampered to join her sister on the oversize armchair, Tessa turned back to Dragan. "Thanks for helping me keep track of these little munchkins. There are so many places to get lost here, and so many things they can get into. I would've packed their toys, but my lawyer said the babysitter she'd hired would bring some. You've done a great job of entertaining them."

Dragan squirmed inwardly. She was doing it again, pulling him into more involvement with her children. "You seem to do fine on your own," he said, steering her toward a different subject. "In fact, if you managed your work the way you manage your children, I can't imagine why anyone would want to fire you."

She stiffened, instantly wary. "Dragan, I'm not sure it's a good idea to talk about the case."

"Why not? I'm one of the major players here and, believe it or not, I want to do right by you. I can't do that unless I know exactly what happened."

Still she hesitated.

"Look," he said, giving her no chance to back out. "The whole story will come out in the trial. How could it matter if I hear it then or now? Give me a minute to put this wood down and make myself a cup of coffee. Then we can talk."

Tessa watched him stride to the far side of the fireplace and lay the wood in the copper tub by the hearth. She knew better than to think she could hold back what he wanted to hear. The Dragon had never been known to take no for an answer—and since she hadn't denied him her body, she could hardly deny him her story.

"Sit down while I get coffee," he said, starting for the kitchen. "Want some?"

"Sure. Why not?" Maybe a hot cup would settle her nerves. As Dragan vanished into the kitchen, she glanced at her daughters. They were nestled against the cushioned arms of the chair, Maddie still clutching her prized stick of kindling. It was late morning, the time of day when they usually went down for their naps. Their eyelids were beginning to droop. Rising, Tessa took the afghan off the couch and laid it over them. They snuggled into the warmth. Tessa watched from the couch as they slowly closed their eyes. With luck, they'd sleep for as long as an hour, after which they'd awaken bright-eyed, recharged and ready for more mischief.

Closing her eyes for a moment's rest, she shifted mental gears to focus on her coming face-off with Dragan. There was no reason to be nervous. She had nothing to hide. But she'd be a fool to trust the man completely. What if she said something in full innocence, and he was able to twist it to his advantage later? Helen would be livid. For all she knew, by telling him her story she could be making the biggest mistake of her life.

He came in from the kitchen, his body shouldering through the swinging doors, each hand balancing a mug of steaming coffee. Even with windblown hair and a shadow of beard he looked like a movie star, so self-confident that it almost made her cringe. How could any mere mortal stand a chance against this man?

"Here you are." Before taking his seat at the opposite end of the couch, he handed her a blue porcelain mug. Its warmth felt soothing between her chilly palms.

He glanced at the sleeping twins. "How do those two little scamps manage to look so angelic?" he mused aloud.

"Because they really are angels," Tessa said. "It's just that now they're learning to be human—and it isn't easy when you're so little."

"Well said." He smiled and took a sip of coffee. "You're a fabulous mother—a fabulous woman."

"And smart. Too smart to fall for your flattery. This is a time for honesty, Dragan. Give me that, at least."

"All right. If you'll give me the same in return. Apart from what it took to lure you onto my plane, I've been straight with you, Tessa. I really do want to understand what's at stake and do the right thing. Right now we've got nothing but time."

As he spoke, a gust of wind rattled the shutters. Another storm was moving in, probably delaying their rescue for at least another day.

Dragan was right. They had nothing but time.

Eight

Late morning wind blasted the lodge, tearing at the shutters and howling down the chimney. Dragan had planned to go out to the plane to try the radio again, but if another storm was blowing in, the trek would probably be a waste of time.

Tessa's hands cradled her coffee cup. Her lovely hazel eyes were wide in the firelight. She looked vulnerable, even a little scared. Dragan found himself imagining how satisfying it would be to sweep her off to his bed and pleasure her until thoughts of fear fled from her mind. But that idea was little more than a fantasy. There was no way Tessa would leave her little ones asleep in the chair, in a house full of dangers. And right now, she'd agreed to tell him her story. He'd be smart to take advantage while she was willing to talk.

"I'm listening," he said. "Start anyplace you like."

Tessa shifted on the couch and took a sip of her coffee.

She stared into the flames, as if gathering her thoughts before she began.

"I already told you how Kevin, my fiancé, was killed. As I said, I didn't even know I was pregnant until after the funeral. Weeks later, when I found out I was carrying twins…" She shook her head. "It was a shock, of course. But I was happy. I loved them from the first moment I knew they were there.

"I'd been working out of Anchorage for six years. I enjoyed my job. It paid well, and I knew I was going to need the insurance. I planned to work as long as I could, then take maternity leave and return afterward."

"We do allow that," Dragan said. "It's company policy."

"I know. That's why I wasn't expecting a problem. I'd planned to keep my pregnancy quiet until I was showing. But then the morning sickness set in. That was when my new supervisor started on me."

"Your supervisor? Was that somebody I know?"

"Tom Roylance, Assistant V.P. of Sales and Contracts. Does it ring a bell?"

"Just barely." As he thought about it, he remembered Roylance from a middle-management conference. Young Turk. Good-looking and overconfident. A climber of the sort who didn't care who he crushed on his way up. From the way she said his name, Dragan had a feeling Tessa had been one of the unfortunate ones Tom had stepped on along the way. Dragan felt an urge to find the man and punch him in the nose.

"You say he started on you. Do you mean it was sexual harassment?"

"I wish!" Her laugh carried a bitter edge. "That would've made this lawsuit a piece of cake, wouldn't it? No, he just became extremely critical. The man's attitude was stuck in the 1800s. He kept mentioning, in front of others, how our Asian clients disliked doing business with a woman, and how they'd walk away before they'd sit down and negotiate with one who was pregnant. I proved him wrong over and over again, but that didn't make any difference. He kept saying how a man could do a better job."

"And you didn't report him?" Dragan asked.

"Report him for what? The man was an annoying jackass, but nothing he said or did was against company policy." Tessa stared into her mug, then set it on the coffee table. "Things went from bad to worse. I was barely five months along when I started bleeding and had to be rushed to the hospital to save the babies. The doctor said I could work at a desk if I was careful, but I wasn't to fly overseas.

"While I was out resting for a week, I used my home computer to apply for a transfer to a desk job in the Seattle office. But when I came back to work the next Monday, my personal things were boxed and waiting in the reception area. I was told that I'd been fired."

It was a rotten way to treat anybody, let alone a valued employee. Dragan fought the impulse to take Tessa in his arms and tell her how sorry he was. Something told him that wouldn't be welcome, and it wouldn't be enough. "Believe me, I knew nothing about this," he said.

"Well, maybe you should have known!" Tears welled in Tessa's eyes. "Most of the people who work for you have never seen your face. Unless they're senior vice presidents, you don't even know their names. You're too busy living your rarified life, driving fast cars, flying your private planes and entertaining rich clients. You don't know what it's like to be the rest of us!"

"I know more than you can imagine," he said. "Listen to me, Tessa. Since you haven't showed up for the trial, I'm guessing your lawyer will request a continuance. Before we walk into that courtroom, I want to learn the whole story behind your being fired. I want to talk to Roylance and to the people over him. Something more was going on in that office. Before I make any decisions, I need to know what it was."

"I'm the plaintiff in this case. Your company is the defendant. Have you forgotten that?" Curled in the corner of the couch, she was both defiant and tender. Dragan ached to hold her, and more. But it wasn't going to happen.

"I haven't forgotten it for a minute," he said. "But you haven't told me the rest of the story."

"The rest?"

He glanced toward her slumbering twins. She nodded her understanding. Wind howled under the eaves of the lodge as she spoke again.

"With no job, and twins on the way, I had no choice except to go home to my parents in Bellingham. They had plenty of room and were happy to have me. But because I was fired I lost my medical insurance. I tried to be careful and rest, but with so much stress and worry, it wasn't enough. When I went into labor seven weeks before my due date, I knew we were in big trouble—all three of us."

Stress and worry. Had Helen Carmichael put those words in her mouth? But of course Tessa would have been under a strain, maybe enough strain to bring on premature labor. The hard, cold question was could it be proved and used as a basis for punitive damages? Dragan couldn't help sympathizing with Tessa. But he had a company to run and that company's reputation to protect. He couldn't afford to let a cutthroat lawyer take advantage of him.

"The girls weighed less than two pounds each," she said. "They were rushed into the NICU before I even had a chance to hold them. At first the question was would they live? Then, would they be normal and healthy? I spent days then weeks, sitting by that incubator, just watching

their tiny bodies struggle and praying the whole time."
Tessa wiped her eyes. "Sorry. I still get weepy when I remember."

Dragan shifted his face away, not wanting her to see
how deeply her story had moved him. He looked over at
the twins, snuggled in the chair. Their eyes were closed,
their cheeks soft and rosy. Missy had flung a plump little
arm over her sister. Maddie was still clutching her kindling
stick. He swallowed the lump in his throat. He'd known
all along, of course, that Tessa loved her children. But he
was just beginning to understand how precious they were.

Not that he could afford to be swayed by sentiment.
When he walked into that courtroom, he meant to be
armed with everything he could learn. He owed that much
to his company and to himself.

Willing his emotions to freeze, he fixed his gaze on
Tessa. "So when the bills started coming in, you decided
to sue."

"I didn't have a choice." She was on the defensive now.
"The NICU alone was almost a million dollars. And with
no job, how could I deal with the expenses of raising two
babies—not only now but in the years ahead? I couldn't
expect my parents to pay. It would have bankrupted them."

"So you hooked up with Helen Carmichael—a feminist lawyer with a national reputation. How did that come
about?" he challenged, knowing others would do the same.

"My parents knew someone who'd worked with her.
She agreed to take my case, with no money up front, on
condition that she be allowed to make an example of Trans
Pacific by going for punitive damages."

None of this came as a surprise. But that didn't mean
Dragan liked hearing it. He scowled his displeasure. "Is
that why you and she refused our settlement offer?"

Her silence was answer enough.

"So, Ms. Carmichael wants to take us to the woodshed. Smart lady. More money for her, more for you, and a big boost for her reputation."

"Helen isn't a bad person," Tessa said. "She truly believes in fighting for women's causes. And she's been wonderful to me. She even booked my charter flight and arranged for a room and a babysitter in Anchorage. She's probably frantic by now."

"Of course she is." Dragan couldn't keep the cynicism out of his voice. "Her little golden goose has flown the coop and disappeared."

Tessa rose from the couch, her eyes blazing. "That was uncalled-for."

"Was it? Why are you letting her run the show, Tessa? What is it you really want from this lawsuit?"

"I want what's best for me and my children. And I want justice." Head high, she turned her back on him and strode into the kitchen.

As the door swung shut behind her, Tessa sank onto a kitchen chair. She'd done it—exactly what Helen would have advised her not to do. And now she knew why she'd been warned.

In her naïveté, she'd hoped that opening up to Dragan might win his sympathy. But she should have known better. The man was as cold and unfeeling as a block of granite.

Had she given him any information he could use against her in court? She couldn't be sure. But Dragan was a clever man. If anything she'd told him could be twisted to Trans Pacific's advantage, he and his team of attorneys would make good use of it.

To make matters worse, she'd slept with him. Knowing Dragan, he'd find a way to use that against her, too. How could she have been such a fool?

Closing her eyes, she took a deep breath to calm her quivering nerves. From the other room, she could hear the sound of Dragan's footsteps crossing to the front door. Was he leaving or just stepping out to check the weather? Either way, she couldn't hide in here. Her babies were asleep in the chair by the fireplace. They could wake at any minute.

As she stood, she heard the sound of the front door opening and closing. Good, he'd left. For the moment, at least, she wouldn't have to walk in and face him.

She entered the great room to find her twins still asleep and Dragan gone. The pistol was missing from the shelf where he'd left it, which suggested he planned to be outside for a while. Maybe he was going to the plane again.

At least his absence would give them both a break. Whether she liked it or not, she and her twins were stuck here with Dragan until rescue arrived. They needed his help. For now, whatever his scheme, she would just have to be civil and tolerate the man.

The wind was still blowing, though not as hard as earlier that morning. When Dragan came back, maybe she could ask him to open the shutters on one of the front windows. The closed-in gloom of the lodge was getting to her. When they'd landed here, she'd expected a rescue plane to come within hours. Now, she realized, they could be stranded here for days.

The twins would be hungry when they woke up. Dragan would likely be hungry, too, since he'd had little more than coffee so far this morning. Returning to the kitchen, she propped the swinging doors open and set about raiding the pantry for lunch.

By now the tide was coming back up the inlet. Since the water had yet to reach the plane, Dragan was still able to cross the long tidal slope on foot. He staggered into the wind, fighting for every step. Another hour and he'd need the raft. He had to find a way to get the plane closer to the dock.

Stepping onto the float, he climbed into the cockpit and turned on the radio. Through the static he could hear muted voices but could make out no words. He sent out a distress signal, giving the location. After a pause he sent it again then listened. There was no way to tell whether the message had been received. He could only hope for the best and try again later.

By the time he'd closed the plane and climbed to the ground, the lapping waves were within a stone's throw of the floats. He paused, staring out at the white-capped inlet and thinking. In the shed, there was a winch and a long, stout rope used for towing the occasional barge, which brought in heavy equipment and supplies, across the shallow water to the dock. He could rig the winch now, wait until the tide was high enough to lift the floats, then tow in the disabled plane.

Racing back to the shed he found what he needed. It felt good to be doing something with a purpose. And all the better that that purpose kept him out of the lodge. He and Tessa needed some time apart after that emotionally bruising session in front of the fire. She'd been through a rough time—he didn't realize how rough until he'd heard her story. She deserved a fair settlement, one that would pay her medical bills and give her enough security to raise her daughters. But the punitive damages, which could amount to several million dollars, were something else. As far as he was concerned, Helen Carmichael was using Tessa's misfortune to fill her pockets and build her reputation.

Dragan was prepared to fight those damages in court. But first he needed to know exactly what was behind Tessa's firing. He needed to talk with Roylance, with the head of Sales and Contracts and with Human Resources. And he couldn't let himself be swayed by sympathy for Tessa. True, there might have been circumstances within the office she wasn't aware of. But what if she wasn't telling him everything she knew—or even if she was lying?

Hard experience had taught him not to trust anyone. That included a ravishing redhead with a siren's body and eyes that could melt any man's heart—even his.

Tessa had strapped the girls into their safety seats and set the seats on the table. Now she was using a teaspoon to offer them little bites of the canned ravioli she'd warmed up. But her daughters weren't having any of it. Missy was spitting out the chunks of pasta as fast as her mother could spoon them in. Maddie had closed her mouth as tight as a clam.

Tessa knew they were hungry. Except for some juice and some dry saltines, which they'd mostly crumbled, they hadn't eaten since breakfast. But her little angels could be stubborn, especially when they wanted things their way. And right now she was outnumbered two to one.

She was scraping a drizzle of tomato sauce off Missy's chin when Dragan walked into the kitchen. Ruddy from the cold, his hair wind-tousled, he looked like an ad for some fancy brand of macho aftershave.

"You seem to have things under control," he said. "How's it going?"

Tessa squelched the urge to fling a spoonful of ravioli in his handsome face. "It may *look* like I'm in control. But they don't like this arrangement. They're on strike—a hunger strike."

He glanced at the dish she was holding in one hand. "Maybe they don't like ravioli."

"They like it at home. It's even the same brand I usually buy. There's more on the stove if you want some. And I warmed up the string beans from last night. The Four Seasons it isn't, but at least it's food. You must be hungry."

"Do you want to strap me to a chair and spoon-feed me, too? That might be fun."

"Stop it, Dragan! I've been trying with these little monkeys for the past twenty minutes without getting a single bite down them. I'm not in the mood for your jokes. These babies need to eat."

"Hmm." She heard him rummaging in the pantry. He came back popping the lid off a can of applesauce. "Try this," he said.

"So now you're an expert." Tessa was reaching the end of her patience. "I've got a better idea." She thrust a clean spoon at him. "*You* feed it to them!"

He backed off a step, shaking his head. "They're your babies. That's your job."

Her frayed nerves snapped. "Not this time. I want to see you do this. I know it sounds crazy, but we're stranded out here in the middle of nowhere. If anything happens to me, I want to know that you'll take care of my children."

Dragan had paled beneath his tan. When she shoved the spoon into his hand, he stared at the utensil as if she'd handed him a live grenade. His throat worked as he swallowed. "No," he said, setting the spoon on the table. "Just no. You do it. I'll be back later."

With that he turned and walked back toward the front door. Tessa heard it open and close behind him.

What had just happened? All she'd done was push him to feed her twins, and he'd reacted as if he'd been threatened with torture.

Had she touched a nerve—some deep, secret pain from his past? She'd already known that Dragan Markovic was a man of dark secrets, a troubling—and troubled—man. But that hadn't stopped her from sleeping with him or leaving him with her children.

Maybe she'd been too trusting. Maybe it was time she started asking questions and demanding answers. She needed to know what he was hiding.

But as her mother had always told her, a woman could catch more flies with honey than with vinegar.

Dragan had harnessed the rope to the plane's struts and rigged the winch to a sturdy post, set deep in the ground for that purpose. Now he sat on the dock, hunched against the wind, watching the tide creep up the inlet. Once the water came in and lifted the floats, he could winch the plane in close.

How hard would it have been to give in to Tessa's demand that he try feeding her twins? He felt like a fool for walking out. But the twenty-year-old memory had kicked him in the gut like a hobnailed boot—the small faces, the hungry, haunting eyes. All he'd wanted was to get away.

Tessa would be upset with him, and he couldn't blame her. He'd behaved like a jerk in there. Maybe he should tell her the truth—the whole, painful story. But that would be one of the most trying things he'd ever done. Only his late uncle Maxim, who'd brought him to America after the war, had heard everything; and telling that good man had been like opening a vein. The idea of going through that again, especially with a woman he'd known less than two days, was unthinkable.

The wind had died down, but the fog was moving in again. By now he could barely see the plane. The cold stung his cheeks and numbed his ears. As he weighed the wisdom of going back into the lodge, a movement to his left, along the tideline, caught his eye. His breath stopped as a big silver wolf, the leader of the resident pack, trotted out of the pines and crossed the inlet through the fog, not thirty yards in front of him. More fascinated than afraid, Dragan watched as the rest of the pack followed—the sleek, black female who was the leader's mate, the gangly half-grown pups and lesser members of the pack, all of them intent on some trail, none of them paying Dragan the least attention.

Only as the last wolf vanished into the trees did Dragan become aware of his own breathing and the pounding of his heart. What a sight! If only Tessa had been outside to see it, too. He glanced back toward the porch, in the hope that she might have come out. But no, she was busy with her twins, or perhaps too cold or too angry to open the front door.

He would tell her about the wolves, of course. But it wouldn't be the same as having shared the experience. That was the irony of his existence, Dragan mused. He could afford to do anything he wanted. But even if he took some companion along on some adventure, there would be no one to share the memory later on. No one lasted long in his life. He always made sure of that. It was the way he wanted things. Wasn't it?

Fog hid the plane completely now, but a tug on the rope reminded him that the tide was rising, lifting the floats off the bottom of the inlet. Standing, he checked the knots and the rigging of the winch. He would go back inside and give the tide another hour, then come out and begin the slow cranking that would bring the plane safely against the dock.

His belly rumbled, reminding him that he hadn't eaten much today. Maybe there'd be some ravioli left over. If not, he could always find something else. After their clash in the kitchen, he didn't look forward to facing Tessa. He owed her an apology—but contrition didn't come easy

for him, and he still didn't want to feed the twins. Maybe
the best plan would be to act as if nothing had happened.

He mounted the steps of the lodge and opened the door.
The aroma that wafted out of the kitchen made his mouth
water. Was this some kind of joke? Or could it really be
chocolate cake?

The twins were racing up and down the hallway, squeal-
ing and giggling. As he closed the door, a small figure
crashed against his legs.

"Hey, watch out there, young lady." He looked down
into Maddie's grinning face. Lifting her off her feet, he
turned her around and set her down, facing the opposite
direction. She scampered down the hall after her sister.

Tessa popped out of the kitchen. "The applesauce was
a good idea," she said. "Once I got them started on that,
they ate the ravioli, too. I hope you don't mind their running around. I put all the breakables out of reach."

"It's fine. Maybe if they burn up enough energy they'll
go right to sleep tonight."

The sudden rush of color to her face told Dragan she'd
caught his unintended double meaning. He hadn't planned
to say it that way, but, yes, as long as the lady was willing, he wanted her in his bed again tonight—preferably
with no interruptions.

"Is that chocolate cake I smell?" he asked, breaking the
awkward silence.

"It is. I found an old box of Betty Crocker in the pantry.
With no eggs, the cake's bound to be heavy, and there'll
be no icing, but—"

"Who cares? It's chocolate cake!"

She laughed—he loved the sound of it. "I'd think a man
like you, who could afford his own plane and anything else
he wanted, would be fussier about what he ate."

Dragan's memory flew back to Sarajevo and a time

when a crust of bread dropped in the street was a banquet for a starving boy. "This is no time to be fussy," he said. "But I'll tell you what. When we get back to Anchorage, you can get a sitter and I'll take you to the best restaurant in town."

"We'll see about that." The smile had faded from her face. Only then did Dragan remember. Returning to Anchorage would change everything. They would be enemies again.

Nine

The wind had stilled, as if sucking in its breath before another blast of storm. In the eerie quiet, Tessa stood at the window, gazing out into the fog. After lunch and a dessert of dense, sweet chocolate cake, Dragan had uncovered the kitchen window and unlocked one set of shutters in the front, letting welcome daylight spill into the lodge. She'd hoped the window would give her a view of the inlet and the plane. But the fog that had moved in was so thick she could barely see past the nearest trees.

Dragan had told her about the wolf pack he'd seen. He hadn't sounded the least bit worried, but as he headed out again to bring the disabled plane in to the dock, she'd kept her eyes on him until he vanished in the mist. He had the pistol tucked into his belt. But what if the wolves came back and attacked him? He couldn't shoot them all.

The lodge was quiet inside—*too* quiet, Tessa suddenly realized. Minutes ago the twins had been with her, playing with a set of poker chips on the coffee table. Now the chips were abandoned and the girls were nowhere in sight. The silence told her they were up to something.

"Missy! Maddie! Where are you?" She checked the kitchen, the pantry and the space behind the bar, then hurried back into the hallway. The two unused guest rooms on her left were securely closed. Her own door stood open, but when she searched inside, her girls weren't in the room, the closet or the adjoining bathroom. Even when she peered under the bed, there was no sign of their mischievous little faces laughing back at her.

Tessa was getting more worried by the minute. Had she made sure the back door was locked? She was sure she had. She'd paid special attention. And if the girls had gone out the front she would have seen them. They had to be somewhere in the lodge.

Farther down the hallway, the door to Dragan's room stood partway open. As she stepped inside, she heard squeals and giggles coming from his bathroom. Tessa groaned, knowing what she was about to find. Her twins were playing their favorite game.

Passing through the bedroom, she averted her eyes from the still-rumpled bed where she'd done things that would make a courtesan blush. Right now she had more urgent priorities.

In the bathroom, she found her daughters standing on either side of the toilet, gleefully splashing their little hands in the bowl. Yards of damp toilet paper spilled across the floor.

Relief clashed with dismay as she snatched them up, turned on the tap, soaped their hands under warm, running water and dried them off. "No! We don't do that!" she scolded, knowing full well that they'd played this game before and, given the chance, would do it again. At least her babies were all right.

Setting them down outside the bathroom she gathered up the soppy toilet paper. She was stuffing it in the wastebasket when she noticed Dragan's leather shaving kit lying open on the vanity. A half-dozen condom packets peeked out of a side pocket.

Her face went hot. The man had certainly come prepared. Had he planned to seduce her all along, or was it simply his practice to be ready for any occasion—and any woman who crossed his path?

Not that she should be surprised, she reminded herself. Dragan Markovic was a player, and she was just another notch on his metaphorical bedpost. She'd do well to remember that the next time he beckoned her to his bed. Maybe it was time to draw the line. Dragan was an accomplished lover, and she'd enjoyed every delicious minute with him. But she had her pride, and it wasn't hard to surmise that she was being used.

Taking her twins in hand, she ushered them out of Dragan's bedroom and closed the door. She would tell him what they'd done, of course. Hopefully he'd laugh about it. At least he might remember not to leave his door ajar.

It was getting close to the time Maddie and Missy took their afternoon naps. They'd probably resist going down, but with luck, if she snuggled with them on the bed, they'd fall asleep and give her a brief chance to unwind.

The afghan was draped over the back of the couch. Tessa took it into the bedroom, curled up with the twins on the bed, and pulled it over the three of them. "Shh," she whispered. "Let's all go to sleep." She began to sing a little lullaby they liked. The song had special meaning for the three of them. She'd sung it to them as they lay in the NICU, with tubes and monitors attached to their tiny bodies. Even now it helped to settle them for sleep.

Tessa could feel them relaxing; feel the deepening of their sweet baby breaths. Once they were asleep she could ease away from them, maybe go make some coffee and spend some time just looking out the window and being quiet. Heaven knows she needed it.

The lullaby faded in her throat. Her eyelids grew heavy. They drooped and closed as she drifted into sleep.

Bringing in the plane had taken more time and effort than Dragan expected, but at last it was done. The sleek craft was moored to the floating dock, lashed securely to the capstans.

Detaching the winch from the post, he finished coiling the long rope. The wind had sprung up again, thinning out the fog but blowing in a huge bank of angry black clouds from the west. From the look of the sky, this storm could be even bigger and meaner than last night's. He wouldn't bet two cents on the odds of their being rescued in the next twenty-four hours. But just in case, he'd radioed one last message from the cockpit. As before, he'd heard nothing but static from the other end. All he could do was keep trying and hope for the best.

At least he and Tessa's little family had warmth and shelter, with enough food to last them for a couple of weeks. But they needed to get out of there and back to their lives. People would already be worried about them.

And then, there was the trial. The more time he spent with Tessa, the less he looked forward to the ordeal. He had a company to protect—with jobs, stockholders and profits at stake. How could he weigh all that against the welfare of a spunky, vulnerable redhead who'd do anything for the babies she loved? Like it or not, he had to make the right decision for the most people.

Putting the thought aside, Dragan lugged the winch and rope to the shed and locked them away. By then the storm front had arrived in full fury. The wind blasted sleet into his face as he gathered up an armload of the firewood he'd cut earlier and carried it around the lodge to the shelter of the front porch. With the storm almost battering him off his feet, he went back for a second load. Burdened under as much wood as he could carry, he staggered onto the porch. Going back for a third load would be out of the question. The storm had become a solid whiteout. In such conditions, men had been known to get lost and freeze within a few yards of shelter.

Stomping his boots clean, he entered the lodge and bolted the door behind him. His thick sweater was coated with sleet. He stripped it off, shook away as much moisture as he could, and hung it over the back of a chair to dry.

The fire had burned down to embers. Dragan stirred the coals with a poker, added more wood and soon had a crackling blaze. Taking off his wet boots and damp wool socks, he set them on the hearth and walked toward the hall to get dry socks and sneakers.

The lodge was quiet. Dragan had never minded solitude, but now he found himself missing Tessa's voice and the happy chaos created by her little girls. He took a detour to check the kitchen. They weren't there, but they couldn't be far.

He continued on down the hall past Tessa's closed bedroom door. Maybe they were napping. As long as he was here, it wouldn't hurt to check.

When no one answered his light rap on the door, he turned the knob and opened it carefully, making sure the hinges didn't creak. Tessa lay on the bed, curled around her twins as he'd seen her the night before. All three were fast asleep.

Something stirred inside him—a surge of protectiveness. His misguided actions had brought them to this isolated place. Now it fell to him to keep them safe and to get them back where they belonged. Their precious lives were in his hands—a truth that frightened him more than Tessa, or anyone, could know. But looking at those sweet, sleeping faces, the long-denied yearning was there—to have someone of his own to love and protect.

How would it feel, he wondered, to lie down on the bed, nestle against Tessa's back and drape an arm across her and her little ones, holding them all in a circle of warmth? He'd never do it, of course. But he could imagine what it might be like. Maybe that was how it felt to be a father.

But that was one role he'd vowed never to play.

Dragan was about to close the door when Tessa opened her eyes and saw him. For a moment he expected her to be upset. But then she touched a finger to her lips to signal silence. Inch by cautious inch, she eased her body away from her sleeping twins, sat up and lowered her feet to the floor. With a few stealthy steps, she joined Dragan in the hall and closed the door behind her.

"I didn't mean to wake you," he said. "I'd just come in from outside and wanted to make sure you three were all right."

"It's fine." Her warm hazel eyes surveyed him up and down. "I heard the wind blowing. It must be bad out there. You look like you could use thawing out. How about some coffee?"

Dragan could think of other ways to be thawed out, but he went along with her invitation. "That sounds good," he said. "While we're at it, I'll have some more of that cake."

She glanced down at his bare feet. "The floor's cold. While you're getting your shoes on, I'll heat some water."

Dragan remembered giving her a foot rub. Too bad she hadn't offered to do the same for him. But right now he'd have to settle for dry sneakers and hot coffee.

He returned to the kitchen to find the kettle boiling and the table set for coffee and cake. "I took a look outside," she said, pouring hot water into mugs and adding measures of instant coffee. "I'm guessing we could be stuck here a while longer. What do you think?"

Dragan opened a packet of powdered creamer and stirred it into his cup. "It's bad out there, all right," he said. "But don't get discouraged. Storms tend to blow through pretty fast this early in the season. Meanwhile, we've got wood, water and plenty of food."

"It's not food I'm worried about," she said, joining him at the table. "It's disposable diapers and clean clothes for the girls. I've tried to go longer between changes, but the supply's getting low. I can always wash their dirty clothes and hang them by the fire to dry. But once we're out of diapers we're in big trouble."

"I hadn't even thought of that," Dragan said. "But we have plenty of sheets. If worse comes to worse, you can cut up one or two of them into diapers and wash them out. I remember my mother doing that for years, the wet diapers hanging on lines…"

His voice trailed off as the memory surfaced, undimmed by time—his parents, his brother, his two lively little sisters. The old wound was too deep to heal.

"Let's hope it won't come to that. I'm not even sure I've got safety pins." Tessa cut slices of cake and put them on two saucers. "You've never told me about your family, Dragan. I'm guessing you must have been the firstborn. I can tell by the way you take charge of—" She broke off as if reading his expression. "Was it a mistake for me to ask?"

"No, it's fine," Dragan said. "You're right, I was the oldest. My parents were schoolteachers. I had a younger brother and two younger sisters."

"You say 'had.'" Something—a knowing sadness, perhaps—flickered in her eyes, as if she'd guessed the truth.

He swallowed a rush of emotion. "That's right. None of them survived the war."

He heard the sharp intake of her breath. "I'm sorry," she said.

"It happens in wartime. People die. Good people. Innocent people."

Tessa's gaze dropped to the table.

Dragan sensed that she was groping for a suitable reply but not finding it.

A cry from the bedroom broke the silence. The twins were awake.

With a murmured apology, she dashed off to take care of them. Knowing she might not be back soon, Dragan went ahead and finished his coffee and cake.

He'd sensed that Tessa had been glad to get away. Not that he blamed her. Nobody would welcome a revelation like the one he'd just given her. That was why he tried to keep his past private. His personal demons were nobody's business. He didn't need people's judgment and he certainly didn't need their pity.

It surprised him that he'd told Tessa as much as he had. The woman had a way of reaching into the raw core of his soul to stir up memories he wanted to forget and emotions he never wanted to feel again.

He didn't like it.

He'd enjoyed her in bed and hoped to have her there again. But once they made it back to civilization, for any number of reasons, it would be best for them both if they went their separate ways. There was the issue of the trial. There was his unwritten rule against dating a woman with children or, for that matter, any woman who played for keeps.

Tessa had "for keeps" written all over her. She needed the kind of faithful, steady man who'd be a good father to her twins. At least she seemed smart enough to know he wasn't that man. But letting her go wouldn't be as simple as kissing her good-night and having a diamond bracelet delivered the next day. Tessa Randall wasn't a diamond bracelet kind of woman.

Both twins needed changing. Tessa wiped their little pink bottoms, sealed the soiled diapers in a plastic trash bag and put on two fresh disposables from her dwindling supply. At this rate, she'd be out in the next couple of days. If they were still stuck here by then, she'd have no choice except to follow Dragan's suggestion to tear up some sheets and go back to the old-fashioned way of diapering babies.

Thinking of Dragan's suggestion dragged her thoughts right back to the man that dominated them so completely. Dragan's revelation about losing his entire family had dismayed her. But it explained a lot about him. A person who'd suffered that kind of bereavement might do anything to protect himself from more of the same. No wife. No children. Probably no close friends. No one in his life whose loss could hurt him again.

How terribly lonely the man must be.

Not that she had any illusions about rescuing him from his loneliness. Dragan was a compelling man whose air of tragedy only added to his appeal. But bitter, wounded heroes only found happy endings in romance novels. In real life they tended to destroy anyone who got too close to them. And right now she had her hands full just being a mother.

By the time she'd finished snapping Missy's coveralls, Maddie had slid off the bed and was making a beeline for the open bathroom door. Grabbing her daughter with one arm she hauled her back onto the bed. The two little girls lay on their backs, grinning up at their mother. Getting into the spirit, Tessa began pushing down and up on the springy mattress, bouncing them until they squealed with laughter.

On impulse, she flung herself down between them and joined the bouncing. Laughing, the three of them flew up and down, up and down.

"What's going on here?" Dragan stood in the doorway, a puzzled frown on his face.

Out of breath, Tessa brushed the hair out of her eyes. He'd caught her acting silly and she was more than a little embarrassed—especially given his disapproving look. But that didn't mean she owed him an apology. She decided to brazen it out. "It's called play. You should try it sometime," she challenged.

His expression suggested he could think of more entertaining things to do on a mattress. He didn't say it out loud, but the unspoken message brought a warm flush to Tessa's cheeks.

She sat up, leaving the twins to tumble on the comforter. "If you're worried about the bed, we won't bounce on it anymore. But unless we can find ways to keep these two little monkeys entertained, they'll just get into mischief. The last time they got away from me I found them in your bathroom, playing in the toilet."

Dragan didn't look amused. "That won't do. I'll remember to keep my doors closed."

"That's all well and good. But I could use some suggestions. I didn't bring any toys, and there aren't any in this place. The poker chips I found under the bar kept them happy until they got bored and wandered off. There must be other things they can play with."

He frowned again, causing her to wonder if she'd gotten through to the man. He seemed to be struggling with something. "Give them anything you see fit," he said in a cold voice. "Consider the place yours. Open any door and take whatever strikes your fancy. I'll trust your judgment. Just don't ask me to help."

With that he turned and walked down the hall to his bedroom. Tessa heard the door open and close. What had she said? What deep, hidden pain had her innocent words touched? Did it have something to do with the loss of his family?

She would never understand Dragan Markovic. But, as she reminded herself, once their rescue arrived it wouldn't make any difference. Her only concern would be winning her suit against his company.

As for tonight… Dragan had left enough hints to let her know he'd welcome her back in his bed. But she'd be a fool to go. Things were already complicated enough.

The twins had stopped bouncing on the bed and were gazing at her with Kevin's beautiful blue eyes, as if to say "What now, Mom?" Tessa gave them a smile.

"Hey," she said, scooping them up in her arms. "What d'you say we go on a treasure hunt?"

Dragan closed the bedroom door. As the latch clicked behind him, he forced himself to exhale the tension from his body. The last encounter with Tessa and her girls had left him shaken. He needed time alone to regain his bearings.

He should never have told Tessa about his family. Mentioning their loss had set off an avalanche of memories—their home in Sarajevo, the warmth, the aroma of soup cooking on the stove. His father's booming voice; his pretty mother bouncing on the bed with his two little sisters, all of them laughing.

The sight of Tessa romping with her twins had struck him like a cold steel blade between his ribs. But worse, even, than that was the guilt—guilt that ate like lye into his conscience.

He'd tried to wipe his memory clean, to go on as if the past had never happened and his being solitary was his natural state. But Tessa and her innocent little girls were all the catalyst it had taken to bring the past back in every detail—the unspeakable loss and his own part in it.

The tragedy was his to own, and there was nothing to be done for it. He would take time to pull himself together, maybe pick up a book and do some reading, even nap. Then he would go back, face Tessa and her babies and make the best of the situation. Until rescue came, it would be his responsibility to keep them safe.

He couldn't fail those who were depending on him. Not this time.

Tessa had pulled pans, lids and a couple of big spoons out of the kitchen cupboards. Hauling the whole mess onto the rug in front of the fireplace, she'd given her twins free rein. Missy and Maddie were having a grand time, banging the pans and lids together, standing on top of them, wearing them as hats. Who needed store-bought toys?

As the cacophony was nearing its loudest, Dragan walked in from the hall. "What is that god-awful racket?" His voice was stern, but his haggard expression was gone. A quiet hour in his room must have done some good.

"It's music. Can't you tell?" Tessa joked.

"Beethoven or Mozart?" He settled on the arm of the sofa.

"You'll have to ask them. I was thinking it sounded more like AC-DC." Tessa turned in her chair to face him. "You did say I could use whatever I found to entertain them."

"I did. And you deserve high marks for creativity. But how much longer do we get to listen to this?"

"Don't worry. Grasshoppers have a longer attention span than these two. Give them another couple of minutes. By then they'll be looking around for something else."

"Like what? Something quiet, I hope."

"Do you have any suggestions?"

"Maybe. I'll be right back."

Tessa watched him disappear into the kitchen. She had to give Dragan credit for making an effort to be nice. Not until he'd told her about his family had she glimpsed how their loss might have forged his character. He'd mentioned two little sisters. Being around her twins might have stirred some painful memories. But there had to be more to the story. Many people who'd suffered loss moved on to find new meaning, new love and new families. Something had held Dragan back and forged a wall against warmth and emotion.

And what about you? an inner voice whispered. *It's been two years. You loved Kevin. You have his babies to keep his memory fresh. But you can't spend your life in mourning. When are you going to move on?*

Ignoring the question, she watched her daughters playing with the pans. Missy was trying to fit a small one inside a large one. Maddie was banging on a skillet lid with a spoon. Her twins were her whole existence, her reason for getting through each day. If she ever let a new man into her life, it would have to be someone who'd love her girls as much as she did—not a man like Dragan who could barely stand being around them.

But why was she even thinking of him in those terms? Dragan Markovic was a ruthless manipulator who would use any means at his disposal to weaken her case against him.

But Tessa knew she wouldn't be satisfied until she'd at least tried to understand this intriguing man.

Dragan came out of the kitchen carrying two large, empty cardboard boxes. "How about these? There's a store-room off the pantry. All I had to do was empty out a few supplies."

"Perfect!" Tessa gave him a smile. "Put them down. I'll pick up the pans."

"I found something else." He dropped the boxes and whipped his free hand from behind his back. He was holding a good-size canned ham.

"Oh, my word!" Tessa had never dreamed she could get so excited about an item she'd seen hundreds of times at the grocery store.

"What do you say I work on cooking while you keep an eye on your girls?" he said. "After they're put to bed for the night, you and I can sit down and enjoy a real dinner. There's plenty of that good wine left."

"That gets my vote. Knock yourself out." As he left the room, Tessa took the two boxes, one deep with high sides, one wide and shallow, and put them on the floor. The twins pounced on them, Missy climbing into the low box, Maddie pulling the high box onto its side and crawling into it, like a little wild creature into a cave.

Dragan was going to need the pans. She gathered up all she could carry and took the armload into the kitchen. The pantry door was open and she could hear the sound of rummaging inside. Deciding not to bother him, she left her burden on the counter and returned to the great room. The man was being unusually pleasant. Maybe he was trying to soften her up for tonight. But she had her own plan that had little to do with his bed. Whatever it took, she was determined to learn the secret of his past.

Ten

Darkness fell at an early hour, with no sign of the storm letting up. Tessa fed the twins their supper of mac and cheese, a dish they loved so much that they even complied with a minimum of mess. Their diet here was too heavy on the pasta, but some things couldn't be helped. At least they were eating.

The savory aroma of baked ham wafted from the stove. Tessa had left the cooking to Dragan, and it smelled heavenly. She was looking forward to whatever surprise he'd prepared from their store of emergency rations. Dragan had already shown himself to be a creative cook. The meal would doubtless be a pleasure. But would there be strings attached? What price would she be asked to pay?

One thing she could count on: the man known as the Dragon never did any favor without a good reason. If he was behaving like a gentleman tonight, it was most likely because he expected something in return. Would it be as simple as a night in his bed? Or would it be part of the bigger picture—the lawsuit, the trial and the chance of a settlement? Whatever he was planning, she couldn't afford to let her guard down.

She'd slipped up once when she'd confided in him about her dismissal and the babies. He'd reacted with sympathy, of course. But she'd be a fool to keep trusting him or to agree to anything without her lawyer present.

After wiping off smears of macaroni and untying their bibs, she lifted her twins out of their safety seats and carried them down the hall for their nightly bath. While she was putting them to bed, Dragan would finish getting dinner ready. Tessa could tell her little ones were tired. She hoped they wouldn't take too long to fall asleep. She was hungry and she had her own plan for the evening. She meant to learn more about Dragan's hidden past.

True, she was curious. But her need to know went deeper than that—to motive, to trust. What could she expect from the man? If he made her an offer or a promise, would he keep his word?

As she bathed the twins, Tessa could hear the faint clatter of plates and cutlery from the dining area. She looked forward to a leisurely meal without the demands of her little ones. But tonight's dinner would hardly be relaxing. It would be more like a chess game—move and counter move.

She diapered the babies, zipped them into their pajamas and tucked them into the big bed. Lying next to them, she sang a whispered lullaby until their eyes closed and their sweet breathing deepened. Then she eased off the bed and went back in the bathroom to splash her face and run a comb through her hair. The black turtleneck she'd put on that morning showed the stains and ravages of a day with two toddlers. On impulse, she pulled it off, found a

V-necked black sweater in her suitcase and pulled it over her head. She'd always liked the way it looked on her. More important, it was clean.

The twins had settled into sleep. With luck they'd be down for the night. She checked to make sure the bathroom door was shut. Then, tiptoeing out of the bedroom, she closed the door behind her and walked into the dining room.

The table was set with its customary gold-rimmed china and linen napkins. The glow of candles reflected on the polished wood that covered the walls. From the kitchen she could hear Dragan's footsteps. She stepped through the door to find him lifting a metal pan with the baked ham out of the oven.

"Anything I can do to help?" she asked.

"You've earned a rest," he said. "Sit down, pour yourself some wine and look beautiful while I get this meal on the table."

"I'll pour you some, too." Ignoring the flattery, Tessa returned to the dining room and poured wine into the two crystal goblets. Vintage wine and crystal in a rustic lodge with the storm blowing outside—it was like something out of a soap opera. Not that there was anything melodramatic about Dragan's intentions, she reminded herself. He had a captive audience and he was prepared to take full advantage.

But that didn't mean she couldn't enjoy a good meal when it was offered. As Dragan brought in the dishes he'd improvised from the emergency stash, Tessa's mouth began to water. The ham was cooked to a flawless golden brown with gravy made from the drippings. There were candied yams, fluffy, seasoned mashed potatoes and flaky biscuits. "No butter," Dragan apologized, "but I did find a little pot of blackberry jam."

"This is amazing!" Tessa took her first bite of potatoes and gravy. "Where did you learn to cook like this?"

He shrugged. "After the war, when fresh food was still scarce, I worked as a cook in one of the refugee camps. I learned to make the best of what was available. I still enjoy cooking. But with nobody to cook for, I don't do it much."

"What a waste of talent." Tessa gave him an appreciative smile. She wanted to question him more about the war but that could darken his mood and risk spoiling the dinner he'd worked so hard to prepare.

Clearly he'd wanted to please her. The only question was why. It was hard to believe the Dragon would do anything out of simple kindness.

"Tell me something, Tessa," he said, taking a sip of wine. "If you could create any life for yourself—any life you wanted, live anyplace, do anything—what would it be like?"

"That's a strange question."

"Is it?" His slate-gray eyes probed hers. "Why do you find it strange that I want to know your thoughts and desires—and that the simplest way is to ask?"

"Since you put it that way, maybe it's not so strange." Tessa weighed her words. "But if I tell you, I want something in return."

One expressive eyebrow tilted upward. "Name it," he said with mock graciousness. "Anything to please a lady."

"There's a question I'm not ready to ask you," she said. "But when I do ask—and I will—I want an honest answer."

A wary look flickered across his face. Then he shrugged. "Why not? What do I have to hide?"

Plenty, Tessa thought. The man had to be bluffing. "Do you promise?" she asked.

He frowned. "I promise. But you haven't answered my

question," he said. "Tell me what you imagine as a perfect life."

Tessa was silent for a moment. Her answer might not please him, but at least it would be honest. "For me, a perfect life would be the one I would've had if Kevin, my fiancé, hadn't been killed—a peaceful home with a man who'd love me and be a good father to our girls. It wouldn't matter where we lived or how much money we had. Being part of a warm, loving family would be enough."

A surprising sadness deepened in his eyes. He shook his head. "Tessa, I was going to offer you enough money to buy the life you dreamed of—a luxury home, servants, expensive cars, travel and a fine education for your girls, if that would make you happy. But I should have known better. What you want isn't for sale."

"I know," Tessa whispered, her throat tight. "But I haven't lost hope. Maybe someday, when I'm ready…"

"Your fiancé…you must have loved him."

"I did."

"He was a lucky man."

"I always thought I was the lucky one." She sipped her wine, fighting to hold back tears.

They finished the meal, making awkward small talk. When they were finished, Tessa insisted on clearing the table and taking everything to the kitchen. "That was a magnificent dinner," she said. "You outdid yourself. At least let me do the cleanup."

"Fine," he said. "But don't take time to wash up. I'll do that in the morning while you're busy with your girls."

He wandered toward the fireplace and sank onto the couch. Tessa's hands felt unsteady as she stacked the dishes in the sink. So Dragan had been prepared to make a deal with her; a generous settlement that would give her enough to set her in style for life. No doubt he would still be glad to settle—anything to avoid the publicity of a trial. But if nothing else, her answer—a true answer—had let him know that her suit wasn't just about money. At least she'd given the Dragon something to think about.

She put the candles away and polished the table with a clean cloth. In the flickering light of the fireplace, she could see Dragan leaning back on the couch with his feet on the ottoman. Glancing around, he caught her watching him.

"Leave that, Tessa," he said. "Come over here and keep me company."

Coming from Dragan, even an invitation could sound like an order. Tessa was tempted to ignore him for a short time, just to prove she could. But then she remembered the promise she'd forced him to make. She crossed the room and settled next to him on the couch.

He'd laid a fresh log on the fire. Flames crackled as they licked at the splintered wood. His arm slipped around her shoulders, easing her closer. Next to her tired body, he felt strong and warm.

His lips grazed her forehead. "Rest," he murmured. "You've had a long day."

Tessa closed her eyes and sank against his shoulder. He wanted to make love to her. His actions were making that clear. Now, in the glow of the firelight, with her feet resting next to his on the ottoman, it would be all too easy to turn, move into his arms and let herself fall into the bliss she knew he could give her.

But now, while she still had her wits about her, she mustn't abandon her quest to learn about his past. She forced herself to stir. "Dragan, you made me a promise," she said.

"Did I now?" His voice was lazy, teasing.

"You know you did. You promised to answer my question."

"You haven't asked it." His voice was the same, but she felt a thread of tension invade his body.

"I'm asking now." She sat up, facing him in the firelight. "I need to know this. What happened to you in Sarajevo? What hurt you so deeply that you can't let anyone get too close to you, not even me, not even my children?"

He'd gone rigid. "What if I told you that I wasn't the one who was hurt? That I was the one who did the hurting?"

He'd meant to shock her and he had. But there had to be more to the story. "Even if it's bad, I want to understand," she said. "Tell me."

"You don't want to hear this, Tessa."

"I need to. And you promised."

Turning away from her, he stared into the fire. Taking a deep breath, he let it out in a slow, ragged exhalation. "How much do you know about Sarajevo?"

"Only what I learned in school. I know the city was under siege for four years, but the people never gave up. Being there all that time, it must've been terrible for you."

"It was. Serbian artillery shells blasting from the hills, buildings collapsing, people starving. The only thing that saved us was the tunnel, dug by hand the first year, all the way under the enemy lines to a spot where people could drop supplies. It became our connection to the outside world—to life.

"I was thirteen when the siege began—too young for the army but old enough to work. I helped haul dirt out of the tunnel and, after it was finished, I spent my nights hauling cargo into the city. In the morning I'd go home to my family—my parents, my younger brother and my two little sisters. We'd have a little time together before my father had to go out on patrol."

He fell silent, staring down at his clenched hands.

Tessa checked the impulse to lay a comforting hand on his shoulder. Dragan was reliving a nightmare. Like an animal in pain, he would lash out at her touch.

"One morning I came home to find that our house had been hit by a shell in the night. There was nothing left of it but a pile of rubble."

Tessa had meant to keep silent, but the words escaped her. "Oh, Dragan…"

"It gets worse." His voice was flat, emotionless. "The police were there. They told me my parents and brother had died in the explosion. But my little sisters had been sleeping in the cellar. They were safe.

"I took those little girls away. They were two and four years old, and I was all the family they had. Lord, I was fourteen. We had no home, no food and winter was coming. The nights were getting cold. How could I take care of them?

"For the first few days I tried keeping us together. I stole food when I could. We slept wherever we could find shelter—a box, an alley, the cab of a wrecked truck. But soon I had to face the truth. I couldn't keep them alive by myself."

Tessa forced back tears. She was beginning to understand. Every time Dragan looked at her twins he thought of those helpless little girls.

"There was an orphanage in the city, run by nuns. Good women who made do with what little they had. Taking my sisters there, I thought, would be the only way to save them. So that's what I did. I promised to come back for them soon and walked away. I can still hear them crying, begging me not to go. I can still see their eyes, their sad little faces." He took an anguished breath. "I never saw them again."

"What happened to them?" Tessa whispered. Something had, she knew. Dragan had already told her his entire family had died in the war.

"I went back to my work in the tunnel. When I came to visit a few days later, the nuns told me there'd been an outbreak of fever. With no medicines and no doctor, it had swept through the place, killing many of the younger, weaker children. My sisters were gone."

His voice sounded as if every word had to be forced from his throat. Tessa realized she was quietly weeping.

"It wasn't your fault," she said. "You were just a boy. You did all you could."

He turned toward her, eyes blazing with helpless anger. "My sisters were my responsibility. They were counting on me, but I wasn't man enough to save them. I turned my back and left them in that place to die."

"But you couldn't have known what would happen." Tessa wanted to seize his shoulders and grip them until he winced. "You gave them the best chance they had, maybe the only chance."

"*Did I*? I could have stayed with them and helped out at the orphanage, maybe taken them away when the fever started. I could at least have been there to comfort them when they closed their eyes for the last time."

But you weren't there. So your punishment was to deny yourself love for the rest of your days. And you made up your mind to never be responsible for anyone again, especially children.

Tessa thought those words, but she didn't say them. Dragan was already in torment. He didn't need a lecture from her. And what would she have done in his place? Could she have walked away from her twins if it seemed to be the only hope of saving their lives? Would she have been any less bitter than Dragan to learn that her sacrifice had failed?

In her eyes the man was blameless. But it was clear that he would go on blaming himself for the rest of his life.

Dragan had turned away from her to stare into the flames. "So, are you satisfied?" he asked after a long silence. "Did you get what you wanted?"

Tessa dared to lay a hand on his back. When he didn't pull away she left it there. She could feel the pulsing of his heart as she struggled to answer.

"I'm sorry," she said. "I wanted to know what had affected you so deeply. And I appreciate your honesty. But I had no idea what I'd be putting you through."

"I warned you about sharing the images in my memory." He poured two fingers of wine into his glass and emptied it in a single gulp. "I've only told that story to two people—my uncle who brought me to America and you. Now you know why."

He put down his glass and rose from the couch. His eyes were cold stone. "It's getting late, and I know you're tired, Tessa. You might as well get some sleep. I'll take care of the dishes."

His message was clear. After what he'd told her, he didn't expect her to feel like making love. But he was wrong. Understanding him made her feel closer to him—gave her insight into the pain he carried. Made her want to soothe it. As a result, she needed him more than ever. And, proud man that he was, she couldn't help believing that he needed her.

Rising to her feet, she watched him walk away, toward the kitchen. The moment was passing. If she didn't stop him now it could be too late.

"Dragan!"

He turned at the sound of her voice. Their gazes met

across the firelight-shadowed room; his asking silent questions.

"Don't go," she said. "Please, I want you to stay with me."

His stern expression crumbled. He hesitated an instant, then strode back, caught her in his arms and crushed her close.

When his mouth found hers, the kiss was tender but hungry, seeking but urgent, his wind-chapped lips utterly possessing her. She closed her eyes, softening in his arms, lips parting to the thrust of his tongue, offering him everything she had to give. Long-dormant yearnings surged like wildfire through her body. She wanted him with a hunger that went deeper than passion, deeper than desire.

With a muffled groan he slid his hand under her sweater and unhooked her bra. His big hands splayed on her back, as if seeking comfort from the feel of her skin. This was nothing like last night's smooth seduction. Dragan had shared a piece of his broken soul. Now he quivered with need. His wound was too raw for her to heal. But if she could ease the pain, maybe that would be enough.

"I think we're in the wrong room," she murmured, reaching down to fumble with his belt buckle.

"I can fix that." With a rough sound that could have been a laugh, a growl or a moan, he swept her up in his arms and strode down the hall and into his room. Their hands tore at each other's clothes, throwing them helter-skelter on the floor in their haste. He took seconds to add protection, then flung her on the bed and entered her in one hard, gliding thrust.

The confident, manipulative near-stranger who'd taken her to bed last night was gone. Tessa's arms held the child who'd been forced to grow up too soon, the boy who'd lost everything and the man who'd locked himself behind a wall of guilt and mourning. He made love to her with a tender savagery that held nothing back. She responded from the deepest part of her, giving him all she had, opening herself to his hurt and taking it in, making his pain her own.

Their shattering climax shook her to the core. When it was done they lay side by side in the dark, touching but not speaking. The storm still roared outside, filling the silence between them. As Dragan's breathing deepened, she realized he'd drifted into exhausted slumber. Tessa knew she had to get back to her babies soon. But she needed a moment to gather her thoughts.

What now? She could easily fall in love with Dragan Markovic, if she hadn't already. But aside from their closeness tonight, what else had changed? Sooner or later the storm would pass, their rescue would arrive and the outside world would come crashing in. Once more he would become the Dragon, her intimidating, untouchable former boss. She would be the ex-employee who was suing him. And he would still be the man who couldn't abide children.

Not very good odds for a lasting relationship.

Easing away from him, she swung her feet off the bed and tiptoed to her room. Her little girls were sleeping peacefully; Missy curled tight on her side, Maddie sprawled on her back. Tessa pulled her flannel nightgown down over her head and slipped under the comforter, curling her body to make a nest around them. With so much on her mind she didn't expect to sleep much, but she was more tired than she'd realized. Within minutes she was sinking into sleep.

Tessa's eyes shot open in the dark. She had no idea what time it was or how long she'd slept, but a sound had awakened her—a terrifying sound, one she knew all too well.

It was Missy, struggling to breathe.

Jerking awake, she sat up, grabbed her daughter, held her close and pressed an ear against her chest. Her body was warm, too warm. With every breath, Tessa could hear the congestion bubbling in her small lungs.

Dear God, she prayed silently. Not here. Anyplace but here!

Missy's lungs had been an issue from the time of her premature birth. From the start she'd been the weaker of the twins. Her underdeveloped lungs had kept her in the NICU longer than Maddie and they were still fragile. Even now, the slightest cold was enough to bring on viral pneumonia.

At home, Tessa kept a vaporizer handy for such emergencies. Rather than pack the bulky device, she'd planned to buy another one in Anchorage. But fate and Dragan had intervened and now, when it was desperately needed, she was without one.

Tessa switched on the flashlight she kept by the bed. Pneumonia in a child Missy's age was life threatening. She had to find some way to ease her lungs before it was too late.

"Mama?" Maddie sat up. She had a runny nose, too, but otherwise seemed all right.

"Stay here," Tessa told her, hoping Maddie would understand. "I won't be far away."

Clutching Missy close, she rushed down the hall to Dragan's room. She needed help and he was all the help she had.

Eleven

"**D**ragan, wake up!"

The frantic voice startled Dragan out of a sound sleep. He sat up, shielding his eyes from the glare of the flashlight. Tessa was standing in the doorway, clutching the light and one of her twins.

Alarm shocked him fully awake. Only some dire emergency would bring her here like this, in the middle of the night. "What is it?" he muttered.

"It's Missy." Fear strained her voice. "She's sick. I'm afraid it's pneumonia."

"How can you tell?" He flung back the covers. The room was frigid. The battery clock on the nightstand said 3:00 a.m.

"She's had it before. I know the signs. Fever, congested lungs. She can barely breathe. We've got to do something for her."

Fear jerked tight around Dragan's heart. He groped on the floor for his clothes. "What's worked before?"

"If I were home, I'd take her to the hospital. I've got some over-the-counter baby meds in my bag. They might help her feel better but they won't do enough to clear her lungs. Have you got anything like a vaporizer here? It won't cure the pneumonia, but it will help her breathe."

"No vaporizer." His mind scrambled for a solution as he found his pants and shirt, yanked them on and jammed his feet into his sneakers. "I remember my brother had bad lungs. My mother used to get him under a blanket with pans of steaming water. We could try that." He glanced around the dark room. "Where's Maddie?"

"I left her in the bed. But she won't stay."

"I'll get her." Dragan stepped out into the dim hallway. It was no surprise to see Maddie, in her pajamas, toddling toward him. "Come here, you little scamp." He scooped her into his arms and headed back toward his bedroom. She had a runny nose, which he wiped on his shirtsleeve, but she didn't feel feverish. Not yet, at least.

As he neared the open doorway, he could hear Missy coughing. Dread was a cold lump in the pit of his stomach. Getting marooned here in a storm was bad enough. But getting marooned with a critically sick baby was terrifying. Tessa was depending on him to help her. What if he couldn't do enough? What if the unimaginable happened and they lost her precious little girl? The shock and grief would destroy her—and it would be his fault for stranding them here in the first place.

It was as if his worst nightmare had come back to haunt him.

But he couldn't dwell on that now. He needed to stay clearheaded, to focus on whatever could be done.

Tessa came out of the bedroom to meet them. "Maddie's all right," he said. "I'll take her with me. Get your medicines and meet us in the kitchen."

Clutching her coughing baby, Tessa rushed down the hall. Dragan carried Maddie to the kitchen, buckled her into her safety seat on the table and covered her with his leather jacket to keep her warm. Then he lit the lantern, set it on the counter and began filling pans with water and setting them on the stove to heat. To hold the little girl's attention and calm his own nerves, he began talking to her.

"So what do you think, Miss Maddie? If you were going to make a steam tent, how would you do it? You say you'd start with a couple of tall chairs for a frame? Great idea. Wait right here."

He pushed through the swinging doors, returning in seconds with two high-backed, dining-room chairs. After moving the kitchen table out of the way he set them face-to-face in the middle of the floor. Checking Maddie again, he wiped her runny nose with a damp paper towel. Then he hurried to the storeroom off the pantry, where fishing gear and extra supplies were stored. He remembered seeing a green canvas tarpaulin stuffed in a corner. If it was big enough it might do for what he needed.

Returning to the kitchen, he unfolded the tarp. "Will you look at that, Miss Maddie!" He spoke to allay his own fears. "It seems to be about the right size, doesn't it?" She didn't blow a raspberry at him, so he chose to take that as agreement.

He draped it over the chairs to create a makeshift tent, and checked the edges to make sure they touched the floor on all sides. "With that runny nose, maybe it'll help you, too," he said to Maddie. "I just hope it helps your sister."

Steam was rising from the pans on the stove, but there was no sign of Tessa. Dragan was about to pick up Maddie to go look for her when she walked into the kitchen with Missy in her arms. She was still in her nightgown, her hair mussed, her eyes laced with red. From where he stood, Dragan could hear Missy's rapid, shallow breathing. The sound sent a bone-deep chill of fear through his body.

"I got some baby ibuprofen and a decongestant down her, and suctioned out her nose. But you can tell she's still bad. Here, you can give these to Maddie, too." She handed him two dropper bottles of medicine. "I'm scared, Dragan," she said.

He ached to tell her everything would be all right. But that was one promise he couldn't make. "I'm scared, too," he said, lifting up one side of the canvas. "Get under here, sit on one of the chairs and I'll put the pans of hot water in around you. Hold her in the steam if you can. Don't worry. I'll keep an eye on Maddie."

Holding Missy tight, she crouched low and then paused. For an instant her gaze locked with his. "Do you pray?" she asked.

Dragan had lost his religious faith in Sarajevo. Unwilling to lie to her, he shook his head.

"Maybe you should try it. Missy needs all the help she can get." Cradling her sick baby, she ducked out of sight.

Dragan began the task of moving pans of boiling water from the stove and sliding them under the edge of the canvas, then refilling more in a cycle that went on for an hour, then two, then longer. While the next batch of water was heating, he dosed Missy with the medicine drops, re-lit the fire in the fireplace and added more wood. The main part of the lodge was warm now, but the stack of logs was getting low. At least the storm seemed to be ebbing. With luck, it would be gone by the time he needed to go out back for more wood.

By now it was almost morning. Gray light filtered through the kitchen window. Maddie, still in her safety seat, had fallen asleep after a dose of Benadryl. Damp curls clung to her forehead. Dragan brushed a fingertip down her cheek. No fever. Just a nose that needed wiping. That would have to wait until she woke up.

The water on the stove had begun to steam. Dragan dropped to his knees and lifted the hem of the tarp to replace the cooled pans. In the faint light he could make out Tessa, huddled on a chair with Missy in her arms. Her damp nightgown clung to her body. Her hair hung down in wet strings.

"How's Missy?" he asked.

"Asleep. I think she's doing better but it's hard to tell in here."

Dragan raised the tarp higher, draping it over the back of the empty chair. "Give her to me and come on out. You need a break."

Tessa didn't argue. She lifted her sleeping child and passed her into Dragan's arms. Missy's hair and pajamas were soaked from the steam, but her breathing was regular, her skin cool. Dragan exhaled a long breath of relief. "She seems fine," he said.

"For now, maybe." Tessa crawled out of the makeshift tent, looking as if she'd just been pulled from a shipwreck. "But I know from experience, she's not out of the woods. She needs oxygen. We need to get her to a hospital."

The fear, which had eased some, clenched Dragan's stomach again. "The storm's letting up," he said. "Once it starts to clear I'll go out and try the radio again. I won't stop trying until I get through. Meanwhile, you and Missy need to stay warm and get into some dry clothes. Here, take her. I'll be right back."

Racing to his room, he yanked the comforter off the bed, returned to the kitchen and wrapped it around Tessa and Missy. By now Maddie was awake, squirming and fussing. She'd been amazingly good, sleeping in her seat. But now she wanted attention—and freedom.

The water was boiling on the stove. Dragan turned off the gas burners. "Go on. I'll bring her," he told Tessa. "You're exhausted. You need to get out of that wet nightgown and into bed, or you'll be sick, too."

As Tessa vanished toward the hall with Missy, Dragan unbuckled Maddie's harness and lifted her up. The odor that rose from her pants told him she was in urgent need of changing.

"Noz!" She grabbed his nose, giggling.

"No, you don't." Dragan pulled her hand away. "Come on, let's find your mother and get you into a clean diaper." He strode down the hall, holding her at arms' length. Entering Tessa's bedroom he found her still in her wet nightgown, getting Missy into dry clothes.

"Oh, heavens!" She wrinkled her nose as she caught Maddie's smell. Reaching into her pink bag, she tossed Dragan a fresh disposable diaper.

"You want *me* to change her?" he asked in disbelief.

"Yes." Tessa's teeth chattered as she shoved a pack of baby wipes toward him. "Get a towel out of the bathroom to lay her on."

Still holding Maddie, Dragan grabbed a towel off the bathroom rack and returned to the bedroom. Tessa was shivering as she zipped Missy into clean pajamas. If she'd brought along a spare nightgown, Dragan couldn't see it in her open suitcase.

With his free hand he laid the towel on the bed and then rummaged in the dresser for a set of thermals, like the ones he'd given her when they'd first arrived. "Put these on and get into bed," he ordered. "Don't worry. I'll take care of Maddie."

While Tessa tucked Missy into the bed and shed her wet nightgown, Dragan laid Maddie on the towel and unzipped her pajamas. He'd never changed a messy baby in his life. But he'd watched his mother do it when he was growing up. How hard could it be?

If he could just get past that ungodly smell…

Maddie knew the drill. She giggled and jabbered while he wiped her off, put on the clean diaper and stowed the soiled one in the bag. When he looked up, Tessa had put on the thermals and climbed into bed. She gave him a tired smile. "Good job. Her clothes and shoes are on the dresser. You might as well put them on her. She won't nap until later."

"No problem. I'll watch her while you get some rest."

"Thanks—oh, and she'll be hungry." She turned over, wrapped a protective arm around the sleeping Missy and closed her eyes.

Dragan washed Maddie's face and wiped her nose, then carried her and her clothes to the warm couch by the fire. It took some time to get her into her coveralls, sweater, socks and shoes, mostly because she kept trying to dress herself. But at last she was ready for breakfast.

Dragan had put her back in her safety seat, tied on her bib and was spooning canned applesauce into her mouth when he realized he could no longer hear the storm outside. He glanced out the window. A light breeze was stirring the pines. Pencil-thin rays of morning sun poked through the blanket of clouds. Was the weather about to truly clear or would the fog thicken again?

Fog or no fog, he'd soon need to get to the plane to try the radio again. But what about Maddie? It wouldn't be safe to turn her loose in the plane and, with her mother asleep, he wouldn't dare leave her here unsupervised.

He would let Tessa rest a little longer, he decided. Meanwhile he'd keep an eye out the window. If the weather showed more signs of clearing, he'd wake her. Meanwhile there were other things he could do.

The stack of wood he'd carried inside before the storm was getting low. There was more cut wood behind the lodge but it might need time indoors to dry. Now would be a good time to bring some in. Maddie would have to come with him, but she'd stayed on the back porch without any trouble yesterday. As long as he gave her another piece of kindling to hold, she should be fine.

Lowering her from her seat, he took her hand and led her out the back door and onto the open porch. The air was warming fast, a good sign. "Stay right here, Maddie," he told her.

"Phhht!" Maddie plopped down on the top step, watching him with eyes the color of his mother's Delft china cups.

The open yard behind the lodge was still foggy, the woodpile glazed with frozen sleet. Dragan kicked the top logs aside. The kindling underneath was mostly dry. He found a smooth, clean piece for Maddie, then piled his arms with all he could carry. "Come on," he said to Maddie. "Yes, you can carry your piece. That's a good girl."

He nudged the door open with his shoulder, let Maddie through and kicked the door shut behind them. Then he carried the wood to the hearth and piled the pieces in the big copper tub.

By the time he turned around, Maddie had abandoned her kindling and found a deck of playing cards on a shelf behind the wet bar. When she shook the box, the cards slid out on the floor. Giggling, she plopped down in the middle of the pile, with cards scattered all around her.

Dragan sighed. He was going to have to entertain this child until her mother woke up. He pulled the ottoman close to her and sat. "Hey, Maddie, let me show you something."

Taking a card, he bent it in the middle, allowing it to

stand on its side. Doing the same thing again, he balanced a second card atop the first, then more, until he had a three-foot tower. Maddie watched in fascination. Then her eyes took on a mischievous gleam. She batted the tower with her hand, toppling cards in all directions. She crowed with laughter.

Dragan built the tower again, then again, until she tired of the game. With a little yawn, she picked up her kindling piece and crawled onto the couch. Hallelujah, was she going to sleep? Tessa had mentioned something about a midmorning nap.

As she snuggled into the pillow, he tucked the afghan around her. Turning, he laid more wood on the fire. By the time he turned around again, her eyes were closed. Her breathing—except for her stuffy nose—was deep and even.

A glance through the front window confirmed that the fog was lifting. Maybe today somebody would answer his distress call. Maybe they'd be lucky enough to get out of there.

He rubbed his stubbled chin. Only then did it strike him that he'd been up most of the night, and that this morning he'd been too busy to brush his teeth or even relieve his bladder. Maddie was fast asleep. Surely she'd be all right while he paid a quick visit to the bathroom.

With a final glance at Maddie, he turned away and headed down the hall. Tessa's door stood partway open. Stepping inside to check, Dragan saw that she was still sleeping. Missy opened her eyes as he bent over the bed; but she didn't try to sit up, which wasn't like her at all. When he reached out to touch her cheek, her skin felt warm. He could hear the faint gurgle of congestion as she breathed.

He mouthed a curse of frustration. Dammit, she needed

to be in the hospital, and it was up to him to get her there. He would make a quick visit to the bathroom, check on Maddie once more and then go back and wake Tessa. If he could get through on the radio, they could steam Missy again before the rescue plane arrived.

He was out of the bathroom in minutes, without bothering to shave. Passing Tessa's door he walked back to the great room where he'd left Maddie and moved around to the front of the couch. His breath caught in his throat.

There was nothing on the couch but the rumpled afghan, the pillow and a familiar stick of kindling. Maddie was gone.

Dragan glanced around the room and checked behind the wet bar. He could see the front door, still bolted from last night. No chance she'd gotten out that way. More than likely she'd gone back to Tessa's room to look for her mother and sister.

Confident of finding her there, he hurried down the hall. Tessa's door was ajar, the way he'd left it. Tessa and Missy were asleep. There was no sign of Maddie.

Remembering the twins' earlier misadventure, he checked the bathroom. Everything was in order. Maddie would have left the place in chaos. She hadn't been here.

Fighting panic, he stepped out into the hall and forced himself to think. He hadn't looked in the kitchen. Maybe she'd gotten hungry. Or maybe she'd wanted to play under the makeshift canvas tent, which was still set up in the middle of the kitchen floor.

He rushed through the dining room and passed through the swinging doors into the kitchen. He didn't see Maddie. But what he did see chilled his blood.

The back door was open.

The memory came clear now, how he'd come in earlier with Maddie beside him and his arms full of wood. With no hands free, he'd kicked the door shut behind him and continued on into the next room.

If the door had failed to latch, Maddie's tiny fingers could have taken advantage of the narrowest crack to pry it open.

Dragan stepped through the door onto the back porch. Maddie hadn't been gone long. She couldn't have gotten far, he told himself. But she'd surprised him before.

His eyes scanned the area behind the lodge, not seeing her at first. Then, a stone's throw away, near the edge of the trees, he spotted her. His heart lurched.

Face-to-face with the little girl was a half-grown black bear cub.

The two were mere inches apart. The cub seemed more curious than aggressive. But a young cub like this one wouldn't venture far from its mother. From somewhere close by, the protective mother bear would likely be watching.

"Maddie," Dragan called softly. "Come here."

Maddie glanced around at him, a delighted smile on her face. "Goggy!" she said.

"Come here right now, Maddie!"

Ignoring him, Maddie had turned around. She reached out and touched the cub's nose. "Noz," she said, giggling.

Dragan was sweating bullets. He had to assume the mother bear was watching. So far, she didn't seem to see Maddie as a threat to her cub. But that could change—and if he walked out to get the little girl, it *would* change in a heartbeat. Even stepping off the porch could provoke a charge, and Maddie would be in the way.

His gaze traced the edge of the forest. A clump of ferns moved slightly against the wind and he saw the huge dark shape behind them, blending with the shadows. The mother bear was there, and she was close—close enough to reach Maddie in a split second.

Dragan's pistol was on the shelf near the front door. And even if he had it, the small caliber wouldn't be enough to stop a charging bear. He swore under his breath. There had to be something he could do.

God, help me...

The unvoiced phrase was as close to a prayer as he'd come in decades. The life of this precious little girl was in his hands. If need be, he would gladly sacrifice himself to save her. But if the mother bear charged, even laying down his own life might not be enough.

Suddenly he remembered the leftover ham from last night's dinner. Lightly wrapped in plastic it was sitting on the counter just inside the door. Bears had keen noses, and ham would smell like a banquet to them. The scent could have drawn them here while he was outside earlier, gathering wood.

Holding his breath, and keeping his eyes on Maddie, he backed through the doorway, far enough to reach out and grab the ham. His fingers peeled off the plastic wrap. The next part of the plan would be harder. He'd had a good throwing arm as a youth, but that had been a long time ago and he was out of practice. He'd have just one chance to do this right.

Maddie was still playing with the cub, laughing and poking at its face. Dragan saw the larger black shape move, edging closer. Running out of time, he hurled the ham with all his strength. It made a high arc, crashed through the trees and landed a dozen yards behind the mother bear.

Her head jerked up as she caught the tantalizing scent. With a beckoning *whuff!* to her cub, she wheeled and lumbered off into the trees. Deserting its new playmate, the cub scampered after its mother.

Alone now, Maddie began to cry. In a flash, Dragan flew down the steps, sprinted across the yard and snatched her up under his arm. She was still howling as he raced through the back door, slammed it shut behind them and locked the dead bolt.

"Goggy!" Furious tears streamed down her face. Dragan caught her close, holding her against his beating heart. "It's all right, little one," he murmured against her soft hair. "It's all right. You're safe." Only as the words left his lips did he realize he was speaking in Croatian. He felt something break inside him, felt the wetness of tears on his face. The tears weren't Maddie's. They were his own. Years ago, he'd failed to save his sisters. At least he'd found a way to save this fearless little girl.

But another little girl remained in peril. It would be up to him to keep Missy alive and to get her to a hospital.

Should he tell Tessa what had happened with Maddie and the bear? Not yet, he decided. She was already under enough stress. By now the sun was coming out. The weather was clearing. He needed to wake her and to get to the plane.

"Come on, Maddie. Let's go find your mother." He carried her to Tessa's bedroom. Tessa was awake, sitting up, holding Missy. Her lovely face was shadowed with fatigue and worry.

"Missy's still sick," she said. "I gave her more medicine, but she's going to need more steaming."

"We can do that. The canvas is still set up in the kitchen," Dragan said. "But give me a few minutes to run out to the plane. The sky's clearing. This might be my best chance to get through on the radio. Can you watch Maddie?"

It was a needless question. Tessa had already reached out and gathered Maddie close. She held her girls with a tenderness that made Dragan ache. How would it feel to be part of that circle of love?

Never mind, right now he had more pressing concerns. "I'll be back as soon as I can," he said, and left them there. He paused a moment to get his pistol then unlocked the front door and stepped outside.

The weather was clearing fast, with patches of blue showing through the clouds. That was definitely a good sign, but it was no guarantee that he'd be able to get the radio to work. He'd hoped to have more time to try. If the signal could reach Ketchikan or Sitka, a rescue plane could be here before the morning was out. But getting Missy back into the steam tent was even more urgent, and Tessa couldn't do it by herself, especially with Maddie on the loose.

The tide was out, the plane still moored to the end of the floating dock, which now lay at a downward slope to the beach. The sun shone with welcome brightness, but the morning was still cold. The wind chilled his face as he strode toward the water. Farther out, above the inlet, a bald eagle dived for a fish and flapped to the top of a tree with its prey.

Dragan had just reached his plane when he heard it. A faint but familiar sound he recognized at once. It was the churning drone that one of his pilot friends had compared to the sound of an old-fashioned Maytag washer— the sound of a de Haviland Beaver, the workhorse plane of the Alaskan bush.

But where was it? He could hear the vintage single-engine prop plane clearly now, but he couldn't see it.

He scanned the clearing sky. Was the plane headed here, in response to one of his earlier calls, or was it just passing overhead? No time to wonder. He had to get the pilot's attention. Short of setting the Porter on fire, the surest way was to call on the radio.

He was scrambling into the plane when the Beaver came in low over the treetops behind the lodge. The engine roared in his ears as it passed overhead, banked into a U-turn above the inlet and touched down on the water as smoothly as a gull. Dragan waited as the little plane taxied up to the water's edge on its floats. The pilot cut the engine and swung out of the cockpit. Grizzled and bearded, he looked as if he'd been flying for the past forty years, and probably had.

"You got my distress signal?" Dragan asked.

"Hell, we got a bunch of 'em in Sitka, where I fly out of. But there was no gettin' out here 'til the weather cleared. I brought you some fuel. Are you folks all right?"

"We've got a sick baby who needs to get to a hospital. You're here just in time. Come on in, I'll make you some coffee while my…" *My what? Not my wife. Not my girlfriend.* "While my friend gets herself and the girls ready to go."

"Let me help you refuel first. It's easier with two pairs of hands." The pilot glanced at the Porter. "Quite an airplane you got here. I've heard of 'em but I never seen one for real."

"Well, it's not much good without fuel," Dragan said. "How much did you bring me?"

"Just enough for you to get to Sitka and fill up. It's all I could carry."

"That'll do." Dragan thrust his cold hands into his pockets. He would not be leaving with Tessa and the girls, he knew. The lodge needed to be closed up, the trash bagged, the pipes drained, the propane turned off. That done, he would fly his own plane to Sitka, fuel up and head for Anchorage.

Whatever had happened with Tessa was already over. The next time they faced each other would be in court— as enemies.

Twelve

From the bedroom, Tessa heard the roar of the Beaver passing over the lodge. As the bush plane glided in for a landing and the pilot cut the engine, she murmured a quiet prayer of thanks. At last their rescue had arrived.

Dizzy with relief she pulled on jeans and a clean sweater and jammed her feet into her shoes. She'd been frantic with worry about Missy; but Sitka, where the plane would likely be taking them, couldn't be more than an hour away. There was a small hospital there, part of Alaska's health care network. Her sick little girl would get the care she needed.

From Sitka she could catch a commercial flight or charter to Anchorage, but she wouldn't be going anywhere until Missy was out of danger. Meanwhile, she would be able to phone her parents to let them know she was safe. Then she would call Helen to find out what was happening with the trial.

Dragan, she assumed, would stay here to shut down the

lodge, then fly his plane out. Where he went from there would be up to him. As far as she was concerned it no longer mattered, Tessa told herself. Still, the thought of Dragan stirred the memory of being in his arms.

The last time it had happened, she'd felt the kind of closeness she'd never expected to feel again. But she knew better than to think it would last. During their time here he'd been kind, thoughtful, even tender. But get him back in his own world, and he would become the Dragon once more; arrogant, forceful and a royal pain in the rear.

By the time Dragan and the pilot walked into the lodge, she'd brushed her teeth, changed both babies into the last of the diapers, and was throwing things helter-skelter into her luggage. Through the open doorway she could hear the voices of the two men.

"Want some coffee, Tessa?" Dragan called.

"Right now, all I want is to get Missy to the nearest hospital." Packing finished, she snapped her suitcases shut. "That would be Sitka, right?"

"That's right, ma'am," the pilot's gruff voice answered from the other room. "It's where I fly out of. If you want, I can radio the hospital ahead so they can meet the plane with an ambulance."

"Thank you. That would be wonderful."

"Tell them to bill everything to me," Dragan said. "The hospital, a hotel room for you and Maddie in Sitka, the meals, anything that comes up. You're not to pay a cent, Tessa."

"Thanks, but right now that's the least of my worries." Tessa walked into the great room. One arm cradled Missy, wrapped in a blanket. The other kept a firm grip on Maddie. Missy's eyes were open and she was looking around, but her skin was flushed and her breathing still congested.

The pilot's bearded face broke into a grin. "I'll be

damned! Two of the little mites, like peas in a pod! And with that red hair. Begging your pardon, ma'am, they must be a handful!"

"They are, most of the time," Tessa said. "We're ready to go. Our luggage is on the bed. Dragan, would you get the safety seats? They're in the kitchen—oh, and I believe we left the stroller in your plane."

"Got it." Dragan didn't meet her gaze. He would know, as she did, that the game had changed and they were different players now.

"Hope you'll take a rain check on the coffee," he told the pilot. "The lady's in a hurry."

"I understand."

The pilot retrieved Tessa's luggage and Dragan followed him out to the plane with the two baby seats. Tessa took a final look around, checking for anything she might have left behind. Then she walked out of the lodge for the last time, the diaper bag over her shoulder and her twins in her arms.

The wind was chilly but the sky had cleared, with vast patches of blue showing through the clouds. Sunlight gleamed on the blue water of the inlet. A lone seagull bobbed on the ripples of the incoming tide.

By the time Tessa reached the Beaver it was loaded and ready to leave. Dragan took the twins and passed them, one at a time, up to the pilot, who buckled them into their safety seats. Then Tessa was left alone on the ground with Dragan.

What should she say to him? Thank you? But that would be insincere, since his meddling was responsible for this whole messy debacle. Goodbye? But she would likely see him again in court. Good luck? Since she was suing his company, she wanted luck on her side, not his. Good riddance? She wouldn't really mean that.

Torn by conflicting emotions, she faced him—a man she could have loved under different circumstance. But, things being what they were, that would never be possible.

He took her hand, his grip cool and impersonal. "Let me help you into the plane, Tessa," he said.

He balanced her while she stepped up onto the float, found the metal hand grip inside the frame of the open door and swung up into the copilot's seat. She glanced away as he closed the door behind her. What could she have communicated to him, even with a look?

There was nothing left to say.

Dragan stood watching as the Beaver taxied into the wind and roared off the water, its floats just clearing the tall pines. He kept his eyes on the little bush plane as it became a dot in the sky and vanished into the clouds. Only then did he turn away and walk back toward the lodge. It was a relief to be done with this misadventure, especially knowing that Tessa and her babies were safe and that little Missy was on her way to the hospital.

But it was strange how alone he suddenly felt.

He mounted the front steps and opened the door to silence. No sound of little running feet or mischievous giggles. No Tessa playing with her twins… Tessa sipping her wine in the candlelight… Tessa in his arms, giving him her beautiful body and fiercely loving spirit, then stealing away in the night to keep her little ones safe.

Damn! This wasn't like him. He'd never had any trouble moving on after it ended with a woman—and it had definitely ended with Tessa. She hadn't even bothered to say goodbye. So why couldn't he stop thinking about her?

Feeling hollow and detached, he closed the front door, wandered to the wet bar and poured himself three fingers of bourbon. No need to rush. After the long night and stressful day, he was too tired to fly out of here before nightfall. The Beaver pilot had told him the weather looked good for tomorrow. He'd spend the rest of today getting the lodge cleaned up and winterized. Then he'd get a good night's sleep and take off for Sitka in the morning. From there he could make some phone calls and decide what to do next.

If the trial in Anchorage was still on, he might be better off skipping it. Let his lawyers and Helen Carmichael duke it out. He could find less punishing things to do than sit in a courtroom and watch Tessa tell the judge how she was waylaid, virtually kidnapped and seduced by the CEO of Trans Pacific.

Sipping his bourbon, he crossed the room to the couch, sat partway down, then paused and straightened. Under the rumpled afghan, in the place where he'd meant to sit, there was something hard. Moving the afghan aside, he found it—a short, smooth stick of kindling, one of Maddie's treasures.

Something quivered in his chest like a heart trying not to break. Tessa's little girls had repelled him, terrified him, beaten down his resistance and ultimately won him over. Now they had left him with an ache in a place so deep not even whiskey could reach it.

Dragan set the half-finished glass on the coffee table. Holding the kindling stick between his hands, he settled back against the cushions and gazed into the dying fire as he tried to fathom the crazy thing that had happened.

Against all odds, he'd fallen in love.

Tessa leaned over the hospital crib and gazed through the oxygen tent at her sleeping daughter. Missy's color was good, her fever down. After a night on oxygen and intravenous fluids, she was responding well. But because of her medical history, the doctors in the pediatric unit of Sitka's Mt. Edgecumbe Hospital wanted to keep her for a few more days to make sure her lungs were clear.

They'd also checked Maddie for signs of pneumonia, but the virus that had made Missy so ill had only given her more robust sister a runny nose.

Tessa had spent the night at Missy's bedside. The nursing staff had brought her blankets and a pillow and wheeled in a portable crib for Maddie. But trying to sleep in a reclining chair, listening to the hiss of oxygen and the beep of monitors while trying to keep Maddie in her crib, was the farthest thing from restful. By the next morning she was exhausted.

But that was fine, Tessa told herself as she glimpsed her haggard face in the mirror above the sink. As long as Missy was doing all right, nothing else mattered.

She'd had her luggage brought up to the hospital room, so at least she had clean clothes for Maddie; and the hospital had given her enough diapers to last until she could get to a store. Maybe later she'd get a hotel room. But right now she couldn't bear to leave Missy alone with strangers.

Yesterday, after Missy was admitted, Tessa had put in a call to her frantic parents and then phoned her lawyer. Helen, understandably upset, had let her know that their case had been granted a continuance, pending her safe return. "But the judge won't allow us more than a few extra days," she'd warned Tessa. "Between now and then, we've got a lot to talk about."

"Fine," Tessa had told her. "But my first priority is Missy. Until she's out of danger, I can't even think about the trial."

Now, as she finished sharing her hospital breakfast with Maddie, she recalled their brief conversation. Helen Carmichael was not a patient woman—a trait that had helped make her a successful attorney. Tessa couldn't imagine her waiting around for other people to take action if she could move things forward herself.

As if the thought could conjure her up in the flesh, there was a brusque knock on the door. Before Tessa could rise from her chair, Helen walked in. Petite, slightly plump, with short, silver hair, she'd always reminded Tessa of the actress, Dame Judy Dench. Today she was dressed in an immaculate navy blue pantsuit. Her hawk-sharp, brown-eyed gaze swept the hospital room, coming to rest on Tessa.

"I took the earliest flight I could get," she said. "Heavens, girl, you look like you've been dragged through a war zone! I can't imagine what you've been through, being kidnapped by that man! But at least his actions have given us plenty of ammunition for our case!"

Tessa put Maddie on the floor and stood. In yesterday's phone conversation, she'd given Helen a brief summary of what had happened. But there was plenty she hadn't told the woman—and didn't plan to.

"We could threaten to press charges," Helen said. "That would really put the fire to Markovic's feet. He'd do anything to save himself from being arrested."

Tension tightened a knot in the pit of Tessa's stomach. Winning her lawsuit against Trans Pacific was one thing. Sending Dragan to jail, or even threatening him with arrest, was something else.

"Isn't that stooping a little low?" she asked.

Helen looked surprised. "It wouldn't be stooping any lower than what he did to you."

"But he didn't really mean to kidnap me. He only wanted to fly me to Anchorage and learn a few things about me and our case. Getting stranded in that fishing lodge was an accident. We were out of fuel. We were lucky we didn't crash."

"You're *defending* him?" Helen's penciled eyebrows arched higher. "Don't you want to win your lawsuit?"

"Of course I do!" Tessa struggled with clashing emotions. "I need the money. And it was wrong, what Trans Pacific did to me. They shouldn't be allowed to get away with that. But we've got a good case. Can't we win without resorting to blackmail?"

"Blackmail? My dear girl, kidnapping is a federal offense, especially since he took you and your twins over a state line! We have enough on him to nail the man to the wall!"

Helen's words sent a chill through Tessa. What if Dragan's actions came out in the trial? What if, despite her own testimony, he was actually charged with kidnapping?

"No," Tessa insisted. "Dragan never meant to kidnap us. While we were in the lodge, he took good care of us. He was amazing. We couldn't have survived without him."

Helen was silent for a moment, her eyes focusing like lasers on Tessa's face. "Oh, Lord, I should have guessed. You slept with him, didn't you?"

The color that burned in Tessa's cheeks was enough to answer the question. Tessa shook her head. "I can't go through with the trial, Helen. I want you to negotiate a settlement, for an amount that will be fair to you as well as to me."

Helen frowned. "That wasn't what we discussed. We wanted your voice to be heard. We wanted to punish Trans Pacific and strike a blow for women's employment rights. What happened to that?"

"I'm sorry. I can't risk having Dragan go to jail for something he never intended to do."

"You're in love with him, aren't you?"

The question struck Tessa like a lightning bolt. Was she so transparent that others could sense what she hadn't even admitted to herself? *Was* she in love with Dragan? Was that why she couldn't bear to see him hurt?

She lowered her gaze. Only then did she realize Helen had left the door open and Maddie was nowhere in sight.

"Oh, no!" She was about to rush out into the hall when Missy woke and started to cry. Torn, Tessa hesitated.

"You stay here," Helen said. "I'll go look for our little runaway." She bustled out the door, heels clicking on the waxed tiles.

Tessa reached under the oxygen tent and cradled Missy in her arms. "There, little love," she murmured. "Don't cry. Everything's all right. You're going to be fine."

How she wished she could say those words to herself and mean them.

Dragan had taken off early and arrived in Sitka around nine. A call to the home office in Seattle had assured him that no crises required his immediate attention. Another call to his legal team brought him up to date on the status of the trial. Everything was on hold, pending the appearance of the plaintiff. No emergency there, either.

It had occurred to him on the flight that if he wanted Tessa's hospital bill and other expenses charged to him, he would need to authorize those charges, most readily done in person. A visit to the small hospital would take a little time but he welcomed any excuse to check on Missy's condition and to make sure Tessa had everything she needed.

After renting a car at the airport, he drove to the hospital, parked and found the admissions desk inside. It was no surprise to learn that Tessa had listed herself as the financially responsible party. She was as proud and stubborn as she was beautiful.

It took about twenty minutes for the busy receptionist to take his billing information, redo the paperwork and give him the room number. He was told he'd find Tessa and her twins in Room 322.

Dragan's pulse quickened as he rode the elevator up to the third floor. They'd been apart less than twenty-four hours, but it was surprising how much he missed Tessa and her twins. He would never have planned on this, but in three short days they'd become part of his life. He didn't want to let them go.

Things would be complicated at first. One way or another, Tessa's lawsuit would have to be settled and put to rest. After that he would try to be patient—a difficult thing for him—and give her time to get to know him in the real world. Only then, if she'd have him, would he ask her to be his wife. He loved her, but in some ways he was a cautious man. He wanted to be sure he could make her happy and be a good father to her children.

The elevator stopped. Dragan crossed the waiting area and followed the direction arrows to a long corridor with doors on both sides. He was checking the room numbers when a small figure in blue coveralls came barreling down the hall and slammed into his legs.

"Maddie!" He picked her up. She giggled and reached for his nose, all smiles and dimples. Delighted, he gave her a gentle hug. Glancing at the room numbers he realized she'd wandered quite a distance.

"What are you doing out here, you little scamp?" he asked. "Come on. Let's go find your mother and sister."

Balancing her against his shoulder, he walked toward the end of the hall, where Room 322 would be. Partway there, he came face-to-face with a sturdy-looking, silver-haired woman in a blue pantsuit. Dragan's mood darkened. He'd seen enough news photos to recognize Helen Carmichael.

"Mr. Markovic." She'd know him, of course. That had

to be why she stood like an armed guard in the middle of the hall, making sure he couldn't pass without shoving her aside. "What are you doing here?" she demanded.

Dragan forced himself to speak calmly. "I was worried about Missy. I came to see how she was doing and to see if her mother needed anything."

"Missy is going to be fine. As for my client, if she needs anything, I'll get it for her myself." She squared her bulldog stance in front of him. "If you mean to speak to Miss Randall, I can't let you do that. She's exhausted and confused. This would be the worst possible time for you to see her—and it could cast a shadow over the legal proceedings."

Dragan struggled to rein in his temper. If he so much as laid a finger on the woman, or even threatened to, she'd have a field day with it. "At least tell her I came by. I want her to know I'm concerned."

The celebrated attorney lifted her chin. "I won't be telling her anything. The last thing she needs right now is your influence, Mr. Markovic. Don't plan on speaking to her until after the lawsuit is resolved. Consider this a warning. If you try to interfere with her in any way, I have the means to get you in more legal trouble than you've ever seen in your life—and if you're wondering how…try kidnapping, for starters."

Dragan went cold inside. Interpreted by the wrong people, his actions could indeed land him behind bars. And Helen Carmichael was skilled at getting people to believe her interpretation of events. He spoke cautiously, weighing his words. "What do you want from me?"

"I want you to leave Tessa Randall alone. Anything you have to say to her can be passed through your lawyers to me. Now give me that child so I can take her back to her mother."

Seeing a stranger reach for her, Maddie locked her arms

around Dragan's neck and began to cry. Her high-pitched wails echoed up and down the long corridor. Other people in the hall turned around to look.

A few feet away, Dragan saw a door open. A figure stepped out. It was Tessa, looking so tired and fragile that it almost broke his heart. She walked toward him, holding out her arms for Maddie. Their eyes met.

"Not a word, either of you." Helen stood between them. "Not unless you want to turn this into the worst media spectacle since the Hindenburg. As far as this case is concerned, you never saw each other today."

Gazing into Tessa's eyes, Dragan gave a silent nod of his head. Helen was right. There were other people in the hall. If his relationship with Tessa became known, it could compromise them both in the eyes of the court. He could only hope Tessa would understand, too.

As far as the legalities were concerned, they were strangers. The past three days had never happened.

Pressing his lips together, he gave the little girl in his embrace one last squeeze, then peeled Maddie loose and passed her into Tessa's arms. Tessa gathered her daughter close. Without speaking, she walked back into her room and closed the door.

"That was smart," Helen said. "I'm glad you took my advice. Sorry if I came down a little hard on you. I was just doing my job."

Dragan turned back toward the elevator. "Walk with me," he said, shortening his stride.

Helen fell into step beside him. "So, do you have any ideas for straightening out this mess?"

"You know the trial would be a nightmare," Dragan said. "It's not about women's rights anymore. If the past three days came out, it would be about the private things that happened between two people and whether there was collusion involved. The press would have a field day, and no one would escape public condemnation."

"So what are you suggesting?" Helen's eyes narrowed. Smart woman. She'd backed him into a corner and she knew it.

"I don't want to put Tessa through that ordeal, and if you've a scrap of regard for your client, neither do you."

"I'm not a coldhearted monster, Mr. Markovic. Much as I'd enjoy hanging you out to dry, I do have Tessa's best interests at heart. She's told me some things in confidence—things I can't pass on, but I think I know what she'd want. So what can you do for us?"

"My legal team offered to settle once and you turned us down. What about now? All I want is to do the right thing. What will you and Tessa accept?"

They had reached the elevator. Helen turned to face him. "A public apology would go a long way. As for the rest…" Her sharp brown eyes twinkled. "Make us an offer we can't refuse."

Dragan pushed the down button and stepped into the elevator. "Give me a couple of days," he said. "I'll let you know."

Thirteen

Dragan revved the Porter's engine, taxied into the wind and lifted off for Anchorage. Clouds scudded across the sky, casting shadows on the white-capped harbor. Was the weather clearing, or, after two days of calm, was another storm moving in?

As he banked and corrected his course, his thoughts churned like the water below him. All he wanted was to get this damned lawsuit over with and to make Tessa his wife. To accomplish that, he would gladly apologize on TV and pay any amount of money that would satisfy Helen Carmichael. But that thought triggered other worries. What would Tessa think if he paid her several million dollars, then turned around and proposed marriage? Would she believe he was just trying to get his money back? Or worse, would she think the money and his petition to marry her were just to prevent her from testifying about the alleged kidnapping?

The reality was he couldn't control what Tessa thought of him. All he could do was make sure she received the settlement she needed and deserved. The rest would be up to her. If it didn't go well, losing her would shatter his heart. But at least he'd know that she and her little girls were well provided for. Maybe that was the real definition of love—not so much having as caring.

The vast harbor at Anchorage bustled with fishing boats, float planes, cruise ships and huge container ships, several of them Trans Pacific's. Dragan landed the Porter and taxied to the company wharf, where an attendant was waiting to take care of the plane. From there he strode to the waiting chauffeured car that would take him to Trans Pacific's Alaska headquarters.

Before he met with the legal team and decided on a fair settlement, there was one thing he needed to do. He had to find out why Tessa had had problems with her supervisor, Tom Roylance, and why the man had fired her.

An office on the top floor was kept ready for him. Dragan seated himself at the desk, ordered coffee and put in a call to Bethany Ferguson, the director of human resources. He'd phoned her yesterday from Sitka, asking for her help. Now he was hoping for answers. If anyone in the company could learn what had happened, it would be Bethany.

Fifteen minutes later she walked into his office. Tall and athletic, with gray-streaked blond hair, she'd been with Trans Pacific since his uncle's time, twenty years ago.

"So how are you these days, Bethany?" Dragan asked. "Have a chair. Want some coffee?"

"Thanks." She sat across from him and accepted the coffee Dragan poured her. "I'm fine. But I may not be here much longer. My husband's talking retirement in Boca Raton. He wants to go where it's warm. How's Tessa? We thought the world of her here. It was a sad day when she left. I bet her twins are adorable."

"They are. Spunky little redheads like their mother."

"And you and she—?" Bethany was an old friend or she might not have ventured to ask.

"Let's table that question for another time," Dragan said. "Right now I'm interested in the story of how and why she was fired. What can you tell me?"

"I did some detective work after you called me yesterday. As you know, Roylance claimed he fired her because she couldn't do her job."

"What about her request for transfer to a desk job in Seattle?"

"There's no trace of it. Either it was never entered or somebody made it go away. But here's another thing, and it's not in her file. I talked to Saul Cooper, the V.P. of Contracts. Tessa hadn't been informed, but she was at the top of a short list for promotion here. If it had gone through, she wouldn't have been transferred. She'd have been offered a desk job here in Anchorage, with her own office. And, get this, she would have become Tom Roylance's boss."

Dragan gave a low whistle. "So Roylance got wind of it and fired her while he still had the power to do it. But how did he know about her prospects?"

"Saul's secretary, Carly, was Roylance's girlfriend. I'm pretty sure she told him. They're both gone, by the way. Roylance moved her into Tessa's old job, and the girl wasn't up to it. Besides that, there was some hanky-panky in the supply closet. Somebody complained."

"So why didn't Roylance just let Tessa transfer to Seattle?"

"Because that might not have been enough to stop the promotion. He wanted her out of the picture entirely. The man said some damaging things about her after she left—

all lies, I'm positive, but they may have kept her from being contacted and rehired."

"So Tessa's pregnancy was just an excuse. The real reason she was fired was jealousy."

"It certainly looks that way." Bethany put down her coffee cup. "Sorry to break this off, Dragan, I've got a meeting scheduled in a few minutes, and I'm in charge. I hope I've given you what you need."

Dragan thanked her and wished her well. After she left, he buzzed the receptionist and asked her to summon his legal team. Tessa wouldn't have known why Roylance fired her. But one thing was certain. She'd been dealt a gross injustice—and she deserved every penny of the generous settlement he planned to give her.

After four days and three nights in the hospital, Missy was finally well enough to be discharged. She would still need rest, but her fever was gone and her lungs were clear. It only remained for the doctor to come by on his morning rounds, give her a final checkup and sign the paperwork. Based on past experience, Tessa knew the wait might be a long one.

She was feeding the twins some scrambled eggs when Helen stepped into the room, closing the door carefully behind her. In her hand she carried a copy of the Anchorage paper. "Take a look at this!" She thrust the business section under Tessa's nose.

Tessa glanced at the headline: CEO Apologizes for Firing of Pregnant Employee.

She didn't need to read the rest. She'd watched Dragan's statement to the press on the local TV news last night. As part of the settlement, he'd promised a public apology. Now he'd kept his word.

He'd also agreed to a payment so generous that it made

Tessa's head spin. It was more than double the previous set-tlement offer—and almost as much as Helen had planned to ask for in punitive damages. Once the check arrived, she'd be going from struggling single mother to multimil-lionaire. If she chose to, she could pay cash for a beautiful home, buy a quality vehicle, hire some help for the twins and invest money for their education. Unless she wanted to, she would never have to work another day in her life.

The money was so much more than she needed, let alone deserved. But was it what she really wanted?

Last night, watching Dragan on TV, she'd felt the urge to reach out and smooth the care lines from his face. Only then, seeing him at an untouchable distance, did she re-alize what a nightmare this experience had been for him. The damage to his reputation and his company, the spec-ter of possible arrest, to say nothing of the money, had all taken their toll in worry. And she'd been the cause of it.

If, after this, he never wanted to see her face again, she wouldn't blame him.

"I'll be running along," Helen said. "I've got a flight to catch. I do hope this has worked out all right for you, Tessa."

"It still feels unreal," Tessa said. "Do you know how the money's supposed to be paid? I should probably make some kind of arrangement. I can't imagine just walking around with the check in my pocket."

"My share is already in the bank," Helen said. "I ar-ranged to have it paid by electronic transfer. But since you haven't designated a payment method, a representa-tive from the company will be here to discuss it with you."

"Here?" Tessa's thoughts flew to her rumpled clothes, her finger-combed hair, face bare of makeup and children looking like little urchins. "But I'm not—"

"Never mind, dear. Remember, you're a rich woman."

Helen squeezed her shoulder. "He's waiting outside right now. I'll send him in as I leave. Ta-ta." Blowing Tessa an air kiss, she opened the door and strutted out into the hall.

There was a moment of hushed silence. Then Dragan walked into the room, immaculately dressed in jeans, a sport shirt and a leather jacket. He was carrying a briefcase.

Tessa's first impulse was to snatch up the twins and lock herself in the bathroom. But, no, she had to face him. And she had to contain the surge of emotion that flooded her whole being at the sight of him.

Her troubles had brought this man to his knees, cost him millions of dollars and subjected him to public humiliation. He had every reason to despise her.

But all she felt for him was love.

It was the twins who broke the awkward tension. Maddie slipped to the floor and raced across the room to fling herself against Dragan's legs. Missy stayed where she was, on Tessa's lap, but her little face broke into a grin. "Da!" she said, giggling.

Dragan smiled as he untangled Maddie from his legs, but Tessa couldn't miss the flicker of uncertainty in his eyes. "That's the kind of welcome I was hoping for," he said, looking straight at Tessa. "What about you?"

Tears welled in her eyes. She struggled for words. "This isn't what I wanted, Dragan. I was hoping for justice, and enough security to pay my bills and take care of my children. But this…all this—" Her voice broke. "This wasn't your fault. I never meant to see you hurt. All that money, so much more than I need."

His expression darkened. "I don't give a damn about the money!" he growled.

She stared at him.

"You crazy little redhead!" he said. "Can't you see that

I'm in love with you? I'd have given you the whole blasted company if you'd asked for it. Staying away these past few days has almost driven me out of my mind. But I'm here now, for you and those two little scamps of yours. If you don't want me in your life, say so. I'll walk away and leave you a rich woman. End of story."

Tessa rose and set Missy in her crib. Her heart was pounding. "And if I do want you?" she whispered. "What then?"

"Then come here." He opened his arms.

Tessa walked into them and felt his embrace close around her. His kiss left her weak-kneed and aching for more. Much more.

His arms held her tight. They were two complicated people, Tessa knew. Their lives would never be simple. But as long as they loved each other, and loved their children, they could make this work.

"The money—" she murmured. "As long as we have each other, I don't care about it. You can take it back."

He lifted her chin and looked into her eyes. "Oh, no, you don't," he said. "It's yours. Call it your mad money. You can do anything you want with it."

"Anything? Like what?"

"Surprise me." He kissed her again. She would think about the money later, Tessa resolved as she melted in his arms. For now, only one thing mattered. They were on their way to becoming a family.

Epilogue

Seattle, one year later

Holding one twin by each hand, Dragan stood next to the mayor to watch his wife cut the ceremonial ribbon on the new women and children's clinic. He couldn't have been more proud of her. The Markovic Foundation, using invested money from the settlement, had been Tessa's idea. The idea of building free or low-cost clinics in poor neighborhoods had been hers, too. She'd done everything from finding the site and choosing the architect to hiring the contractor. Now that the first clinic was a reality, there would be more scheduled.

He suppressed a smile as she reached around her swollen belly to manipulate the scissors. At nine months pregnant, she hadn't been sure she would make it to the ribbon-cutting. Just to be safe, Dragan had the new family Volvo parked close by.

As the ribbon parted and the applause broke out, two-year-old Maddie tore loose from his hand and ran to her mother's side. "Pretty!" she said, grabbing a cut end of the red satin ribbon. "Mine!"

Laughing, the mayor took the scissors and cut her a two-foot length of ribbon. But Maddie wasn't finished. She pointed to the other half of the ribbon. "Missy!" she demanded.

"I'm sorry," Tessa said. "She wants a piece for her sister, too."

Still laughing, the mayor cut more ribbon. Maddie took it and scampered back to her sister. Tessa was laughing, too, but suddenly a startled look came over her face.

Dragan's heart dropped. Scooping up the twins, he reached her side in three long strides.

"Now?" he asked, leaning close to Tessa's ear.

She gave him a pain-laced smile. "I'm afraid so. Get me to the car."

Still holding the twins, he bulled his way through the crowd, reached the car and helped her into the passenger seat. "Let's go, girls," he said, buckling them into their safety seats. "I think we're about to meet your little brother."

Dragan eased the car onto the street, driving fast but carefully. He had precious cargo aboard—his family.

Tessa's hand tightened on his knee, gripping hard as a contraction passed. She'd had a worry-free pregnancy. The baby was healthy, and their doctor had assured him all would go well. Still, it would be a great relief to see the baby delivered safely and a joy to hold his son in his arms for the first time.

They hadn't planned to have the twins along when they went to the hospital. But there was no time to drop them off at home, so Dragan would have to figure out what to do when they got there. That was typical. Things seldom went by plan in the Markovic household.

The past year had been a crazy roller-coaster ride, with the small, private wedding, the passionate honeymoon, the move to a new home, the pregnancy and the ongoing chaos of raising twin redheads. What would the coming year be like with a new baby in the house?

Never mind, bring it on, Dragan told himself. For twenty years, until Tessa and her twins had dropped into his life, he'd been emotionally frozen. He'd forgotten how to feel, how to live. Now every day was a new adventure, and he faced each morning with gratitude—so much gratitude. It was as if Tessa and her little ones had brought him back from the dead. They had saved him.

Her hand tightened on his knee again. "I love you," she whispered.

Dragan felt the welling of tears. "I love you, too," he said. "All four of you."

* * * * *

All of the raw power he projected was clearly—and safely—locked down.

He turned her hand over and kissed the back of it. In the enclosed space of the office, with no one to witness his chivalrous gesture, she couldn't tell if the kiss was a threat or a seduction. Or both.

Then he raised his gaze and looked her in the eyes. Suddenly, the room was much warmer, the air much thinner. Frances had to use every ounce of her self-control not to start taking huge, gulping breaths just to get some oxygen into her body. Oh, but he had nice eyes, warm and determined and completely focused on her.

She might have underestimated him. "I'm not going to take the job."

He laughed then. It was a warm sound, full of humor and honesty. It made her want to smile.

"I wasn't going to offer it to you again. You're right—it is beneath you."

Here it came—the trap he was waiting to spring. He leaned forward, his gaze intent on hers.

"I don't want to hire you. I want to marry you."

* * *

Falling for Her Fake Fiancé
is part of the Beaumont Heirs series:
One Colorado family, limitless scandal!

FALLING FOR HER
FAKE FIANCÉ

BY
SARAH M. ANDERSON

MILLS & BOON

Published in Great Britain 2015
by Mills & Boon, an imprint of Harlequin (UK) Limited,
Eton House, 18-24 Paradise Road, Richmond, Surrey, TW9 1SR

© 2015 Sarah M. Anderson

ISBN: 978-0-263-25281-1

51-0915

Award-winning author **Sarah M. Anderson** may live east of the Mississippi River, but her heart lies out West on the Great Plains. With a lifelong love of horses and two history teachers for parents, she had plenty of encouragement to learn everything she could about the tribes of the Great Plains.

When she started writing, it wasn't long before her characters found themselves out in South Dakota among the Lakota Sioux. She loves to put people from two different worlds into new situations and to see how their backgrounds and cultures take them someplace they never thought they'd go.

Sarah's book *A Man of Privilege* won the 2012 RT Reviewers' Choice Award for Best Harlequin Desire. Her book *Straddling the Line* was named Best Harlequin Desire of 2013 by *CataRomance*, and *Mystic Cowboy* was a 2014 Booksellers' Best Award finalist in the Single Title category as well as a finalist for the Gayle Wilson Award of Excellence.

When not helping out at her son's school or walking her rescue dogs, Sarah spends her days having conversations with imaginary cowboys and American Indians, all of which is surprisingly well tolerated by her wonderful husband. Readers can find out more about Sarah's love of cowboys and Indians at www.sarahmanderson.com.

To Jennifer Porter, who took me under her wing
before I was published and helped give me a
platform to talk about heroes in cowboy hats.
Thank you so much for supporting me!
We'll always have dessert at Junior's together!

One

"*Mis*-ter Logan," the old-fashioned intercom rasped on Ethan's desk.

He scowled at the thing and at the way his current secretary insisted on hissing his name. "Yes, Delores?" He'd never been in an office that required an intercom. It felt as if he'd walked into the 1970s.

Of course, that was probably how old the intercom was. After all, Ethan was sitting in the headquarters of the Beaumont Brewery. This room—complete with hand-carved everything—probably hadn't been redecorated since, well...

A very long time ago. The Beaumont Brewery was 160 years old, after all.

"*Mis*-ter Logan," Delores rasped again, her dislike for him palatable. "We're going to have to stop production on the Mountain Cold and Mountain Cold Light lines."

"What? Why?" Logan demanded. The last thing he could afford was another shutdown.

Ethan had been running this company for almost three months now. His firm, Corporate Restructuring Services, had beat out some heavy hitters for the right to handle the reorganization of the Beaumont Brewery, and Ethan had to make this count. If he—and, by extension, CRS—could turn this aging, antique company into a modern-day business, their reputation in the business world would be cemented.

Ethan had expected some resistance. It was only natural. He'd restructured thirteen companies before taking the helm of Beaumont Brewery. Each company had emerged from the reorganization process leaner, meaner and more competitive in a global economy. Everyone won when that happened.

Yes, thirteen success stories.

Yet nothing had prepared him for the Beaumont Brewery.

"There's a flu going around," Delores said. "Sixty-five workers are home sick, the poor dears."

A flu. Wasn't that just a laugh and a half? Last week, it'd been a cold that had knocked out forty-seven employees. And the week before, after a mass food poisoning, fifty-four people hadn't been able to make it in.

Ethan was no idiot. He'd cut the employees a little slack the first two times, trying to earn their trust. But now it was time to lay down the law.

"Fire every single person who called in sick today."

There was a satisfying pause on the other end of the intercom, and, for a moment, Ethan felt a surge of victory.

The victorious surge was short-lived, however.

"*Mis*-ter Logan," Delores began. "Regretfully, it seems that the HR personnel in charge of processing terminations are out sick today."

"Of course they are," he snapped. He fought the urge to throw the intercom across the room, but that was an impulsive, juvenile thing to do, and Ethan was not impulsive or juvenile. Not anymore.

So, as unsatisfying as it was, he merely shut off the intercom and glared at his office door.

He needed a better plan.

He always had a plan when he went into a business.

His method was proven. He could turn a flailing business around in as little as six months.

But this? The Beaumont freaking Brewery?

That was the problem, he decided. Everyone—the press, the public, their customers and especially the employees—still thought of this as the Beaumont Brewery. Sure, the business had been under Beaumont management for a good century and a half. That was the reason All-Bev, the conglomerate that had hired CRS to handle this reorganization, had chosen to keep the Beaumont name a part of the Brewery—the name-recognition value was through the roof.

But it wasn't the Beaumont family's brewery anymore. They had been forced out months ago. And the sooner the employees realized that, the better.

He looked around the office. It was beautiful, heavy with history and power.

He'd heard that the conference table had been custom-made. It was so big and heavy that it'd been built in the actual office—they might have to take a wall out to remove it. Tucked in the far corner by a large coffee table was a grouping of two leather club chairs and a matching leather love seat. The coffee table was supposedly made of one of the original wagon wheels that Phillippe Beaumont had used when he'd crossed the Great Plains with a team of Percheron draft horses back in the 1880s.

The only signs of the current decade were the flat-screen television that hung over the sitting area and the electronics on the desk, which had been made to match the conference table.

The entire room screamed Beaumont so loudly he was practically deafened by it.

He flipped on the hated intercom again. "Delores."

"Yes, *Mis*—"

He cut her off before she could mangle his name again.

"I want to redo the office. I want all this stuff gone. The curtains, the woodwork—and the conference table. All of it." Some of these pieces—hand carved and well cared for, like the bar—would probably fetch a pretty penny. "Sell it off."

There was another satisfying pause.

"Yes, sir." For a moment, he thought she sounded subdued—cowed. As if she couldn't believe he would really dismantle the heart of the Beaumont Brewery. But then she added, "I know just the appraiser to call," in a tone that sounded...smug?

He ignored her and went back to his computer. Two lines shut down was not acceptable. If either line didn't pull double shifts tomorrow, he wouldn't wait for HR to terminate employees. He'd do it himself.

After all, he was the boss here. What he said went.

And that included the furniture.

Frances Beaumont slammed her bedroom door behind her and flopped down on her bed. Another rejection—she couldn't fall much lower.

She was tired of this. She'd been forced to move back into the Beaumont mansion after her last project had failed so spectacularly that she'd had to give up her luxury condo in downtown Denver. She'd even been forced to sell most of her designer wardrobe.

The idea—digital art ownership and crowdsourcing art patronage online by having buyers buy stock in digital art—had been fundamentally sound. Art might be timeless, but art production and collection had to evolve. She'd sunk a considerable portion of her fortune into Art Digitale, as well as every single penny she'd gotten from the sale of the Beaumont Brewery.

What an epic, crushing mistake. After months of delays and false starts—and huge bills—Art Digitale had been live for three weeks before the funds ran out. Not a single transaction had taken place on the website. In her gilded life, she'd never experienced such complete failure. How could she? She was a Beaumont.

Her business failure was bad enough. But worse? She couldn't get a job. It was as if being a Beaumont suddenly counted for nothing. Her first employer, the owner of Galerie Solaria, hadn't exactly jumped at the chance to have Frances come back, even though Frances knew how to flatter the wealthy, art-focused patrons and massage the delicate egos of artists. She knew how to sell art—didn't that count for something?

Plus, she was a *Beaumont*. A few years ago, people would have jumped at the chance to be associated with one of the founding families of Denver. Frances had been an in-demand woman.

"Where did I go wrong?" she asked her ceiling.

Unsurprisingly, it didn't have an answer.

She'd just turned thirty. She was broke and had moved back in with her family—her brother Chadwick and his family, plus assorted Beaumonts from her father's other marriages.

She shuddered in horror.

When the family still owned the Brewery, the Beaumont name had meant something. *Frances* had meant something. But ever since that part of her life had been sold, she'd been…adrift.

If only there was some way to go back, to put the Brewery under the family's control again.

Yes, she thought bitterly, that was definitely an option. Her older brothers Chadwick and Matthew had walked away and started their own brewery, Percheron Drafts. Phillip, her favorite older brother, the one who had gotten her into parties and helped her build her reputation as the Cool Girl of Denver high society, had ensconced himself out on the Beaumont Farm and gotten sober. No more parties with him. And her twin brother, Byron, was starting a new restaurant.

Everyone else was moving forward, pairing off. And Frances was stuck back in her childhood room, alone.

Not that she believed a man would solve any of her problems. She'd grown up watching her father burn through marriage after unhappy marriage. No, she knew love didn't exist. Or if it did, it wasn't in the cards for her.

She was on her own here.

She opened up a message from her friend Becky and stared at the picture of a shuttered storefront. She and Becky had worked together at Galerie Solaria. Becky had no famous last name and no social connections, but she knew art and had a snarky sense of humor that cut through the bull. More to the point, Becky treated Frances like she was a real person, not just a special Beaumont snowflake. They had been friends ever since.

Becky had a proposition. She wanted to open a new gallery, one that would merge the new-media art forms with the standard classics that wealthy patrons preferred. It wasn't as avant-garde as Frances's digital art business had been, but it was a good bridge between the two worlds.

The only problem was Frances did not have the money to invest. She wished to God she did. She could co-own and comanage the gallery. It wouldn't bring in big bucks, but it could get her out of the mansion. It could get her back to being a somebody. And not just any somebody. She could go back to being Frances Beaumont—popular, respected, *envied*.

She dropped her phone onto the bed in defeat. *Right*. Another fortune was just going to fall into her lap and she'd be in demand. *Sure*. And she would also sprout wings.

True despair was sinking in when her phone rang. She

answered it without even looking at the screen. "Hello?" she said morosely.

"Frances? Frannie," the woman said. "I know you may not remember me—I'm Delores Hahn. I used to work in accounting at—"

The name rang a bell, an older woman who wore her hair in a tight bun. "Oh! Delores! Yes, you were at the Brewery. How are you?"

The only people besides her siblings who called her Frannie were the longtime employees of the Beaumont Brewery. They were her second family—or at least, they had been.

"We've been better," Delores said. "Listen, I have a proposal for you. I know you've got those fancy art degrees."

In the safety of her room, Frances blushed. After today's rejections, she didn't feel particularly fancy. "What kind of proposal?" Maybe her luck was about to change. Maybe this proposal would come with a paycheck.

"Well," Delores went on in a whisper, "the new CEO that AllBev brought in?"

Frances scowled. "What about him? Failing miserably, I hope."

"Sadly," Delores said in a not-sad-at-all voice, "there's been an epidemic of Brew Flu going around. We had to halt production on two lines today."

Frances couldn't hold back the laugh that burst forth from her. "Oh, that's fabulous."

"It was," Delores agreed. "But it made Logan—that's the new CEO—so mad that he decided to rip out your father's office."

Frances would have laughed again, except for one little detail. "He's going to destroy Daddy's office? He wouldn't dare!"

"He told me to sell it off. All of it—the table, the bar,

everything. I think he'd even perform an exorcism, if he thought it'd help," she added.

Her father's office. Technically, it had most recently been Chadwick's office. But Frances had never stopped thinking of her father and that office together. "So what's your proposal?"

"Well," Delores said, her voice dropping past whisper and straight into conspirator. "I thought you could come do the appraisals. Who knows—you might be able to line up buyers for some of it."

"And..." Frances swallowed. The following was a crass question, but desperate times and all that. "And would this Logan fellow pay for the appraisal? If I sold the furniture myself—" say, to a certain sentimental older brother who'd been the CEO for almost ten years "—would I get a commission?"

"I don't see why not."

Frances tried to see the downside of this situation, but nothing popped up. Delores was right—if anyone had the connections to sell off her family's furniture, it'd be Frances.

Plus, if she could get a foothold back in the Brewery, she might be able to help all those poor, flu-stricken workers. She wasn't so naive to think that she could get a conglomerate like AllBev to sell the company back to the family, but...

She might be able to make this Logan's life a little more difficult. She might be able to exact a little revenge. After all—the sale of the Brewery had been when her luck had turned sour. And if she could get paid to do all of that?

"Let's say Friday, shall we?" That was only two days away, but that would give her plenty of time to plan and execute her trap. "I'll bring the donuts."

Delores actually giggled. "I was hoping you'd say that."

Oh, yes. This was going to be great.

* * *

"*Mis*-ter Logan, the appraiser is here."

Ethan set down the head count rolls he'd been studying.
Next week, he was reducing the workforce by 15 percent.
People with one or more "illness absences" were going to
be the first to find themselves out on the sidewalk with
nothing more than a box of their possessions.

"Good. Send him in."

But no nerdy-looking art geek walked into the office.
Ethan waited and then switched the intercom back on. Before he could ask Delores the question, though, he heard a
lot of people talking—and laughing?

It sounded as though someone was having a party in
the reception area.

What the hell?

He strode across the room and threw open his office
door. There was, point of fact, a party going on outside.
Workers he'd only caught glimpses of before were all
crowded around Delores's desk, donuts in their hands and
sappy smiles on their faces.

"What's going on out here?" he thundered. "This is a
business, people, not a—"

Then the crowd parted, and he saw her.

God, how had he missed her? A woman with a stunning mane of flame-red hair sat on the edge of Delores's
desk. Her body was covered by an emerald-green gown
that clung to every curve like a lover's hands. His fingers
itched to trace the line of her bare shoulders.

She was not an employee. That much was clear.

She was, however, holding a box of donuts.

The good-natured hum he'd heard on the intercom died
away. The smiles disappeared, and people edged away
from him.

"What is this?" he demanded. The color drained out

of several employees' faces, but his tone didn't appear to have the slightest impact on the woman in the green gown.

His eyes were drawn to her back, to the way her ass looked sitting on the edge of the desk. Slowly—so slowly it almost hurt him—she turned and looked at him over her shoulder.

He might have intimidated the workers. He clearly had not intimidated her.

She batted her eyelashes as a cryptic smile danced across her deep red lips. "Why, it's Donut Friday."

Ethan glared at her. "What?"

She pivoted, bringing more of her profile into view. *Dear God, that dress—that body.* The strapless dress came to a deep V over her chest, doing everything in its power to highlight the pale, creamy skin of her décolletage.

He shouldn't stare. He *wasn't* staring. Really.

Her posture shifted. It was like watching a dancer arrange herself before launching into a series of gravity-defying pirouettes. "You must be new here," the woman said in a pitying tone. "It's Friday. That's the day I bring donuts."

Individually, he understood each word and every implication of her tone and movement. But together? "Donut Friday?" He'd been here for months, and this was the first time he'd heard anything about donuts.

"Yes," she said. She held out the box. "I bring everyone a donut. Would you like the last one? I'm afraid all I have left is a plain."

"And who are you, if I may ask?"

"Oh, you may." She lowered her chin and looked up at him through her lashes. She was simply the most beautiful woman he'd ever seen, which was more than enough to turn his head. But the fact that she was playing him for the fool—and they both knew it?

There were snickers from the far-too-large audience as

she held out her hand for him—not to shake, no. She held it out as though she expected him to kiss it, as if she were the queen or something.

"I'm Frances Beaumont. I'm here to appraise the antiques."

Two

Oh, this *was* fun.

"Donut?" she asked again, holding out the box. She kept as much innocence as she could physically manage on her face.

"You're the *appraiser*?"

She let the donut box hang in the space between them a few more moments before she slowly lowered the box back to her lap.

She'd been bringing donuts in on Fridays since—well, since as long as she could remember. It'd been her favorite part of the week, mostly because it was the only time she ever got to be with her father, just the two of them. For a few glorious hours every Friday morning, she was Daddy's Little Girl. No older brothers taking up all his time. No new wives or babies demanding his attention. Just Hardwick Beaumont and his little girl, Frannie.

And what was more, she got to visit all the grown-ups—including many of the same employees who were watching this exchange between her and Logan with rapt fascination—and hear how nice she was, how pretty she looked in that dress, what a sweetheart she was. The people who'd been working for the Brewery for the past thirty years had made her feel special and loved. They'd been her second family. Even after Hardwick had died and regular Donut

Fridays had faded away, she'd still taken the time to stop in at least once a month. Donuts—hand-delivered with a smile and a compliment—made the world a better place.

If she could repay her family's loyal employees by humiliating a tyrant of an outsider, then that was the very least she could do.

Logan's mouth opened and closed before he ordered, "Get back to work."

No one moved.

She turned back to the crowd to hide her victorious smile. They weren't listening to him. They were waiting on her.

"Well," she said graciously, unable to keep the wicked glint out of her eye. Just so long as Logan didn't see it. "It has been simply wonderful to see everyone again. I know I've missed you—we all have in the Beaumont family. I do hope that I can come back for another Donut Friday again soon?"

Behind her, Logan made a choking noise.

But in front of her, the employees nodded and grinned. A few of them winked in silent support.

"Have a wonderful day, everyone," she cooed as she waved.

The crowd began to break up. A few people dared to brave what was no doubt Logan's murderous glare to come close enough to murmur their thanks or ask that she pass along their greetings to Chadwick or Matthew. She smiled and beamed and patted shoulders and promised that she'd tell her brothers exactly what everyone had said, word for word.

The whole time she felt Logan's rage rolling off him in waves, buffeting against her back. He was no doubt trying to kill her with looks alone. It wouldn't work. She had the upper hand here, and they both knew it.

Finally, there was only one employee left. "Delores,"

Frances said in her nicest voice, "if Mr. Logan doesn't want his donut—" She pivoted and held the box out to him again.

Oh, yes—she had the advantage here. He could go right on trying to glare her to death, but it wouldn't change the fact that the entire administrative staff of the Brewery had ignored his direct order and listened to hers. That feeling of power—of importance—coursed through her body. God, it felt *good*.

"I do not," he snarled.

"Would you be a dear and take care of this for me?" Frances finished, handing the box to Delores.

"Of course, Ms. Frances." Delores gave Frances a look that was at least as good as—if not better than—an actual hug, then shuffled off in the direction of the break room, leaving Frances alone with one deeply pissed-off CEO. She crossed her legs at the ankle and leaned toward him, but she didn't say anything else. The ball was firmly in his court now. The only question was did he know how to play the game?

The moment stretched. Frances took advantage of the silence to appraise her prey. This Logan fellow was *quite* an attractive specimen. He was maybe only a few inches taller than Frances, but he had the kind of rock-solid build that suggested he'd once been a defensive linebacker—and an effective one at that. His suit—a very good suit, with conservative lines—had been tailored to accommodate his wide shoulders. Given the girth of his neck, she'd put money on his shirts being made-to-order. Bespoke shirts and suits were not cheap.

He had a square jaw—all the squarer right now, given how he was grinding his teeth—and light brown hair that was close cut. He was probably incredibly good-looking when he wasn't scowling.

He was attempting to regain his composure, she realized. Couldn't have that.

Back when she'd been a little girl, she'd sat on this very desk, kicking her little legs as she held the donut box for everyone. Back then, it'd been cute to hop down off the desk when all the donuts were gone and twirl in her pretty dress.

But what was cute at five didn't cut it at thirty. No hopping. Still, she had to get off this desk.

So she extended her left leg—which conveniently was the side where one of the few designer dresses she'd hung on to was slit up to her thigh—and slowly shifted her weight onto it.

Logan's gaze cut to her bare leg as the fabric fell away.

She leaned forward as she brought her other foot down. The slit in the dress closed back over her leg, but Logan's eyes went right where she expected them to—her generous cleavage.

In no great hurry, she stood, her shoulders back and her chin up. "Shall we?" she asked in a regal tone. "My cloak," she added, motioning with her chin toward where she'd removed the matching cape that went with this dress.

Without waiting for an answer from him, she strode into his office as if she owned it. Which she once had, sort of.

The room looked exactly as she remembered it. Frances sighed in relief—it was all still here. She used to color on the wagon wheel table while she waited for the rest of the workers to get in so she could hand out the donuts. She'd played dolls on the big conference table. And her father's desk…

The only time her daddy hugged her was in this room. Hardwick Beaumont had not been a hard-driven, ruthless executive in those small moments with her. He'd told her things he'd never told anyone else, like how his father, Frances's grandfather John, had let Hardwick pick out the color of the drapes and the rug. How John had let Hardwick try a new beer fresh off the line, and then made him tell the older man why it was good and what the brewers should do better.

"This office," her daddy used to say, "made me who I am." And then he'd give her a brief, rare hug and say, "And it'll make you who you are, too, my girl."

Ridiculous how the thought of a simple hug from her father could make her all misty-eyed.

She couldn't bear the thought of all this history—all *her* memories—being sold off to the highest bidder. Even if that would result in a tidy commission for her.

If she couldn't stop the sale, the best she could do was convince Chadwick to buy as much of his old office as possible. Her brother had fought to keep this company in the family. He'd understand that some things just couldn't be sold away.

But that wasn't plan A.

She tucked her tenderness away. In matters such as this one, tenderness was a liability, and God knew she couldn't afford any more of those.

So she stopped in the middle of the office and waited for Logan to catch up. She did not fold herself gracefully into one of the guest chairs in front of the desk, nor did she arrange herself seductively on the available love seat. She didn't even think of sprawling herself out on the conference table.

She stood in the middle of the room as though she was ruler of all she saw. And no one—not even a temporary CEO built like a linebacker—could convince her otherwise.

She was surprised when he did not slam the door shut. Instead, she heard the gentle whisper of it clicking closed. *Head up, shoulders back*, she reminded herself as she stood, waiting for him to make the next move. She would show him no mercy. She expected nothing but the same returned in kind.

She saw him move toward the conference table, where he draped her cape over the nearest chair. She felt his eyes on her. No doubt he was admiring her body even as he debated wringing her neck.

Men were so easy to confuse.

He was the kind of man, she decided, who would need to reassert his control over the situation. Now that the audience had dispersed, he would feel it a moral imperative to put her back in her place.

She could not let him get comfortable. It was just that simple.

Ah, she'd guessed right. He made a wide circle around her, not bothering to hide how he was checking out her best dress as he headed for the desk. Frances held her pose until he was almost seated. Then she reached into her small handbag—emerald-green silk, made to match the dress, of course—and pulled out a small mirror and lipstick. Ignoring Logan entirely, she fixed her lips, making sure to exaggerate her pouts.

Was she hearing things or had a nearly imperceptible groan come from the area behind the desk?

This was almost too easy, really.

She put the lipstick and mirror away and pulled out her phone. Logan opened his mouth to say something, but she interrupted him by taking a picture of the desk. And of him.

He snapped his mouth shut. "Frances *Beaumont*, huh?"

"The one and only," she purred, taking a close-up of the carved details on the corner of the desk. And if she had to bend over to do so—well, she couldn't help it if this dress was exceptionally low-cut.

"I suppose," Logan said in a strangled-sounding voice, "that there's no such thing as a coincidence?"

"I certainly don't believe in them." She shifted her angle and took another shot. "Do you?"

"Not anymore." Instead of sounding flummoxed or even angry, she detected a hint of humor in his voice. "I suppose you know your way around, then?"

"I do," she cheerfully agreed. Then she paused, as if she'd just remembered that she'd forgotten her manners. "I'm so sorry—I don't believe I caught your name?"

My, *that* was a look. But if he thought he could intimidate her, he had no idea who he was dealing with. "My apologies." He stood and held out his hand. "I'm Ethan Logan. I'm the CEO of the Beaumont Brewery."

She let his hand hang for a beat before she wrapped her fingers around his. He had hands that matched his shoulders—thick and strong. This Ethan Logan certainly didn't look a thing like the bean-counting lackey she'd pictured.

"Ethan," she said, dropping her gaze and looking up at him through her lashes.

His hand was warm as his fingers curled around her smaller hand. Strong, oh yes—he could easily break her hand. But he didn't. All the raw power he projected was clearly—and safely—locked down.

Instead, he turned her hand over and kissed the back of it. The very thing she'd implied he should do earlier, when they'd had an audience. It'd seemed like a safe move then, an action she knew he'd never take her up on.

But here? In the enclosed space of the office, with no one to witness his chivalrous gesture? She couldn't tell if the kiss was a threat or a seduction. Or both.

Then he raised his gaze and looked her in the eyes. Suddenly, the room was much warmer, the air much thinner. Frances had to use every ounce of her self-control not to take huge gulping breaths just to get some oxygen into her body. Oh, but he had nice eyes, warm and determined and completely focused on her.

She might have underestimated him.

Not that he needed to know that. She allowed herself an

innocent blush, which took some work. She hadn't been innocent for a long time. "A pleasure," she murmured, wondering how long he planned to kiss her hand.

"It's all mine," he assured her, straightening up and taking a step back. She noted with interest that he didn't sit back down. "So you're the appraiser Delores hired?"

"I hope you won't be too hard on her," she simpered, taking this moment to put another few steps between his body and hers.

"And why shouldn't I be? Are you even qualified to do this? Or did she just bring you in to needle me?"

He said it in far too casual a tone. *Damn.* His equilibrium was almost restored. She couldn't have that.

And what's more, she couldn't let him impinge on her ability to do this job.

Then she realized that his lips—which had, to this point, only been compressed into a thin line of anger or dropped open in shock—were curving into a far-too-cocky grin. He'd scored a hit on her, and he knew it.

She quickly schooled her face into the appropriate demureness, using the excuse of taking more pictures to do so.

"I am, in fact, highly qualified to appraise the contents of this office. I have a bachelor's degree in art history and a master's of fine art. I was the manager at Galerie Solaria for several years. I have extensive connections with the local arts scene."

She stated her qualifications in a light, matter-of-fact tone designed to put him at ease. Which, given the little donut stunt she'd pulled, would probably actually make him more nervous—if he had his wits about him. "And if anyone would know the true value of these objects," she added, straightening to give him her very best smile, "it'd be a Beaumont—don't you think? After all, this was ours for *so* long."

He didn't fall for the smile. Instead, he eyed her suspiciously, just as she'd suspected he would. She would have to reconsider her opinion of him. Now that the shock of her appearance was wearing off, he seemed more and more up to the task of playing this game.

Even though it shouldn't, the thought thrilled her. Ethan Logan would be a formidable opponent. This might even be fun. She could play the game with Ethan—a game she would win, without a doubt—and in the process, she could protect her family legacy and help out Delores and all the rest of the employees.

"How about you?" she asked in an offhand manner.

"What about me?" he asked.

"Are you qualified to run a company? This company?" She couldn't help it. The words came out a little sharper than she had wanted them to. But she followed up the questions with a fluttering of her eyelashes and another demure smile.

Not that they worked. "I am, in fact," he said in a mocking tone as he parroted her words, "highly qualified to run this company. I am a co-owner of my firm, Corporate Restructuring Services. I have restructured thirteen previous companies, raising stock prices and increasing productivity and efficiency. I have a bachelor's degree in economics and a master's of business administration, and I *will* turn this company around."

He said the last part with all the conviction of a man who truly believed himself to be on the right side of history.

"I'm quite sure you will." Of course she agreed with him. He was expecting her to argue. "Why, once the employees all get over that nasty flu that's been going around…" She lifted a shoulder, as if to say it was only a matter of time. "You'll have things completely under control within days." Then, just to pour a little lemon juice in the wound, she leaned forward. His gaze held—he didn't even glance at her cleavage. *Damn. Time to up the ante.*

She let her eyes drift over those massive shoulders and the broad chest. He was quite unlike the thin, pale men who populated the art world circles she moved within. She could still feel his lips on the back of her hand.

Oh, yes, she could play this game. For a short while, she could feel like Frances Beaumont again—powerful, beautiful, holding sway over everyone in her orbit. She could use Ethan Logan to get back what she'd lost in the past six months and—if she was very lucky—she might even be able to inflict some damage on AllBev through the Brewery. Corporate espionage and all that.

So she added in a confidential voice, "I have faith in your abilities."

"Do you?"

She looked him up and down again and smiled. A real smile this time, not one couched to elicit a specific response. "Oh, yes," she said, turning away from him. "I do."

Three

He needed her.

That crystal clear revelation was quickly followed by a second—and far more depressing one—Frances Beaumont would destroy him if he gave her half the chance.

As he watched Frances move around his office, taking pictures of the furniture and antiques and making completely harmless small talk about potential buyers, he knew he would have to risk the latter to get the former.

The way all those workers had been eating out of her hand—well, out of her donut box? The way not a single damn one of them had gotten back to work when he'd ordered them to—but they'd all jumped when Frances Beaumont had smiled at them?

It hurt to admit—even to himself—that the workers here would not listen to him.

But they would listen to her.

She was one of them—a Beaumont. They obviously adored her—even Delores, the old battle-ax, had bowed and scraped to this stunningly beautiful woman.

"If you wouldn't mind," she said in that delicate voice that he was completely convinced was a front. She kicked out of her shoes and lined one of the conference chairs up beneath a window. She held out her hand for him. "I'd like to get a better shot of the friezes over the windows."

"Of course," he said in his most diplomatic voice.

This woman—this stunning woman who's fingertips were light and warm against his hand as he helped her balance onto the chair, leaving her ass directly at eye level—had already ripped him to shreds several times over.

She was gorgeous. She was clearly intelligent. And she was obviously out to undermine him. That's what the donuts had been about. Announcing to the world in general and him in particular that this was still the Beaumont Brewery in every sense of the word.

"Thank you," she murmured, placing her hand on his shoulder to balance herself as she stepped down.

She didn't stick the landing, although he couldn't say if that was accidental or on purpose.

Before he could stop himself, his arm went around her waist to steady her.

Which was a mistake because electricity arced between them. She looked up at him through those lashes—he'd lost count of how many times she'd done that so far—but this time it hit him differently.

After almost a month of dealing with passive-aggressive employees terrified of being downsized he suddenly felt like a very different man altogether.

"Thank you," she said again, in a quiet whisper that somehow felt more honest, less calculated than almost every other word she'd uttered so far. Imperceptibly, she leaned into him. He could feel the heat of her breasts through his suit.

As soon as he was sure she wouldn't fall over, he stepped well clear of her. He needed her—but he could not need her like that. Not now, not ever. Because she *would* destroy him. He had no doubt about that. None.

Still…an idea was taking shape in his mind.

Maybe he'd been going about this all wrong. Instead of trying to strip the Beaumont out of the Beaumont Brewery, maybe what he needed to do was bring in a Beaumont. The moment the idea occurred to him, he latched on to it with both hands.

Yes. What he really needed was to have a Beaumont on board with the management changes he was implementing. If the workers realized their old bosses were signing off on the reorganization, there wouldn't be any more mass food poisonings or flu or whatever they'd planned for next week. Sure, there'd still be grumbling and personnel turnover, but if he had a Beaumont by his side...

"So!" Frances said brightly, just as she leaned over to adjust the strap on her shoe.

Ethan had to slam his eyes shut so he wouldn't be caught staring at her barely contained cleavage. If he was going to pull this off, he had to keep his wits about him and his pants zipped.

"How would you like to proceed? Ethan?" It was only when she said his name that he figured it was safe to look.

As safe as it got, anyway. More than any other woman he'd seen in person, Frances looked as if she'd walked right off a movie screen and into his office. Her hair fell in soft waves over her shoulders and her eyes were a light blue that took on a greenish tone that matched her dress. She was the stuff of fantasies, all luscious curves and soft skin.

"I want to hire you."

Direct was better. If he tried to dance around the subject, she'd spin him in circles.

It worked, too—at least for a second. Her eyes widened in surprise, but she quickly got herself back under control. She laughed lightly, like a chime tinkling in the wind. "Mr. Logan," she said, beaming a high-wattage smile at him. "You already have hired me. The furniture?" she reminded him, looking around the room. "My family's legacy?"

"That's not what I mean," he replied. "I want you to come work for me. Here. At the Brewery. As..." His mind spun for something that would be appropriate to a woman like her. "As executive vice president of human resources. In charge of employee relations." *There*. That sounded fancy without actually meaning anything.

A hint of confusion wrinkled her forehead. "You want me to be a…manager?" She said the word as if it left a bad taste in her mouth. "Out of the question." But she favored him with that smile he'd decided she wielded like other people might wield a knife in a street fight. "I'm so sorry, but I couldn't possibly work for the Beaumont Brewery if it wasn't owned by an actual Beaumont." With crisp efficiency, she snatched up her cape and elegantly swirled it around her shoulders, hiding her body from his eyes.

Not that he was looking at it. He felt the corners of his mouth curve up in a smile. He had her off balance for possibly the first time since she'd walked onto the Brewery property.

"I'll work up an appraisal sheet and a list of potential buyers for some of the more sentimental pieces," she announced, not even bothering to look over her shoulder as she strode toward the door.

Before he realized what he was doing, he ran after her. "Wait," he said, getting to the door just as she put her hand on the knob. He pushed the door shut.

And then realized he basically had her trapped between the door and his body.

She knew it, too. Moving with that dancer's grace, she pivoted and leaned back, her breasts thrust toward him and her smile coy. "Did you need something else?"

"Won't you at least consider it?"

"About the job offer?" She grinned. It was too victorious to be pretty. "I rather think not."

What else would she be thinking about? His blood began to pound in his veins. He couldn't admit defeat, couldn't admit that a beautiful woman had spun him around until he hadn't realized he'd lost until it was too late. He had to come up with something to at least make her keep her options open. He could not run this company without her.

"Have dinner with me, then."

If this request surprised her, it didn't show. Instead, she tilted her head to one side, sending waves of beautiful red hair cascading over her cloaked shoulders. Then she moved. A hand emerged from the folds of her cloak and she touched him. She touched the line of his jaw with the tips of her fingers and then slid them down to where his white shirt was visible beneath the V of his suit jacket.

Heat poured off her as she flattened her palm against him. He desperately wanted to close his eyes and focus on the way her touch made his body jump to full attention. He wanted to lower his head and taste her ruby-red lips. He wanted to pull her body into his and feel her skin against his.

He did none of those things.

Instead, he took it like a man. Or he tried to. But when she said, in that soft whisper of hers, "And why would I agree to *that*?" it nearly broke his resolve.

"I'd like the chance to change your mind. About the job offer." Which was not strictly true, not any longer. Not when her palm moved in the smallest of circles over his heart.

"Is that all?" she breathed. He could feel the heat from her hand burning his skin. "There's nothing else you want from me?"

"I just want what's best for the company." Damn it all; his voice had gotten deeper on him. But he couldn't help it, not with the way she was looking up at him. "Don't you?"

Something in her face changed. It wasn't resignation, not really—and it wasn't surrender.

It was engagement. It was a *yes*.

She lightly pushed on his chest. He straightened and

dropped his arm away from the door. "Dinner. For the company," she agreed. He couldn't interpret that statement, not when his ears were ringing with desire. "Where are you staying?"

"I have a suite at the Hotel Monaco."

"Shall we say seven o'clock tomorrow night? In the lobby?"

"It would be an honor."

She arched an eyebrow at him, and then, with a swirling turn, she was gone, striding into the reception area and pausing only to thank Delores again for all her help.

He had to find a way to get Frances on his side.

It had nothing to do with the way he could still feel her touch burned into his skin.

Four

In the end, it'd come down to one of two dresses. Frances only had four left after the liquidation of her closet anyway. The green one was clearly out—it would reek of desperation to wear the same dress twice, even if Ethan's eyes had bugged out of his head when he'd looked at her in it.

She also had her bridesmaid's dress from her brother Phillip's wedding, a sleek gray one with rhinestone accents. But that felt too formal for dinner, even if it did look good on her.

Which meant she had to choose between the red velvet and the little black dress for her negotiation masquerading as dinner with Ethan Logan.

The red dress would render him completely speechless; that she knew. She'd always had a fondness for it—it transformed her into a proper lady instead of what she often felt like, the black sheep of the family.

But there was nothing subtle about the red dress. And besides, if the evening went well, she might need a higher-powered dress for later.

The little black dress was really the only choice. It was a halter-top style and completely backless. The skirt twirled out, but there was no missing the cleavage. The dark color made it appear more subdued at first, which would work to her advantage. If she paired it with her cropped bolero jacket, she could project an air of seriousness, and then, when she needed to befuddle Ethan, she could slip off the jacket. *Perfect*.

She made it downtown almost twenty minutes late, which meant she was right on schedule. Ethan Logan could sit and cool his heels for a bit. The more she kept him off balance, the better her position would be.

Which did beg the question—what was her position? She'd only agreed to dinner because he'd said he wanted what was best for the company. And the way he'd said it…

Well, she also wanted what was best for the company. But for her, that word was a big umbrella, under which the employees were just as important as the bottom line.

And after all, if something continued to be named the Beaumont Brewery, shouldn't it still be connected to the Beaumonts?

So dinner was strictly about those two objectives. She would see what she could get Ethan to reveal about the long-term plan for the Brewery. And if there was something in those plans that could help her get her world back in order, so much the better.

Yes, that was it. Dinner had nothing to do with how she'd felt Ethan's chest muscles twitch under her touch, nothing to do with the simmering heat that had rolled off him. And it had even less to do with the way he'd looked down at her, like a man who'd been adrift at sea for too long and had finally spotted land.

She was Frances Beaumont. She could not be landed. For years, she'd had men look at her as if they were starving and she was a banquet. It was nothing new. Just a testament to her name and genetics. Ethan Logan would be no different. She would take what she needed from him—that feeling that she was still someone who mattered, someone who wielded power—and leave the rest.

Which did not explain why, for the first time in what felt

like years, Frances had butterflies in her stomach as she strode into the lobby of the Hotel Monaco. Was she nervous? It wasn't possible. She didn't get nervous, especially not about something like this. She'd spent her entire life navigating the shark-infested waters of wealthy and powerful men. Ethan was just another shark. And he wasn't even a great white. He was barely a dogfish.

"Good evening, Ms. Beaumont."

"Harold," she said to the doorman with a warm smile and a big tip.

"Ms. Beaumont! How wonderful to see you again!" At this rather loud pronouncement, several other guests in the immediate vicinity paused to gape at her.

Frances ignored the masses. "Thank you, Heidi," she said to the clerk at the front desk with another warm smile. The hotel had been catering to the Beaumont family for years, and Frances liked to keep the staff on her side.

"And what can we do for you tonight?" Heidi asked.

"I'm meeting someone for dinner." She scanned the crowd, but she didn't see Ethan. He wouldn't be easy to miss—a man as massively built as he was? All those muscles would stand out.

Then she saw him. And did a double take. Yes, those shoulders, that neck, were everything she remembered them being. The clothing, however? Unlike the conservative gray suit and dull tie he'd had on in the office, he was wearing a pair of artfully distressed jeans, a white button-up shirt without a tie and…a purple sports coat? A deep purple—plum, maybe. She would not have figured he was the kind of man who would stand outside a sartorial box with any great flair—or success.

When he saw her, he pushed himself off the column he was leaning against. "Frances, hello." Which was a perfectly normal thing to say. But he said it as if he couldn't quite believe his eyes—or his luck—as she strode toward him.

He should feel lucky. "Ethan." When he held out his hand, she took it and used it to pull herself up so she could kiss him on the cheek.

His free hand rested against her side, steadying her. "You look amazing," he murmured, his mouth close to her ear.

Warmth that bordered on heat started where his breath kissed her skin and flamed out over her body. That was what made her nervous. Not the man, not the musculature—not even his position as CEO of her family's company.

It was the way her body reacted to him. The way a touch, a look—a whispered word—could set her fluttering.

Ridiculous. She was not flattered by his attentions. This was not a date. This was corporate espionage in a great dress. This was her using what few resources she had left at her disposal to get her life back on track. This was about her disarming Ethan Logan, not the other way around.

So she clamped down on the shiver that threatened to race across her skin as she lowered herself away from him. "That's a great color on you. Very…" She let the word hang in the air for a beat too long. "Bold," she finished. "Not just any man could pull off that look."

He raised his eyebrows. She realized he was trying not to laugh at her. "Says the woman who showed up in an emerald evening gown to hand out donuts. Have no fear, I'm comfortable in my masculinity. Shall we? I made reservations at the restaurant." He held out his arm for her.

"We shall." She lightly placed her hand in the crook of his elbow. She didn't need his help—she could walk in these shoes just fine—but this was part of setting him up. It had nothing to do with wanting another flash of heat from where their bodies met.

The restaurant was busy, as was to be expected on a Saturday night. When they entered, the diners paused. She and Ethan must have made quite a pair, her with her red hair and him in his purple jacket.

People were already forming opinions. That was something she could use to her advantage. She placed her free hand on top of Ethan's arm and leaned into him. Not much, but just enough to create the impression that this was a date.

The maître d' led them to a small table tucked in a dim corner. They ordered—she got the lobster, just to be obnoxious about it, and he got the steak, just to be predictable—and Ethan ordered a bottle of pinot grigio.

Then they were alone. "I'm glad you came out tonight."

She demurely placed her hands in her lap. "Did you think I would cancel?"

"I wouldn't have been surprised if you'd tried to string me along a little bit. Just to watch me twist." He said it in a jovial way but she didn't miss the edge to his voice.

So he wasn't totally befuddled. And he was more than sharp enough to know they were here for something much more than dinner.

That didn't mean she had to own up to it. "Whatever do you mean?"

His smile sharpened. The silence carried, and she was in serious danger of fidgeting nervously under his direct gaze.

She was saved by the sommelier, who arrived with the wine. Frances desperately wanted to take a long drink, but she could not let Ethan know he was unsettling her. So she slowly twirled the stem of her wineglass until he said, "I propose a toast."

"Do you now?"

"To a long and productive partnership." She did not drink. Instead, she leveled a cool gaze at him over the rim of her glass and waited for him to notice. Which, admittedly, did not take long. "Yes?"

"I'm not taking that job, you know. I have 'considered' it, and I can't imagine a more boring job in the history of employment," she told him.

She would not let the world know she was so desperate as to take a job in management at a company that used to belong to her family. She might be down on her luck, but she wasn't going to give up.

Then, and only then, did she allow herself to sip her wine. She had to be careful. She needed to keep her wits about her and not let the wine—and all those muscles— go to her head.

"I figured as much," he said with a low chuckle that Frances felt right in her chest. What was it with this man's voice?

"Then why would you toast to such a thing?" Maybe now was the time to take the jacket off? He seemed entirely too self-aware. She did not have the advantage here, not like she'd had in the office.

Oh, she did not like that smile on him. Well, she did— she might actually like it a great deal, if she wasn't the one in the crosshairs.

He leaned forward, his gaze so intense that she considered removing her jacket just to cool down. "I'm sure you know why I want you," he all but growled.

It *was* getting hotter in here. She tried to look innocent. It was the only look she could pull off with the level of blush she'd probably achieved by now. "My sparkling wit?"

There was a brief crack in his serious facade, as if her sparkling wit was the correct answer. "I consider that a fringe benefit," he admitted with a tilt of his head. "But let's not play dumb, you and I. It's far too beneath a woman with your considerable talents. And your talents…" She straightened her back and thrust her chest out in a desperate attempt to throw him off balance. It didn't work. His gaze never left her face. "Your talents are considerable. I'm not sure I've ever met a woman like you before."

"Are you hitting on me?"

The corner of his mouth quirked up, making him look like a predator. She might have to revise her earlier opinion of him. He was *not* a dogfish. More like…a tiger shark, sleek and fast. Able to take her down before she even realized she was in danger.

"Of course not."

"Then why do you want me?" Because honestly—for the first time in her adult life—she wasn't sure what the answer would be.

Men wanted her. They always had. The moment her boobs had put in an appearance, she'd learned about base male lust—how to provoke it, how to manage it, how to use it for her own ends. Men wanted her for a simple, carnal reason. And after watching stepmother after stepmother come and go out of her father's life, she had resolved never to be used. Not like that.

The upside was that she'd never had her heart broken. But the downside?

She'd never been in love. Self-preservation, however vital to survival, was a lonely way to live.

"It's simple, really." He leaned back, his posture at complete ease. "Obviously, everyone at the Brewery hates me. I can't blame them—no one likes change, especially when they have to change against their will." He grinned at her, a sly thing. "I should probably be surprised that Delores hasn't spiked my coffee with arsenic by now."

"Probably," she agreed. Where was he going with this?

"But you?" He reached over and picked up her hand, rubbing his thumb along the edges of her fingertips. Against her will, she shivered—and he felt it. That smile deepened—his voice deepened. Everything deepened. *Oh, hell.*

"I saw how the workers—especially the lifers—responded to you and your donut stunt," he went on, still stroking her hand. "There's nothing they wouldn't do for you, and probably wouldn't do for any Beaumont."

"If you think this is going to convince me to take that job, you're sorely mistaken," she replied. She wanted to jerk her hand out of his—she needed to break that skin-to-skin contact—but she didn't. If this was how the game was going to go, then she needed to be all in.

So instead she curled her fingers around his and made small circles on the base of his palm with her thumb. She was justly rewarded with a little shiver from him. *Okay, good. Great.* She wasn't entirely at his mercy here. She could still have an impact even without the element of surprise. "Especially if you're going to call them 'lifers.' That's insulting. You make them sound like prisoners."

He notched an eyebrow at her. "What would you call them?"

"Family." The simple reply—which was also the truth—was out before she could stop it.

She didn't know what she expected him to do with that announcement, but lifting her hand to his lips and pressing a kiss against her skin wasn't it. "And that," he whispered against her skin, "is exactly why I need you."

This time, she did pull her hand away. She dropped it into her lap and fixed him with her best polite glare, the one that could send valets and servers scurrying for cover. Just then, the waiter appeared with their food—and did, in fact, pause when Frances turned that glare in his direction. He set their plates down with a minimum of fanfare and all but sprinted away.

She didn't touch her food. "I'm hearing an awful lot about how much you need me. So let us, as you said, dispense with the games. I do not now, nor have I ever, formally worked for the Beaumont Brewery. I do not now, nor have I ever, had sex with a man who thought he was entitled to a piece of the Beaumont Brewery and, by extension, a piece of me. I will not take a desk job to help you win the approval of people you clearly dislike."

"They disliked me first," he put in as he cut his steak.

What she really wanted to do was throw her wine in his face. It'd feel so good to let loose and let him have it. Despite his claims that he recognized her intelligence, she had the distinct feeling that he was playing her, and she did not like it. "Regardless. What do you want, Mr. Logan? Because I'm reasonably certain that it's no longer just the dismantling and sale of my family's history."

He set his knife and fork aside and leaned his elbows on the table. "I need you to help me convince the workers that joining the current century is the only way the company will survive. I need you to help me show them that it doesn't have to be me against them or them against me—that we can work together to make the Brewery something more than it was."

She snorted. "I'll be sure to pass such touching sentiments along to my brother—the man you replaced."

"By all accounts, he was quite the businessman. I'm sure that he'd agree with me. After all, he made significant changes to the management structure himself after his father passed. But he was constrained by that sense of family you so aptly described. I am not."

"All the good it's doing you." She took another sip of wine, a slightly larger one than before.

"You see my problem. If the workers fight me on this, it won't be only a few people who lose their jobs—the entire company will shut down, and we will all suffer."

She tilted her head from side to side, considering. "Perhaps it should. The Beaumont Brewery without a Beaumont isn't the same thing, no matter what the marketing department says."

"Would you really give your blessing to job losses for hundreds of workers, just for the sake of a name?"

"It's *my* name," she shot at him.

But he was right. If the company went down in flames, it'd burn the people she cared for. Her brothers would be safe—they'd already ensconced themselves in the Percheron Drafts brewery. But Bob and Delores and all the rest? The ones who'd whispered to her how nervous they were about the way the wind was blowing? Who were afraid for their families? The ones who knew they were too old to start over, who were scared that they'd be forced into early retirement without the generous pension benefits the Beaumont Brewery had always offered its loyal employees?

"Which brings us back to the heart of the matter. I need you."

"No, you don't. You need my approval." Her lobster was no doubt getting cold, but she didn't have much of an appetite at the moment.

Something that might have been a smile played over his lips. For some reason, she took it as a compliment, as if he was acknowledging her intelligence for real this time, instead of paying lip service to it. "Why didn't you go into the family business? You'd have made a hell of a negotiator."

"I find business, in general, to be beneath me." She cast a cutting look at him. "Much like many of the people who willingly choose to engage in it."

He laughed then, a real thing that she wished grated on her ears and her nerves but didn't. It was a warm sound, full of humor and honesty. It made her want to smile. She didn't. "I'm not going to take the job."

"I wasn't going to offer it to you again. You're right—it is beneath you."

Here it came—the trap he was waiting to spring. He leaned forward, his gaze intent on hers and in the space of a second, before he spoke, she realized what he was about to say. All she could think was, *Oh, hell*.

"I don't want to hire you. I want to marry you."

Five

The weight of his statement hit Frances so hard Ethan was surprised she didn't crumple in the chair.

But of course she didn't. She was too refined, too schooled to let her shock show. Even so, her eyes widened and her mouth formed a perfect O, kissable in every regard.

"You want to…what?" Her voice cracked on the last word.

Turnabout is fair play, he decided as he let her comment hang in the air. She'd caught him completely off guard in the office yesterday and had clearly thought she could keep that shock and awe going. But tonight? The advantage was his.

"I want to marry you. More specifically, I want you to marry me," he explained. Saying the words out loud made his blood hum. When he'd come up with this plan, it had seemed like a bold-yet-risky business decision. He'd quickly realized that Frances Beaumont would absolutely not take a desk job, but the unavoidable fact was he needed her approval to validate his restructuring plans.

And what better way to show that the Beaumonts were on board with the restructuring than if he were legally wed to the favored daughter?

Yes, it had all seemed cut-and-dried when he'd formulated the plan last night. A sham marriage, designed to bolster his position within the company. He'd done a little digging into her past and discovered that she had tried to launch some sort of digital art gallery recently, but it'd gone under. So she might need funding. No problem.

But he'd failed to take into account the actual woman he'd just proposed to. The fire in her eyes more than matched the fire in her hair, and all of her lit a hell of a flame in him. He had to shift in his chair to avoid discomfort as he tried not to look at her lips.

"You want to get married?" She'd recovered some, the haughty tone of her voice overcoming her surprise. "How very flattering."

He shrugged. He'd planned for this reaction. Frankly, he'd expected nothing less, not from her.

He hadn't planned for the way her hand—her skin—had felt against his. But a plan was a plan, and he was in for far more than a penny. "Of course, I'm not about to profess my undying love for you. Admiration, yes." Her cheeks colored slightly. Nope, he hadn't planned for that, either.

Suddenly, his bold plan felt like the height of foolishness.

"My," she murmured. Her voice was soft, but he didn't miss the way it sliced through the air. "How I love to hear sweet nothings. They warm a girl's heart."

He grinned again. "I'm merely proposing an…arrangement, if you will. Open to negotiation. I already know a job in management is not for you." He sat back, trying to look casual. "I'm a man of considerable influence and power. Is there something you need that I can help you with?"

"Are you trying to *buy* me?" Her fingertips curled around the stem of her wineglass. He kept one hand on the napkin in his lap, just in case he found himself wearing the wine.

"As I said, this isn't a proposal based on love. It's based on need. You're already fully aware of how much I need you. I'm just trying to ascertain what you need to make this arrangement worth your time. Above and beyond making sure that your Brewery family is well taken care of, that is." He leaned forward again. He enjoyed negotiations like this—probing and prodding to find the other party's breaking point. And a little bit of guilt never hurt anything.

"What if I don't want to marry you? Surely you can't think you're the first man who's ever proposed to me out of the blue." The dismissal was slight, but it carried weight. She was doing her level best to toy with him.

And he'd be lying if he said he didn't enjoy it. "I have no doubt you've been fending off men for years. But this proposal isn't based on want." However, that didn't stop his gaze from briefly drifting down to her chest. She had *such* an amazing body.

Her lips tightened, and she fiddled with the button on her jacket. "Then what's it based on?"

"I'm proposing a short-term arrangement. A marriage of convenience. Love doesn't need to play a role."

"Love?" she asked, batting her eyelashes. "There's more to a marriage than that."

"Point. Lust also is not a part of my proposal. A one-year marriage. We don't have to live together. We don't have to sleep together. We need to occasionally be seen in public together. That's it."

She blinked at him. "You're serious, aren't you? What kind of marriage would *that* be?"

Now it was Ethan's turn to fidget with his wineglass. He didn't want to get into the particulars of his parents' marriage at the moment. "Suffice it to say, I've seen long-distance marriages work out quite well for all parties involved."

"How delightful," she responded, disbelief dripping off every word. "Are you gay?"

"What? No!" He jolted so hard that he almost knocked

his glass over. "I mean, not that there's anything wrong with that. But I'm not."

"Pity. I might consider a loveless, sexless marriage to a gay man. Sadly," she went on in a not-sad voice, "I don't trust you to hold up your sexless end of the bargain."

"I'm not saying we couldn't have sex." In fact, given the way she'd pressed her lips to his cheek earlier, the way she'd held his hand—he'd be perfectly fine with sex with her. "I'm merely saying it's not expected. It's not a deal breaker."

She regarded him with open curiosity. "So let me see if I understand this proposal, such as it is. You'd like me to marry you and lend the weight of the Beaumont name to your destruction of the Beaumont Brewery—"

"Reconstruction, not destruction," he interrupted.

She ignored him. "In a starter marriage that has a built-in sunset at one year, no other strings attached?"

"That sums it up."

"Give me one good reason why I shouldn't stab you in the hand with my knife."

He flinched. "Actually, I was waiting for you to give me a good reason." She looked at him flatly. "I read on-line that your digital art gallery recently failed." He said it gently. He could sympathize with a well-thought-out project going sideways—or backward.

She rested her hand on her knife. But she didn't say anything. Her eyes—beautiful light eyes that walked the line between blue and green—bore into him.

"If there was something that I—as an investor—could help you with," he went on, keeping his voice quiet, "well, that could be part of our negotiation. It'd be venture capi-tal—*not* an attempt to buy you," he added. She took her hand off her knife and put it in her lap, which Ethan took as a sign that he'd hit the correct nerve. He went on, "I wouldn't—and couldn't—cut you a personal check. But as an angel investor, I'm sure we could come to terms you'd find satisfactory."

"Interesting use of the word *angel* there," she said. Her voice was quiet. None of the seduction or coquettishness that she'd wielded like a weapon remained.

Finally, he was talking to the real Frances Beaumont. No more artifice, no more layers. Just a beautiful, intelligent woman. A woman he'd just proposed to.

This was for the job, he reminded himself. He was only proposing because he needed to get control of the Beaumont Brewery, and Frances Beaumont was the shortest, straightest line between where he was today and where he needed to be. It had nothing to do with the actual woman.

"Do you do this often? Propose marriage to women connected with the businesses you're stripping?"

"No, actually. This would be a first for me."

She picked up her knife, and he unwittingly tensed. One corner of her perfect rosebud mouth quirked into a smile before she began to cut into her lobster tail. "Really? I suppose I should be flattered."

He began to eat his steak. It had cooled past the optimal temperature, but he figured that was the price one paid for negotiating before the main course arrived. "I'm never in one city for more than a year, usually only for a few months. I have, on occasion, made the acquaintance of a woman with whom I enjoy doing things such as this—dining out, seeing the sights."

"Having sex?" she asked bluntly.

She was trying to unnerve him again. It might be working. "Yes, when we're both so inclined. But those were short-term, no-commitment relationships, as agreed upon by both parties."

"Just a way to pass the time?"

"That might sound harsh, but yes. If you agree to the

arrangement, we could dine out like this, maybe attend the theater or whatever it is you do for fun here in Denver."

"This isn't exactly a one-horse town anymore, you know. We have theaters and gala benefits and art openings and a football team. Maybe you've heard of them?" Her gaze drifted down to his shoulders. "You might consider trying out for the front four."

Ethan straightened his shoulders. He wasn't a particularly vain man, but he kept himself in shape, and he'd be lying if he said he wasn't flattered that she'd noticed. "I'll keep it in mind."

They ate in silence. He decided it was her play. She hadn't stabbed him, and she hadn't thrown a drink in his face. He put the odds of getting her to go along with this plan at fifty-fifty.

And if she didn't… Well, he'd need a new plan.

Her lobster tail was maybe half-eaten when she set her cutlery aside. "I've never fielded a marriage proposal like yours before."

"How many have you fielded?"

She waved the question away. "I've lost count. A quickie wedding, a one-year marriage with no sex, an irreconcilable-differences, uncontested divorce—all in exchange for an investment into a property or project of my choice?"

"Basically." He'd never proposed before. He couldn't tell if her no-nonsense tone was a good sign or not. "We'd need a prenup."

"Obviously." She took a much longer pull on her wine. "I want five million."

"I'm sorry?"

"I have a friend who wants to launch a new art gallery, with me as the co-owner. She has a business plan worked up and a space selected. All we need is the capital." She pointed a long, red-tipped nail at him. "And you did offer to invest, did you not?"

She had him there. "I did. Do we have a deal?" He stuck out his hand and waited.

She must be out of her ever-loving mind.

As Frances regarded the hand Ethan had extended toward her, she was sure she had crossed some line from desperation into insanity to even consider his offer.

Would she really agree to marry the living embodiment of her family's downfall for what, essentially, was the promise of job security after he was gone? With five million—a too-large number she'd pulled out of thin air—she and Becky could open that gallery in grand style, complete with all the exhibitions and parties it took to wine and dine wealthy art patrons.

This time, it'd be different. It was Becky's business plan, after all. Not Frances's. But even that thought stung a bit. Becky's plan had a chance of working. Unlike all of Frances's grand plans.

She needed this. She needed something to go her way, something to work out right for once. With a five-million-dollar investment, she and Becky could get the gallery operational and Frances could move out of the Beaumont mansion. Even if she only lived in the apartment over the gallery, it'd still be hers. She could go back to being Frances Beaumont. She could feel like a grown-up in control of her own life.

All it'd take would be giving up that control for a year. Not just giving it up, but giving it to Ethan.

She felt as if she was on the verge of passing out, but she refused to betray a single sign of panic. She did not breathe in deep gulps. She did not drop her head in her hands. And she absolutely did not fiddle with anything.

She kept herself serene and calm and did all her panicking on the inside, where no one could see it.

"Well?" Ethan asked. But it wasn't a gruff demand for an answer. His tone was more cautious than that.

And then there was the man himself. This was all quite noble, this talk of no sex and no emotions. But that didn't change the fact of the matter—Ethan Logan was one hell of a package. He could make her shiver and shake with the kind of heat she hadn't felt in a very long time.

Not that it mattered, because it didn't.

"I don't believe in love," she announced, mostly to see what kind of reaction it'd get.

"You don't? That seems unusually cynical for a woman of your age and beauty."

She didn't try to hide her eye roll. "I only mention it because if you're thinking about pulling one of those 'I'll make her love me over time' stunts, it's best to nip it in the bud right now."

She'd seen what people did in the name of love. How they made grand promises they had every intention of keeping until the next pretty face came along. As much as she'd loved her father, she hadn't been blind to his wandering eye or his wandering hands. She'd seen exactly what had happened to her mother, Jeannie—all because she'd believed in the power of love to tame the untamable Hardwick Beaumont.

"I wouldn't dream of it." Ethan's hand still hung in the air between them.

"I won't love you," she promised him, putting her palm in his. "I'd recommend you not love me."

Something in his eyes tightened as his fingers closed around hers. "I hope admiration is still on the table?"

She let her gaze drift over his body again. It wasn't desire, not really. She was an art connoisseur, and she was merely admiring his form. And wondering how it'd function. "I suppose."

"When do you want to get married?"

She thought it over. *Married.* The word felt weird rattling around her head. She'd never wanted to be married, never wanted to be tied to someone who could hurt her.

Of course, her brother Phillip had recently had a fairy-tale wedding that had been everything she might have ever wanted, if she'd actually wanted it. Which she didn't.

No, a big public spectacle was not the way to go here. This was, by all public appearances, a whirlwind romance, starting yesterday when she'd sashayed into his office. "I think we should cultivate the impression that we are swept up in the throes of passion."

"Agreed."

"Let's get married in two weeks."

Just saying it out loud made her want to hyperventilate. What would her brothers say to this, her latest stunt in a long line of stunts? "Frannie," she could practically hear Chadwick intone in his too-serious voice. "I don't think…" And Matthew? He was the one who always wanted everyone to line up and smile for the cameras and look like a big happy family. What would he say when she up and got herself hitched?

Then there was Byron, her twin. She'd thought she'd known Byron better than any other person in the world, and vice versa. But in the matter of a few weeks, he'd gone from her brother to a married man with a son and another baby on the way. Well, if anyone would understand her sudden change in matrimonial status, it'd be Byron.

Everyone else—especially Chadwick and Matthew—would just have to deal. This was her life. She could damn well do what she pleased with it.

Even if that meant marrying Ethan Logan.

Six

Ethan didn't know if it was the wine or the woman, but throughout the rest of dinner, he felt light-headed.

He was going to get married. To Frances Beaumont. In two weeks.

Which was great. Everything was going according to plan. He would demonstrate to the world that the Beaumonts were behind the restructuring of the Beaumont Brewery. That would buy him plenty of goodwill at the Brewery.

Yup. It was a great plan. There was just one major catch.

Frances leaned toward him and shrugged her jacket off. The sight of her bare shoulders hammered a spike of desire up his gut. He wasn't used to this sort of craving. Even when he found a lady friend to keep him company during his brief stints in cities around the country, he didn't usually succumb to this much *lust*.

His previous relationships were founded on...well, on *not* lust. Companionship was a part of it, sure. The sex was a bonus, definitely. And the women he consorted with were certainly lovely.

But the way he reacted to Frances? That was something else. Something different.

Something that threatened to break free from him.

Which was ridiculous. He was the boss. He was in control of this—all of this. The situation, his desires—

Well, maybe not his desires, not when Frances leaned forward and looked up at him coyly through her lashes. It shouldn't work, but it did.

"Well, then. Shall we get started?"

"Started?" But the word died on his lips when she reached across the table and ran her fingertips over his chin.

"Started," she agreed. She held out her hand, and he took it. He had no choice. "I happen to know a thing or two about creating a public sensation. We're already off to a great start, what with the confrontation outside your office and now this very public dinner. Kiss my hand again."

He did as he was told, pressing her skin against his lips and getting a hint of expensive perfume and the underlying taste of Frances.

He looked up to find her beaming at him, the megawatt smile probably visible from out on the sidewalk. But it wasn't real. Even he could tell that.

"So, kissing hands is on the table?" He didn't move her hand far from his mouth. He didn't want to.

When had he lost his head this much? When had he been this swamped by raw, unadulterated want? He needed to get his head back out of his pants and focus. He had explicitly promised that he would not make sex a deal breaker. He needed to keep his word, or the deal would be done before it got started.

"Oh, yes," she purred. Then she flipped her hand over in his grip and traced his lower lip with her thumb. "I'd imagine that there are several things still on the table."

Such as? His blood was beating a new, merciless rhythm in his veins, driving that spike of desire higher and higher until he was in actual pain. His mind helpfully supplied several vivid images that involved him, Frances and a table.

He caught her thumb in his mouth and sucked on it, his tongue tracing the edge of her perfectly manicured nail. Her eyes widened with desire, her pupils dilating until he could barely see any of the blue-green color at all. He swore he could see her nipples tighten through the fabric of her dress. Oh, yeah—a table, a bed—any flat surface would do. It didn't even have to be flat. Good sex could be had standing up.

He let go of her thumb and kissed her hand again. "Do you want to get out of here?"

"I'd like that," she whispered back.

It took a few minutes to settle the bill, during which every single look she shot him only made his blood pound that much harder. When had he been this overcome with lust? When had a simple business arrangement become an epic struggle?

She stood, and he realized the dress was completely backless. The wide swath of smooth, creamy skin that was Frances's back lay bare before him. His fingers itched to trace the muscles, to watch her body twitch under his touch.

He didn't want her to put her jacket back on and cover up that beautiful skin. And, thankfully, she didn't. She waited for him to assist her with her chair and then said, "Will you carry my jacket for me?"

"Of course." He folded it over one arm and then offered his other to her.

She leaned into his touch, her gorgeous red curls brushing against his shoulder. "Did you ever play football?" she asked, running her hands up and down his forearms. "Or were you just born this way?"

There was something he was supposed to be remembering, something that was important about Frances. But he couldn't think about anything but the way she'd looked in that green dress yesterday and the way she looked right now. The way he felt when she touched him.

He flexed under her hands and was rewarded with a little gasp from her. "I played. I got a scholarship to play in college, but I blew out my knee."

They were walking down the long hallway that separated the restaurant from the hotel. Then it'd be a quick turn to the left and into the elevators. A man could get into a lot of trouble in an elevator.

But they didn't even make it to the elevator. The moment they got to the middle of the lobby, Frances reached across his chest and slid her hand under his coat. Just like it had in the office yesterday, her touch burned him.

"Oh, that sounds awful," she breathed, curling her fingers around his shirt and pulling him toward her.

The noise of the lobby faded away until there was only the touch of her hand and the beating of his heart.

He turned into her, lowering his head. "Terrible," he agreed, but he no longer knew what they were talking about. All he knew was that he was going to kiss her.

Their lips met. The kiss was tentative at first as he tested her and she tested him. But then her mouth opened for him, and his control—the control he'd maintained for years and years, the control that made him a savvy businessman with millions in the bank—shattered on him.

He tangled his hands into her hair and roughly pulled her up to his mouth so he could taste her better—taste all of her. Dimly, somewhere in the back of his mind where at least three brain cells were doing their best to think about something beyond Frances's touch, Frances's taste—dimly, he realized they were standing in the middle of a crowd, although he'd forgotten exactly where they were.

There was a wolf whistle. And a second one—this one accompanied by laughter.

Frances pulled away, her impressive chest heaving and her eyes glazed with lust. "Your suite," she whispered, and then her tongue darted out, tracing a path on her lips that he needed to follow.

"Yeah. Sure." She could have suggested jumping out of an airplane at thirty thousand feet and he would have done it. Just so long as she went down with him.

Somehow, despite the tangle of arms and jackets, they made it to the elevators and then onto one. Other people were waiting, but no one joined them on the otherwise-empty lift. "Sorry," Frances said to the waiting guests as she curled up against his chest. "We'll send it back down," she added as the doors closed and shut them away from the rest of the world.

Then they were alone. Ethan slid his hands down her bare back before he cupped her bottom. "Where were we?"

"Here," she murmured, pressing her lips against his neck, right above his collar. "And here." Her teeth scraped over his skin as she pressed the full length of her body against his. "And…here."

She didn't touch him through his pants, not with her hands—but with her body? She shifted against him, and the pressure drove those last three rational brain cells out of his mind. "God, yes," he groaned, fisting his hands into her curls and tilting her head back. "How could I forget?"

He didn't give her time to reply. He crushed his mouth against hers. There wasn't any more time for testing kisses—all that existed in the safe space of this little moving room was his need for her and, given the way she was kissing him back, her need for him.

He liked sex—he always had. He prided himself on being good at it. But had he ever been this excited? This consumed with need? He couldn't remember. He couldn't think, not with Frances moaning into his mouth and arching her back, pushing her breasts into his body.

He reached up and started to undo the tie at the back of her neck, but she grabbed his hand and held it at waist height. "We're almost there," she murmured in a coy tone. "Can you wait just a little longer?"

No. "Yes."

Love and sex and, yes, marriage—that was all about waiting. There'd never been any instant gratification in it for him. He'd waited until he'd been eighteen before losing his virginity because it was a test of sorts. Everyone else was going as fast as they could, but Ethan was different. Better. He could resist the fire. He would not get burned.

Frances shifted against him again, and he groaned in the most delicious agony that had ever consumed him. Her touch—even through his clothing—seared him. For the first time in his life, he wanted to dance with the flames.

One flame—one flame-haired woman—in particular. Oh, how they would dance.

The elevator dinged. "Is this us?" Frances asked in a shaky whisper.

"This way." He grabbed her hand and strode out of the elevator. It was perhaps not the most gentlemanly way of going about it—essentially dragging her in her impossible shoes along behind him—but he couldn't help himself. If she couldn't walk, he'd carry her.

His suite was at the end of a long, quiet hall. The only noise that punctuated the silence was the sound of his blood pounding in his temples, pushing him faster until he was all but running, pulling Frances in his wake. Each step was pain and pleasure wrapped in one, his erection straining to do anything but walk. Or run.

After what felt like an hour of never-ending journeying, he reached his door. Torturous seconds passed as he tried to get the key card to work. Then the door swung open and he was pulling her inside, slamming the door shut behind them and pinning her against it. Her hands curled into his shirt, holding him close.

He must have had one lone remaining brain cell functioning, because instead of ripping that dress off her body so he could feast himself upon it, he paused to say, "Tell me what you want."

Because whatever she wanted was what he wanted.

Or maybe she wasn't holding him close. The thought occurred to him belatedly, just about the time her mouth curved up into what was a decidedly nonseductive smile. She pushed on his chest, and he had no choice but to let her. "Anything I want?"

She'd pushed him away, but her voice was still colored with craving, with a need he could feel more than hear. Maybe she wanted him to tie her up. Maybe she wanted to tie him up instead. Whatever it was, he was game.

"Yeah." He tried to lean back down to kiss her again, but she was strong for a woman her size. She held him back.

"I wonder what's on TV?"

It took every ounce of her willpower to push Ethan back, to push herself away from the door, but she did it anyway. She forced herself to stroll casually over to the dresser that held the flat-screen television and grab the remote. Then, without daring to look at Ethan, she flopped down on the bed. It was only after she'd propped herself up on her elbows and turned on the television that she hazarded a look at him.

He was leaning against the door. His jacket was half off; his shirt was a rumpled mess. He looked as though she'd mauled him. She was a little hazy on the details, but, as best she could recall, she had.

She turned her attention back to the television, randomly clicking without actually seeing what was on-screen. She'd only meant to put on a little show for the crowd. If they were going to do this sham marriage thing in two weeks, they needed to start their scandalous activities right now. Kissing in a lobby, getting into the elevator together? She was unmistakable with her red hair. And Ethan—he wasn't that hard to look up. People would make the connection. And people, being reliable, would talk.

When she'd stroked his face at dinner, she'd seen the headlines in her mind. "Whirlwind Romance between Beaumont Heir and New Brewery CEO?" That was what Ethan wanted, wasn't it? The air of Beaumont approval. This was nothing but a PR ploy.

Except…

Except for the way he'd kissed her. The way he'd kept kissing her.

At some point between when he'd sucked on her thumb and the kiss in the lobby—the first one, she mentally corrected—the game they'd been playing had changed.

It was all supposed to have been for show. But the way he had pinned her against the door in this very nice room? The way his deep voice had begged her to tell him what she wanted?

That hadn't felt like a game. That hadn't been for show.

The only thing that had kept her from spinning right over the edge was the knowledge that he didn't want her. Oh, he wanted her—naked, that was—but he didn't want *her*, Frances—complicated and crazy and more than a little lost. He'd only touched her because he wanted something, and she could not allow that to cloud her thinking.

"What—" He cleared his throat, but it didn't make his voice any stronger. "What are you doing?"

"Watching television." She kicked her heels up.

She cut another side glance at Ethan. He hadn't moved. "Why?"

It took everything Frances had to make herself sound glib and light. "What else are we going to do?"

His mouth dropped down to his chest. "I don't mean to sound crass, but...sex?"

Frances couldn't help it. Her gaze drifted down to the impressive bulge in his pants—the same bulge that had ground against her in the elevator.

Sex. The thought of undoing those pants and letting that bulge free sent an uncontrollable shiver down her back. She snapped her eyes back to the television screen. "Really," she said in a dismissive tone.

There was a moment where the only noise in the room was the sound of Ethan breathing heavily and some salesman on TV yelling about a cleaning cloth.

"Then what was that all about?" Ethan gruffly demanded.

"Creating an impression." She did not look at him.

"And who were we impressing in the elevator?"

She put on her most innocent look—which, granted, would have been a lot easier if her nipples weren't still chafing against the front of her dress. "Fine. A test, then."

Ethan was suddenly in front of the television, arms crossed as he glared down at her. "A *test*?"

"It has to be convincing, this relationship we're pretending to have," she explained, making a big show of looking around his body, rather than at the still-obvious bulge in his pants. "But part of the deal was that we don't have sex." She let that sink in before adding, "You're not going to back out of the deal, are you?"

Because that was a risk, and she knew it. There were many ways a deal could go south—especially when sex was on the line.

"You're testing *me*?" He took a step to the side, trying to block her view of the screen again.

"I won't marry just anyone, you know. I have standards."

She could feel the weight of his glare on her face, but

she refused to allow her skin to flush. She leaned the other way. Not that she had any idea of what she was watching. Her every sense was tuned into Ethan.

It'd be so easy to change her mind, to tell him that he'd passed his first test and that she had another test in mind—one that involved less clothing for everyone. She could find out what was behind that bulge and whether or not he knew how to use it.

She could have a few minutes where she wouldn't have to feel alone and adrift, where she could lose herself in Ethan. But that was all it would be. A few minutes.

And then the sex would be done, and she'd go back to being broke, unemployed Frances who was trading on her good looks even as they began to slip away. And Ethan? Well, he'd probably still marry her and fund her art gallery. But he'd know her in a way that felt too intimate, too personal.

Not that she was a shy, retiring virgin—she wasn't. But she had to keep her eye on the long game here, which was reestablishing herself and the Beaumont name and inflicting as much collateral damage on the new Brewery owners and operators as possible.

So this was her, inflicting a little collateral damage on Ethan—even if the dull throb that seemed to circle between her legs and up to her nipples felt like a punishment in its own right.

Okay, so it was a lot of collateral damage.

She realized she was holding her breath as she waited. Would he render their deal null and void? She didn't think so. She might not always be the best judge of men, but she was pretty sure Ethan wasn't going to claim sex behind tired old lines like "she led me on." There was something about him that was more honorable than that.

Funny. She hadn't thought of him as honorable before this moment.

But he was. He muttered something that sounded like a curse before he stalked out of her line of vision. She heard the bathroom door slam shut and exhaled.

The score was Frances: two and Ethan: one. She was winning.

She shifted on the bed. If only victory wasn't taking the shape of sexual frustration.

Frances had just stumbled on some sort of sporting event—basketball, maybe?—when Ethan threw the bathroom door open again. He stalked into the room in nothing but his trousers and a plain white T-shirt. He went over to the desk, set against the window, and opened his computer. "How long do you need to be here?" he asked in an almost-mean voice.

"That's open to discussion." She looked over at him. He was pointedly glaring at the computer screen. "I obviously didn't bring a change of clothing."

That got his attention. "You wouldn't stay the night, would you?"

Was she wrong, or was there a note of panic in his voice? She pushed herself into a sitting position, tucking her feet under her skirt. "Not yet, I don't think. But perhaps by next week, yes. For appearances."

He stared at her for another tight moment and then ground the heels of his palms into his eyes. "This seemed like *such* a good idea in my head," he groaned.

She almost felt bad for him. "We'll need to have dinner in public again tomorrow night. In fact, at least four or five nights a week for the next two weeks. Then I'll start sleeping over and—"

"Here?" He made a show of noticing there was only one bed and a pullout couch. "Shouldn't I come to your place?"

"Um, no." The very last thing she needed was to parade her fake intended husband through the Beaumont mansion. God only knew what Chadwick would do if he caught wind of this little scheme of hers. "No, we should stick to a more public setting. The hotel suits nicely."

"Well." He sagged back in his chair. "That's the evenings. And during the day?"

She considered. "I'll come to the office a couple of times a week. We'll say that we're discussing the sale of the antiques. On the days I don't stop by, you should have Delores order flowers for me."

At that, Ethan cocked an eyebrow. "Seriously?"

"I like flowers, and you want to look thoughtful and attentive, don't you?" she snapped. "Fake marriage or not, I expect to be courted."

"And what do I get out of this again?"

"A wife." A vein stood out on his forehead, and she swore she could see the pulse in his massive neck even at this distance. "And an art gallery." She smiled widely.

The look he shot her was hard enough that she shrank back.

"So," she said, unwilling to let the conversation drift back to sex just quite yet. "Tell me about this successful long-distance relationship that we're modeling our marriage upon."

"What?"

"You said at dinner that you've seen long-distance relationships work quite well. Personally, I've never seen any relationship work well, regardless of distance."

The silence between them grew. In the background, she heard the whistles and buzzers of the game on the TV.

"It's not important," he finally said. "So, fine. We won't exactly be long-distance for the next two weeks. Then we get married. Then what?"

"Oh, I imagine we'll have to keep up appearances for a month or so."

"A *month*?"

"Or so. Ethan," she said patiently. "Do you want this

to be convincing or not? If we stop being seen together the day after we tie the knot, no one will believe it wasn't a publicity stunt."

He jumped out of his chair and began to pace. "See—when I said long-distance, I didn't actually anticipate being in your company constantly."

"Is that a bad thing?" She batted her eyes when he shot her an incredulous look.

"Only if you keep kissing me like you did in the elevator."

"I can kiss you less, but we have to spend time together." She shifted so she was cross-legged on the bed. "Can you do that? At the very least, we have to be friends."

The look he gave her was many things—perhaps angry, horny—but "friendly" was not on the list.

"If you can't, we can still call it off. A night of wild indiscretion, we'll both 'no comment' to the press—it's not a big deal." She shrugged.

"It's a huge deal. If I roll into the Brewery after everyone thinks I had a one-night stand with you and then threw you to the curb, they'll hang me up by my toenails."

"I am rather well liked by the employees," she said, not a little smugly. "Which is why you thought up this plan in the first place, is it not?"

He looked to the ceiling and let out another muttered curse. "Such a good idea," he said again.

"Best laid plans of mice and men and all that," she agreed. "Well?"

He did a little more unproductive pacing, and she let him think. Honestly, she didn't know which way she wanted him to go.

There'd been the heat that had arced between them, heat that had melted her in places that hadn't been properly melted in a very long time. She'd kissed before, but Ethan's mouth against hers—his body against hers—

She needed the money. She needed the fresh start that an angel investor could provide. She needed to feel the power and prestige that went with the Beaumont name—or had, before Ethan had taken over. She needed her life back. And if she got to take the one man who embodied her fall from grace down a couple of pegs, all the better.

It was all at her fingertips. All she had to do was get married to a man she'd promised not to love. How hard could that be? She could probably even have sex with him—and it would be *so* good—without love ever entering into the equation.

"No more kissing in the elevator."

"Agreed." At least, that's what she said. She would be lying if she didn't admit she was enjoying the way she'd so clearly brought him to his knees with desire.

"What do people do in this town on a Sunday afternoon?"

That was a yes. She'd get her funding and make a few headlines and be back on top of the world for a while.

"I'll take it easy on you tomorrow—we need to give the gossip time to develop."

He shot her a look and, for the first time since dinner, smiled. It appeared to be a genuine smile even. It set off his strong chin and deep eyes nicely. Not that she wanted him to know that. "Should I be worried that you know this much about manipulating the press?"

She brushed that comment aside. "It comes with the territory of being a Beaumont. I'll leave after this game is over, and then I'll stop by the office on Monday. Deal?"

"Deal."

They didn't shake on it. Neither of them, it seemed, wanted to tempt fate by touching again.

Seven

"Becky? You're not going to believe this," Frances said as she stood in front of her closet, weighing the red evening gown versus something more…restrained. She hated being restrained, but on her current budget, it was a necessary concession.

"What? Something good?"

Frances grinned. Becky was easily excitable. Frances was pretty sure she could hear her friend bouncing up and down. "Something great. I found an investor."

There was some screaming. Frances held the phone as far away from her face as she could until the noise died down. She flicked through the hangers. She needed something sexy that didn't look as if she was trying too hard. The red gown would definitely be trying too hard for a Monday at the office. "Still with me?"

"Ohmygosh—this is so exciting! How much were they willing to invest?"

Frances braced herself for more screaming. "Up to five."

"Thousand?"

"Million." She immediately jerked the phone away from her head, but there was no sound. She cautiously put it back to her ear. "Becky?"

"I—it—what? I heard you wrong," she said with a nervous laugh. "I thought you said…"

"Million. Five million," Frances repeated, her fingers landing on her one good suit—the Escada. It was a conservative cut—at least by her standards—with a formfitting pencil skirt that went below her knee and a close-cropped jacket with only a little peplum at the waist.

It was the color, however—a warm hot pink—that made her impossible to miss.

Oh—this would be perfect. All business but still dramatic. She pulled it out.

"What—how? *How?*" Frances had never heard Becky this speechless before. "Your brothers?"

Frances laughed. "Oh no—you know Chadwick cut me off after the last debacle. This is a new investor."

There was a pause. "Is he cute?"

Frances scowled—not that Becky could see it, but she did anyway. She did not like being predictable. "No." And that wasn't a lie.

Ethan was *not* cute. He existed in the space between handsome and gorgeous. He wasn't pretty enough to be gorgeous—his features were too rough, too masculine. But handsome—that wasn't right, either. He exuded too much raw sexuality to be handsome.

"Well?" Becky demanded.

"He's…nice."

"Are you sleeping with him?"

"No, it's not like that. In fact, sex isn't even on the table." Her mind oh so helpfully provided a mental picture that completely contradicted that statement. She could see it now—Ethan bending her over a table, yanking her skirt up and her panties down and—

Becky interrupted that thought. "Frannie, I just don't want you to do something stupid."

"I won't," she promised. "But I have a meeting with

him tomorrow morning. How quickly can you revise the business plan to accommodate a five-million-dollar investment?"

"Uh… Let me call you back," Becky said.

"Thanks, Becks." Frances ended the call and fingered the fine wool of her suit. This wasn't stupid, really. This was…marriage with a purpose. And that purpose went far beyond funding an art gallery, although that was one part of it.

This was about putting the Beaumonts back in control of their own destiny. Okay, this was about putting one Beaumont—Frances—back in control of her destiny. But that still counted for a lot. She needed to get over this slump she was in. She needed her name to mean something again. She needed to feel as if she'd done something for the family honor instead of being a deadweight.

Marrying Ethan was the means to a bunch of different ends. That was all.

Those other men who'd proposed, they'd wanted what she represented, too—the Beaumont name, the Beaumont fortune—but they'd never wanted her. Not the real her. They had wanted the illusion of perfection she projected. They wanted her to look good on their arm.

What was different about Ethan? Well, he got points for being up front about his motivations. Nothing couched in sweet words about how special she was or anything. Just a straight-up negotiation. It was refreshing. Really. She didn't want anything sweet that was nothing but a lie. She didn't want him to try and make her love him.

She had not lied. She would not love him.

That was how it had to be.

"Delores," Frances said as she swept into the reception area. "Is Ethan—I mean, Mr. Logan—in?" She tried to blush at the calculated name screw-up, but she wasn't sure she could pull it off.

Delores shot her an unreadable glance over the edge of her glasses. "Had a good weekend, did we?"

Well. That was all the confirmation Frances needed that the stunt she'd pulled back in the hotel had done exactly as she'd intended. People had noticed, and those people were talking. Of course, there'd been some online chatter, but Delores wasn't the kind of woman who existed on social media. If she'd heard about the "date," then it was a safe bet the whole company knew all the gritty details.

"It was lovely." And that part was not calculated at all. Kissing Ethan had, in fact, been quite nice. "He's not all bad, I don't think."

Delores snorted. "Just bad enough?"

"Delores!" This time, her blush was more unplanned. Who knew the older lady had it in her?

"Yes, he's in." Delores's hand hovered near the intercom.

"Oh, don't—I want to surprise him," Frances said.

As she swept open the massive oak door, she heard Delores say, "Oh, we're all surprised," under her breath.

Ethan was sitting at her father's desk, his head bent over his computer. He was in his shirtsleeves, his tie loosened. When she flung the door open, his head popped up. But instead of looking surprised, he looked pleased to see her. "Ah, Frances," he said, rising to his feet.

None of the strain that she'd inflicted on him two days ago showed on his face now. He smiled warmly as he came around the desk to greet her. He did not, she noticed, touch her. Not even a handshake. "I was expecting you at some point today."

Despite the lack of physical contact, his eyes took in her hot-pink suit. She did a little twirl for him, as if she needed his approval when they both knew she didn't. Still, when he murmured, "I'm beginning to think the black dress is the most conservative look you have," she felt her cheeks warm.

For a second, she thought he was going to lean forward and kiss her on the cheek. He didn't. "You would not be wrong." She waltzed over to the leather love seats and spread herself out on one. "So? Heard any of the chatter?"

"I've been working. Is there chatter?"

Frances laughed. "You can be adorably naive. Of course there's chatter. Or did Delores not give you the same look she gave me?"

"Well…" He tugged at his shirt collar, as if it'd suddenly grown a half size too small. "She was almost polite to me this morning. But I didn't know if that was because of us or something else. Maybe she got lucky this weekend."

Unlike some of us. It was the unspoken phrase on the end of that statement that was as loud as if he'd pronounced the words.

She grinned and crossed her legs as best she could in a skirt that tight. "Regardless of Delores's private life, she's aware that we had an intimate dinner. And if Delores is aware of it, the rest of the company is, as well. There were several mentions on the various social media sites and even a teaser in the *Denver Post* online."

His eyes widened. "All of that from one dinner, huh? I am impressed."

She shrugged, as if this were all just another day at the office. Well, for her, it sort of was. "Now we're here."

He notched an eyebrow at her. "And we should be doing…what?"

She slipped the computer out of her bag. "You have a choice. We can discuss art or we can discuss art galleries. I've worked up a prospectus for potential investors."

Ethan let out a bark of laughter. "I've got to stop being surprised by you, don't I?"

"You really do," she agreed demurely. "In all honesty, I'm not that shocking. Not compared to some of my siblings."

"Tell me about them," he said, taking a perfectly safe seat to her right—not within touching distance. "Since we'll be in-laws and all that. Will I get to meet them?"

"It does seem unavoidable." She hadn't really considered the scene where the Beaumonts welcomed Ethan into the family fold with open arms. "I have nine half siblings from my father's four marriages. My older brothers are aware of other illegitimate siblings, but it's not unreasonable that there are more out there." She shrugged, as if that were normal.

Well, it was for her, anyway. Marriages, children, more children—and love had nothing to do with it.

Maybe there'd been a time, back when she was still a little girl who'd twirled in this office, when she'd been naive and innocent and had thought that her father loved her—and her brothers, their mother. That they were a family.

But then there'd been the day... She'd known her parents weren't happy. It was impossible to miss, what with all the screaming, fights, thrown dishes and slammed doors.

And it'd been Donut Friday and she'd been driven to the office with all those boxes and had bounced into the office to see her daddy and found him kissing someone who wasn't her mommy.

She'd stood there, afraid to yell, afraid to not yell—or cry or scream or do something that gave voice to the angry pain that started in her chest and threatened to leak out of her eyes. In the end, she'd done nothing, just like Owen, the driver who'd brought her and was carrying the donuts. Nothing to let her father know how much it hurt to see his betrayal. Nothing to let her mother know that Frances knew now what the fights were about.

But she knew. She couldn't un-know it, either. And

if she called her daddy on it—asked why he was kissing the secretary who'd always been so nice to Frances—she knew her father might put her aside like he'd put her mother aside.

So she said nothing. She showed nothing. She handed out donuts on that day with the biggest, best smile she could manage. Because that's what a Beaumont did. They went on, no matter what.

Just like now. So what if Ethan would eventually have to meet the family? So what if her siblings would react to this marriage with the same mix of shock and horror she'd felt when she'd walked in on her father that cold gray morning so long ago? She would go on—head up, shoulders back, a smile on her face. Her business failed? She couldn't get a job? She'd lost her condo? She'd been reduced to accepting the proposal of a man who only wanted her for her last name?

Didn't matter. Head up, shoulders back, a smile on her face. Just like right now. She called up the prospectus that Becky had put together yesterday in a flurry of excited phone calls and emails. Becky was the brains of the operation, after all—Frances was the one with the connections. And if she could deliver Ethan gift wrapped…

An image of him in nothing but a strategically placed bow popped before her. Christmas might be long gone, but there'd be something special about unwrapping *him* as a present.

She shook that image from her mind and handed the computer over to Ethan. "Our business plan."

He scrolled through it, but she got the distinct feeling he was barely looking at it. "Four wives?"

"Indeed. As you can see, my partner, Rebecca Rosenthal, has mocked up the design for the space as well as a cost-benefit analysis." She leaned over to click on the next tab. "Here's a sampling of the promotion we have planned."

"Ten siblings? Where do you fall in that?"

"I'm fifth." For some reason, she didn't want to talk about her family.

Detailing her father's affairs and indiscretions in this, his former office, felt wrong. This was where he'd been a good father to her. Even after she'd walked in on him cheating with his secretary, when she hadn't thrown a fit and hadn't tattled on him, he'd still doted on her when she was here. The next Donut Friday, she remembered, he'd had a pretty necklace waiting for her, and once again she'd been Daddy's girl for a few special minutes each week.

She didn't want to sully those memories. "Chadwick and Phillip with my father's first wife, Matthew and then Byron and me—we're twins—with his second wife." She hated referring to her mother by that number, as if that's all Jeannie had contributed. Wife number two, children three, four and five.

"You have a twin?" Ethan cut in.

"Yes." She gave him humorous look. "He's very protective of me." She did not mention that Byron was busy with his new wife and son. Better to let him worry about how her four older brothers would deal with him if he crossed a line.

Ethan's eyebrows jumped up. "And there were five more?"

"Yup. Lucy and Harry with my father's third wife. Johnny, Toni and Mark with his fourth. The younger ones are in their early twenties, for the most part. Toni and Mark are still in college and, along with Johnny, they all still live at the Beaumont mansion with Chadwick and his family." She rattled off her younger siblings' names as if they were items to be checked off a list.

"That must have been…interesting, growing up in that household."

"You have no idea." She made light of it, but *interesting* didn't begin to cover it.

She and Byron had been in an odd position in the household, straddling the line between the first generation of Hardwick Beaumont's sons and the last. Being five years older than she and Byron, Matthew was Chadwick and Phillip's contemporary. And since Matthew was their full brother, Byron and Frances had grown closer to the two older Beaumont brothers.

But then, her first stepmother—May, the not-evil one—had harbored delusional fantasies about how Frances and May's daughter, Lucy, would be the very best of friends, a period of time that painfully involved matching outfits for ten-year-old Frances and three-year-old Lucy. Which had done the exact opposite of what May intended—Lucy couldn't stand the sight of Frances. The feeling was mutual.

And the youngest ones—well, they'd been practically babies when Frances was a teenager. She barely knew them.

They were all Beaumonts, and, by default, that meant they were all family.

"What about you? Any strings of siblings floating around?"

Ethan shook his head. "One younger brother. No stepparents. It was a pretty normal life." Something in the way he said it didn't ring true, though.

No stepparents? What an odd way to phrase it. "Are you close? With your family, I mean." He didn't answer right away, so she added, "Since they'll be my in-laws, too."

"We keep in touch. I imagine the worst-case scenario is that my mother shows up to visit."

We keep in touch. What was it he'd said, about long-distance relationships working?

It was his turn to change the subject before she could

drill for more information. "You weren't kidding about an art gallery, were you?"

"I am *highly* qualified," she repeated. This time, her smile was more genuine. "We envision a grand space with enough room to highlight sculpture and nontraditional media, as well as hosting parties. As you can see, a five-million-dollar investment will practically guarantee success. I think that, as a grand opening, it would be ideal to host a showing of the antiques in this room. I don't want to auction off these pieces. Too impersonal."

He ignored the last part and focused instead on the one part Frances would have preferred to gloss over. "Practically?" He glanced at her. "What kind of track record do you have with these types of ventures?"

Frances cleared her throat as she uncrossed and re-crossed her legs before leaning toward Ethan. Her distraction didn't work this time. At least, not as well. His gaze only lingered on her legs for a few seconds. "This is a more conservative investment than my last ventures," she said smoothly. "Plus, Rebecca is going to be handling more of the business side of the gallery—that's her strong suit."

"You're saying you won't be in charge? That doesn't seem like you."

"Any good businesswoman knows her limitations and how to compensate for them."

His lips quirked up into a smile. "Indeed."

There was a knock at the door. "Come in," Ethan said. Frances didn't change her position. She wasn't exactly sitting in Ethan's lap, but her posture indicated that they were engaged in a personal discussion.

The door opened and what looked like two-dozen red roses walked into the room. "The flowers you ordered, Mr. Logan." Delores's voice came from behind the blooms. "Where should I put them?"

"On the table here." He motioned toward the coffee

table, but Delores couldn't see through that many blooms, so she put them on the conference table instead.

"That's a lot of roses," Frances said in shock.

Delores fished the card out of the arrangement and carried it over to her. "For you, dear," she said with a knowing smile.

"That'll be all, Delores. Thank you," Ethan said. But he was looking at Frances as he said it.

Delores smirked and was gone. Ethan stood and carried the roses over to the coffee table while Frances read the note.

Fran—here's to more beautiful evenings with a beautiful woman—E.

It hadn't been in an envelope. Delores had read it, no doubt. It was thoughtful and sweet, and Frances hadn't expected it at all.

With a sinking feeling in her stomach, Frances realized she might have underestimated Ethan.

"Well?" Ethan said. He sounded pleased with himself.

"Don't call me Fran," she snapped. Or she tried to. It came out more as a breathless whisper.

"What should I call you? It seems like a pet name would be the thing. Snoogums?"

She shot him a look. "I thought I said you should send me flowers when I didn't come to the office. Not when I was already here."

"I always send flowers after a great first date with a beautiful woman," he replied. He sounded sincere about it, which did not entirely jibe with the way he'd acted after she'd left him hanging.

In all honesty, it did sound sweet, as if the time they'd spent together had been a real date. But did that matter?

So what if this was a thoughtful gesture? So what if it

meant he'd been paying attention to her when she'd said she liked flowers and she expected to be courted? So what if the roses were gorgeous? It didn't change the fact that, at its core, this was still a business transaction. "It wasn't a great date. You didn't even get lucky."

He didn't look offended at this statement. "I'm going to marry you. Isn't that lucky enough?"

"Save it for when we're in public." But as she said it, she buried her nose in the roses. The heady fragrance was her favorite.

It'd been a while since anyone had sent her flowers. There was a small part of her that was more than a little flattered. It was a grand gesture—or it would have been, if it'd been sincere.

Honest? Yes. Ethan was being honest with her. He'd been totally up front about the reasons behind his interest in her.

But his attention wasn't sincere. These were, if possible, the most insincere roses ever. Just all part of the game— and she had to admit, he was playing his part well.

The thought made her sadder than she'd thought it might. Which was ridiculous. Sincerity was just another form of weakness that people could use to exploit you. Her mother had sincerely loved her father, and see where that had gotten her? Nowhere good.

The corners of Ethan's eyes crinkled, as if her less-than-gracious response amused him. "Fine. Speaking of, when would you like to be seen together in public again?"

"Tomorrow night. Mondays are not the most social day of the week. I think the roses today will accomplish everything we want them to."

"Dinner? Or did you have something else in mind?"

Did he sound hopeful? "Dinner is good for now. I'm keeping my eyes open for an appropriate activity this weekend."

He nodded, as if she'd announced that the sales projections for the quarter were on target. But then he stood and handed her computer back to her. As he did so, he leaned down and whispered, "I'm glad you liked the roses," in her ear. And, damn it all, heat flushed her body.

She tilted her head up to him. "They're beautiful," she murmured. There was no audience for this, no crowd to guess and gossip. Here, in the safety of this office, there was only him and her and dozens of honest roses.

He was close enough to kiss—more than close enough. She could see the golden tint to his brown eyes that made them lighter, warmer. He had a faint scar on the edge of his nose and another one on his chin. Football injuries or brawls? He had the body of a brawler. She'd felt that for herself the other night.

Ethan Logan was a big, strong man with big, strong muscles. And he'd sent her flowers.

She could kiss him. Not for show but for herself. She was going to marry him, after all. Shouldn't she get something out of it? Something beyond an art gallery and a restored sense of family pride?

His fingers slid under her chin, lifting her face to his. His breath was warm on her cheeks. Many things were warm at this point.

Not for the Beaumonts. Not for the gallery. Just for her. Ethan was just for *her*.

They held that pose as Frances danced right up to the line of kissing Ethan because she wanted to. But she didn't cross it. And after a moment, he relinquished his hold on her. But the warmth in his eyes didn't dim. He didn't act as if she'd rejected him.

Instead, he said, "You're welcome."

And that?

That was sincere.

Oh, hell.

Eight

First thing Tuesday morning, Ethan had Delores order lilies and send them to Frances. Roses every day felt too clichéd and he'd always liked lilies, anyway.

"Any message?" the old battle-ax asked. She sounded smug.

Ethan considered. The message, he knew, was as much for Delores's loose lips as it was for Frances. And no matter what Frances said, they needed pet names for each other. "Red—until tonight. E."

Delores snorted. "Will do, boss. By the way…"

Ethan paused, his hand on the intercom switch. *Boss?* That was the most receptionist-like thing Delores had said to him yet. "Yes?"

"The latest attendance reports are in. We're operating at full capacity today."

A sense of victory flowed through him. After four days, the implied Beaumont Seal of Approval was already working its magic. "I'm glad to hear it."

He switched off the intercom and stared at it for a moment. But instead of thinking about his next restructuring move, his thoughts drifted back to Frances.

She was going to kill him for the Red bit; he was reasonably confident about that. But there'd been that moment yesterday where he'd thought all her pretense had fallen away. She'd been well and truly stunned that he'd had flowers delivered for her. And in that moment, she'd seemed...vulnerable. All of her cynical world-weariness had fallen away, and she'd been a beautiful woman who'd appreciated a small gesture he'd made for her.

Marriage notwithstanding, she wasn't looking for anything long term. Neither was he. But that didn't mean the short term couldn't mean *something*, did it? He didn't need the fire to burn for long. He just needed it to burn bright.

He flipped the intercom back on. "Delores? Did you place that order yet?"

He heard her murmur something that sounded like, "One moment," before she said more clearly, "in process. Why?"

"I want to change the message. Red—" Then he faltered. "Looking forward to tonight. Yours, E." Which was not exactly a big change and he felt a little foolish for making it. He switched off the intercom again.

His phone rang. It was his partner at CRS, Finn Jackson. Finn was the one who pitched CRS to conglomerates. He was a hell of a salesman. "What's up?"

"Just wanted to let you know—there's activity," Finn began without any further introduction. "A private holding company is making noise about AllBev's handling of the Beaumont Brewery purchase."

Ethan frowned. "Link?"

"On its way." Seconds later, the email with the link popped up. Ethan scanned the article. Thankfully, it wasn't an attack on CRS's handling of the transition. However, this private holdings company, ZOLA, had written a letter stating that the Brewery was a poor strategic purchase for AllBev and they should dump the company—preferably on the cheap, no doubt.

"What is this?" he asked Finn. "A takeover bid? Is it the Beaumonts?"

"I don't think so," Finn replied, but he didn't sound convinced. "It's owned by someone named Zeb Richards—ring any bells for you?"

"None. How does this impact us?"

"This mostly appears to be an activist shareholder making noise. I'll keep tabs on AllBev's reaction, but I don't think this impacts you at the moment. I just wanted to keep you aware of the situation." Finn cleared his throat, which was his great tell. "You could ask your father if he knows anything."

Ethan didn't say a damned thing. His father? *Hell no.* He would never show the slightest sign of weakness to his old man because, unlike the Beaumonts, family meant nothing to Troy Logan. It never had, it never would.

"Or," Finn finally said, dragging out the word, "you could maybe see if anyone on the ground knows anything about this Zeb character?"

Frances. "Yeah, I can ask around. If you hear anything else, let me know. I'd prefer for the company not to be resold until we've fulfilled our contract. It'd look like a failure on the behalf of CRS—that we couldn't turn the company around fast enough."

"Agreed." With that, Finn hung up.

Ethan stared at his computer without seeing the files. He was just starting to get a grip on this company, thanks to Frances.

This ZOLA, whatever the hell it was, *felt* like it had something to do with the Beaumonts. Who else cared about this beer company? Ethan did a quick search. Privately held firm located in New York, a list of their successful investments—but not much else. Not even a picture of Zeb Richards. Something about it was off. This could easily be a shell corporation set up with the express purpose of wrestling the Brewery away from AllBev and back into Beaumont hands.

Luckily, Ethan happened to have excellent connections here on the ground. He'd have to tread carefully, though.

He needed Frances Beaumont. The production lines at full capacity today? That wasn't his keen management skills in action, as painful as it was to admit. That was all Frances.

But on the other hand…her sudden appearance happening so closely to this ZOLA business? It couldn't be a coincidence, could it?

Maybe it was; maybe it wasn't. One thing was for sure. He was going to find out *before* he married her and *before* he cut her a huge investment check.

He sent a follow-up message to his lawyers about protecting his assets and then glanced over Frances's art gallery plans again. He knew nothing about art, which was surprising, considering his mother was the living embodiment of "artsy-fartsy." So as an art space, it didn't mean much to him. But as a business investment?

It wasn't that he couldn't spot her the five million. He had that and much more in the bank—and that didn't count his golden-parachute bonuses and stock options. Restructuring corporations was a job that paid extremely well. It just felt…

Too familiar. Like he was hell-bent on replicating his parents' unorthodox marriage. And that wasn't what he wanted.

He pushed the thoughts of his all-business father and flighty mother out of his brain. He had a company to run, a private equity firm to investigate and a woman to woo, if people still did that. And above all that, tonight he had a date.

This really wasn't that different from what he normally did, Ethan told himself as he waited at the bar of some hip restaurant. He rolled into a new town, met a woman and did the wining-and-dining thing. He saw the sights, had a little fun and then, when it was time, he moved on. This was standard stuff for him.

Which did not explain why he was sipping his gin and tonic with a little more enthusiasm than the drink required. He was just…bracing himself for another evening of sexual frustration, that was all. Because he knew that, no matter what she was wearing tonight, he wouldn't be able to take his eyes off Frances.

Maybe it wouldn't be so bad if she were just another pretty face. But she wasn't. He'd have to sit there and look at her and then also be verbally pummeled by her sharp wit as she ran circles around him. She challenged him and pushed him to his very limits of self-control, and that was something he could honestly say didn't happen much. Oh, the women he'd seen in the past were all perfectly intelligent ladies, but they didn't see their role of temporary companion as one that included the kind of conversation that bordered on warfare.

But Frances? She was armed like a Sherman tank, and she had excellent aim. She knew how to take him out with a few well-chosen words and a tilt of her head. He was practically defenseless against her.

His only consolation—aside from her company—was that he'd managed to slip past her armor a few times.

Then Frances was there, framed by the doorway. She had on a thick white coat with a fur collar that was belted tightly at the waist and a pair of calf-high boots in supple brown leather. Her hair was swept into an elegant updo and—Ethan blinked. Did she have flowers in her hair? Lilies?

Perhaps the rest of the restaurant was pondering the same question because he would have sworn the whole place paused to note her arrival.

She spotted him and favored him with a small personal

smile. Then she undid the belt of her coat and let it fall off her shoulders.

This wasn't normal, the way he reacted to what had to be the calculated revelation of her body. Hell, it wasn't even that much of a reveal—she had on a slim brown skirt and a cream-colored sweater. The sweater had a sweetheart neckline and long sleeves. Nothing overtly sexual about her appearance tonight.

She was just a gorgeous woman. And she was headed right for him. The restaurant was so quiet he could hear the click of her heels on the parquet flooring as she crossed to the bar.

He couldn't take his eyes off her.

What if things were different? What if they'd met on different terms—him not trying to reconstruct her family's former company, her not desperate for an angel investor? Would he have pursued her? Well, that was a stupid question—of course he would have. She was not just a feast for the eyes. She was quite possibly the smartest woman he'd ever gone head-to-head with. He couldn't believe it, but he was actually looking forward to being demolished by her again tonight. Blue balls be damned.

He rose and greeted her. "Frances."

She leaned up on her tiptoes and kissed his cheek. "What," she murmured against his skin. "Not Red?"

He turned his head slightly to respond but just kissed her instead. He kissed her like he'd wanted to kiss her in his office the other day. The taste of her lips burned his mouth like those cinnamon candies his mother preferred—hot but sweet. And good. *So* good. He couldn't get enough of her.

And that was a problem. It was quickly becoming *the* problem. He was having trouble going a day or two without touching her. How was he supposed to make it a year in a sexless marriage?

She pulled away, and he let her. "Still trying to find the right name for you," he replied, hoping that how much she affected him didn't show.

"Keep trying." She cocked her head to one side. "Shall we?"

Ethan signaled for the hostess, who led them back to their private table. "How was your day, darling?" Frances asked in an offhand way as she accepted the menu.

The casual nature of the question—or, more specifically, the lack of sexual innuendo—caught him off guard. "Fine, actually. The production lines were producing today." She looked at him over the edge of her menu, one eyebrow raised. "And, yes," he said, answering the unspoken question. "I give you all the credit for that."

He wanted to ask about ZOLA and Zeb Richards, but he didn't. Maybe after they'd eaten—and shared a bottle of wine. "How about you?"

They were interrupted by the waitress, so it wasn't until after they'd placed their orders that she answered. "Good. We met with the Realtors about the space. Becky's very excited about owning the space instead of renting."

Ah, yes. The money he owed her. "Have you been monitoring the chatter, as you put it?"

At that, she leaned forward, a winning smile on her face. Ethan didn't like it. It wasn't real or true. It was a piece of armor, a shield in this game they were playing. She wasn't smiling for him. She was smiling for everyone else. "So far, so good," she purred, even though there was no one else who could have heard her. "I think this weekend, we should attend a Nuggets game."

He dimly remembered her watching a basketball game on Saturday when she'd been pointedly not sleeping with him. "Big fan?"

"Not really," she replied with a casual shrug. "But sports

fans drink a lot of beer. It'd signal our involvement to a different crowd and boost the chatter significantly."

All of that sounded fine in a cold, calculated kind of way. He found he didn't much care for the cold right now. He craved her heat.

It was his turn to lean forward. "And after that? I seem to recall you saying something about how you were going to start sleeping over this weekend. Of course, you're always welcome to do so sooner."

That shield of a smile fell away, and he knew he'd slipped past her defenses again. But the moment was short. She tilted her head to one side and gave him an appraising look. "Trying to change the terms of our deal again? For shame, Ethan."

"Are you coming back to the room with me tonight?"

"Of course." Her voice didn't change, but he thought he saw her cheeks pink up ever so slightly.

"Are you going to kiss me in the lobby again?"

Yes, she was definitely blushing. But it was her only tell. "I suppose you could always kiss me first. Just for a little variety."

Oh, he'd love to show her some variety. "And the elevator?"

"You *are* trying to change the terms," she murmured as she dropped her gaze. "We discussed that—at your request. There's no kissing in elevators."

He didn't respond. At the time, it'd seemed like the shortest path to self-preservation. But now? Now he wanted to push the envelope. He wanted to see if he could get to her like she was getting to him. "I like what you've done with the lily," he said, nodding toward where she'd worked the bloom into her hair. Because thus far, the flowers were by far the best way to get to her.

There was always a chance that she wasn't all that attracted to him—that the heat he felt when he was around her was a one-way street.

Damn, that was a depressing thought.

"They were beautiful," she said. And it could have easily been another too-smooth line.

But it wasn't.

"Not as beautiful as you are."

Before she could respond to that their food arrived. They ate and drank and made polite small talk disguised as sensual flirting.

"After the game, we'll have to deal with my family," she warned him over the lip of her second glass of wine after she'd pushed her plate away. "I'm actually surprised that my brother Matthew hasn't called to lecture me about the Beaumont family name."

Ethan was wrapped in the warm buzz of his alcohol. "Oh? That a problem?"

Frances waved her hand. "He's the micromanager of our public image. Was VP of marketing before you showed up. He did a great job, too."

She didn't say it as if she was intentionally trying to score a hit, but he felt a little wounded anyway. "I didn't fire him. He was gone before I got there."

"Oh, I know." She took another drink. "He left with Chadwick."

Ethan was pondering this information when someone said, "Frannie?"

At the name, Frances's eyes widened, and she sat bolt upright. She looked over Ethan's shoulder and said, "Phillip?"

Phillip? Oh, right. He remembered now. Phillip was one of her half brothers.

Oh, hell. Ethan was one sheet to the wind and about to meet a Beaumont.

Frances stood as a strikingly blond man came around

the table. He was holding the hand of a tall, athletic woman wearing blue jeans. "Phillip! Jo! I didn't expect to see you guys here."

Phillip kissed his sister on the cheek. "We decided it was time for our once-a-month dinner date." As the woman named Jo hugged Frances, Phillip turned a gaze that was surprisingly friendly toward Ethan. "I'm Phillip Beaumont. And you are?" He stuck out his hand.

Ethan glanced at Frances, only to find that both she and Jo were watching this interaction with curiosity. "I'm Ethan Logan," Ethan said, giving Phillip's hand a firm shake.

He tried to pull his hand back, but it didn't go anywhere. "Ah," Phillip said. His smile grew—at the same time he clamped down on Ethan's hand. "You're running the Brewery these days."

The strength with which Phillip had a hold on him was more than Ethan would have given him credit for. Ethan would have anticipated her brother to be someone pampered and posh and not particularly physically intimidating. But Phillip's grip spoke of a man who worked with his hands for a living—and wasn't afraid to use them for other purposes.

"Phillip manages the Beaumont Farm," Frances said, her voice slightly louder than necessary. Ah, that explained it. "He raises the Percherons. And this is Jo, his wife. She trains horses."

It was only then that Phillip let go of Ethan so Ethan could give Jo's hand a quick shake. "A pleasure, Ms. Beaumont."

To his surprise, Jo said, "Is it?" with the kind of smile that made no pretense of being polite. But she linked arms with Phillip and physically pulled him a step away.

"Would you like to join us?" Ethan offered, because it seemed like the sociable thing to do and also because he absolutely did not want Phillip Beaumont to catch a hint of fear. Ethan would act as though having his hot date with Frances suddenly crashed by an obviously overprotective older brother was the highlight of his night if it killed him.

And given the look on Phillip's face, it just might.

"No," Jo said. "That's all right. You both look like you're finishing up, anyway."

Phillip said, "Frannie, can I talk with you—in private?"

That was a dismissal if Ethan had ever heard one. "I'll be right back," he genially offered. This called for a tactical retreat to the men's room. "If you'll excuse me," he added to Frances.

"Of course," she murmured, nodding her head in appreciation.

As Ethan walked away, he heard nothing but chilly silence.

"What are you doing?" Phillip didn't so much say the words as hiss them. His fun-times smile never wavered, though.

In that moment Phillip sounded more like stuck-up Matthew than her formerly wild older brother. "I'm on a date. Same as you."

Beside her, Jo snorted. But she didn't say anything. She just watched. Sometimes—and not that Frances would ever tell her sister-in-law this—Jo kind of freaked her out. She was so quiet, so watchful. Not at all the kind of woman Frances had envisioned with Phillip.

Which was not a complaint. Phillip was sober now and, with Jo beside him, almost a new man.

A new man who'd tasked himself with making sure Frances toed the family line. *Ugh*.

"With the man who's running the Brewery? Are you drunk?"

"That is *such* a laugh riot, coming from you," she stiffly

replied. She felt Jo tense beside her. "Sorry." But she said it to Jo. Not to Phillip. "But no, thanks for asking, I'm not drunk. I'm not insane, and, just to head you off at the pass, I'm not stupid. I know exactly who he is, and I know exactly what I'm doing."

Phillip glared at her. "Which is *what*, exactly?"

"None of your business." She made damn sure to say it with her very best smile.

Phillip was not swayed. "Frannie, I don't know what you think you're doing here—either you're completely clueless and setting yourself up for yet another failure or—"

"And thank you for that overwhelming vote of confidence," she hissed at him, her best smile cracking unnaturally. "I liked you better when you were drunk. At least then you didn't assume I was an idiot like everyone else does."

"Or," Phillip went on, refusing to be sidetracked by her attack, "you think you're going to accomplish something at the Brewery." He paused, and when Frances didn't respond immediately to that spot-on accusation, his eyes widened. "What on earth do you think you're doing?"

"I don't see what it matters to you. You don't drink beer. You don't work at any brewery, old or new. You've got the farm, and you've got Jo. You don't need anything." He had his happy life now. He couldn't begrudge her this.

Phillip did grab her then, wrapping his hand around her upper arm. "Frannie—corporate espionage?"

"I'm just trying to restore the Beaumont name. You may not remember it, but our name used to mean something. And we lost that."

Unexpectedly, Phillip's face softened. "We didn't lose anything. We're still Beaumonts. You can't go back—why would you even want to? Things are better now."

If that wasn't the most condescending thing Phillip had

ever said to her, she didn't know what was. "Better for who? Not for me."

He was undaunted, damn him. "We've moved on—we *all* have. Chadwick and Matthew have their new business. Byron's back and happy. Even the younger kids are doing okay. None of us want the Brewery back, honey. If that's what you're trying to do here..."

A rush of emotions Frances couldn't name threatened to swamp her. It was what she wanted, but it wasn't. This was about *her*. She wanted Frances Beaumont back.

She turned to Jo, who'd been watching the entire exchange with unblinking eyes. "I'm sorry if this interrupted your night out. Ethan and I were almost done anyway."

"It's not a problem," Jo said. Frances couldn't tell if Jo was saying it to her husband or to Frances. Jo then slid her arm through Phillip's. "Let it be, babe."

Phillip gave his wife an apologetic look. "My apologies. I'm just surprised. I'd have thought..."

She knew what Phillip would have thought—and she knew what Chadwick and Matthew and even Byron would all be thinking, just as fast as Phillip could text them. Another Frances misadventure. "Trust me, okay?"

Phillip's gaze cut back over her shoulder. Even without looking, Frances could tell Ethan had returned. She could *feel* his presence. Warm prickles raised the hairs on the back of her neck as he approached.

Then his arm slid around her waist in an act that could only be described as possessive. Phillip didn't miss it, curse his clean-and-sober eyes. "Well. Logan, a pleasure to meet you. Frances..."

She could hear the unspoken *be careful* in his tone. She gave Jo another quick hug and Phillip a kiss on the cheek. Ethan's hand stayed on her lower back. "I'll come out soon," she promised, as if that was what their little chat had been about.

Phillip smirked at the dodge. But he didn't say anything else. He and Jo moved off to their own table.

"Everything okay?" Ethan said. His arm was firmly back around her waist and she wanted nothing more than to lean into him.

"Oh, sure." It wasn't a lie, but it wasn't the whole truth. For someone who'd been playing a game calculated on public recognition, Frances suddenly felt overexposed.

Ethan's fingertips tightened against her side, pulling her closer against his chest. "Do you want to go?"

"Yes."

Ethan let go of her long enough to fish several hundred-dollar bills out of his wallet, and then they were walking toward the front. He held her coat for her before he slid his own back on. Frances could feel the weight of Phillip's gaze from all the way across the room.

Why did she feel so…weird? It wasn't what Phillip thought. She wasn't being naive about this. She wasn't betraying the family name—she was rescuing it, damn it. She was keeping her friends—and family—close and her enemies closer, by God. That's all this was. There was nothing else to it.

Except…except for the way Ethan wrapped his strong arm around her and hugged her close as they walked out of the restaurant and into the bitterly cold night air. As they walked from the not-crowded sidewalk to the nearly empty parking lot, where he had parked a sleek Jaguar, he held her tighter still. He opened her door for her and then started the car.

But he didn't press. He didn't have to. All he did was reach over and take her hand in his.

When they arrived at the hotel, Ethan gave the keys to the valet, who greeted them both by name. They walked into the lobby, and this time, she did rest her head on his shoulder.

She shouldn't feel weird, now that someone in the family was aware of her...independent interests. Especially since it was Phillip, the former playboy of the family. She didn't need their approval, and she didn't want it.

But...she felt suddenly adrift. And what made it worse? Ethan could tell.

They didn't stop in the middle of the lobby and engage in heavy petting as planned. Instead, he walked her over to the elevator. While they waited, he lifted her chin with one gloved hand and kissed her.

Damn him, she thought even as she sighed into his arms. Damn Ethan all to hell for being exactly who he was—strong and tough and good at the game, but also honest and sincere and thoughtful.

She did not believe in love. She struggled with believing in *like*. Infatuation, yes—she knew that existed. And lust. Those entanglements that burned hot and fast and then fizzled out.

So no, this was not love. Not now, not ever. This was merely...fondness. She could be fond of Ethan, and he could return the sentiment. Perhaps they could even be friends. Wouldn't that be novel, being friends with her soon-to-be-ex husband?

The elevator doors pinged open, and he broke the kiss. "Shall we go up?" he whispered, his gaze never leaving hers as his fingers stroked her cheek. Why did he have to be like this? Why did he have to make her think he could care for her?

Why did he make her want to care for him?

"Yes," she said, her voice shaky. "Yes, let's."

They stepped onto the elevator.

The doors closed behind them.

Nine

Before she could sag back against the wall of the elevator, Ethan had folded her into his arms in what could only be described as a hug.

She sank into his broad and warm and firm chest. When was the last time she'd been hugged? Not counting when she went to visit her mother. Men wanted many things from her—sex, notoriety, sex, a crack at the Beaumont fortune and, finally, sex. But never something as simple as a hug, especially one seemingly without conditions or expectations.

"I'm fine," she tried to say, but her words were muffled by all his muscles.

His chest moved, as if he'd chuckled. "I'm sure you are. You are, without a doubt, the toughest woman I know."

Against her wishes, she relaxed into his embrace as they rode up and up and up. "You're just saying that."

"No, I'm not." He loosened his hold on her enough to look her in the eyes. "I'm serious. You've got some of the toughest, most effective armor I've ever seen a woman wear, and you hardly ever expose a chink."

Something stung at her eyes. She ignored it. "Save it for when we have an audience, Ethan."

Something hard flashed over his eyes. "I'm not saying this for the general public, Frances. I'm saying it because it's the truth." He traced his fingertips—still gloved—down the side of her face. "This isn't part of the game."

Her breath caught in her throat.

"But every so often," he went on, as if stunning her speechless was just par for the course, "something slips past that armor." She was not going to lean into his touch. Any more than she already had, that was. "It's subtle, but I can tell. You weren't ready for your brother just then. God knows I wasn't, either." His lips—lips she'd kissed—quirked into a smile. "I'd have loved to see what you'd done with him if you'd been primed for the battle."

"It's different when it's family," she managed to get out in a breathy whisper. "You have to love them even when they think you're making a huge fool of yourself."

She felt his body tense against hers. "Is that what he told you?"

"No, no—Phillip has far more tact than that," she told him. "But I don't think he approves."

The elevator slowed, and then the doors opened on Ethan's floor. Ethan didn't make a move to exit. "Does that bother you?"

She sighed. "Come on." It took more effort than she might have guessed to pull herself out of his arms, but when she held out her hand, he took it. They walked down the long hall like that, hand in hand. She waited while he got the door unlocked, and then they stepped inside.

This time, though, she didn't make a move for the remote. She just stood in the middle of his suite—the suite that she would be spending more and more time in. Spending the night in—until they got married. Then what? They'd have to get an apartment, wouldn't they? She couldn't live in a hotel suite. Not for a year. And she couldn't see moving Ethan into the Beaumont mansion with her. Just trying to picture that made her shudder in horror.

Good God, she was going to marry this man. In…a week and a half.

Ethan stepped up behind her and slid his hands around her waist. He'd shucked his gloves and coat, she saw as his fingers undid the belt at her waist. Then he removed her coat for her.

This wasn't an act. Or was it? He could still be working an angle, one in which his interests would best be served by making her think he was really a decent man, a good human being. It was possible. He could be looking to pump more information out of her. Looking to take another big chunk of power or money away from the Beaumonts. He could be building her up to drop her like a rock and put her in her place—especially after the stunt she'd pulled with Donut Friday.

Then his arms were around her again, pulling her back into him. "Does it bother you?" he asked again. "That they won't approve of this. Of us."

"They rarely approve of anything I do—but don't worry," she hurried to add, trying to speak over the catch in her voice. "The feeling is often mutual. Disapproval is the glue that holds the Beaumonts together." She tried to say it as if it were just a comical fact of nature—because it was.

But she felt so odd, so not normal, that it didn't come out that way.

"Is he your favorite brother? Other than your twin, I mean."

"Yes. Phillip threw the best parties and snuck me beers and…we were friends, I guess. We could do anything together, and he never judged me. But he's been sober for a while now. His wife helps."

"So he's not the same brother you knew." Ethan pulled the lily out of her hair and set it on the side table. Half of her hair fell out of the twist, and he used his fingers to unravel the rest.

"No, I guess not. But then, nothing stays the same. The only thing that never changes is change itself, right?"

She knew that better than anyone. Wasn't that how she'd been raised? There were no constants, no guarantees. Only the family name would endure.

Right up until it, too, had stopped meaning what it always had.

Unexpectedly, Ethan pressed his lips against her neck. "Take off your shoes," he ordered against her skin.

She did as he said, although she didn't know why. The old Frances wouldn't have followed an order from an admirer.

Maybe, an insidious little voice in the back of her head whispered, *maybe you aren't the same old Frances anymore*. And this quest, or whatever she wanted to call it, to undermine Ethan and strike a blow against the new owners of her family's brewery—all of that was to make her feel like the old Frances again. Even the art gallery was a step back to a place where she'd been more secure.

What if she couldn't go back there? What if she would never again be the redheaded golden girl of Denver? Of the Brewery? Of her family?

Ethan relinquished his hold on her long enough to peel back the comforter from the bed. Then he guided her down. "Scoot," he told her, climbing in after her.

She would have never done so, not back when she was at the top of her form. She would have demanded high seduction or nothing at all. Champagne. Wild promises. Diamonds and gems. Not this *fondness*, for God's sake.

He pulled the covers over them and wrapped his arm around her shoulder. She curled into his side, feeling warmer and safer by the moment. For some reason, it was what she needed. To feel safe from the winds of change that had blown away her prospects and her personal fortune. In Ethan's arms, she could almost pretend none of it had happened. She could almost pretend this was normal.

"What about you?" she asked, pressing her hand against his chest.

He covered her hand with his. Warm. Safe. "What about me?"

"You must be used to change. A new company and a new hotel in a new city every other month?" She curled her fingers into the crisp cotton of his shirt. "I guess change doesn't bother you at all."

"It doesn't feel like that," he said. "It's the same thing every time, with slightly different scenery. Hotel rooms all blend together, executive offices all look the same…"

"Even the women?"

The pause was long. "Yes, I guess you could say that. Even the women were all very similar. Beautiful, good conversationalists, cultured." He began to stroke her hair. "Until this time."

"This time?" Something sparked in her chest, something that didn't feel cynical or calculated. She didn't recognize what it was.

"The hotel is basically the same. But the company? I usually spend three to six months restructuring. I've already been here for three months and I've barely made any headway. The executive office—hell, the whole Brewery—is unlike any place I've ever worked before. It's not a sterile office building that's got the same carpeting and the same crappy furniture as every other office. It's like it's this…*thing* that lives and breathes on its own. It's not just real estate. It's alive."

"It's always been that way," she agreed, but she wasn't thinking about the Brewery or the antique furniture or the people who'd made it a second home to her.

She was thinking about the man next to her, the one

who'd just told her that women were as interchangeable as hotel rooms. Which was a cold, soulless thing to admit and also totally didn't match up with the way he was holding her.

"And?"

"And…" His voice trailed off as he wrapped his fingers more tightly around hers.

She swallowed. "The woman?"

For some reason, she needed to know that she wasn't like all the rest.

Please, she thought, *please say something I can believe. Something real and honest and sincere, even if it kills me.*

"The woman," he said, lifting her hand away from his chest and pressing a kiss to her palm, "the woman is unlike any other. Beautiful, a great conversationalist, highly cultured—but there's something else about her. Something that runs deeper."

Frances realized she was holding her breath, so she made herself breathe normally. Or as close to normal as she could get, what with her heart pounding as fast as it was. "You make her sound like a river."

"Then I'm not doing a very good job," he said with a chuckle. "I'm not used to whispering sweet nothings."

"They're not nothing." Her voice felt as if it were coming from somewhere far away.

His hand trailed down from her hair to her back, where he rubbed her in long, even strokes. "Neither are you."

She wasn't, was she? She was still Frances. Hell, in a few weeks, she wouldn't even be a Beaumont anymore. She'd be a Logan. And then after that… Well, nothing stayed the same, after all.

"We can call it off," he said, as if he'd been reading her mind.

She pushed herself up and stared down at him. *"What?"* Was he serious?

Or was this the real, honest, true thing she'd asked for? Because if this was it, she took it back.

"Nothing official has changed hands. No legal commitments have been made." She saw him swallow. He stared up at her with such seriousness that she almost panicked because the look on his face went so far beyond fond that she didn't know what to do. "If you want."

She sat all the way up, pushing herself out of what had been the safe shelter of his arms. She sat back on her heels, only vaguely aware that her skirt had twisted itself around her waist. "No. No! We can't end this!"

"Why not? Relationships end all the time. We had a couple of red-hot dates and it went nowhere." He tilted his head to the side. "We just walk away. No harm, no foul."

"*Just* walk away? We can't. *I* can't." Because that was the heart of the matter, wasn't it? She couldn't back out of this deal now. This was her ticket back to her old life, or some reasonable facsimile thereof. With Ethan's angel investment, she could get the gallery off the ground, she could get a new apartment and move out of the Beaumont mansion. She could go back to being Frances Beaumont.

He sat up, which brought their bodies into close proximity again. She didn't like being this aware of him. She didn't like the fact that she wanted to know what he'd look like without the shirt. She didn't want to like him. Not even a little.

He reached over and stroked her hair tenderly. She didn't want tenderness, damn it. She didn't want feelings. She wanted cutting commentary and wars of words and… She wanted to hate him. He was the embodiment of her family's failures. He was dismantling her second home piece by piece. He was using her for her familial connections.

And he was making it damned near impossible to hate him. Stupid tender fondness.

It only got worse when he said, "I'd like to keep seeing

you," as if he thought that would make it better when it only made everything worse. "I don't think it's an exaggeration to say that I haven't stopped thinking about you since the moment you offered me a donut. But we don't have to do this rush to the altar. We don't have to get married. Not if you'd like to change the deal. Since," he added with a wry smile, "things do change."

"But you need me," she protested, trying vainly to find some solution that would not lead to where she'd started—alone, living at the family home, broke, with no prospects. "You need *me* to make the workers like you."

His lips quirked up into a tender smile, and then he was closing the distance between them. "I need more than just that."

He was going to kiss her. He was being sweet and thoughtful and kind and he was going to kiss her and it was wrong. It was all wrong.

"Ethan," she said in warning, putting her hand on his chest and pushing lightly. "Don't do this."

He let her hold him back, but he didn't let go of her hair. He didn't let go of *her*. "Do what?"

"This—*madness*. Don't start to like me. I won't like you back." His eyes widened in shock. She dug deeper. "I won't love you."

Ever so slightly, his fingers loosened their hold on her hair. "You already said that."

"I meant it. Love is for fools, and I refuse to be one. Don't lower my opinion of you by being one, too." The words felt sharp on her tongue, as if she were chewing on glass.

Cruel to be kind, she told herself. If he got infatuated with her—if real emotions came into play—well, this whole thing would fall apart. This was not a relationship, not a real one. This was a business deal. They couldn't afford to forget that.

Well, she couldn't, anyway.

If she'd expected him to pull away, to be pissed at her blanket rejection, she was sorely disappointed. He did, in fact, lean back. And he did let his fingers fall away from her hair.

But he sat there, propped up on hotel pillows that were just like any other hotel pillows, and he smiled at her. A real smile, damn him. Honest and true.

"If you want out, that's fine," she pressed on. She would not be distracted by real emotions. "But don't take pity on me and don't like me, for God's sake. We had a deal. Don't patronize me by deciding what's best for me. If I want out of the deal, I'll tell you. In the meantime, I'll hold up my end of the bargain and you'll hold up yours—unless you've changed your mind?"

"I haven't," he said after a brief pause. His mouth was still slightly curved into a smile.

She wanted to wipe that smile off his face, but she couldn't think of a way to do it without kicking and screaming. So all she said was, "Fine."

They sat there for a few moments. Ethan continued to stare at her, as if he were trying to see into her. "Yes?" she demanded as she felt her face flush under his close scrutiny.

"The woman," he murmured in what sounded a hell of a lot like approval, "is a force unto herself."

Oh, she definitely took it back. She didn't want real or honest out of him. No tenderness and, for the love of everything holy, not a single hint of fondness.

She would not *like* him. She simply would not.

She had to nip this in the bud *fast*.

"Ethan," she said, baring her teeth in some approximation of a smile, "save it for when we're in public."

Ten

The next day, Ethan had Delores send a bird of paradise floral arrangement with a note that just read, "Yours, E." Then he sent Frances a text message telling her how much he was looking forward to seeing her again that night.

He wasn't surprised when she didn't respond. Not after the way she'd stalked out of his hotel room last night.

As hard as it was, he tried to put the events of the previous evening aside. He had work to do. The production lines were up to full speed. He checked in with his department heads and was stunned by the complete lack of pushback he got when he asked about head count and department budgets. A week ago, people would have been staring at the table or out the window and saying that the employees who had those numbers were out with the flu or on vacation or whatever lame excuse they assumed wouldn't be too transparent.

But now? After less than a week of having Frances Beaumont in his life, people were making eye contact and saying, "I've got those numbers," and smiling at him. Actually smiling! Even when a turnaround was going well, there weren't a lot of smiles in the process.

Then there was what happened at the end of the last meeting of the day. He'd been discussing the marketing budget in his office with the department managers. The men and women seated around the Beaumont conference table looked comfortable, as though they belonged there. For the briefest moment, Ethan was jealous of them. He didn't belong there, and they all knew it.

It was 4:45 and the marketing people were obviously ready to go home. Ethan wrapped things up, got the promises that he'd have the information he'd requested on his desk first thing in the morning and dismissed everyone.

"So, Mr. Logan," an older man said with a smile. Ethan thought his name was Bob. Larsen, maybe? "Are you going to get a donut on Friday?"

The room came to a brief pause, everyone listening for the answer. For what was quite possibly the first time, he grasped what Frances kept talking about when she said he should save it for the public.

Still, he had to say something. People were waiting for a reaction. More than that, they were waiting for the reaction that told them their trust in Ethan's decisions wasn't about to be misplaced. They were waiting for him to admit he was one of them.

"I hope she saves me a chocolate éclair this time," he said in a conspiratorial whisper. He didn't specify who "she" was. He didn't have to.

This comment was met with an approving noise between a chuckle and a hum. *Whew*, Ethan thought as people cleared out. At least he hadn't stuck his foot in it. Not like he had with Frances last night.

She'd been right. He *did* need her. If they walked away right now, whatever new, tenuous grip he had on this company would float away as soon as the last donut had been consumed. He'd gotten more accomplished in the past week than he had in three months, and, as much as it pained him to admit it, it had nothing to do with his keen managerial handling.

So why had he offered to let her out of their deal?

He didn't know the answer to that, except there'd been a chink in her armor and instead of looking like a worthy opponent, Frances had seemed delicate and vulnerable. There'd been this pull—a pull he wasn't sure he'd ever felt before—to take care of her. Which was patently ridiculous. She could take care of herself. Even if she hadn't seen fit to remind him of that fact, he knew it to be true.

But the look on her face after they'd left her brother behind…

Ethan hadn't lied. There were similarities between Frances and all his previous lady friends. Cultured, refined—the sort of woman who enjoyed a good meal and a little evening entertainment, both the kind that happened at the theater and in the hotel room.

So what was it about her that was so damn different?

It wasn't her name. Sure, her name was the starting point of this entire relationship, but Ethan was no sycophant. The Beaumont name was only valuable to him as long as it let him do his job at the Brewery. He had no desire to get in with the family, and Ethan had his own damn fortune, thank you very much.

Was it the fact that, for the first time in his life, he was operating with marriage in mind? Was that alone enough to merit this deeper…engagement, so to speak? He would be tied to Frances for the next calendar year. Maybe it was only natural to want to take care of the woman who would be his wife.

Not that he knew what that looked like. His father had certainly never taken care of his mother, aside from providing the funds for her to do whatever she liked. Troy Logan's involvement with the mother of his two sons was strictly limited to paying the bills. Maybe that was why his mother never stayed home for longer than a few months at a time. Troy Logan wasn't capable of deeper feeling, so

Wanda had sought out that emotional connection somewhere else. Anywhere else, really.

Ethan went to the private bathroom and splashed cold water on his face. This wasn't supposed to be complicated, not like his parents' relationship. This was cut-and-dried. No messy emotions. Just playing a game with one hell of an opponent who made him want to do things that were completely out of character. No problem.

He checked his jaw in the mirror—maybe he wouldn't shave before dinner tonight. As he was debating the merits of facial hair, he heard his office door shut with a decent amount of force.

"Frances?" he called out. "Is that you?"

There was no response.

He unrolled his sleeves and slid his jacket back on. The only other person who walked into his office without being announced by Delores was Delores herself. Even if it was near quitting time, he still needed to maintain his professional image.

But as he walked back into his office, he knew it wasn't Delores. Instead, a tall, commanding man sat in one of the two chairs in front of the desk.

The man looked like Phillip Beaumont—until he gave Ethan such an imperious glare that Ethan realized it wasn't the same Beaumont.

He recognized that look. He'd seen it on the covers of business magazines and in the *Wall Street Journal*. None other than Chadwick Beaumont, the former CEO of the Beaumont Brewery, was sitting in Ethan's office. The man every single employee in this company wanted back.

Ethan went on high alert. Beaumont had, until this very moment, been more of a ghost that Ethan had to work around than an actual living man to be dealt with. Yet here he was, months after Ethan had taken over. This couldn't be a coincidence, not after the interaction with Phillip last night.

"I had heard," Beaumont began with no other introduction, "that you were going to tear this office out."

"It's my prerogative," Ethan replied, keeping his voice level. He had to give Beaumont credit—at least he hadn't said *my office*. "As I am the current CEO."

Beaumont tilted his head in acknowledgment.

"To what do I owe the honor?" Ethan asked, as if this were a social call when it was clearly anything but. He took his seat behind his desk, leaving both hands on the desktop, as if all his cards were on the table.

Beaumont did not answer immediately. He crossed his leg and adjusted the cuff of his pants. Which was to be expected, Ethan figured. Beaumont was a notoriously tough negotiator, much like his father had been.

Well, two could play at this game. Troy Logan had earned his reputation as a corporate raider during the 1980s the hard way. His name alone could make high-powered bankers turn tail and run. Ethan had learned at the feet of the master. If Beaumont thought he could gain something with this confrontation, he was going to be sorely disappointed.

While Beaumont tried to wait Ethan out, Ethan studied him.

Chadwick Beaumont—the scion of the Beaumont family—was taller and blonder than Frances or even his brother Phillip. His hair held just a shine of redness, whereas Frances's was all flame. There was enough similarity that, even if Ethan hadn't met Phillip the night before, he would have recognized the Beaumont features—the chin, the nose, the ability to command a room just by existing in it.

How had the company been sold away from this man? Ethan tried to recall. An activist shareholder had precipitated the sale. Beaumont had fought against it tooth and nail, but once the sale had been finalized, he'd packed up and moved on.

So, yeah—this wasn't about the company. This was about Frances.

Which Beaumont proved when he tried out something that was probably supposed to be a smile but didn't even come close. "You're making me look bad. Flowers every day? My wife is beginning to complain."

Ethan didn't smile back. "My apologies for that." He was not sorry. "That's not my intention."

One eyebrow lifted. "What are your intentions?"

Damn, Ethan had walked right into that one. "I'm sorry—is that any of your business?"

"I'm making it my business." The statement was made in a casual enough tone, but there was no missing the implicit threat. Beaumont tried to stare him down for a moment, but Ethan didn't buckle.

"Good luck with that."

Beaumont's eyes hardened. "I don't know what your game is, Logan, but you really don't know what you're getting into with her."

That might be a true enough observation, but Ethan wasn't about to concede an inch. "As far as I can tell, I'm getting into a relationship with a grown woman. Still don't see how that's any of your concern."

Beaumont shook his head slowly, as if Ethan had blundered into admitting he was an idiot. "Either she's using you or you're using her. It won't end well."

"Again, not your concern."

"It is my concern because this will be just another one of Frances's messes that I have to clean up after."

Ethan bristled. "You talk as if she's a wayward child."

Beaumont's glare bore into him. "You don't know her like I do. She's lost more fortunes than I can count. Keeping her out of the public eye is a challenge during the best of times. And you," he said, pointing his chin at Ethan, "are pushing her back into the public eye."

Ethan stared at Beaumont. Was he serious? But Chadwick Beaumont did not look like the kind of man who made a joke. Ever.

What had Frances said last night? "Don't patronize me by deciding what's best for me." Suddenly, that statement made sense. "Does she know you're here?"

"Of course not," Beaumont replied.

"Of course not," Ethan repeated. "Instead, you took it upon yourself to decide what was best not only for her but for me, as well." He gave his best condescending smile, which took effort. He did not feel like smiling. "You'll have to excuse me, but I'm trying to figure out what gives you the right to be such a patronizing asshole to a pair of consenting adults. Any thoughts on that?"

Beaumont gave him an even look.

"I suppose," Ethan went on, "that the only surprising thing is that you came alone to intimidate me, instead of with a herd of Beaumont brothers."

"We don't tend to travel in a pack," Beaumont said coolly.

"And I'm equally sure you didn't think you'd need any help in the intimidation department."

Beaumont's eyes crinkled a little at the corners, as if he might have actually found that observation amusing. "How's the Brewery doing?"

Ethan blinked at the subject change, but only once. "We're getting there. You cultivated an incredibly loyal staff. The ones that didn't follow you to your new company were not happy about the changes."

Beaumont tilted his head at the compliment. "I imagine not. When I took over after my father's death, there was a period of about a year where we verged on total collapse. Employee loyalty can be a double-edged sword."

Ethan didn't bother to hide his surprise. *"Really."*

Beaumont nodded. "The club of Beaumont Brewery CEOs is even more exclusive than the Presidents' Club. There are only two of us alive in the world. You're only the fifth person to helm this company." He stared down at Ethan, but the intimidation wasn't as overbearing. "It's not a position to be taken lightly."

Honest to God, Ethan had never thought about it in those terms. The companies he usually restructured had often gone through a new CEO every two or three years as part of their downhill spiral. He'd never been anything special, in terms of management. He'd waltzed in, righted the sinking ship and moved on—just another CEO in a long line of them. There'd been nothing for the other employees to be loyal to except a paycheck and benefits.

Beaumont was right. Frances was right. Everything about this place, these people—this was different.

"If you need any help with the company…"

Ethan frowned. Accepting help was not something he did, especially not when it came to his job.

Except for Frances, a silky voice in the back of his head whispered. It sounded just like her.

"Actually, I do have a question. Have you ever heard of ZOLA?"

"ZOLA?" Beaumont mouthed the word like it was foreign. "What's that?"

"A private holdings company. They're making noise about the Brewery. I think they're trying to undermine—well, I'm not sure who they're trying to undermine. Not you, obviously, since you're no longer the boss around here. But it could be my company, or it could be AllBev." He fought the urge to get up and pace. "Unless, of course, ZOLA is representing your interests."

"I have no interest in reclaiming the Brewery. I've

moved on." His gaze was level, and his hands and feet were calm. Beaumont was telling the truth, damn it.

"And the rest of your family?"

"I don't speak for the entire Beaumont family."

"I'll be sure and pass that information along to Frances."

Beaumont's eyes widened briefly in surprise at this barb. "Phillip has no interest in beer. Matthew is one of my executives. Byron has his own restaurant in our new brewery. The younger Beaumonts never had anything to do with the Brewery in the first place. And you seem to be in a position to form your own opinion of Frances's motivations."

Point. Ethan was quite proud that his ears didn't burn under that one. "I appreciate your input."

Beaumont stood and held out his hand. Ethan rose to shake it. "Good to meet you, Logan. Stop by the mansion sometime."

"Likewise. Anytime." He was pretty sure they were both lying through their teeth.

Beaumont didn't let go of his hand, though. If anything, his grip tightened down. "But be careful with Frances. She is not a woman to be trifled with."

Ethan cracked a real smile. As if anyone could trifle with Frances Beaumont and hope to escape with their dignity—or other parts—intact.

Still, this level of meddling was something new to Ethan. No wonder seeing her other brother last night had shaken her so badly. Ethan hadn't really anticipated this much peer pressure. He increased his grip right back. "I think she can take care of herself, don't you?"

He waited for Beaumont to make another thinly veiled threat, but he didn't. Instead, he dropped Ethan's hand and turned toward the door.

Ethan watched him go. If Beaumont had shown up here,

had anyone been designated to give Frances a talking-to? Hopefully she'd had her armor on.

Then Beaumont paused at the door. He turned back, his gaze sweeping the entirety of the room. Instead of another pronouncement about how they were members of the world's smallest club, he only gave Ethan a little grin that was somehow tinged with sadness before he turned and was gone.

Ethan got the feeling that Beaumont wouldn't come back to the Brewery again.

Ethan collapsed back into his chair. What the ever-loving hell was that all about, anyway? He still wasn't going to rule out Beaumont—any Beaumont—of having direct involvement with ZOLA. Including Frances. There were no such things as coincidences—she'd said so herself. Frances had waltzed into his life just as ZOLA had started making noise. There had to be a connection—didn't there? But if that connection didn't run through her brothers, what was it?

Frances. His thoughts always came back to her. He couldn't wait to see her at dinner tonight, but he got the feeling that she might need something a little more than a floral arrangement, if she'd gotten half the pushback Ethan had today.

He checked his watch. He had time to make a little side trip, if he didn't shave.

Hopefully Frances liked stubble.

Eleven

Frances was unsurprised to find Byron waiting for her when she got back to the mansion after a long day of going over real estate contracts.

"Phillip called you, didn't he?" she began, pushing past her twin brother on her way up to her room. She had a date tonight, and she was already on edge. This would be a great night to put on the red dress. That'd drive any thoughts of affection right out of Ethan's mind. He'd be nothing but a walking, talking vessel of lust, and that was something she knew how to deal with.

No more tenderness. End of discussion.

"He might have," Byron admitted as he followed her into her room.

She was about to tear Byron a new one when she saw the huge floral arrangement on her nightstand table. "Oh!"

The card read, "Yours, E." Of course it did.

Those two little words—a mere six letters—made her smile. Which was just another sign that she needed a shower and a stiff drink. Ethan was not hers any more than she was his. She would not like him.

It would be easier to hold that line if he could just stop being so damn perfect.

"George said you've gotten flowers every day this week."

Frances rolled her eyes. George was the chef at the mansion and far too close with Byron. "So?" she said, pointedly ignoring the massive arrangement of blooms. "It's not like I haven't gotten flowers before."

"From the guy running the Brewery?"

She leveled a tired look at Byron. It was not a stretch to pull it off. "Why are you here? Aren't you running a restaurant or something? It's almost dinnertime, you know."

Byron flopped down on her bed. "We haven't officially opened yet. If you're going to flounce all around town with this new guy, you could at least plan on stopping by next week when we open. We could use the boost."

Frances stalked to her closet and began wrenching the hangers from side to side. "Excuse me? I do not *flounce*, thank you very much."

"Look," Byron said, staring at her. "Phillip seemed to think you were making a fool of yourself. I'm sure Chadwick has been updated. But whatever's going on, you're more than capable of dealing with it. If you're seeing this guy because you like him, then I want to meet him. And if you're seeing him for some other reason…"

The jerk had the nerve to crack his knuckles.

"Oh, for God's sake, Byron," she huffed at him. "Ethan could break you in half. No offense."

"None taken," Byron said without a trace of insult in his voice. "All I'm saying is that Phillip asked me to talk to you, and I've done that. Consider yourself talked to."

She pulled out the red dress and hung it on the closet door. "Seriously?"

Byron looked at the dress and then whistled. "Damn, Frannie. You either really like him or…"

This was part of the game, wasn't it? Convincing other people that she did like Ethan a great deal. Even if those people were Byron. She wasn't admitting to anything, not really. Not as long as she knew the truth deep down inside.

"I do, actually." It was supposed to come out strong and powerful because she was a woman in control of the situation.

It didn't. And Byron heard the difference. He wrinkled his forehead at her.

She was suddenly talking far more than was prudent. But this was Byron, damn it. She'd been sharing with him since their time in the womb, for crying out loud. "I mean, I do like him. There's something about him that's not your typical multimillionaire CEO. But I don't like *like* him, you know?" Which did not feel like the most honest thing to say. Because she might like him, even if it were a really bad idea.

Wasn't that what had almost happened last night? She'd let her guard down, and Ethan had been right there, strong and kind and thoughtful and she almost liked him.

Byron considered her juvenile argument. "So if you don't like *like* him, you're busting out the red dress because…"

Her mouth opened, and she almost admitted to the whole plan—the sham wedding, the angel investment, how she'd originally agreed to the whole crazy plan so she could inflict a little collateral damage on the current owners of the Brewery. For the family honor. If anyone would understand, it'd be Byron. She could always trust her brother and, no matter how crazy the situation was, he'd always stand behind her. *Always*.

But…

She couldn't do it. She couldn't admit she was breaking out the red dress because this was all a game, with high-dollar, high-power stakes, and she needed to level the playing field after the disaster that had been last night.

Her gaze fell on the bird of paradise arrangement. It was beautiful and had no doubt cost Ethan a fortune. She couldn't admit to anyone that she might not be winning the game. Not to Byron. Not to herself.

She decided it was time for a subject change. "How's the family?" Byron had recently married Leona Harper, an old girlfriend who was, awkwardly, the daughter of the Beaumonts' nemesis. Leona and Byron had a baby boy and another baby on the way. "Any other news from Leon Harper?"

"No," Byron said. "I don't know what we're paying the family lawyers these days, but it's worth it. Not a peep." He dug out his phone and called up a picture. "Guess what?"

Frances squinted at the ultrasound. "It's a...baby? I already knew Leona was pregnant, you goof."

"Ah, but did you know this? It's a girl," he said, his voice brimming with love. It almost hurt Frances to hear it—and to know that was not what she had with Ethan. "We're going to name her Jeannie."

"After Mom?" Frances didn't have a lot of memories of her mother and father together—at least, not a lot of memories that didn't involve screaming or crying. But Mom had made a nice, quiet life for herself after Hardwick.

There had been times when Frances had been growing up in this mansion that she'd wanted nothing more than to move in with Mom and live a quiet life, too. Frances bore the brunt of the new wives' dislike. By then, her older brothers had been off at college or, in Byron's case, off in the kitchen. Frances was the one who'd been expected to make nice with the new wives and the new kids—and Frances was the one who was supposed to grin and bear it when those new wives felt the need to prove that Hardwick loved them more than he'd loved anyone else. Even his own daughter.

Love had always been a competition. Never anything more.

Until now, damn it. Chadwick had married his assistant,

and no matter which way Frances looked at it, the two of them seemed to be wildly in love. And Phillip—her former partner in partying—had settled down with Jo. He had never been the kind of man to stick to one woman, and yet he was devoted to Jo. Matthew had decamped to California to be with his new wife. And now this—Byron and his happy, perfect little family.

Were you winning the game if you were the only one still playing it?

Byron nodded. "Mom's going to move in with us."

Frances looked at him in surprise. "Really?"

"Dad was such a mess, and God knows Leona's parents are, too. But Mom can be a part of the family again. And we've got plenty of room," he added, as if that were the deciding factor. "A complete mother-in-law apartment. Percy adores her, and I think Leona is thrilled to have Mom around. She never had much of a relationship with her own mother, you know."

Frances, as jaded as she was, felt tears prick at her eyes. The one thing their mother had never gotten over was losing her sense of family when Hardwick Beaumont had steamrolled her in court. When she'd lost her game, she'd lost *everything*.

That wasn't going to be how Frances wound up. "Oh, Byron—Mom's going to be *so* happy."

"So," Byron said, standing and taking his phone back. "I know you. And I know that you are occasionally prone to rash decisions."

She narrowed her eyes at him. "Is this the part where I get to tell you to go to hell, so soon after that touching moment?"

But Byron held up his hands in surrender. "All I'm saying is, if you do something that some people *might* consider rash, just call Mom first, okay? She was there when

Matthew got married and when I got married. And I get dibs on walking you down the aisle."

Frances stared at him. *"What?"* Where had he gotten *that*? The impending wedding was something that she and Ethan had only discussed behind closed doors. No one else was supposed to have a clue.

No one but Byron, curse him. She'd never been able to hide anything from him for long, anyway, and he knew it. He gave her a wry smile and said, "You heard me. And come to the restaurant next week, okay? I'll save you the best table." He kissed her on the cheek and gave her shoulders a quick hug. "I've got to go. Take care, Frannie."

She stood there for several moments after Byron left. *Rash?* This wasn't rash. This was a carefully thought-out plan. A plan that did not necessarily include her mother watching her get married to Ethan Logan or having Byron—or any other brother—walk her down the aisle.

She didn't want her mother to think she'd found a happily-ever-after. Maybe she should call Mom and warn her that this whole thing wasn't real and it wouldn't last.

Frances found herself sitting on her bed, staring at the flowers. She was running out of room in here—the roses were on the dresser, the lilies on the desk. He didn't have to spend this much on flowers for her.

She plucked the card out and read it again. It didn't take long to process the two words. *Yours, E.*

She grinned as her fingertip traced the *E*. No, he was not particularly good at whispering—or writing—sweet nothings.

But he was hers, at least for the foreseeable future.

She needed to call her mom. And she would. Soon.

Right now, however, she had to get ready for a date.

Ethan knew the moment Frances walked into the restaurant. Not because he saw her do it, but because the entire place—including the busboy passing by and the bartender pouring a glass of wine—came to a screeching halt. There wasn't a sound, not even a fork scraping on a plate.

He knew before he even turned around that he wasn't going to make it. He wasn't going to be able to wall himself off from whatever fresh hell Frances had planned for him tonight. And what only made it worse? He didn't want to. God help him, he didn't want to.

While he finished his whiskey he took a moment to remind himself that part of the deal was that sex was not part of the deal. It didn't matter if she were standing there completely nude—he would give her his present and take her up to his hotel room and lock himself in the bathroom if he had to. He'd control himself. He'd never succumbed to wild passion before. Now was not the time to start.

After a long, frozen moment, everyone moved again. Ethan took a deep breath and turned around.

Oh, Jesus. She was wearing a strapless fire-engine-red dress that hugged every curve. And as good as she looked, all he wanted to do was strip that dress off her and see the real her, without armor—or anything else—on.

Even across the dim restaurant, he saw her smile when their eyes met. She did not like him, he reminded himself. That smile was for public consumption, not for him. But damned if it didn't make him smile back at her.

He got off his stool and went to meet her. He knew he needed to say things—for the diners who were all not so subtly listening in. He needed to compliment Frances's dress and tell her how glad he was to see her.

He couldn't get his stupid mouth to work. Even as part of his brain knew that was the whole point of that dress, he couldn't fight it.

He couldn't fight her.

So instead of words, he did the next best thing—he pulled her into his arms and kissed her like he'd been thinking of doing all damn day long. And it wasn't for the viewing public, either.

It was for her. All for her.

Somehow, he managed to pull away before he slid his hands down her back and cupped her bottom in the middle of the restaurant. "I missed you today," he whispered as he touched his forehead to hers.

"Did you?"

Maybe it was supposed to sound dismissive, but that's not how it hit his ears. Instead, she sounded as if she couldn't quite believe he was being sincere—but she wanted him to be.

"I did. Our table's ready." He took her hand in his and led her to the waiting table. After they were seated, he asked, "Anything interesting happen today?"

She arched an eyebrow at him. "Yes, actually. My twin, Byron, came to see me."

"Oh?" Had it been the same kind of visit he'd gotten from Chadwick?

Frances was watching him closely. "His new restaurant opens next week. He'd appreciate it if we could put in an appearance. Apparently, we're great publicity right now."

"Which was the plan," he said, more to remind himself than her. Because he had to stick to that plan, come hell or high water.

She leaned forward on her elbows, her generous cleavage on full display. He felt his pulse pick up a notch. "Indeed. You? Anything interesting today?"

"A few things," he tried to say casually. "Everyone at the Brewery is waiting to see if you bring me my very own donut this Friday."

A dazzling—and, he hoped, genuine—smile lit up her face. "Oh, really? I guess I should plan on coming, then?" Her tone was light and teasing.

This was what he'd missed today. She could talk circles

around him, and all he could do was keep up. He reached over and cupped her cheek in his hand, his thumb stroking her skin.

She leaned into his touch—a small movement that no one else could see. It was just for him, the way she let him carry a little of her weight. Just for him, the way her eyelashes fluttered. "I requested a chocolate éclair."

"Maybe I'll bring you a whole box, just to see what they say."

She would not like him. He should not like her.

But he did, damn it all. He liked her a great deal.

He didn't want to tell her the other interesting thing. He didn't want to watch her armor snap back into place at the mention of one of her brothers. Hell, for that matter, he didn't really want to be sitting in this very nice restaurant. He wanted to be someplace quiet, where they could be alone. Where her body could curl up against his and he could stroke her hair and they could talk about their days and kiss and laugh without giving a flying rat's ass what anyone else saw, much less thought.

"Chadwick came by the office today."

It was a hard thing to watch, her reaction. She sat up, pulling away from his touch. Her shoulders straightened and her eyes took on a hard look. "Did he now?"

Ethan let his hand fall away. "He did."

She considered this new development for a moment. "I suppose Phillip talked to him?"

"I got that feeling. He also said I'm making him look bad, with all the flowers."

Frances waved this excuse away as if it were nothing more than a gnat. "He can afford to buy Serena flowers— and does, frequently." Her eyes closed and, elbows back on the table, she clasped her hands in front of her. She looked as though she was concentrating very hard—or praying. "Do I even want to know what he said?"

"The usual older-brother stuff. What are my intentions, I'd better not break his little sister's heart—that sort of thing." He shrugged, as if it'd been just another day at the office..

She opened her eyes and stared at him over the tops of her hands. "What did you say? Please tell me you didn't kowtow to him. It's not good for his already-massive ego."

Ethan leaned back. "I merely informed him that what happens between two consenting adults is none of his business and for him to presume he knows best for either of us was patronizing at best. A fact I have recently been reminded of myself."

Frances's mouth opened, but then what he said registered and she closed it again. A wry smile curved her lips. He wanted to kiss that smile, those lips—but there was a table in the way. "You didn't."

"I did. I don't recall any kowtowing."

She laughed at that, which made him feel good. It wasn't as if he'd fought to the death for her honor or anything, but he'd still protected her from a repeat of what had happened last night.

She shifted and the toes of her foot came into contact with his shin. Slowly, she stroked up and down. His pulse kicked it up another notch—then two.

"I got you something," he said suddenly. He had decided it would be better to wait to give her the jewelry until after dinner, but the way she was looking at him? The way she was touching him? He'd changed his mind.

"The flowers were beautiful," she murmured. Her foot moved up and then down again, stroking his desire higher.

The room was too warm. Too hot. He was going to fall into the flames and get burned, and he couldn't think of a better way to go.

He reached into his pocket and pulled out the long, thin

velvet box. "I picked it out," he told her, holding it out to her. "I thought it suited you."

Her foot paused against his leg, and he took advantage of the break to adjust his pants. Sitting had suddenly become uncomfortable.

Her eyes were wide as she stared at the box. "What did you do?"

"I bought my future wife a gift," he said simply. The words felt right on his tongue, like they belonged there. *Wife.* "Open it."

She hesitated, as if the box might bite her. So he opened it for her.

The diamond necklace caught the light and glittered. He'd chosen the drop pendant, a square-cut diamond that hung off the end of a chain of three smaller diamonds, all set in platinum. Tiffany's had some larger solitaires, but this one seemed to fit Frances better.

"Oh, Ethan," she gasped as he held the box out toward her. "I didn't expect this."

"I like to keep you guessing," he told her. He set the box down and pulled the platinum chain out of its moorings. "Here," he said, his voice deeper than he remembered it being. "Allow me."

He stood and moved behind her, draping the necklace in front of her. She swept her mane of hair away from her neck, exposing the smooth skin. Ethan froze. He wanted nothing more than to lean down and taste her, to run his lips over the delicate curve where her neck met her shoulders—to see how she would react if he trailed kisses lower, pulling the dress down farther until...

She tilted her head down, pulling him back to the reality of standing in a crowded restaurant, holding nine thousand dollars' worth of diamonds. As he tried to fasten the clasp, his hands began to shake with need—the need to hold her, the need to stroke her bare shoulders. The need to make her *his*.

He'd had other lady friends, bought them nice gifts—usually when it was time for him to move on—but he had never felt this much need before. He didn't know what it was—only that it was because of her.

He willed his hands—and other body parts—to stand down. This was just a temporary madness; that was all. A beautiful woman in a gorgeous dress designed to inspire lust—nothing more, really.

Except it wasn't. No matter what he told himself, he knew he wasn't being honest—not with himself, not with her.

Honesty was not supposed to figure into this, after all. The whole premise of their relationship was based on a stack of lies that only got taller with each passing day and each passing floral arrangement. No, it was not supposed to be honest, their relationship. It was, however, supposed to be simple. She needed the money. He needed the Beaumont seal of approval. Everyone came out a winner.

That was possibly the biggest lie of all. Nothing about Frances Beaumont had been simple since the moment he'd laid eyes on her.

Finally, he got the clasp hooked. He managed to restrain himself enough that he did not press a kiss to her neck, did not wind her long hair into his hands.

But he was not exactly restrained. His fingertips drifted over the skin she'd exposed when she'd moved her hair and then down her bare shoulders with the lightest of touches. It shouldn't have been overtly sexual, shouldn't have been all that erotic—but unfamiliar need hammered through his gut.

It only got worse when she let go of her hair and that mass of fire-red silk brushed over the backs of his hands. Without meaning to—without meaning any of this—he dug his fingers into her skin, pulling her against him. She was soft and warm, and she leaned back and looked up at him.

Their gazes met. He supposed that, with another woman, he'd be staring down her front, looking at how his diamonds were nestled between her breasts, so large and firm and on such display at this angle.

But he was only dimly aware of her cleavage because Frances was staring up at him, her lips parted ever so slightly. Color had risen in her cheeks, and her eyes were wide. One of her hands reached up and found his. It was only when she pressed his hand flat against her skin that he realized his palms were moving along her skin, moving to feel everything about her—to learn everything about her.

He stroked his other thumb over her cheek. She gasped, a small movement that he felt more than saw. His body responded to her involuntary reaction with its own. Blood pounded in his ears as it raced from his brain to his erection as fast as it could. And, given how she was leaning against it, she knew it, too.

This was the moment, he thought dimly—as much as he could think, anyway. She could say something cutting and put him in his place, and he'd have to sit down and eat dinner with blue balls and not touch her like he meant it.

"Ethan," she whispered as she stared up at him. Her eyes seemed darker now, the pupils widening until the blue-green had almost disappeared.

Yes, he wanted to shout, to groan—yes, yes. He wanted to hear his name on her lips, over and over, in the most intimate of whispers and the loudest of passionate shouts. He wanted to push her to the point where all she could do, say—think—was his name. Was him.

His hand slipped lower, stroking the exposed skin of her throat. Lower still, tracing the outline of the necklace he'd bought for her.

Her grip on his hand tightened as his fingers traced the pendant. She didn't tell him to stop, though. She didn't lean away, didn't give a single signal that he should stop touching her. His hand started to move even lower, stroking down into the body of her dress and—

"Are we ready to order?" a too-bright, too-loud voice suddenly demanded.

Frances and Ethan both jumped. Suddenly he was aware that they were still in public, that at least half the restaurant was still watching them—that he'd been on the verge of sheer insanity in the full view of anyone with a cell phone. What the hell was wrong with him?

He tried to step away from her, to put at least a respectable three inches between their bodies—but Frances didn't let go of his hand.

Instead—incredibly—she stood and said, "Actually, I'm not hungry. Thanks, though." Then she turned to give him a look over her shoulder. "Shall we?"

"We shall," was the most intelligent thing he was capable of coming up with. The waiter smirked at them both as Ethan fished a fifty out of his wallet to cover his bar tab.

Every eye was on them as they swept up to the front together. Ethan took Frances's coat from the coat check girl and held it as Frances slipped her bare arms into it. They didn't speak as they braved the cold wind and waited for the valet to bring his car around. But Ethan put his arm around her shoulders and pulled her close. She leaned her head against his chest. Was he imagining things, or was she breathing hard—or at least, harder than normal? He wasn't sure. Maybe that was his chest, rising and falling faster than he normally breathed.

He didn't feel normal. Sex was always fun, always enjoyable—but something he could take or leave. He liked the release of it, and, yeah, sometimes he needed that release more than other times. But that's all it was. A pressure valve that sometimes needed to be depressurized a bit.

It wasn't this pain that made thinking rationally impossible—a pain that could only be erased by burying himself in her body over and over again until he was finally sated.

This wasn't about a simple release. He could achieve that with anyone. Hell, he didn't even need another person.

But this? Right now? This was about Frances and this unknown need she inspired in him. And the more he tried to name that need, the more muddled his head became. He wanted to show her what he could do for her, how he could take care of her, protect her and honor her. That they could be good together. For each other.

Finally, the car arrived. Ethan held her door for her and then got behind the wheel. He gunned it harder than he needed to, but he didn't want to waste another minute, another second, without Frances in his arms.

They weren't far from the hotel. He wouldn't have even bothered with the car if it'd been twenty degrees warmer. The drive would take five minutes, tops.

Or it would have—until Frances leaned over and placed her hand on his throbbing erection. Even through the layers of his boxers and wool trousers, her touch burned hot as she tested his length. Ethan couldn't do anything but grip the steering wheel as she made her preliminary exploration of his arousal.

It was when she squeezed him, shooting the pain that veered into pleasure through his whole body, that he forced out the words. "This isn't a game, Frances."

"No, it's not," she agreed, her voice breathy as her fingers stroked him. His body burned for her. If she stopped, he didn't know if he could take it. "Not anymore."

"Are you coming up to my room?" It came out far gruffer than he'd intended—not a request but not quite a demand.

"I don't think the hotel staff would appreciate it if we had sex in the lobby." She didn't let go of him when she said it. If anything, her hand was tighter around him.

"Is that what you really want? Sex, I mean. Not the lobby part." Because he was honor-bound to ask and more than honor-bound to accept her answer as the final word on the matter. Even if it killed him. "Because it wasn't part of the original deal."

That pushed her away from him. Her hot hand was gone, and he was left aching without her touch. "Ethan," she said in the most severe voice he'd heard her use all night long. "I don't want to talk about the damned deal. I don't want to think about it."

"Then what do you want?" he asked as they pulled up in front of the hotel.

She didn't answer. Instead, she got out, and he had no choice but to follow her, handing his keys to the valet. They walked into the hotel without touching, waited for the elevator without speaking. Ethan was thankful his coat was long enough to hide his erection.

They walked into the elevator together. Ethan waited until the doors were closed before he moved on her. "Tell me what you want, Frances," he said, pinning her against the back of the elevator. Her body was warm against his as she looked up at him through her lashes and he saw her. Not her armor, not her carefully constructed front— he saw *her*. "To hell with the deal. Tell me what you want right now. Is it sex? Is it *me*?"

"I shouldn't want you," she said, her voice soft, almost uncertain. She took his face in her hands, their mouths a whisper away. "I shouldn't."

"I shouldn't want you, either," he told her, an unfamiliar flash of anger pushing the words out of his mouth. "You drive me mad, Frances. Absolutely freaking mad. You undermine me at the Brewery and work me into a lather, and you turn my head around so fast that I get dizzy every time I see you. And, damn it all, you do it with that smile that lets me know it's easy for you. That *I'm* easy for you." He touched his thumb to her lips. She tried to kiss his thumb, and when he pulled it away, she tried to kiss him, pulling his head down to hers.

He didn't let her. He peeled her hands off his face and pinned them against the elevator walls. For some reason, he had to tell her this now before they went any further. "You *complicate* things. God help me—you make everything harder than it has to be, and I don't want you any other way."

Her eyes were wide, although he didn't know if that was because he was holding her captive or what he'd said. "You…don't?"

"No, I don't. I want you complicated and messy." He leaned against her, so she could feel exactly how much he wanted her. "I want you taunting and teasing me, and I want you with your armor up because you're the toughest woman I know. And I want you with your armor off entirely because—" Abruptly, the flash of anger that gave him all of those words was gone, and he realized that instead of telling a beautiful woman how wonderful she was, he was pretty sure he'd been telling her that she irritated him. "Because that's how I want you," he finished, unsure of himself.

Her lips parted and her mouth opened—right as the elevator did the same. They were on Ethan's floor. He held her like that for just a second longer, then released his hold in time to keep the doors from closing on them.

He held out his hand for her.

And he waited.

Twelve

"You *want* me complicated?" Frances stood there, staring at Ethan as if he'd casually announced he wore a cape in his off time while fighting crime.

No one had wanted her messy and complicated before. They wanted her simply, as an object of lust or as a step up the social ladder. It was when things got messy or complicated or—God help her—both that men disappeared from her life. When Frances dared to let her real self show through—that was when the trouble began. She was too dramatic, too high-maintenance, her tastes and ambitions too expensive. Her family life was far too complex—that was always rich, coming from the ones who wanted an association with the prestige of the Beaumont name but none of the actual work that went into maintaining it.

She'd heard it all before. *So* many times before.

The elevator beeped in warning. Ethan said, "I do," and grabbed her, hauling her past the closing doors.

She didn't know what to say to that, which was a rarity in itself. They stood in the middle of the hallway for a moment, Ethan holding on to her hand tightly. "Do you?" he asked in a gentle voice. "Want me, that is."

She felt the cool weight of the diamonds he'd laid against her skin. How many thousands of dollars had he spent on them? On her? It was not supposed to be complicated. If they had sex, then it was supposed to be this simple quid pro quo. This was the way of her world—it always had been. The man buys an expensive, extravagant gift and the woman takes her clothes off. It was not messy.

Except it was.

"You're ruining the last of my family's legacy and business," she told him. "You're everything that went wrong. When we lost the Brewery, I lost a part of my identity and I should hate you for being party to that. God, how I wanted to hate you."

Oh, Lord—were her eyes watering? No. Absolutely not. There was no crying in baseball or in affairs of the heart. At least, not in her affairs of the heart, mostly because her affairs never actually involved her heart.

She kept that locked away from everyone, and no one had ever realized it—until Ethan Logan had shown up and seen the truth of the matter. Until he'd seen the truth of her.

"You can still hate me in the morning," he told her. "I don't expect anything less from you."

"But what about tonight?" Because it was all very well and good to say that he liked her messy, but that didn't mean she wasn't still a mess. And that wore on a man after a while.

He stepped into her. His body was strong and warm, and she knew if she gave first and leaned against him, breathed in his woodsy scent, that she would be lost to him.

She'd already lost so much. Could she afford to lose anything else?

He stroked his fingers down her face, then slid them back through her hair, pulling her up to him. "Let me love you tonight, Frances. Just you and me. Nothing else."

It was real and honest and sincere, damn him to hell. It was true because he was true. None of those little lies and half glosses of compliments that hid the facts better than they illuminated them. And for a man who did not grasp the finer points of sweet nothings, it was the sweetest damn something she'd ever heard.

A door behind them opened. She didn't know if it was the elevator or another guest and she didn't much care. She took off down the hall toward Ethan's room without letting go of his hand.

He got the door open and pulled her inside. "I won't like you in the morning," she told him, her voice shaking as he undid the belt at her waist and pushed the coat from her shoulders.

"But you like me now," he replied, shucking his own coat in the process. "Don't you?"

She did. Oh, this was a heartache waiting to happen, this thing between her and Ethan.

"I don't want to talk anymore," she said in as commanding a voice as she could muster. More than that, she didn't want to think anymore. She only wanted to feel, to get lost in the sweet freedom of surrendering to her baser lust.

She grabbed him by the suit jacket and jerked it down his arms, trying to get him as naked as possible as fast as possible. He let her, but he said, "Don't you dare hide behind that wall, Frances."

"I'm not hiding," she informed him, grabbing his belt and undoing it. "I'm getting you naked. That's generally how sex works best."

The next thing she knew, they were right back to where they'd been in the elevator, with the full weight of his body pinning her against the door, her wrists in his hands. "Don't," he growled at her. "I don't want to sleep with your armor. I want to sleep with you, damn it. I *like* you. Just the way you are. So don't try to be some flippant, distant princess who's above this. Above us."

Her breath caught in her throat. "You don't know what you're asking of me." It didn't come out confident or cocky or even flippant.

"Maybe I do." He kissed her then, with enough force to knock her head back. "Sorry," he murmured against her lips.

"It's okay," she replied because if they were getting to the sex part, they'd stop talking and she could just feel. Even the small pain in the back of her head was okay because she didn't have to talk about it, about what it really meant. "Just keep kissing me hard."

"Is that how you want it?"

She tested her wrists against his grip. There was a little give, but not much. "Yes," she said, knowing full well that he was a man who knew exactly what that meant. "That's how I want *you*." Hard and fast with no room to stop and think. None.

A deep sound came out of his chest, a growl that she felt in her bones. His hips shifted and his erection ground against her. Yes, she wanted to feel all of that.

But then he said, "Tell me if something doesn't work," and she heard his control starting to fray. "Promise me that, babe."

She blinked up at him through a haze of desire. Had anyone ever said that to her before? "Of course," she said, trying to make it sound as though all of her previous lovers had put her orgasms first—had put her first.

He raised an eyebrow at her. He didn't even have to say it—she could still hear him telling her not to pretend.

Then he moved. "Whatever else," he said as he slid her hands up over her head and put both her wrists under one of his massive hands, "I expect complete and total honesty in bed."

"We aren't currently in bed," she reminded him. She tested her wrists again, but he wasn't playing around. He had her pinned.

It wasn't that she wasn't turned on—she was. But a new kind of excitement started to build underneath the standard sexual arousal that she normally felt. Ethan had her pinned. He had a free hand. He could do anything that he wanted to her.

And he'd stop the moment she told him to.

For once in her life, she wouldn't have to think about anything except what he was going to do next.

"Turn around," he ordered as he lifted her wrists away from the door just enough that she could spin in place. Then he swept her hair away from her neck and—and— oh, God. He didn't just kiss her there, he scraped his teeth over her exposed skin, raw and hungry.

Frances sucked in air at the unexpected sensation. "Good?" he asked.

"Yeah."

"Good," he said, biting a little harder this time, then kissing the sore spot.

Frances shifted, the weight between her legs growing hotter and heavier as he worked over her skin. Then he was pulling the zipper down on her dress, and the whole thing fell to her feet, leaving her in nothing but a white lace pair of panties that left very little to the imagination.

"Oh, babe," Ethan said in undisguised appreciation. She started to turn so she could see his face when he said it, but he gave her bottom a light smack and then used his body to keep hers flat against the door. "No, don't look," he ordered. "Just feel."

"Yeah," she moaned, her skin slightly stinging from where he'd smacked her. "I want to feel you."

His hand popped against her bare bottom again—not hard. He wasn't hurting her. But the unexpected contact made her body involuntarily tighten, and the anticipation of the next touch drove everything else from her mind.

Ethan's free hand circled her waist, pushing her just far enough away from the door that he could cup one of her breasts, teasing the nipple until it was hard with desire.

Then he tugged at it with more force. "Yeah?" he asked, his breath hot against her neck. He shoved one of his knees between her legs and she sagged onto it, grinding her hips, trying to take the pressure off the one spot in her body that made standing hard.

"Yeah," she moaned, her body moving without her permission, trying to find release, that moment where there was a climax that only Ethan could bring her to.

"You want more?" he demanded, tugging at her nipple again.

"Ethan, please," she panted, for no matter how she shifted her hips, the only pressure she felt did not push her over the edge.

He pulled away from her. "Don't move," he said. Then her wrists were free and his knee was gone and she felt cold, pressed up against this impersonal hotel door. Behind her, she heard the sound of plastic tearing. The condom. *Good.*

Then Ethan put his hand on the back of her neck and pulled her away from the door. "Hard?" he asked again, as if he wanted to make absolutely sure.

"Hard," she all but begged. "Hard and fast and—"

He led her to the bed, but instead of laying her out on it, he bent her over the edge. Her panties were pulled down, and she was exposed before him.

Her body quivered with need and anticipation and excitement because this was not gentle and sweet, not when he grabbed her by the hips and lifted her bottom against his rock-hard erection. His fingers dug into her flesh in a hungry way.

"Ethan," she moaned as he smacked her bottom again, just hard enough that her muscles tightened and she almost came right then. She fisted the bedclothes in her hands and tensed, hoping and praying for the next touch. "Hard and fast and now. Now, Ethan, or I won't like you in the morning, I swear to God, I'll hate you. *Now*, Ethan, *now*."

Then he was against her, and, with a moan of pure masculine satisfaction, he was in her, thrusting hard. Frances gasped at the suddenness of him—oh, he was huge—but her body took him in as he pounded her with all the aggression she needed so badly.

She hit her peak, moaning into the sheets as the wave cascaded over her. *Thank heavens*, she thought, going soft after it'd passed. She'd wanted to come so badly and—and—

And Ethan didn't stop. He didn't sputter to a finish. Instead, he paused long enough to reach forward and tangle his hands in her hair and pull so that her head came off the bed. "Are you nice and warmed up now?" he demanded, and a shiver ran through her body. He felt it, too—she could tell by the way he twined her hair around his fingers. "That's it, babe. Ready?"

He wasn't done. Oh, he wasn't done with her. He was going to make her come again, so fast and so hard that when he began to thrust again, all she could do was take him in. He kept one hand tangled in her hair, lifting her head up and back so that she arched away from him and her bottom lifted up to his greedy demands.

All she could do was moan—she wanted to cry out, but the angle of her neck made that too hard. Everything about her tightened as Ethan gave her exactly what she wanted—him, hard and fast.

This time, when he brought his hand against her ass in time with his thrusting, she came equally as hard. She couldn't help it. Her body acted without her input at all. All she was, all she could feel, was what Ethan did to her. The climax was unlike anything she'd ever felt before, so intense she forgot to breathe even.

Ethan held her there as waves of pleasure washed her

clean of everything but satisfaction. When she sagged against the bed, spent and panting, he let go of her hair, dug his fingertips back into her hips and pumped into her three more times before groaning and falling forward onto her.

They lay there for a moment, his body pressing hers against the mattress while she tried to remember how to breathe like a normal human. She didn't feel normal anymore; that was for sure.

She didn't know how she felt. Good—oh, yes. She felt wonderful. Her body was limp and her skin tingled and everything was amazing.

But when Ethan rolled off her and then leaned down and pressed a kiss between her shoulder blades—she felt decidedly not normal. She didn't turn her head to look at him. She didn't know what to say. Her! Frances Beaumont! Speechless! That was hard enough to accomplish by itself—but to have had sex so intense and so satisfying that she had not a single snappy observation or cutting comeback?

Not that he was waiting for her to say something. He kissed her on the shoulder and said, "I'll be right back," before he hefted himself off the bed. She heard the bathroom door click shut, and then she was alone in the hotel room with only her feelings.

Now what was she going to do?

Thirteen

Ethan splashed cold water on his face, trying to get his head to clear. He felt like a jackass. That wasn't how he normally took a woman to bed. Not even close. He usually took his time, making sure the foreplay left everyone satisfied before the actual sex.

But pinning Frances against the door and then bending her over the edge of the bed? Pawing at her as if he were little more than a lust-crazed animal? That hadn't been tender and sweet.

He didn't want to be responsible for his actions. He'd smacked her bottom—more than once! That wasn't like him. He wanted that to be her fault—she'd worn the red dress, she'd been this *siren* that pushed him past sanity, past responsibility.

But that was crap, and he knew it. All she'd said was that she wanted it hard and fast. He could have still been a gentleman about it. Instead, he'd gotten rough. He'd never done that before. He didn't know…

Well, he just didn't know.

And he wasn't going to find out hiding in the bathroom.

He'd apologize; that was all there was to it. He'd gotten carried away. It wouldn't happen again.

He finished up and headed out. He hadn't even gotten undressed. He'd stripped her down, but aside from shoving his pants out of the way, he was still dressed. Yes, that was quite possibly the best sex of his life, but still. He couldn't shake the feeling that he'd gone too far.

That feeling got even stronger when he saw her. Frances had curled up on her side. She looked impossibly small against the expanse of white sheets. She watched him, her eyes wide. Was she upset? *Hell.*

Then her nose wrinkled, and he was pretty sure she smiled. "You're not naked," she said. Her voice was raw, as if she'd been shouting into the wind for hours.

"Is that a problem?" He tried to keep it casual sounding. He wasn't sure he made it.

She uncurled from the bed like a flower opening for him. "I wanted to see you. And I didn't get to."

"My apologies for the disappointment." He started to jerk open the buttons on his shirt, but she stood and closed the distance between them. His hands fell around her waist, still warm from the sex. He wanted to fold her into his arms and hold her for as long as he could.

Where was all this ridiculous sentiment coming from? He wasn't a sentimental guy.

"Let me," she said. He saw that her hands were trembling. "And it wasn't disappointing. It was wonderful. Except that I couldn't see you."

Ethan blinked twice, trying to process that. "I didn't go too far?"

"No," she said, giving him a nervous smile. "I—" She paused and took a deep breath. "Honestly?"

"Even though we're still not in bed," he said with a grin, tilting her chin up so he could look her in the eyes.

She held his gaze for a moment before forcibly turning her attention back to his buttons. "Thank you," she said quietly.

That was not quite what he'd been expecting. "For what? I think I got just as much out of that as you did."

She undid the last button and pushed the shirt off him. Then his T-shirt followed. Finally she shoved his pants down, and Ethan kicked out of them.

"Oh, my," she whispered, skimming her fingers over his chest and ruffling his hair.

He fought the urge to flex. The urge won. She giggled as his muscles moved under her hands. "Ethan!"

"Sorry," he said, walking her back toward the bed. "I can't seem to help myself around you."

This time, they actually got under the covers. Ethan pulled her on top of him. He didn't mean it in an explicitly sexual way, but her body covering his? Okay, it was more than a little sexual. "Why did you thank me?"

She laid out on him, her head tucked against his chest. "You really want me messy and complicated?"

"Seems to be working so far."

She sighed, tracing small circles against his skin. "No one's ever wanted me. Not the real me. Not like this."

"I find that hard to believe. You are a hell of a woman."

"They don't want me," she insisted. "They want the fantasy of me. Beautiful and sexy and rich and famous. They want the mystique of the Beaumont name. That's what I am to people." When he didn't have a response to that, she propped herself up on one elbow and stared down at him. "That's what I was to you, wasn't I?"

There was no point in playing games about it. "You were. But you're not anymore."

Her smile was tinged with sadness. "I'm not used to being honest, I guess."

He cupped her face in his hands and kissed her. He didn't intend for it to be a distraction, but she must have taken it that way because she pulled back. "Why did you agree to a sham marriage? And don't give me that line about the workers loving me."

"Even though they do," he put in.

"Most men do not agree to sham marriages as business deals," she went on as if he hadn't interrupted her. "I seem to recall you making quite a point of saying love wasn't a part of marriage when we came to terms. So spill it."

She had him trapped. Sure, he could throw her off him, but then she shifted and straddled him, and his body stirred at the thought of her bare legs wrapped around his waist, her body so close to his.

So, with mock exasperation, he flopped back against the bed. "My parents have an…unusual relationship," he said.

She leaned down on him, her arms crossed over her chest, her chin on her arms. "I don't want you to take this the wrong way, but so? I mean, my mom was second out of four wives for my dad. I wouldn't know a usual relationship if it bit me. Present company included."

He wrapped his arms around her body, enjoying the warmth she shared with him. No, this wasn't usual, not even close. But he was enjoying it anyway. "Have you ever heard of Troy Logan?"

"No. Brother or father?"

He wasn't surprised. Her brother Chadwick would probably recognize the name, but that wasn't Frances's world. "Father. Notorious on Wall Street for buying companies and dismantling them at a profit."

She tilted her head from side to side. "I take it the apple did not fall terribly far from the tree?"

"I don't take companies apart. I restructure them." She gave him an arch look, and he gave in. "But, yes, you're correct. We're in nearly the same line of work."

"And…" she said. "Your mother?"

"Wanda Kensington." He braced for the reaction.

He didn't have to wait long. She gasped, which made him wince. "What? You don't mean—*the* Wanda Kensington? The artist?"

"I can't tell you how rare it is that someone knows my

mother's name but not my father's," he said, stroking her hair away from her face.

"Don't change the subject," she snapped, sitting all the way up. Which left her bare breasts directly in Ethan's line of sight. The diamonds he'd bought for her glittered between those perfect breasts. "Your mother is—but Wanda's known for her art installations! Massive performance pieces that take like a year to assemble! I don't ever remember reading anything about her having a family."

"She wasn't around much. I don't know why they got married, and I don't know why they stayed married. I'm not even sure they like each other. They never made sense," he admitted. "She'd be gone for months, a year—we had nannies that my father was undoubtedly sleeping with—and then she'd walk back in like no time at all had passed and pretend to be this hands-on mother who cared."

He was surprised to hear the bitterness in his voice. He'd long ago made peace with his mother. Or so he'd thought. "And she'd try, I think. She'd stick it out for a few weeks—once she was home for almost three months. She made it to Christmas, and then she was gone again. We never knew, my brother and I. Never had a clue when she'd show up or when she'd disappear again."

"So you were—what? Another piece of performance art? The artist as a mother?"

"I suppose." Not that he'd ever thought about it in those terms. "It wasn't bad. Dad wasn't jealous of her. She wasn't jealous of him. It wasn't like there was drama. It was just… a marriage on paper."

"It was a sham," Frances corrected.

He skimmed his hands up and down her thighs, shifting her weight against him. His erection was more than interested in the shifting. "Didn't seem like it'd be hard to replicate," he agreed.

But that was before—before he'd seen past Frances's

armor, before he'd stupidly begun to like the real woman underneath.

She rocked her hips, and his body responded. He stroked her nipples—this time, without the roughness—and Frances moaned appreciatively. He shouldn't want her this much, shouldn't *like* her this much. Passion wasn't supposed to figure into his plans. It never had before.

He lifted her off long enough to roll on another condom, and then she settled her weight back onto him, taking him in with a sigh of pure pleasure. *This* was honesty. This was something real between them because she meant something more to him than just her last name.

She rode him slowly, taking her time, letting him play with her breasts and her nipples until she was panting and he was driving into her. He leaned forward enough to catch one of her breasts in his mouth and sucked her nipple hard between his teeth.

She might not like him in the morning, and she'd be well within her rights.

But he was going to like her. Hell, he already did. It was going to be a huge problem.

As she shuddered down on him, urging him to suck her nipples harder as she came apart, he didn't care. Complicated and messy and his.

She was his.

After she'd collapsed onto him and he'd taken care of the condom, they lay in each other's arms. He had things he wanted to say to her, except he didn't know what those things were, which wasn't like him. He was a decisive man. The buck stopped with him.

"Are we still going to get married next week?" she asked in a drowsy voice.

"If you want," he said, feeling even as he said it that it was not the best response. He tried again. "I thought we weren't going to talk about the deal tonight."

"We aren't," she agreed and then immediately qualified that statement. "It's just that...this changes things."

"Does it?" He leaned over and turned out the light and
then pulled the covers up over them both. When was the
last time he'd had a woman spend the night in his arms?
He couldn't think of when. His previous relationships were
not spend-the-night relationships.

He tucked his arm around her body and held her close.
Something cold and metallic poked at his side—the necklace. It was all she had on.

"We were supposed to barely live together," she reminded him. "We weren't supposed to sleep together. We
weren't..."

He yawned and shrugged. "So we'll be slightly more
married than we planned on. The marital bed and all that."

"And you're okay with that?"

"I'm okay with you." He kissed the top of her head. "I
guess... Well, when we made the deal, I didn't think I'd
enjoy spending time with you."

"You mean sex. You didn't think you'd enjoy sleeping with me." She sounded hurt about that, although he
couldn't tell if she was playing or actually pouting.

"No, I don't," he clarified. "I mean, I didn't think I'd
want to spend time with you. I didn't think I'd like you
this much."

The moment the words left his mouth, he knew that he'd
said too much. Damn it, they were supposed to roll over
and go to sleep and not have deep, meaningful conversations until he'd recovered from the sex and had some more.

Instead, Frances tensed and then sat up, pulling away
from him. "Ethan," she said, her voice a warning. "I told
you not to like me."

"You make it sound like I have a choice about it," he
said.

"You do."

"No, I don't. I can't help it." She didn't reply, didn't curl back into his arms. "We don't have to rush to get married. I'm willing to wait for you."

"Jesus," she said. The bed shifted, and then she was out of it, fumbling around the room in the dark. "Jesus, you sound like you *want* to marry me."

He turned on the light. "What's wrong?"

She threw his words back at him. "What's wrong?" She grabbed her dress and started to shimmy into it. Any other time, watching Frances Beaumont get dressed would be the highlight of his day. But not now, not when she was angrily trying to jerk up the zipper.

"Frances," he said, getting out of bed. "Where are you going?"

"This was a mistake," was the short reply.

He could see her zipping into her armor as fast as the dress—if not faster. "No, it wasn't," he said defensively, trying to catch her in his arms. "This was good. Great. This was us together. This is what we could be."

"Honestly, Ethan? There is no us. Not now, not ever. My God," she said, pushing him away and snagging her coat. "I thought you were smarter than this. Good sex and you're suddenly in love—in like?" she quickly corrected. "Unacceptable."

"Like hell it is," he roared at her.

"This is causal at best, Ethan. *Casual.* Casual sex, casual marriage." She flung her coat over her barely zipped dress and hastily knotted the belt. "I warned you, but you didn't listen, did you?"

"Would you calm the hell down and tell me what's wrong?" he demanded. "I did listen. I listened when you told me you expected to be courted with flowers and gifts and thoughtfulness."

"I did not—"

But he cut her off. "I listened when you told me about

your plans for a gallery. I listened when your family caught you off guard."

"I do not like you." She bit the words off as if she were killing them, one syllable at a time.

"I don't believe you. Not anymore. I've seen the real you, damn it all."

She drew herself up to her full height, a look on her face like a reigning monarch about to deliver a death sentence. "Have you?" she said. "I thought you were better at the game than this, Ethan. How disappointing that you're like all the rest."

And then she was gone. The door to the room swung open and slammed shut behind her, leaving Ethan wondering what the holy hell had just happened.

Fourteen

When had Frances lost control? That was the question she kept asking herself on the insanely long elevator ride down to the hotel lobby. She asked it as the valet secured a cab for her, and she asked it again on the long ride out to the mansion.

Because she had. She'd lost all sorts of control.

She slipped into the mansion. The place was dark and quiet—but then, it was late. Past midnight. The staff had left hours ago. Chadwick and Serena and their little girl were no doubt asleep, as were Frances's younger siblings.

She felt very much alone.

She took off her shoes and tiptoed up to her room. She jerked her zipper down so hard she heard tearing, which was a crying shame because this dress was her best one. But she couldn't quite care.

Frances dug out her ugly flannel pajamas, bright turquoise plaid and baggy shapelessness. They were warm and soft and comforting, and far removed from the nothing she'd almost fallen asleep wearing when she'd been in bed with Ethan.

God, what a mess. And, yes, she was aware that she was probably making it messier than it had to be, just by virtue of being herself.

But was he serious? Sure, she could have believed it if

he'd said he loved being with her and she was special and wonderful before the sex. It was expected, those words of seduction. Except he hadn't said them then. He'd said things that should have been insults—that she made his life harder than he wanted her to, that she drove him mad, that she was a complicated hot mess.

Those were not the words of a man trying to get laid.

Those were the words of an honest man.

And then after? To lay there in his arms and feel as if she'd exposed so much more than her body to him and to have him tell her that he enjoyed being with her, that he liked her, that—

That he'd happily push back their agreed-on marriage because she was worth waiting for?

It was all supposed to be a game. A game she'd played before and a game she'd play again. Yes, this was the long game—a wedding, a yearlong marriage—but that didn't change the rules.

Did it?

She climbed under her own covers in her own bed, a bed that was just as large as Ethan's. It felt empty compared with what she'd left behind.

Ethan wasn't following the rules. He was changing them. She'd warned him against doing so, but he was doing so anyway. And it was all too much for Frances. Too much honesty, too much realness. Too much intimacy.

Men had proposed before. Professed their undying love and admiration for her. But no one had ever meant it. No one ever did, not in her world. Love was a bargaining chip, nothing more. Sex was calling a bluff. All a game. Just a game. If you played it right, you got diamonds and houses and money. And if you lost…you got nothing.

Nothing.

She curled up into a tight ball, just like she'd always done back when she was little and her parents were fighting. On bad nights, she'd sneak into Byron's room and curl up in his bed. He took the top half and she took the bottom, their backs touching. That's how they'd come into this world. It felt safer that way.

Once, Mom had loved Dad. And Dad must have had feelings for Mom, right? That's why he'd married her and made their illegitimate child, Matthew, legitimate.

But they couldn't live together. They couldn't share a roof. They'd have been better off like Ethan's folks, going their separate ways 85 percent of the time and only coming together when the stars aligned just so. And in the end, her father had won and her mother had lost, and that had been the game.

She almost got up and got her phone to call Byron. To tell him she might have been rash and that she needed to come hang out for a couple of days until things cooled off. Mom was out there, anyway.

It was late. Byron was probably still asleep.

And then there was Friday. Donut Friday.

She had to face Ethan again. With an audience. Just like they'd planned it.

She had nothing to wear.

Delores walked in with a stack of interoffice envelopes. Ethan glared at her, trying to get his heart to calm down.

He hadn't heard from Frances since she'd stormed out of his room two nights ago, and it was making him jumpy. He did not like being jumpy.

"Any donuts yet?" he made himself say casually.

"Haven't seen her yet, but I can check with Larry to find out if she's on the premises," Delores said in a genial manner. She handed him a rather thick envelope. It had no return address. It just said, "E. Logan."

"What's this?"

"I'm sure I don't know." When Ethan glared at her, she said, "I'll go check on those donuts."

The old battle-ax, he thought menacingly as he undid the clasp and slid out a half-inch-thick manila folder.

"Potentially of our mutual interest—C. Beaumont," proclaimed a small, otherwise benign yellow sticky note on the front of the folder.

The only feeling that Ethan did not enjoy more than jumpiness was uncertainty. And that's what the manila folder suddenly represented. What on earth would Chadwick Beaumont consider of mutual interest? The only thing that came to mind was Frances.

And what of Frances could merit a folder this thick?

The possibilities—everything from blackmail to depravities—ran together in his mind. He shoved them aside and opened the file.

And found himself staring at a dossier for one Zeb Richards, owner of ZOLA.

Ethan blinked in astonishment as he scanned the information. Zeb Richards, born in Denver in 1973, graduated from Morehouse College with a bachelor of arts degree and from the University of Georgia with a master's in business administration. Currently resided in New York. There was a small color photo of the man, the first that Ethan had seen.

Wait—had he met Zeb Richards before? There was something about the set of the man's jaw that looked familiar. He had dark hair that was cropped incredibly close to his head, the way many black men wore it.

But Ethan would remember meeting someone named Zeb, wouldn't he?

Then he flipped the page and found another document—a photocopy of a birth certificate. Well, he had to hand it to Chadwick—he was nothing if not thorough. The certificate confirmed that Zebadiah Richards was

born in Denver in 1973. His mother was Emily Richards
and his father was…

Oh, hell.

Under "Father" was the unmistakable name of one
Hardwick James Beaumont.

Ethan flipped back to the photo. Yes, that jaw—that
was like Chadwick's jaw, like Phillip's. Those two men
had been unmistakably brothers—full brothers. The resemblance had been obvious. And they'd looked a fair
deal like Frances. The jaw was softer on her, more femi-
nine—more beautiful.

But if Zeb's mother had been African-American… That
would account for everything else.

Oh, hell.

Suddenly, it all made sense. This agitation on behalf of
ZOLA to sell the Beaumont Brewery? It wasn't a rival firm
looking to discredit Ethan's company, and it wasn't an activist shareholder looking to peel the Beaumont Brewery
off so it could pick it up for pennies on the dollar and sell
it off, like Ethan's father did.

This was personal.

And it had nothing to do with Ethan.

Except he was, as of about two nights ago, sleeping with
a Beaumont. He was probably still informally engaged to
be married to said Beaumont, although he wouldn't be sure
of that until the donut situation was confirmed. And, perhaps most important of all, he was currently running the
Beaumont Brewery.

"Delores," he said into the intercom. "Was this envelope hand-delivered to you?"

"It was on my desk this morning, Mr. Logan."

"I need to speak to Chadwick Beaumont. Can you get
me his number?"

"Of course." Ethan started to turn the intercom off, but
then she added, "Oh, Ms. Beaumont is on the premises."

"Thank you," he said. He flipped the intercom off and stuffed the folder back into the envelope. It was no joke to say he was out of his league here. A bastard son coming back to wreak havoc on his half siblings? Yeah, Ethan was *way* out of his league.

Chadwick must have a sense of humor, what with that note about Zeb Richards being "potentially" a mutual interest.

But Frances—she didn't know anything about her siblings from unmarried mothers, did she? No, Ethan was certain he remembered her saying she didn't know any of them. Just that there were some.

So Zeb Richards was not, at this exact moment, something she needed to know about.

Unless…

He thought back to the way she'd stood before him last night, all of her armor fully in place while he'd been naked in every sense of the word. And she'd said—*No, be honest*, he told himself—*sneered* that she'd thought he'd be better at the game.

Was Zeb Richards part of the game?

Just because Frances said she didn't know any of the illegitimate Beaumonts didn't mean she'd been truthful about it.

She'd asked Ethan why he wanted to marry her. Had he asked why she'd agreed to marry him? Beyond the money for her art gallery?

What else was she getting out of their deal?

Why had she shown up with donuts last week?

The answer was right in front of him, a manila folder in an envelope.

Revenge.

Hadn't she told him that she'd lost part of herself when the family lost the Brewery? And hadn't she said she should hate him for his part in that loss?

What had seemed like a distant coincidence—Frances disrupting his personal life at nearly the exact same time some random investor was trying to disrupt his business—now seemed less like a coincidence and more like directly correlated events.

What if she not only knew Zeb Richards was her half brother—what if she was helping him? Getting insider information? Not from Ethan, necessarily—but from all the people here who loved and trusted her because she was their Frannie?

Did Chadwick know? Or did he suspect? Was that why he'd sent the file?

Ethan had assumed it'd been the encounter with Phillip Beaumont that had prompted Chadwick's appearance at the Brewery the other day. But what if there'd been something else? What if one of Chadwick's loyal employees had tipped him off that Frances was asking around, digging up dirt?

And if that was possible, who's side was Chadwick on? Ethan's? Frances's? Zeb Richards's?

Ethan's head began to ache. This, he realized with a half laugh, was what he was trying to marry into—a family so sprawling, so screwed up that they didn't even have a solid head count on all their relatives.

"She's here," Delores's voice interrupted his train of thought.

Ethan stood and straightened his tie. He didn't know why. He pushed the thought of bastards with an ax to grind out of his head. He had to focus on what was important here—Frances. The woman he'd taken to his bed last night and then promptly chased right out of it, all because he was stupid enough to develop feelings for her.

The woman who might be setting him up to fail because it was a game. Nothing but a game.

He had no idea which version of Frances Beaumont was on the other side of that door.

He wanted to be wrong. He wanted it to be one giant coincidence. He did not want to know that he'd misjudged her so badly, that he'd been played for such a fool.

Because if he had, he didn't know where he would go from here. He was still the CEO of this company. He still had a deal to marry her and invest in her gallery. He had his own company to protect. As soon as the Brewery was successfully restructured, he'd pull up stakes and move on to the next business that needed to be run with an iron fist and an eye to the bottom line. They'd divorce casually and go on with their lives.

And once he was gone, he'd never have to think about anything Beaumont ever again.

He opened his door. Frances was standing there in jeans and boots. She wore a thick, fuzzy cable-knit sweater, and her hair was pulled back into a modest bun. Not a sky-high heel or low-cut silk blouse in sight. She looked…plain, almost, which was something because if there was one thing Frances Beaumont wasn't, it was plain.

And despite the fact that his head felt as if an anvil had just been dropped on it, despite the fact that he was in over his head—despite the fact that, no, he was most likely not as good at the game as he'd thought he was and, no, she did not like him—he was glad to see her. He absolutely shouldn't be, but he was.

It only got worse when she lifted her head. There was no crowd today, no group of eager employees around to stroke her ego or destroy his. Just her and Delores and a box.

"Frances."

"Chocolate éclair?" she asked simply.

Even her makeup was simple today. She looked almost innocent, as if she was still trying to understand what had happened between them last night, just like he was.

But was that the truth of the matter? Or was this part of the game?

"I saved you two," she told him, holding the box out.

"Come in," he said, holding his door open for her. "Delores, hold my calls."

"Even—" she started to say.

"I'll call him back." Yes, he needed to talk to Chadwick, but he needed to talk to Frances more. He wasn't sleeping with Chadwick. Frances came first.

Frances paused, a look on her face that yesterday Ethan would have assumed to be confusion. Today? He couldn't be sure.

She walked past him, her head held high and her bearing regal. Ethan wanted to smile at her. Evening gowns or blue jeans, she could pull off imperial like nobody's business.

But he didn't smile. She did not like him. And liking her? Wanting to take care of her, to spend time with her? That had been a massive error on his part.

So the moment the door shut, he resolved that he would not care about her. He would not pull her into his arms and hold her tight and try to find the right sweet nothings to whisper in her ear to wipe that shell-shocked look off her face.

He would not comfort her. He couldn't afford to.

She carried the donut box over to the wagon-wheel coffee table and set it down. Then she sat on the love seat, tucking her feet up under her legs. "Hi," she said in what seemed like a small voice.

He didn't like it, that small voice, because it pulled at him, and he couldn't afford to let her play his emotions like that. "How are you today?" he asked politely. He went back to his desk and sat. It seemed like the safest place to be, with a good fifteen feet and a bunch of historic furniture between them.

She watched him with those big eyes of hers. "I brought you donuts," she said.

"Thank you." He realized his fingers were tapping on the envelope Chadwick had sent. He made them be still.

She said, "Oh. Okay," in such a disappointed voice that it almost broke him because he didn't want to disappoint her, damn it, and he was anyway.

But then, what was he supposed to do? He'd given her everything he had last night, and look how that had turned out. She'd cut him to shreds. She'd been disappointed that he'd liked her.

So she wasn't allowed to be disappointed that he was keeping his distance right now. End of discussion.

He stared at the envelope again. He had to know—how deep was she in this? "So," he said. "How are the plans for the art gallery going?"

"Fine. Are we…"

"Yes?"

She cleared her throat and stuck out her chin, as if she was trying to look tough and failing, miserably. "Are we still on? The deal, that is."

"Of course. Why would you think it's off?"

She took a deep breath. "I—well, I said some not-nice things last night. You've been nothing but wonderful and I… I was not gracious about it. About you."

Was she apologizing? For hurting his feelings? Not that he'd admit to having his feelings hurt.

Was it possible that, somewhere under the artifice, she actually cared for him, too?

No, probably not. This was just another test, another move. Ethan made a big show of shrugging. "At no point did I assume that this relationship—or whatever you want to call it—is based on 'niceness.'" She visibly winced. "You were right. Affection is irrelevant." This time, he did not offer to let her out of the deal or postpone the farce that would be their wedding. "And a deal's a deal, after all."

A shadow crossed her face, but only briefly. "Of course," she agreed. She wrapped her arms around her waist. She looked as though she was trying to hold herself together. "So we'll need to get engaged soon?"

"Tonight, if that's all right with you. I've made reservations for us as we continue our tour of the finer restaurants in Denver." He let his gaze flick over her outfit in what he hoped was judgment.

"Sounds good." That's what she said. But the way she said it? Anything but good.

"I did have a question," he said. "You asked me last night why I'd agreed to get married to you. To a stranger."

"Because it seems normal enough," she replied. He refused to be even the slightest bit pleased that she recalled their conversation about his parents. "And the workers love me."

He tilted his head in appreciation. "But when we were naked and sharing, I failed to ask what you were getting out of this deal. Why *you* would agree to marry a total stranger."

She paled, which made her red hair stand out that much more. "The gallery," she said in a shaky voice. "It's going to be my job, my space. Art is what I'm good at. I need the gallery."

"Oh, I'm quite sure," he agreed, swiveling his chair so he was facing her fully. His hand was tapping the envelope again. Damn that envelope. Damn Zebadiah Richards. Hell, while he was at it, damn Chadwick Beaumont, too. "But that's not all, is it?"

Slowly, her head moved from side to side, a no that she was apparently unaware she was saying. "Of course that's all. A simple deal."

"With the man who represented the loss of your family business and your family identity."

"Well, yes. That's why I need the gallery. I need a fresh start."

He leveled his stoniest glare at her, the one that produced results in business negotiations. The very look that usually had employees falling all over themselves to do what he wanted, the way he wanted it.

To her credit, she did not buckle. He would have been disappointed if she had, frankly. He watched her armor snap into place. But it didn't stop the rest of the color from draining out of her face.

He had her, and they both knew it.

"You wanted revenge."

The statement hung in the air. Frances's gaze darted from side to side as if she was looking for an escape route. When she didn't find what she wanted, she sat up straighter.

Good, Ethan thought. She was going to brazen this out. For some reason, he wanted it that way, wanted her to go down fighting. He didn't want her meek and apologetic and fragile, damn it. He wanted her biting and cutting, a warrior princess with words as weapons.

He wanted her messy and complicated, and, damn it all, he was going to get her that way. Even if it killed him.

"I don't know what you're talking about." As she said it, she uncurled on the couch. Her legs swung down and stretched out before her, long and lean, the very legs that had been wrapped around him. At the same time, she stretched up, thrusting out her breasts.

This time, he did smile. She was going to give him hell. *This* was the woman who'd walked into his office a week ago, using her body as a weapon of mass distraction.

This was the woman he could love.

He pushed that thought aside.

"How did you plan to do it?" he asked. "Did you plan on pumping me for information, or just gather some from the staff while you plied them with donuts?"

One eyebrow arched up. "*Plied?* Really, Ethan." She shifted forward, which would have worked much better to distract him if she'd been in a low-cut top instead of a sweater. "You make it sound like I was spiking the pastries with truth-telling serum."

He caught the glint of a necklace—his necklace, the one he'd given her last night. She was wearing it. For some reason, that distracted him far more than the seductive pose did.

"What I want to know," he said in a calm voice, "is if Richards contacted you first, or if you contacted him."

Her mouth had already opened to reply, but the mention of Richards's name pulled her up short. She blinked at him, her confusion obvious. Too obvious. "Who?"

"Don't play cute with me, Frances. You said so yourself, didn't you? This is all part of the game. I just didn't realize how far it went until this morning."

Her brow wrinkled. "I don't—who is Richards?"

"This innocent thing isn't working," he snapped.

Abruptly, she stood. "I don't know who Richards is. I didn't ply anyone with donuts to tell me anything they weren't willing to tell me anyway—which, for the most part, was how you were a jerk who didn't know the first thing about running the Brewery. So you can accuse me of plotting some unspecified revenge with some unspecified man named Richards, if that makes you feel better about not being able to do your own job without me smiling like an idiot by your side. But in the meantime, go to hell." She swept out of the room with all the cold grace he could have expected. She didn't even slam the door on the way out, probably because that would have been beneath her.

"Dinner tonight," he called after her, just so he could get in the last word.

"Ha!" he heard her say as she walked away from him.

Damn, that last bit had been more than loud enough that Delores would have heard. And Ethan knew that whatever Delores heard, the rest of the company heard.

The thing was, he was still no closer to an answer about Frances's level of involvement with ZOLA and Zeb Richards than he'd been before she'd shown up. He'd thought he'd learned how to read her, but last night, she'd made him question his emotional investment in her.

He had no idea how to trust anything she said or how to decide if she was telling the truth.

A phone rang. It sounded as if it came from a long way away. Delores stuck her head through the door. "I know you said to hold your calls," she said in a cautious voice, "but Chadwick's on the phone."

"I'll take it," he said because to pretend he was otherwise involved would look ridiculous.

He was going to get engaged tonight. Frances was supposed to start sleeping over. He was going to get married to her next weekend so he could maintain control over his company.

Because that was the deal.

He picked up his phone. "Who the hell is Zeb Richards?"

Fifteen

Frances found herself at the gallery—actually, at what would become the gallery. It wasn't a gallery yet. It was just an empty industrial space.

Becky was there with some contractors, discussing lighting options. "Oh, Frances—there you are," she said in a happy voice. But then she paused. "Are you okay?"

"Fine," Frances assured her. "Why would anything be wrong? Excuse me." She dodged contractors and headed back to the office. This room, at least, was suitable to hide in. It had walls, a door—and a lock.

Why would anything be wrong? She'd only screwed up. That wasn't unusual. That was practically par for the course. Ethan had been—well, he'd been wonderful. She'd spent a week with him. She'd let her guard down around him. She'd even slept with him—and he was amazing.

So of course she'd gone and opened her big mouth and insulted him, and now he was colder than a three-day-old fish.

She sat down at what would be her desk when she got moved in and stared at the bare wooden top. He'd said he liked her messy and complicated. And for a moment, she'd almost believed him.

But he hadn't meant it. Oh, he thought he had, of that she had no doubt. He'd thought he liked her all not simple.

He'd no doubt imagined he'd mastered the complexities of her extended family, besting her brothers in a show of sheer skill and Logan-based manliness.

The fool, she thought sadly. He'd gone and convinced himself that he could handle her. And he couldn't. Maybe no one could.

Then there'd been the conversation today. What the ever-loving hell had that been about? Revenge? Well, yeah—revenge had been part of it. She hadn't lied, had she? She'd told him that she'd lost part of herself when the Brewery had been sold. She just hadn't expected him to throw that back in her face.

And who the hell was this Richards she was supposed to be conspiring with?

Still, a deal was a deal. And as Ethan had made it quite clear that morning, it was nothing but a deal. She supposed she'd earned that.

It was better this way, she decided. She couldn't handle Ethan when he was being tender and sweet and saying absolutely ridiculous things like how he'd happily put the wedding off because she was worth the wait.

The sooner he figured out she wasn't worth nearly that much, the better.

The doorknob turned, but the lock held. This was followed by a soft knock. "Frances?" Becky said. "Can I come in?"

Against her better judgment, Frances got up and unlocked the door for her friend. A deal was a deal, after all—especially since Frances wasn't the only one who needed this gallery. Becky was depending on it just as much as Frances was. "Yes?"

Becky pushed her way into the office and shut the door behind her. "What's wrong?"

"Nothing," Frances lied. Too late, she remembered she

should try to look as if that statement were accurate. She attempted a lighthearted smile.

Becky's eyes widened in horror at this expression. "Ohmygosh—what happened?"

Maybe she wouldn't try to smile right now. It felt wrong, anyway. "Just a...disagreement. This doesn't change the deal. It's fine," Frances said with more force. "I just thought—well, I thought he was different. And I think he's really much the same."

That was the problem, wasn't it? For a short while, she'd believed Ethan might actually be interested in her, not her famous name or famous family.

Why hadn't she just taken him at his word? Why had she pushed and pushed and pushed, for God's sake, until whatever honest fondness he felt for her had been pushed aside under the glaring imperfection that was Frances Beaumont? Why couldn't she have just let good enough alone and accepted his flowers and his diamonds and his offers of affection and companionship?

Why did she have to ruin everything?

She'd warned him. She'd told him not to like her. She just hadn't realized that she'd do everything in her power to make sure he didn't.

She'd screwed up *so* much. She'd lost a fortune three separate times. Every endeavor she'd ever attempted outside of stringing a man along had failed miserably. She'd never had a relationship that could come close to breaking her heart because there was nothing to break.

So this relationship had been doomed from the get-go. Nothing lost, nothing gained. She was not going to let this gallery fail. She needed the steady job and the sense of purpose far more than she needed Ethan to look her in the eye and tell her that he wanted her just as complicated as she was.

Unexpectedly, Becky pulled her into a tight hug. "I'm so sorry, honey," she whispered into Frances's ear.

"Jeez, Becks—it was just a disappointing date. Not the end of the world." And the more Frances told herself that, the truer it'd become. "Now go," she said, doing her best to sound as if it was just another Friday at the office. "Contractors don't stand around for free."

She had to make this gallery work. She had to…

She had to do something to not think about Ethan.

That was going to be rather difficult when they had dinner tonight.

She wore the green dress. She felt more powerful in the green dress than she did in the bridesmaid's dress. And she'd only worn the green dress to the office, not out to dinner, so it wasn't like wearing the same outfit two days in a row.

The only person who would recognize the dress was Ethan, and, well, there was nothing to be done about that.

Frances twisted her hair up. The only jewelry she wore was the necklace. The one he'd gotten for her. It felt odd to wear it, to know he'd picked it out on his own and that, for at least a little while, she'd been swayed by something so cliché as diamonds.

But it was a beautiful piece, and it went with the dress. And, after all, she was getting engaged tonight so it only seemed right to wear the diamonds from her fiancé.

She swept into the restaurant, head up and smile firmly in place. She'd given herself a little pep talk about how this wasn't about Ethan; this was about her and she had to get what she needed out of it. And if that occasionally included mind-blowing sex, then so be it. She needed to get laid every so often. Ethan was more than up to the task. Casual sex in a casual marriage. No big whoop.

Ethan was waiting for her at the bar again. "Frances,"

he said, pulling her into a tight embrace and brushing his lips over her cheek. She didn't miss the way he avoided her lips. "Shall we?"

"Of course." She was ready for him tonight. He was not going to get to her.

"You're looking better," he said as he held her chair for her.

"Oh? Was I not up to your usual high standards this morning?"

Ethan's mouth quirked into a wry smile. "You seem better, too."

She waved away his backhanded compliment. "So," she said, not even bothering to look at the menu, "tell me about this mysterious Richards person. If I'm going to be accused of industrial espionage, I should at least get some of the details."

His smile froze and then fell right off his face. It made Frances feel good, the rush of power that went with catching him off guard.

So she'd had a rough night and a tough morning. She was not going down with a whimper. And if he thought he could steamroll her, well, he'd learn soon enough.

"Actually," he said, dropping his gaze to his menu, "I did want to talk to you about that. I owe you an apology."

He owed her an apology? This morning he'd accused her of betrayal. This evening—apologies?

No. She did not want to slide back into that space where he professed to care about her feelings because that was where she got into trouble. She pointedly stared at her menu.

"Do you know who Zeb Richards is?"

"No. I assume he is the Richards in question, however." She still didn't look at Ethan. She realized she was fiddling with the diamonds at her neck, but she couldn't quite help herself.

"He is." Out of the corner of her eye, she saw Ethan lay down his menu. "I don't feel it's my place to tell you this, but I don't want to come off as patronizing, so—"

"A tad late for that," she murmured in as disinterested a voice as possible.

"A company called ZOLA is trying to make my life harder. They're making noises that my company is failing at restructuring and that AllBev should sell off the Brewery. One presumes that they'll either buy it on the cheap or buy it for scrap. A company like the Brewery is worth almost as much for its parts as it is for its value."

"Indeed," she said. She managed to nail "faux sympathetic," if she did say so herself. "And this concerns me how?"

"ZOLA is run by Zeb Richards."

This time, she did put down her menu. "And...? Out with it, Ethan."

For the first time, Ethan looked unsure of himself. "Zeb Richards is your half brother."

She blinked a few times. "I have many half brothers. However, I don't particularly remember one of them being named Zeb."

"When I found out this morning that he was related to you, I assumed you were working with him."

She stared at him. "How do you know about any supposed half brothers of mine?"

"Chadwick," he added with an apologetic smile.

"I should have known," she murmured.

"I asked him if he knew about ZOLA, and he gave me a file on Richards. Including proof that you and Zeb are related."

"How very nice of him to tell *you* and not *me*." Oh, she was damnably tired of Chadwick meddling in her affairs.

"Hence why I'm trying not to be patronizing." Ethan

fiddled with his silverware. "I did not have all the facts this morning when you got to the office and I made a series of assumptions that were unfair to you."

She looked at him flatly. "Is that so? And what, pray tell, was this additional information that has apparently exonerated me so completely?"

He dropped his gaze and she knew. "Chadwick again?"

"Correct. He believes that you have never had contact with your other half brothers. So, I'm sorry about my actions this morning. I was concerned that you were working with Richards to undermine the Brewery and I know now that simply isn't the case."

This admission was probably supposed to make her feel better. It did not. "*That's* what you were concerned with? *That's* what this morning was about?"

And not her? Not the way she'd insulted him last night, the way she'd stormed out of the hotel room without even pausing long enough to get her dress zipped properly?

He'd been worried about the company. His job.

Not her.

It shouldn't hurt. After all, this entire relationship was built on the premise that he was doing it for the company. For the Brewery and for his private firm.

No, it shouldn't have hurt at all.

Funny how it did.

"I could see how you were trying to get your family identity back. It wasn't a difficult mental leap to make, you understand. But I apologize."

She stared at him. She'd wanted to get revenge. She'd wanted to bring him down several pegs and put him in his place. But she hadn't conspired with some half brother she didn't even know existed to take down the whole company.

She didn't want to take down the company. The people

who worked there were her friends, her second family. Destroying the company would be destroying them.

It'd mean destroying Ethan, too.

"You're serious. You're really apologizing?"

He nodded, the look in his eyes deepening as he leaned forward. "I should have had more faith in you. It's a mistake I won't make again."

As an apology went, it wasn't bad. Actually, it was pretty damned good. There was only one problem with it.

"So that's it? The moment things actually get messy, you assume I'm trying to ruin you. But now that my brother has confirmed that I've never even heard of Zeb Richards or whatever his name is, you're suddenly all back to 'I like you complicated, Frances'?" She scoffed and slouched away from the table.

It must have come out louder than she realized because his eyes hardened. "We are in public."

"So we are. Your point?"

A muscle in his jaw tensed. "This is the night when I ask you to marry me," he said in a low growl that, despite the war of words they were engaged in, sent a shiver down her spine because it was the exact same voice he'd used when he'd bent her over the bed and made her come. Twice.

"Is it?" she growled back. "Do you always ask women to marry you when you're losing an argument?"

He stared hard at her for a second and then, unbelievably, his lips curved into an almost smile, as if he enjoyed this. "No. But I'll make an exception for you."

"Don't," she said, suddenly afraid of this. Of him. Of what he could do to her if she let him.

"This was the deal."

"Don't," she whispered, terrified.

He pushed back from his chair in full view of everyone in the restaurant. He dropped to one knee, just like in the movies, and pulled a robin's-egg-blue box out of his pocket. "Frances," he said in a stage voice loud enough to carry across the whole space. "I know we haven't known each other very long, but I can't imagine life without you. Will you do me the honor of marrying me?"

It sounded rehearsed. It wasn't the fumbling failure at sweet nothings she'd come to expect from him. It was for show. All for show.

Just like they'd planned.

This was where the small part of her brain that wasn't freaking out—and it was a very small part—was supposed to say yes. Where she was publically supposed to declare her love for him, and they were supposed to ride off into the sunset—or, at the very least, his hotel room—and consummate their relationship. Again.

He was handsome and good in bed and a worthy opponent and rich—couldn't forget that. And he liked her most of the time. He liked her too much.

She was supposed to say yes. For the gallery. For Becky. For the Brewery, for all the workers.

She was supposed to say yes so she could make Frances Beaumont important again, so that the Beaumont name would mean what she wanted it to mean—fame and accolades and people wanting to be her friend.

She was supposed to say yes for *her*. This was what she wanted.

Wasn't it?

Ethan's face froze. "Well?" he demanded in a quiet voice. "Frances."

Say yes, her brain urged. *Say yes right now.*

"I…" She was horrified to hear her voice come out as a whisper. "I can't."

His eyes widened in horror or confusion or some unholy mix of the two, she didn't know. She didn't wait around to find out. She bolted out of the restaurant as fast as she could in her heels. She didn't even wait to get her coat.

She ran. It was an act of cowardice. An act of surrender.

She'd ceded the game.

She'd lost everything.

Sixteen

"Frances?"

What the hell just happened? One second, he was following the script because, yes, he damn well had planned out the proposal. It was for public consumption.

The next second, she was gone, cutting an emerald-green swath through the suddenly silent restaurant.

"Frances, wait!" he called out, painfully aware that this was not part of the plan. He lunged to his feet and took off after her. She couldn't just leave—not like that. This wasn't how it was supposed to go.

Okay, today had not been his best work. He'd acted without all the available facts this morning and clearly, that had been a bad move. There were no such things as coincidences—except, it seemed, for right now.

Yes, he should have given her the benefit of the doubt and yes, he probably should have groveled a little more. The relief Ethan had felt when Chadwick had told him the only Beaumonts who knew of Zeb's identity were him and Matthew had been no small thing. Frances hadn't been plotting to overthrow the company. In fact, she'd been apologizing to Ethan. They could reset at dinner and continue on as they had been.

But he hadn't expected her to run away from him—especially not after the way she'd dressed him down after they'd had sex.

If she didn't want to get married, he thought as he gave chase, why the hell hadn't she just said so? He'd given her an out—several outs. And she'd refused his concessions at every turn, only to leave him hanging with a diamond engagement ring in his hand.

This wasn't right, damn it.

He caught up with her trying to hail a cab. He could see her shivering in the cold wind. "For God's sake, Frances," he said, shucking his suit jacket and slinging it around her shoulders. "You'll catch your death."

"Ethan," she said in the most plaintive voice he'd ever heard.

"What are you doing?" he demanded. "This was the deal."

"I know, I know…" She didn't elucidate on that knowledge, however.

"Frances." He took her by the arm and pulled her a step back from the curb. "We agreed—we agreed this *morning*—that I was going to ask you to marry me and you were going to say yes." When she didn't look at him, he dropped her arm and cupped her face in his hands. "Babe, talk to me."

"Don't *babe* me, Ethan."

"Then talk, damn it. What the hell happened?"

"I—I can't. I thought I could, but I can't. Don't you see?" He shook his head. "I thought—I thought I didn't need love. That I could do this and it'd be no different than watching my parents fight, no different than all the other men who wanted to get close to the Beaumont name and money. You weren't supposed to be *different*, Ethan. You were supposed to be the *same*."

Then, as he watched in horror, a tear slipped past her blinking eyelid and began to trickle down her cheek.

"I wasn't supposed to like you. And you, you big idiot, you weren't supposed to like me," she said, her voice quiet and shaky as more tears followed the first.

He tried to wipe the tears away with his thumb, but they were replaced too quickly. "I don't understand how liking each other makes marrying each other a bad thing," he said.

"You're here for your company. You're not here for me," she said, cutting him off before he could protest.

An unfamiliar feeling began to push past the confusion and the frustration—a feeling that he hadn't often allowed himself to feel.

Panic.

And he wasn't sure why. It could be that, if the workers at the Brewery got it in their collective heads that he'd broken their Frannie's heart, they might draw and quarter him. He could be panicking that his foolproof method of regaining control over his business felt suddenly very foolish.

But that wasn't it. That wasn't it at all.

"See?" She sniffed. She was openly crying at this point. It was horrifying because as much as she might have berated him for being lousy at the game when he dared admit that he might have feelings for her, he knew this was not a play on her part. "How long will it last?"

His mouth opened. *A year*, he almost said, because that was the deal.

"I could love you," he told her and it was God's honest truth. "If you'll let me."

Her eyes closed, and she turned her head away. "Ethan…" she whispered, so softly he almost didn't hear it over the sound of a cab pulling up next to them. "I could love you, too." For a moment, he thought she was agreeing; she was seeing the light, and they'd get in the cab and carry on as planned.

But then she added, "I won't settle for *could*. Not anymore. I can't believe I'm saying this, but I want to be in love with the man I marry. And I want him to be in love with me, too. I want to believe I'm worth that—worth something more than a business deal. Worth more than some company."

"You are," he said, but it didn't sound convincing, not even to his own ears. "You *are*, Frances."

She gave him a sad smile full of heartache. "I want to believe that, Ethan. But I'm not a prize to be won in the game. Not anymore."

She slipped his jacket off her slim shoulders and held it out to him.

He didn't want to take it. He didn't want her to go. "Keep it. I don't want you to freeze."

She shook her head no, and the cabbie honked and shouted, "Lady, you need a ride or not?" so Frances ducked into the cab.

He stood there, freezing his ass off as he watched the cab's taillights disappear down the street.

When he'd talked to Chadwick Beaumont on the phone today, he'd barely been able to wait for Chadwick to get done explaining who the hell Zeb Richards was before asking, "Does Frances know about this?" because he'd been desperate to know if she was leading him on or if those moments he'd thought where honesty were real.

"Unless she's hired her own private investigators, the only people who know about my father's illegitimate children are me and Matthew. My mother was the one who originally tracked down the oldest three. She'd long suspected my father was cheating on her," he had added. "There are others."

"And you don't think Frances would have hired her own PI?"

"Problem?" Chadwick had said in such a genial way that

Ethan had almost confided in him that he might have just accused Chadwick's younger sister of industrial espionage.

"No," Ethan had said because, at the time, it hadn't been a problem. A little lover's quarrel, nothing that a thirty-thousand-dollar diamond ring couldn't fix. "Just trying to understand the Beaumont family tree."

"Good luck with that," was all Chadwick had said.

Ethan had thanked him for the information and promised to pass along anything new he learned. Then he'd eaten his donuts and thought about how he'd make it up to Frances.

She'd promised not to love him—not to even like him. She'd told him to do the same. He should have listened to her, but he hadn't lied. When it came to her, he couldn't quite help himself. Everything about her had been an impulse. Even his original proposal had been half impulse, driven by some basic desire to outwit Frances Beaumont.

Their entire relationship had been based on a game of one-upmanship. In that regard, she'd gotten the final word. She'd said no.

Well, hell. Now what? He'd publically proposed, been publically rejected and his whole plan had fallen apart on him. And the worst thing was that he wasn't sure *why*. Was it because he hadn't trusted her this morning when she'd said she didn't know anything about Richards?

Or was it because, despite it all, he did like her? He liked her a great deal. More than was wise, that much was sure.

This morning she'd shown up at his office with the donuts he'd requested. She hadn't had on a stitch of her armor—no designer clothes, no impenetrable attitude. She'd been a woman who'd sat down, admitted fault and apologized for her actions.

She'd been trying to show him that she liked him. Enough to be honest with him.

He'd thrown that trust back in her face. And then cavalierly assumed that a big rock was going to make it up to her.

Idiot. She wanted to know she was worth it—and she hadn't meant worth diamonds and roses.

He was in too deep to let her go. She *was* worth it.

So this was what falling in love was like.

How was he going to convince her that this wasn't part of the game?

Frances was not surprised when no extravagant floral arrangement arrived the next day. No chocolates or champagne or jewels showed up, either.

They didn't arrive the day after that. Or the third, for that matter.

And why would they? She was not bound to Ethan. She had no claim on him, nor he on her. The only thing that remained of their failed, doomed "relationship" were several vases of withering flowers and an expensive necklace.

She had taken off the necklace.

But she hadn't been able to bring herself to return it. Not to him, not to the store for cash—cash she could use, now that the gallery was dead and she had no other job prospects, aside from selling her family's heirlooms on the open market.

The necklace sat on her bedside table, mocking her as she went to sleep every night.

She called Becky but didn't feel like talking except to say, "The funding is probably not going to happen, so plan accordingly."

To which Becky had replied, "We'll get it figured out, one way or the other."

That was the sort of platitude people said when the situation was hopeless but they needed to feel better. So Frances had replied, "Sure, we'll get together for lunch soon and go over our options," because that was the sort of thing rational grown-ups said all the time.

Then she'd ended the call and crawled back under the covers.

Byron had texted, but what could she tell him? That she'd done the not-rash thing for the first time in her life and was now miserable? And why, exactly, was she miserable again? She shouldn't be hiding under the covers in her cozy jammies! She'd won! She'd stopped Ethan in his tracks with a move he couldn't anticipate and he couldn't recover from. She'd brought him firmly down to where he belonged. He wasn't good enough for the Beaumonts, and he wasn't good enough for the Brewery.

Victory was hers!

She didn't think victory was supposed to taste this sour.

She didn't believe in love. Never had, never would. So why, when the next best thing had presented itself—someone who was fond of her, who admired her, and who could still make her shiver with need, someone who had offered to generously provide for her financial future in exchange for a year of her life even—*why* had she walked away?

Because he was only here for the company. And, fool that she was, she'd suddenly realized she wanted someone who was going to be here for her.

"I could love you." She heard his words over and over again, beating against her brain like a spike. He could.

But he didn't.

What a mess.

Luckily, she was used to it.

She'd managed to drag herself to the shower on the fourth day. She had decided that she was going to stop moping. Moping didn't get jobs, and it didn't heal broken hearts. She needed to get up and, at the very least, have lunch with Becky or go see Byron. She needed to do something that would eventually get her out of the Beaumont mansion because she was *done* living under the same roof as Chadwick. She was going to tell him that the very next time she saw him, too.

She'd just buttoned her jeans when she heard the doorbell. She ignored it as she toweled her hair.

Then someone knocked on her bedroom door. "Frannie?" It was Serena, Chadwick's wife. "Flowers for you."

"Really?" Who would send her flowers? Not Ethan. Not at this late date. "Hang on." She threw on a sweater and opened the door.

Serena stood there, an odd look on her face. She was not holding any flowers. "Um… I think you need to get these yourself," Serena said before she turned and walked down the hall.

Frances stood there, all the warning bells going off in her head at once.

Her heart pounding, she walked down the hallway and peered over the edge of the railing. There, in the middle of the foyer, stood Ethan, holding a single red rose.

She must have made a noise or gasped or something because he looked up at her and smiled. A good smile, the kind of smile that made her want to do something ridiculous like kiss him when she absolutely should not be glad to see him at all.

She needed to say something witty and urbane and snarky that would put him in his place, so that for at least a minute, she could feel like Frances Beaumont again.

Instead, she said, "You're here."

Damn. Worse, it came out breathy, as if she couldn't believe he'd actually ventured into the lair of the Beaumonts.

"I am," he replied, his gaze never leaving her face. "I came for you."

Oh. That was terribly close to a sweet nothing—no, it

wasn't a nothing. It was a sweet something. But what? "I'm here. I've been here for a few days now."

There, that was a good thing to say. Something that let him know that his apology—if this even was an apology—was days late and, judging by the single flower he was holding, dollars short.

"I had some things to do," he said. "Can you come down here?"

"Why should I?"

His grin spread. "Because I don't want to shout? But I will." He cleared his throat. *"Frances!"* he shouted, his voice ringing off the marble and the high-vaulted ceilings. *"Can you come down here? Please?"*

"Okay, okay!" She didn't know who else besides Serena was home, but she didn't need to have Ethan yelling at the top of his lungs.

She hurried down the wide staircase with Ethan watching her the entire time. She slowed only when she got to the last few steps. She didn't want to be on his level, not just yet. "I'm here," she said again.

He held out the lone red rose to her. "I brought you a flower."

"Just one?"

"One seemed…fitting, somehow." He looked her over. "How have you been?"

"Oh, fine," she tried to say lightly. "Just hanging out around the house, trying to avoid social media and gossip columns—the normal stuff, really. Just another day in the life of a Beaumont."

He took a step closer to her. It made her tense. "You don't have to do that," he said, his voice soft and quiet and just for her.

"Do what?"

"Put your armor on. I didn't come here looking for a fight."

She eyed him warily. What was this? A single rose? A claim that he didn't want to fight? "Then why did you come?"

He took another step in—close enough to touch her. Which he did. He lifted his hand and brushed his fingertips down her cheek. "I wanted to tell you that you're worth it."

She froze under his touch, the rose between them. "We aren't in public, Ethan. You don't have to do this. It's over. We made a scene. It's fine. We can go on with our lives now." Her words came out in a rush.

"Do you really believe that? That it's fine?"

"Isn't it?" Her voice cracked, damn it.

"It isn't. Three days without you has almost driven me mad."

"I drive you mad when we're together. I drive you mad when we're apart—you know how to make a woman feel special." The words should have sounded flippant. They didn't. No matter how hard she tried, she couldn't convince herself that this was no big deal. Not when Ethan was staring into her eyes with this odd look of satisfaction on his face, not when his thumb was now stroking her cheek.

"Why are you here?" she whispered, desperate to hear the answer and just as desperate to not hear it.

"I came for you. I've never met anyone like you before, and I don't want to walk away from you. Not now, not ever."

"It's all just talk, Ethan." Her voice was the barest of whispers. She was doing a lousy job convincing herself. She didn't think she was convincing him at all.

"Do you know how much you're worth to me?"

She shook her head. "Some diamonds, some flowers. A rose."

He stepped in another bit, bringing her body almost into contact with his. "As of yesterday, I am no longer the CEO of the Beaumont Brewery."

"What?"

"I quit the job. For personal reasons. My second in command, Finn Jackson, flew in today to take over the restructuring project. We're still dealing with a little fallout from AllBev, but it's nothing I can't handle." He said it as if it were just a little speed bump.

"You *quit*? The Brewery?"

"It wasn't my company. It wasn't worth it to me. Not like you are."

"I don't understand." He was saying words that she understood individually. But the way he was stringing them together? It didn't make sense. Not a bit.

Something in his eyes changed—deepened. A small shiver ran down Frances's back. "I do not need to marry you to solidify my position within the company because I no longer work for the company. I do not need to worry about unknown relations trying to overthrow my position because I have given up the position. The company was never worth more than you were."

She blinked at him. All of her words failed her. She had nothing to hide behind now.

"So," he went on, his eyes full of honesty and sincerity and hope. All of those things she hadn't believed she deserved. "Here I am. I have quit the Brewery. I have taken a leave of absence from my company. I could care less if anyone's listening to what we say or watching how we say it. All I care about is you. Even when you're messy and complicated and even when I say the wrong thing at the wrong time, I care about *you*."

"You can't mean that," she whispered, because what if he did?

"I can and I do. I truly never believed I would meet anyone I could care about, much less someone who would mean more to me than the job. But I did. It's you, Frances. I want you when your armor's up because you make sarcasm and irony into high art. I want you when you're feeling vulnerable and honest because I want to be that soft place where you can land after a hard day of putting the world in its place. And I want you all the times in between, when you challenge me and call me on my mistakes and push me to be a better man—one who can keep up with you."

Unexpectedly, he dropped to his knees. "So I'm asking you again. Not for the Brewery, not for the employees, not for the public. I'm asking you for me. Because I want to spend my life with you. Not a few months, not a year— my life. Our lives. Together."

"You want to marry me? *Me?*"

"I like you," he said simply. "I shouldn't, but I do. Even worse, I love you." He gave her a crooked grin. "I love you. I'd recommend you love me, too."

Her mouth opened, but nothing came out. Not a damn thing. Because what was she going to say? That he'd gotten better at sweet nothings? That he was crazy to have fallen for her? That...

That she wanted to say yes—but she was afraid?

"I've seen the real you," he said, still on his knees. "And that's the woman I love."

"Do we get—married? Next week?" That had been the deal, hadn't it? A whirlwind courtship, married in two weeks.

"I'm not making a deal, Frances. All I'm doing right now is asking a simple question. We can wait a year, if you want. You're worth the wait. I'm not going anywhere without you."

"It won't ever be simple," she warned him. "I don't have it in me."

He stood and pulled her into his arms as if she'd said yes, when she wasn't sure she had yet. The rose, she feared, was a total loss. "I don't want you simple. I want to know that every day, I've fought for you and every day, you've chosen me again."

Was it possible, what he was saying? Could a man love her?

"I expect to be wined and dined and courted," she warned him, trying to sound stern and mostly just laughing.

He laughed with her. "And what do I get out of this again?"

"A wife. A messy, complicated wife who will love you until the end of time."

"Perfect," he said, lowering his lips to hers. "That's *exactly* what I wanted."

* * * * *

If you loved Frances's story,
pick up the first four books in the
BEAUMONT HEIRS *series:*

NOT THE BOSS'S BABY
TEMPTED BY A COWBOY
A BEAUMONT CHRISTMAS WEDDING
HIS SON, HER SECRET

MILLS & BOON®

Why shop at millsandboon.co.uk?

Each year, thousands of romance readers find their perfect read at millsandboon.co.uk. That's because we're passionate about bringing you the very best romantic fiction. Here are some of the advantages of shopping at www.millsandboon.co.uk:

* **Get new books first**—you'll be able to buy your favourite books one month before they hit the shops

* **Get exclusive discounts**—you'll also be able to buy our specially created monthly collections, with up to 50% off the RRP

* **Find your favourite authors**—latest news, interviews and new releases for all your favourite authors and series on our website, plus ideas for what to try next

* **Join in**—once you've bought your favourite books, don't forget to register with us to rate, review and join in the discussions

Visit **www.millsandboon.co.uk**
for all this and more today!

MILLS & BOON®

Desire™

PASSIONATE AND DRAMATIC LOVE STORIES

A sneak peek at next month's titles...

In stores from 16th October 2015: